ONE LAST BREATH

By the same author

Black Dog
Dancing with the Virgins
Blood on the Tongue
Blind to the Bones

STEPHEN BOOTH

One Last Breath

HarperCollins*Publishers*

HarperCollins*Publishers*
77–85 Fulham Palace Road, London W6 8JB

www.harpercollins.co.uk

Published by HarperCollins*Publishers* 2004

1 3 5 7 9 8 6 4 2

A catalogue record for this book
is available from the British Library

ISBN 0 00 717202 8

Typeset in Sabon by Palimpsest Book Production Limited,
Polmont, Stirlingshire

Printed in Great Britain by
Clays Ltd, St Ives plc

Dedicated to the men and women
who explore the scariest place there is
– the world beneath our feet

No book would reach this stage without the efforts of a whole team of people, and I particularly owe a debt on this occasion to my editor Julia Wisdom and the team at HarperCollins for their support. As usual, any mistakes are entirely my own.

Castleton, Derbyshire, 9 October 1990

And then she was gone. He heard the final scrape of air as it caught in her throat, and felt her last breath brush his cheek, as if a wisp of smoke had passed through the room. For a moment, she had taken his life in her mouth like a bubble of soap, swollen to bursting and smeared with light. And she'd punctured it with a sigh, that dying whisper. With one last breath, she had blown his life away.

Mansell Quinn knew he'd heard her die. He pulled his hands away from her body, and stared at the blood staining his fingers and pooling in his palms. He turned them from side to side, and watched the blood slide over a coating of white dust on his skin. It ran across his wrists and trickled into the soft flesh of his forearms, teasing the fine hairs like the caress of a fingertip.

He shook his head, trying to clear away the thoughts that buzzed in his brain like flies. He knew there were things he should do. Things he should do *now*. But he couldn't remember what they were. Quinn's mind was whirling and the room had begun to swing around him in dizzying arcs. Painful surges of adrenalin twitched in his veins, churning through his body as if poison had been pumped into his bloodstream.

The words running through his head were no help at all. *Murder. The children. The knife.* He knew what the words were, but couldn't get them in the right order.

For some reason, she was wearing the lime-green sweater. A moment ago, the fabric had been stretching and twisting in his hands where it hung open over her breast. The colour of it looked garish next to the blood. But if someone had asked him what else she was wearing, he wouldn't have been able to say. The sweater and the blood were all he saw.

Quinn sank to the floor and knelt by the body. He could feel sweat soaking from his pores and running down his face like tears. Gas bubbled in his stomach until he thought he'd be sick. He reached to pick up the knife, thinking he should put it out of her reach, hide it, throw it away, keep it safe. He had no idea which. He took her wrist between his fingers to feel her pulse, though he'd heard her die and he knew she was dead. He flinched at the touch of her skin and the slackness of her joints, and he dropped her hand back on the floor, where it landed with a thud. Then he noticed the bloody smears he'd left on her arm; they formed a pattern of red blotches and streaks, like a mark branded on an animal.

He looked up and squinted at the room, trying to place where he was. Her death had changed the world completely, so that nothing was familiar any more. Small impressions jostled his senses, like fragments of a broken picture. Music was playing somewhere, but he didn't recognize it. A door facing him was open, but he couldn't remember where it led. There was light coming through the doorway, yet it ought to be dark. A sweet scent hung on the air that he should know, but he couldn't name it. It was his own house, yet it had become a place he'd never seen before. It was an alien landscape, painted in blood.

Quinn looked down at her face, and the shock hit him a second time. He felt a desperate rush of hope that it might be possible to undo everything and turn the clock back, so that nothing had happened at all. What if he'd come home a bit earlier, or later? Or if he hadn't been held up by the roadworks on Back Street? What if he'd left his tools in the car, instead of taking his time getting the bag out and bringing it into the house, worrying about thieves going by on the road in the night, instead of what might happen in the next few minutes?

If he could take just one step back in time, her body might not be lying on the sitting-room floor, and the blood might magically fade from the carpet, like an advert for a miracle cleaner. She might stand up and laugh, and explain why she'd pretended to be dead. And life would go back to the way it had been before.

But Quinn had heard her die. The sound of her last breath had convinced him, not the sight of the blood or the slackness of her joints. And he knew his mistake had been made much earlier – years before, when he'd first met her and the whole thing had started. And now his life would never be normal again.

In a moment of silence, Quinn became aware of his own breathing. The sound of it seemed to fill the room, harsh and rapid, like the panting of a hunted animal, a rabbit in the jaws of the dog. He had never listened to his breathing before. He had never felt his lungs struggling to find air, or heard the shallow gasp that rushed across the roof of his mouth, like a cold wind inside his head. He didn't like the noise, and he was glad when the music started again to fill the silence in the house.

What *was* that music? Why was it playing? Quinn nodded at someone, though there was no one else in the room. He remembered that he hadn't found what he was looking for. The words had replaced the others in his head. *He still hadn't found what he was looking for.* But he hadn't been looking for the lime-green sweater. That shouldn't be here at all.

Then he noticed the wetness soaking through his jeans to

his knees. He stood up, staring at the purple stains on the denim, and at the blood spreading from the soles of his boots. It was so deep that it welled up from the carpet when he moved his feet.

Unsteadily, he walked round the body, praying it might look different from another angle. But all he saw now were his footprints in the blood. The carpet had been gold once – a gold shadow pattern, one of the first things he and Rebecca had chosen when they were decorating the house. She'd be upset that the carpet was ruined.

Quinn looked at his hands again, and the blood reminded him of something he should do. The phone stood on a table by the door. He dialled 999, and somehow remembered his address.

'Yes, 82 Pindale Road. An ambulance, please.'

He tried hard to listen to the voice of the operator, though he was distracted by the metallic smell of the blood on his hand and the slippery feel of the phone in his fingers.

'Police? Yes, probably.'

When that was done, he felt as though his legs wouldn't support him any longer. He made it back across the carpet and collapsed into an armchair. His eyes were drawn to the clock on the wall over the mantelpiece. He knew the clock was important for some reason. He listened to its ticking, waiting for it to penetrate the fog in his brain and tell him what else to do.

Finally, Quinn remembered the most important thing of all. The children. And he should have hidden the knife. The knife was dangerous.

But then exhaustion overwhelmed him, and his head fell back against the chair. When the first police officers arrived at the house, they found Mansell Quinn asleep. He was dreaming that the whole world could hear him breathing.

1

Monday, 12 July 2004

Today was the day Detective Constable Ben Cooper was supposed to have died. For practical purposes, he was already dead. His feet and hands felt icily cold, as if death might be creeping up on him slowly, claiming his body inch by inch.

For the past half hour, Cooper had been unable to move his arms or his legs, or even his head. Mud-stained rock filled his vision, every crack and protrusion glistening with dampness in the beams of light that swung across the passage. He could smell the mud and sweat around him, and hear the splashing of water as it echoed in the confined space. The rock was so close to his face that his breath condensed on it and fell back on him as mist. It filled his mouth with its taste. The sharp taste of stone.

Cooper had never imagined that he'd feel so helpless. The roof seemed to be sinking closer towards him, pressing down to crush his skull. He could sense the mass of the hill poised overhead. One tiny movement of the earth's crust over Derbyshire, and millions of tons of rock would flatten him where he lay. He'd be squeezed to a juice, reduced to an inexplicable red smear for future geologists to find.

'Only a few more minutes,' said a voice in the darkness, 'and we'll reach the Devil's Staircase.'

Then the light went off the roof, and Cooper could see nothing at all. For a moment, he thought the rock had already crushed him, and he began to panic. His lungs spasmed as if there were no oxygen left for him to breathe.

Cooper felt himself tilted violently backwards, but he was strapped in too tightly to move. Looking up from this angle, he saw a cluster of yellow PVC oversuits glowing in the sporadic light. Lamps created pools of luminescence around them and distorted their shadows on the roofs and walls. But there were no faces visible in darkness.

He was jolted again. He was sure the stretcher would turn over and tip him on to the floor of the passage, where he'd drown lying helpless in two feet of muddy water. And that would be the end of his career in Derbyshire CID. He'd never expected it to be like this.

'I want to die in the daylight,' he said.

But no one was listening to him. As far as they were concerned, he was already dead.

Detective Sergeant Diane Fry stumbled in the middle of the floor and kicked out in irritation. She'd never thought of herself as a tidy person – there were too many messy loose ends in her life for that. And God knew, her flat was a tip; she might have been competing with the students across the landing for the pigsty-of-the-year competition. But the intrusion of someone else's untidiness was a different thing altogether. It made her grit her teeth every time she came home from a shift. She'd barely noticed the mess when it was her own clothes thrown on the bathroom floor, but finding a pair of black jeans halfway across the room from the laundry basket reminded her that she was no longer alone.

Fry's pager was bleeping. She checked the number, scooped up her phone from the edge of the bath and dialled.

'DS Fry here. Yes, sir?'

Her boss at E Division, Detective Inspector Paul Hitchens, was at his desk early this morning. Yet he sounded far from alert.

'Oh, Fry. Are you on your way in?'

'Very shortly.'

'OK.'

Fry waited expectantly, but heard nothing except a metallic whirring in the background, as if Hitchens were having some construction work done on his office.

'Was there something, sir?'

'Oh, just . . . Does the name Quinn mean anything to you, Fry?'

'Quinn?'

'Mansell Quinn.'

'I'm sorry, it doesn't.'

'No. No, it wouldn't do.'

Hitchens sounded as though his mind was on something else entirely. Fry pulled a face and gestured impatiently at the phone, as if she'd been reduced to using sign language to an idiot.

'Well, make sure you come and see me before you do anything else, will you, Fry?'

'Certainly, sir.'

Fry shrugged as she ended the call. It was probably nothing. Hitchens was just losing his grip, like everyone else around E Division. But she'd better not be late. There was no time for clearing up someone else's clothes.

Hold on, though. She looked more closely at the jeans on the floor. These weren't someone else's clothes – they were hers, bought only a couple of weeks ago during a shopping trip to the Meadowhall Centre in Sheffield. Worse, they'd been a comfort purchase on a day when she'd been feeling particularly down. She hadn't even found a chance to wear them yet.

7

'Angie!'

There was no reply from the sitting room, where her sister lay wrapped in a duvet on the sofa. The flat was so small that the distance between the rooms was only a few feet. The fact that her sister was asleep irritated Fry even more.

'Angie!'

She heard a grunt, and a creaking of springs as her sister stirred and turned over. Fry looked at her watch: quarter past eight. She'd better pray the traffic wasn't too bad getting to West Street, or she'd be late.

She called again, more loudly, then picked up the jeans and tried to fold them back into their proper shape before laying them on top of the overflowing laundry basket. They were creased and scuffed across the knees, as if Angie had been crawling around the floor in them. They were hardly worth wearing now, despite the money she'd lashed out for the sake of the designer label stitched to the back pocket.

Cursing, Fry began to fuss about the bathroom, picking up more items of clothing and shoving them into the basket. She rescued a towel from the bottom of the bath and hung it on the rail. She straightened the curtains, swept up an empty toothpaste tube and a Tampax wrapper and threw them into the pedal bin. She dampened a cloth and began wiping splashes of soap off the mirror. Then she caught sight of her own reflection, and stopped. She didn't like what she saw.

'What's all the noise about?'

Angie stood in the doorway wearing only a long T-shirt, scratching herself and peering at her sister through half-open eyes. Fry felt a rush of guilt at the sight of her sister's bare, thin legs.

'Nothing.'

'What are you doing? I thought there must be a fire, or a burglar or something.'

'No. I'm sorry. You can go back to sleep, if you want.'

Angie coughed. 'I'm awake now, I suppose. Are you going out, Sis?'

'I'm on shift this morning.'

'Yeah. Well, I'll get myself a coffee. Do you want anything?'

'I don't have time.'

Angie looked around the bathroom. 'Tidying up? Just before you go to work? You want to slow down, Di. You'll be giving yourself a heart attack if you get so stressed.'

'Yeah, right.'

Angie looked at her, puzzled. 'You were shouting me though, weren't you? I'm sure you were. What did you want?'

'Nothing,' said Fry. 'It doesn't matter. You go and get yourself that coffee.'

Angie turned away. 'I'm sure I heard you shouting me,' she said. 'You sounded just like Ma.'

Fry dropped the damp cloth and leaned on the washbasin for a moment. She listened to Angie shuffling away, her bare feet slapping on the worn tiles in the passage. Fry kept her head lowered. The one thing she didn't want to do was see herself in the mirror again. She didn't want the memories that had been visible for a brief moment in the reflection of her own eyes, in the hard line of her mouth and the frown marks etched into her forehead.

Reluctantly, she looked at her watch. She had to go or she'd be late, and she couldn't afford to be late when she had to set an example for the likes of Ben Cooper and Gavin Murfin, who would go wandering off in their own directions in a second if she didn't keep an eye on them.

Fry walked into her bedroom to fetch her jacket from behind the door. She was annoyed to see that her hand was shaking as she entered the kitchen. Angie was sitting at the table, staring at her fingernails.

'Angie, just now, what did you mean . . . ?'

'What?'

'When you mentioned Ma. What did you mean?'

Angie shrugged. 'Nothing really.'

'But . . .' Fry stopped, defeated. 'I've got to go.'

She went down the wide flight of stairs with its thread-bare treads, and left the house by the back door. Number 12 Grosvenor Avenue was one of a series of detached Victorian villas in a tree-lined street, its front door nestling between mock porticos. It had space at the back for Fry to park her Peugeot, and she was glad to be able to get the car off the street, especially when she lay in bed at night listening to the passing drunks.

Fry wound the windows down to let some air into the car. It might turn out to be one of the few days in the year when she wished she had air conditioning. She plugged her mobile phone into the cigarette lighter to make sure it would be fully charged by the time she got to West Street. Then she drove up to the corner of Castleton Road and waited for the traffic to clear. She looked at her watch again. Almost eight thirty. She might not be too late, after all.

At this point, her mind was trained to switch off anything else and start to think about work. There was plenty to do, as usual. Today's diary included a meeting to plan an operation against Class A drug misuse and a review of a long-running rape enquiry, as well as prioritizing whatever had happened in the last twenty-four hours.

Then Fry frowned. She hated starting the day with irritations that she couldn't classify. And she had one already this morning, thanks to the call from her DI. What was the name he mentioned? Quinn? It still meant nothing to her. But she would have to know – who the hell was Mansell Quinn?

She looked at her phone. There was one person who was sure to know. She didn't really want to talk to him if she could avoid it, but it might be preferable to walking into the DI's office ignorant, and therefore in a position of weakness. Ben Cooper's number was stored in her phone's memory, one

10

of a hundred invisible squiggles on its smart card, so that she carried his presence with her permanently, like a scar.

From the moment she'd arrived at E Division, Cooper had been in her hair, probing into her past, turning over all the memories she'd left the West Midlands to escape. And then this business with her sister. Why had he got himself involved in that? The one thing she wasn't going to do was give Cooper the satisfaction of asking him. It seemed impossible to Fry that there could be any acceptable explanation.

She pulled his number up out of her phone's memory and dialled, ready to pull over to the side of the road if he answered. But the number was unobtainable. Fry grimaced in frustration. Of course, Cooper was on a rest day today. Why shouldn't he turn off his phone and enjoy himself?

Water was pouring through the roof. Splashes of it landed on his face, making him blink. Ben Cooper tried to move a hand to wipe it away, but his arms were held too tightly. Then he felt himself travelling up a slope and saw a larger chamber, lit by artificial lights. At last there was a change in air temperature and a glimpse of daylight as the mouth of the cavern opened above him, then he heard the high-pitched cries of jackdaws.

Giving an exhausted cheer, the six men in yellow oversuits dropped the stretcher with a thump. Cooper's head banged on the plastic cover.

'Hey, I'm a casualty, you know. Where's the ambulance? Don't I get an ambulance?'

After a moment, one of the men came back to the stretcher.

'Sorry, Ben. But you *are* dead, you know.'

'My God, if I'd known it'd be like that, Alistair, I wouldn't have volunteered. In fact, I didn't volunteer – I was talked into it.'

Alistair Page took off his gloves and leaned over to unfasten the buckles on the straps. He was still covered in the

11

smelly silt that coated the caves and had been stirred up from the flooded passages by the rescue party. Like the rest of the team taking part in the exercise, he was protected by elbow and kneepads, and had a heavy tackle bag slung from his belt.

Cooper tried to remember which of his friends had introduced him to Page. Whoever it was, he had a score to settle.

'You're not telling me you're claustrophobic,' said Page. 'It's a bit late for that.'

'I didn't think I was, until an hour ago. But I've changed my mind. I feel quite sick.'

'You'll be all right in a minute.'

At last, Cooper was free of the stretcher. His legs felt numb, and he had to walk up and down and shake them a bit before the painful tingling started, a sign that the blood was flowing back into his limbs. Glad to be using his muscles again, he helped Page to lift a bundle of ropes and slide them into the cave rescue vehicle, an old Bedford van that was kept in the police compound in Edendale. The van was well overdue for replacement, but the Derbyshire Cave Rescue was a voluntary group and relied entirely on donations. They'd have to raise tens of thousands of pounds before they could buy a new vehicle.

The chattering of the jackdaws made Cooper look up. The birds were circling the roofless keep of the castle on the eastern rim of the Peak Cavern gorge, hopping restlessly from tree to tree, or flapping on to the cliff ledges.

'Do they nest on those ledges?'

'Yes. And so do mallard ducks sometimes,' said Page. 'But their ducklings have a habit of falling off. Visitors don't like that very much.'

'I can imagine,' said Cooper, still craning his neck. It was a relief just to be able to move his head and see the sky.

'You did a good job of being dead, by the way. Don't forget – you get a free tour through the show cave for doing this.'

12

'I'm coming down with my two nieces tomorrow afternoon. They've just broken up for the summer holidays, and I promised them a day out.'

'You can cope with that, can you?'

'At least you don't get many real deaths here.'

'There's only ever been one in Peak Cavern. That was a long time ago. And, well . . .' Page hesitated, looking back anxiously over his shoulder at the mouth of the cavern, as if he heard noises in the darkness but couldn't see what was there. 'Well, that was different,' he said. 'It was unique. And a long time ago.'

Some of the rescue team were carrying their gear back to the cavers' clubhouse in Castleton. But Page lived only a couple of hundred yards away, in one of the cottages climbing the hillside on a narrow lane called Lunnen's Back.

'I'll be here between ten and five tomorrow,' he said. 'Just ask for me if I'm not around.'

Since it was impossible to get a car anywhere near the cavern approach, Cooper had left his Toyota in the main car park, near the new visitor centre. From there, he could see a long line of people winding their way up to Peveril Castle. The climb was gruelling, and some of the older visitors stopped to rest at every chance, pretending to admire the view while they eased the pain in their knees. As a child, Cooper had himself visited Castleton on a school outing. In term time, the streets of the town were full of children with worksheets.

In the car park, he turned his face to the sun and breathed deeply. Right now, he couldn't imagine who or what was going to ruin his rest day.

Diane Fry knocked on the door of the DI's office at West Street, and walked straight in. Paul Hitchens was leaning back in his chair, gazing out over the roof of the east stand at Edendale Football Club. He barely moved when she entered.

'Sir? You said you wanted to see me.'

Hitchens was silent for a moment, lost in some thoughts of his own that he wasn't going to let Fry interrupt. So she waited until he was ready. She watched the sunlight from his window cast shadows on his face, making him look older than the DI she'd met when she first transferred to Derbyshire Constabulary, not all that long ago. Since setting up home with a nurse in Chesterfield he'd become middle-aged almost overnight, preoccupied with finding the right wallpaper for the bathroom and tending his lawn at weekends. Hitchens himself had seemed to sense the difference, too. He was a man settling into his position in life.

But now Fry noticed him fingering the scar across the middle knuckles of his left hand, as if remembering an old injury.

'I hear Mansell Quinn is due out today,' said Hitchens finally.

Fry felt a surge of irritation and fought to contain it. 'Who,' she said, 'is Mansell Quinn?'

The DI spun a little on his chair, glanced at Fry as if checking who she was. She had a feeling that he'd have said the same thing no matter who had walked into his office. He might have been having this conversation with the cleaner.

'You won't remember him, DS Fry,' he said. 'Quinn got a life sentence for murder some years ago. He lived in Castleton, a few miles up the road from here, in the Hope Valley. Do you know it?'

'A tourist honeypot, isn't it?'

'Interesting place, actually. I went there as a kid. I remember being particularly impressed by the sheep – they came right down into the centre of the town. I suppose they must have been looking for food. I hadn't seen one up close before.'

'Sir?' said Fry. 'You were talking about somebody called Quinn . . .'

'Yes, Mansell Quinn.' Hitchens swung his chair back again

and gazed out of the window. His eyes seemed to go out of focus, as if he were staring beyond Edendale to the country further north – towards Hope Valley, on the fringes of the Dark Peak. 'Well, Castleton's quiet most of the year, when the tourists aren't there. People know each other very well. Quinn's case caused quite a stir. It was a pretty violent killing – blood on the sitting-room carpet, and all that.'

Fry hadn't been asked to sit down, so she leaned against the wall by the door instead.

'A domestic?'

'Well, sort of,' said Hitchens. 'The thing was, Quinn denied the charge at first, but entered a guilty plea at trial. Then he changed his mind again when he'd been inside for a while. He said he didn't do it after all.'

'A bit perverse. Did he get parole?'

'No.'

'He ruined his own case, then. The parole board would have thought he was in denial.'

'It doesn't work like that any more. Early release depends on an assessment of any future risk you might pose, not on whether you've accepted the court's verdict. The Home Office makes an issue of it in its policy for lifers these days.'

'They were forced into that, weren't they?'

'That's a sore point around here, Fry.'

'Sorry.'

'Risk assessment,' said Hitchens. 'That's what it comes down to. We know about risk assessment, don't we?'

Fry nodded. Too often, it meant covering your back, a means of avoiding litigation or compensation payouts. But that was one thought she didn't articulate. It might not have been what the DI meant.

'Mansell Quinn had behaviour issues,' said Hitchens. 'He had to undertake anger-management training in prison.'

'And he still didn't get parole?'

'No. Quinn served thirteen years and four months, until

15

he reached his automatic release date.' Hitchens turned round fully in his chair and leaned forward on his desk. 'And that date is today. Mansell Quinn was due to collect his belongings and walk out of HMP Sudbury at half past eight this morning.' Hitchens looked at his watch. 'Half an hour ago, in fact.'

'So?'

'Quinn will be on licence. He's supposed to move into temporary hostel accommodation in Burton on Trent, and he has an appointment with his probation officer this afternoon. One of the conditions of his licence is that he stays away from this area. We've been asked to keep an eye out for him, in case he breaches his conditions.'

Fry shrugged. 'So what if he does turn up here? Sometimes prisoners get a bit over-excited about being out and decide to celebrate. We might find him in a pub somewhere, but it will mean nothing.'

'Probably.'

She straightened up to leave the DI's office. But then Fry hesitated, feeling there might be something more that he hadn't told her.

'Anger management? So Quinn is a violent man, would you say, sir?'

'No doubt about it,' said Hitchens. 'He has a long history of violent incidents in his past. In fact, he got knockback early in his sentence because he assaulted a fellow prisoner. He broke the man's arm and removed a couple of his teeth. And he couldn't explain why he did it. Or wouldn't.'

'And what about the original murder?'

'Well, there was certainly enough blood at the scene. The place was like an abattoir. Not what you'd want your sitting room to look like – especially in your nice new three-bedroom detached house in Castleton. Pindale Road, that was the place.'

Fry settled back against the wall with a sigh. 'What happened exactly?'

'Well, it seems that Quinn had made his way home from the pub, where he'd been drinking with his mates all afternoon. There was a row; he lost his temper, grabbed a handy kitchen knife . . . And bingo – a body on the floor, blood on the shag-pile, and the suspect still on the premises when a patrol responds to the 999 call. Terrible scenes with the kids arriving home. The whole street hanging out of their doors to see what was going on and generally getting in the way. All the usual mess. The victim was dead at the scene. She had multiple stab wounds to her body.'

'An ordinary domestic, then,' said Fry, irrationally disappointed. 'One like thousands of others. I suppose the reasons for the argument might vary a bit, but the choice of household object doesn't usually show much imagination. And it's always the wife who ends up dead on the floor.'

'Except there was one big difference in the Quinn case.'

Fry lifted her head.

'What?'

'The body on Quinn's sitting-room floor,' said Hitchens. 'It wasn't his wife's.'

2

Sudbury Prison, Derbyshire

There used to be poppies in every cornfield once – they were bright red, like splashes of fresh blood. Mansell Quinn was sure he'd seen them all through the summer. As soon as the sun came out, they were everywhere in little clusters, peering from among the yellow stalks, nodding their bloodied heads in the sun, waiting for the combine to scythe them down. For a few hot days each year, a field in the bottom of the valley would be filled with entire red rivers of poppies, pooling and streaming, moving slowly in the breeze.

This morning, he noticed for the first time that there was a cornfield right across the road, its acres of brown stalks just starting to seed. The fences around it were strung barbed wire. Quinn looked for poppies in the corn, needing that glimpse of red. But there were no poppies.

As he walked towards the outer gate clutching a plastic carrier bag and his travel warrant, Quinn began to realize that even his liberty clothing was too big for him, and too stiff to be comfortable. He'd lost weight during the last fourteen years, and his body had hardened, as if a callus had grown over his skin, the way it had grown over his heart.

Past the gatehouse, he turned to look back for the last

time. Above a bank of flowers was the white sign with its slogan *Custody with Care* and a mission statement: *committed to rehabilitation and resettlement of prisoners.*

Eight thirty was time for the morning collection. Right now, a court van was turning in through the gate and slowing for the speed hump, its steel grilles and reinforced doors making it look like an armoured personnel carrier. As Quinn stepped on to the grass to let it pass, the driver gave him a cautious glance, though the van would be empty yet this morning, its cage still smelling of too much disinfectant.

'I'll be home in an hour or so. And I can't bloody wait. What about you?'

The man who fell into step alongside him was at least twenty years younger than Quinn, somewhere in his mid-twenties. He had short, gelled hair and a tattoo on the side of his neck, and he looked freshly shaved and scrubbed. He could have mingled with any bunch of lads in town on a Saturday night – which was just what he'd be doing by tonight, no doubt.

'It'll take me a bit longer than that,' said Quinn.

'Eh?'

'A bit longer to get home.'

'Oh? You sound like a Derbyshire bloke, though.'

'That's exactly what I am.'

'Right.'

But Quinn had been born in the Welsh borders. It was there that the poppies had filled his summers. He supposed they must have found their way into the seed that the farmers sowed, or lay hidden in the ground until disturbed by the plough. Then they would flower before the wheat ripened, flourishing secretly between sowing and harvest. For the young Mansell Quinn, those poppies had been like a glimpse of wicked things existing where they shouldn't be.

But when his father had got himself a new job as a forester on a country estate near Hathersage, his family had moved

19

north to the Hope Valley. There were no cornfields among the gritstone hills and shale valleys of the Dark Peak.

The young man laughed. 'You mean you're getting right away from the old place? I don't blame you, mate. Not for a minute.'

Quinn had no idea who the lad was. Yet in a way, they were as close as brothers. There were things that created a bond, ties that didn't need to be talked about in these few minutes between the prison gate and the outside world.

'Have you got somebody waiting at home for you?' said Quinn.

'Bloody right. I told her we'd get married when I came out. It's only right, for the sake of the kids. We've got a council house and everything.'

'Lucky.'

'Yeah. I won't be going back, that's for sure.'

Quinn had stopped listening. His mind was on another house and another family.

'Sometimes,' he said, 'you have to go back.'

'You what? What are you saying? You know nothing about me, mate.'

'No,' said Quinn. 'Nothing.'

The young man's edginess subsided. It was only tension born of a fear of the unknown.

'I'm Rick. You?'

'Quinn.'

'I've seen you around, I think. But I've not spoken to you before.'

'Make the most of it.'

They walked across the road from the gate. This road was a dead end, created to serve the prison when the Sudbury bypass had been built. Ahead of them was the entrance to a concrete underpass.

'So where are you heading?' said Rick.

'Burton on Trent. Some hostel my probation officer fixed up.'

20

The underpass was damp and smelly, a dim tunnel leading towards a patch of light. Their voices echoed from the walls, but the sound of their footsteps was muffled by the dirt floor.

'First thing tomorrow,' said Rick, 'I'll be off to Meadowhall to get myself a load of new gear. Well, after I've slept off the hangover from tonight, anyway. Getting pissed is the first priority.' He laughed. 'You too, I bet.'

'Me too what?'

'You'll be getting some new clothes.'

Quinn looked down at what he was wearing. One of the first things he should do was find one of those charity shops where they sold second-hand stuff for a couple of pounds – the places he'd seen on his escorted absences: Oxfam, Cancer Research, Help the Aged. In one of those shops, he could pick up some jeans and a couple of shirts, maybe an old jacket that smelled of fag smoke, and a pair of boots. Dead men's clothes probably, but who cared? They'd make him less noticeable. He had his discharge grant in his pocket, but there were other things he might need money for. Dead men could provide his clothes for now. It would be appropriate, in a way.

'I've even got a job lined up,' said Rick. 'What a stroke of luck, eh? My probation officer helped me. He's a decent enough bloke. A bit of money in your pocket, that makes all the difference, doesn't it? A home to go to and your family around you. I'm going to get my life sorted out, just you watch.'

'Good for you.'

'I mean, I'm only twenty-five – I've got my whole future ahead of me. Besides, you can't waste your life away when you're a dad. I want my two to be proud of me some day. I don't want them to think they've got a dad who's a waster because he's spent most of his life in the nick, do I?'

'No.'

21

'Have you got kids yourself, then?'

Mansell Quinn grimaced, and his jaw tightened. He said nothing. But the young man hadn't really been interested in an answer.

'I want them to do better for themselves than I've done,' said Rick. 'I want them to work hard and get on in the world. So I'm going to set them an example from now on. I promised Sharon I would. My lad wants to be a doctor, and I'm going to help him do that.'

The A50 was dusty, and the passing traffic stank of petrol and hot metal. Quinn had inhaled more fumes in the past five minutes than in the last fourteen years. He wished there had been poppies in the field. They would have been a good omen – blood in the fields matching the blood in his mind. But their absence made him uneasy. For the first time it occurred to him that life in the outside world might have changed in too many ways while he'd been gone.

These days, he supposed farmers treated their seed with chemicals to kill the poppies, to make every crop they planted perfectly pure and golden, totally sterile and dull. There was no more scarlet among the yellow, no more blood in the cornfields. Now, the blood moved only in his memory.

Rick looked at Quinn, leaving his own fantasy world for a moment.

'Have you been inside for a while, like?'

'Thirteen years and four months.'

'Thirteen years? That's tough.'

Quinn could see him working it out. You learned to do that in prison – to calculate parole and automatic release dates, all the stuff that the system hid with acronyms, as if they were no more than letters on the page of a report, rather than the days of a man's freedom. Rick could work it out for himself. Thirteen years and four months meant his sentence must have been at least twenty years, even without parole.

'A lifer, then?'

They had emerged from the underpass, back into the light. Quinn turned slowly, trying to orientate himself. The busy stretch of trunk road above him was new, and he didn't know which direction anything was from the underpass. It was almost as if the prison existed in a strange little universe of its own, created to keep it away from the rest of the world.

'Yes, a lifer.'

He knew that Rick wanted to ask the next question, but something was stopping him – maybe he was distracted by the slight stirring of the air between them, a draught blowing up from the underpass, causing a swirl of dust at their feet. Rick opened his mouth to speak, but a look of doubt clouded his eyes and he didn't ask.

'*Who did you kill?*' he wanted to say. But he didn't.

And that was a good thing. Because Mansell Quinn might not have been able to tell him.

There must be a way for the buses to come down off the A50, because there was a stop right here near the underpass and another across the road. In fact, there was a bus coming now, on his side of the road, heading for Burton upon Trent.

'Here we go, then. Here we go.'

Rick took a firmer grip on his carrier bag. He spat into the gutter and watched his saliva seep into the dust.

'Good luck, mate,' said Quinn.

His companion looked at him oddly, but his attention was diverted by the approach of the bus. As soon as it pulled up to the stop and the doors folded open, he jumped on board.

Suddenly, Quinn took a step back from the bus stop. He gave the driver a blank stare as the man met his eye expectantly. Rick turned to watch him, not understanding what was happening, perhaps even a bit hurt. Then the doors closed, and the driver accelerated away from the stop.

Quinn watched the bus until it was out of sight. Despite the noise of traffic, all the cars were passing above him, on the main road. He looked for a moment at the exit from the concrete underpass, at the barbed-wire fences and the pale, bland acres of corn. Then he crouched, picked up a lump of stone that had fallen from the banking, and hurled it at the bus shelter. A glass panel shattered and crazed, its broken fragments showering on to the tarmac like crushed ice.

For a moment, Quinn smiled at the noise that exploded into the silence. And then he began to walk. Behind him, four words still seemed to echo amid the sound of shattering glass: *Who did you kill?*

3

Rebecca Lowe's new house in Aston had been built to be almost airtight. The insulation created a difference in the internal air pressure from the outside world, so that the back door opened with a soft little cough as it parted from its draught-proof lining. The air was sticky outside, and the thunder flies were swarming. The tiny black insects covered everything when she wasn't looking, and even the thought of them made her skin prickle, so that she constantly wanted to wash her face.

Inside the house, she had air conditioning. It had been one of the things Rebecca had insisted on after the discomfort of the previous summer and its record high temperatures. She couldn't bear the humidity, which made her head ache, her temples throb and her hands slippery with perspiration. She'd slept badly for weeks, and changed her bedclothes every morning. The rumble of the washing machine had become a permanent background accompaniment to the long summer days.

In the new house, she could be cool. Parson's Croft had been built of breeze-block on the inside, but with local grit-stone on the outside, so that it blended in with the older houses and the landscape, as well as meeting the national park planning regulations. The site had a belt of mature sycamores and chestnut trees to screen the house and provide shade when the sun was in the west. But the air conditioning only worked properly if she kept all the doors and windows closed. Sometimes, the atmosphere in the house tasted stale, as if she were breathing the same air over and over again. It created its own kind of oppressiveness, a feeling that was almost as bad as the humidity outside.

Her dog Milly felt it, too. She lay in her basket all day, dozing restlessly, until it was time for her evening walk. And even when she got outside, she was bad tempered. She would yap at strangers, or worry obsessively at a stick or a piece of stone lying on the grass verge.

Today, Rebecca felt she would even welcome rain to bring a bit of freshness. As she finished washing up and wiped her hands, she walked into the lounge to look out through the double-glazed picture window. She examined the view down into the Hope Valley and up the slopes of Bradwell Moor and Abney Moor, her gaze skirting quickly past the tall chimney of the cement works in Pindale. Grey clouds were gathering over the moors, with darker patches among them, like blue bruises in the sky. There might be a shower later, with a bit of luck.

The phone rang in the still air. Rebecca put her towel down on the window ledge before she answered it, immediately identifying a familiar voice.

'Mum, you know what day it is today?'

'Monday,' said Rebecca. 'There, you see – I'm not entirely ga-ga yet. Try me with another one.'

She heard her daughter sigh at the other end of the line. She could picture Andrea sitting in a coffee bar somewhere, or striding along a London street with her mobile phone clamped to her ear. Living independently in the city and being good at her job as a buyer for a big retail chain had turned her into a formidable young woman.

'Today's the day he's coming out, Mum,' she said.

'Yes, they told me.'

'Aren't you worried?'

'No.'

'You're not? But, Mum, what if he comes out there?'

Rebecca was still looking out of the lounge window. She could see nothing but the flowering cherry tree and buddleias at the bottom of her garden, and a pair of mature lime trees. Red-and-black butterflies fluttered around the buddleias, bright and gaudy in the sun. A flycatcher dipped from his perch on the telephone wire, caught a mouthful of food on the wing, and landed back on the wire in one graceful movement.

'I don't think he'll come here,' she said.

'A change of name isn't going to fool *him*, you know.'

'Of course not, Andrea.'

'So what will you do, Mum? What precautions are you taking?'

'Well, I haven't fed Milly for days,' said Rebecca lightly.

'Mum, a geriatric Shih Tzu isn't going to do much to protect you from an intruder, no matter how hungry she is.'

'I was joking, dear.'

Rebecca moved a little to the right and lifted the curtain aside. Beyond the lime trees, she could see part of the field that backed on to the garden of Parson's Croft. The field sloped away towards a stone barn where the farmer kept hay as winter fodder for his sheep.

'This is nothing to joke about, Mum. You're remembering to set the burglar alarms, aren't you?'

'Oh yes,' said Rebecca.

'Mum, if you're not taking any precautions, I'm going to have to come up there and make sure you do.'

'No. I don't want you to.' But then Rebecca heard her daughter's intake of breath, and realized she might have sounded rude and ungrateful. 'Not that I wouldn't be pleased

27

to see you. I always am, dear, any time. But I'm all right. Really.'

'What about Simon? He'll come and stay with you for a while. You know he will.'

'Yes, he offered, but I told him not to. He's not very far away, and I can always phone him. But I don't want you *or* your brother to think you have to drop what you're doing. You're both much too busy.'

She heard her daughter sigh. 'But, Mum –'

'Look, I'm sure he won't come here.'

'Mum, remember what happened. You *do* remember what happened?'

'Of course, dear. I was involved at the time. You weren't.'

'Not involved? I was twelve years old. You may not have been paying much attention to me, but I knew exactly what was going on.'

'Not exactly,' said Rebecca. 'I don't think you can have known *exactly* what was going on, can you?'

'Well, OK. Just don't tell me I wasn't involved, Mum.'

Rebecca leaned to the left and let her forehead touch the glass of the window. This way, she could just make out the gable end of her neighbours' roof. It was another new house, but much bigger than hers, with a fishpond, stone terraces, and a vast billiard-table lawn with sprinklers that ran eighteen hours a day in the hot weather. She rarely spoke to them, but they would occasionally smile and wave if they passed her in their Jaguar as she walked Milly on the lane.

'I'm sorry, Andrea,' she said. 'You're right. It must have been very traumatic for you.'

Her daughter went away from her phone for a couple of seconds. Rebecca could hear background chatter, and wondered if Andrea was mouthing a commentary at some-body sitting with her, wherever she was, exclaiming in exasperation at the impossible eccentricity of her mother back home in Derbyshire.

'Well, anyway,' said Andrea when she came back to the phone, 'what on earth could you have to talk to him about *now*, Mum?'

'There are things,' said Rebecca, 'that you might say were still unresolved.'

'Oh God, Mum. I despair of you.'

Rebecca smiled. Her daughter really didn't know everything.

'But, in any case,' Rebecca said, 'he won't come here.'

With an effort, Raymond Proctor smiled and nodded, forcing himself to be pleasant despite the anxiety in his stomach. These people were customers, after all. And customers were too few these days at Wingate Lees. They were a family from Hertfordshire – mum, dad and two kids. Their car stood near the roadway in front of one of the static caravans, ready to go.

'Where are you off to today, then? Somewhere nice? The weather should be all right for you, I reckon.'

The woman stopped for a moment, ushering her children ahead of her to the car. 'The kids want to go to one of the caverns,' she said. 'We thought we'd visit the one you suggested to us yesterday, Peak Cavern.'

'Ah. The Devil's Arse,' said Proctor, grinning.

'Pardon?'

'That's what they call it these days. I suppose they thought it would be more marketable.' Then Proctor saw she wasn't smiling. 'Sorry.'

'It's not the sort of language we think suitable for the children to hear.'

Proctor shrugged. 'I'm afraid you'll see it on the signs.'

'Perhaps we'll go somewhere else, then. There's Speedwell.'

'Well, that's interesting, too. But Peak Cavern's best. Let me know what you think of it when you get back. Say hello to the guide for me while you're there. And don't forget to ask him –'

'Yes, thank you.' The woman turned to go.

'It's a pleasure,' said Proctor, maintaining his smile. 'Of course, if you're going underground, it won't matter what the weather's like, will it? I said, it won't matter . . .'

But the woman didn't answer him. She fussed over the children's seat belts and snapped something at her husband as she got into the passenger seat next to him.

'Unless it rains really, really hard,' said Proctor through gritted teeth, after they'd started the engine. 'And then the caves might flood, and you could all *drown*.'

He kicked the head off a wallflower growing in a bed near the phone box, and winced at a twinge of pain in his leg. His arthritis was troubling him this morning, which meant it probably *would* rain later, after all. Slowly he walked past the shop and the TV lounge, irritated as always by their log-effect façades. The design had been Connie's idea – she said it would go with the style of the cabins and give the site a theme. But Proctor thought it made the place look like a Wild West frontier town. Just too bloody tacky for the sort of guest he was trying to attract to Wingate Lees.

There was a lot of competition from other caravan parks in the Hope Valley, and Wingate Lees was a bit off the main road for passing trade. People had to turn off the A625 for half a mile, then drive over Killhill Bridge and under the railway line to find his little site tucked into the edge of Win Hill. The nearest village was Aston, but there was no way of getting there from the site except by walking – and nothing to do if you went there, anyway.

The reputation of Wingate Lees was important if it was going to survive. He didn't have endless amounts of money to spend on marketing, so he relied on word of mouth to get him business. He needed his guests to be happy. Though, God knew, it was difficult to be polite to some of them when what they really deserved was a kick up the backside. A lot of the time, he hardly felt like bothering.

Proctor supposed he might feel differently about the business if Alan were here to run it with him. Having somebody to pass it on to – that was what mattered. But all he had was Connie and her kids, and it wasn't the same at all. Nothing was the same as your own son.

He stopped to check on the girl who helped in the shop and looked after the coin-op laundry. Then he glared across the grass to where Henry, the maintenance man, was raking the gravel around the hardstandings. He couldn't find fault with either of them, so he kept on walking, passing along the lines of mobile homes to the touring caravan pitches, and past them to the pond, which his promotional leaflets called a water amenity. A copse of trees lay across the pond, and an area of grass where visitors could walk their dogs. Convenient exercise facilities available for the use of pet owners.

Four old caravans were pitched here, well away from the rest of the site and in the shadow of the railway embankment. He only let these out to visitors when the rest of the place was full – which was a rare occurrence these days – or if he had a bunch of students on the site he didn't like the look of. If they wrecked an old 'van, it would be a lot cheaper to replace than one of the family units, which had to be in good condition or he'd lose his customers.

This was where Proctor came to get away from the family. He could see the house from here, allowing him advance warning if Connie was on the prowl.

Because there was no demand, he hadn't maintained the old 'vans properly, and now some of the joints in the shells had developed leaks. The lad who came in to wash the caravans must have noticed, because he hadn't bothered to clean these two. Moss had started to grow on their surfaces, staining the paintwork green. The heavy rain in the last few days had streaked the dirt, making their deteriorating condition even more obvious.

31

Proctor was breathing heavily by the time he reached this part of the site. He'd been getting overweight ever since he married Connie. She fed him junk food every day, then told him he ought to get more exercise.

He'd come this far feeling calm enough, but now he felt uneasy as he reached out to try the handle on the door of the first caravan. He rattled it quickly, withdrawing his fingers as if he might get burned. He peered through the orange curtains, using his hands to cut out reflections from the window. Then he moved on to the next caravan and did the same.

'What are you doing, Ray?'

Proctor jumped guiltily. His wife was standing on the other side of the pond. She was wearing a baggy white sweatshirt and yellow pedal pushers that emphasized the muscles of her thighs. And her feet were shoved into those ridiculous trainers with enormous tongues and lights in the heels. That was why he hadn't heard her coming.

'Just checking the old 'vans,' he said.

'Why?'

'In case we need them.'

'Ray, take a look around you – half the site is empty.'

'You never know.'

Connie stared at him in open disbelief. 'Really.'

'I'm making sure everything is OK down here, that's all. We mustn't let them get too neglected.'

She looked at the mould and streaks of dirt on the nearest caravan. 'Neglected? You should have got rid of them years ago. If you want something useful to do, there's still that leak in cabin six that needs fixing.'

'I know, I know. I'll see to it in a minute.'

But Connie stood watching him until he sighed, moved away, and went back through the trees. She would have put her hands on her hips like an old schoolmistress – if she had any hips.

A cement train ran southwards across the bridge, with a long line of Blue Circle tankers coming away full from the Hope works. As they rattled over the stone arch, their wheels rumbled like approaching thunder. The sound went on for so long that Raymond Proctor found it hard to resist breaking into a run.

Down at the cement works, Will Thorpe had watched the line of tankers leave. Now, an excavator was trundling along the skyline, a black outline against the afternoon sun as it worked its way along the edge of the quarry. Beneath Thorpe's feet, dead bracken branches snapped, releasing puffs of cement dust. Decaying leaves still lay on the ground from the previous autumn, but now they were white, as if they'd been covered in frost.

Thorpe licked his lips. They were dry and cracked from the sun and dust. He knew he should stay away from the Hope works. His lungs hurt badly enough without the abrasive powder that hung in the air. But at night, it was irresistible. Here, the night-time world was a window on to another reality. The works was lit up like a city in a science fiction film, full of glittering towers and glaring lights, with drifting spurts of steam and mysterious rumbles and screeches from hidden machinery.

When he spread his hand flat against the ground, Thorpe could feel the vibration that went with the noise. It reminded him of the movement of a column of armoured vehicles on a desert road, their steel tracks grinding the surface into dust, and their gun barrels swollen and heavy, like ripe fruit. The recollection was so clear that he could almost taste the sand in his mouth and feel the sun on his neck below the band of his beret.

Thorpe would have liked to be able to step into another reality. If ever it was possible, it ought to be possible now. He'd checked the date when he was in Castleton earlier in the day, and he knew it was 12 July. Somehow, he'd convinced himself that the day would never arrive, but here it was.

Will Thorpe had seen enough death to believe that he could sense it in the air when it was coming. Not slow, drawn-out death, drugged against the pain and hooked up to drips in a hospital bed. But sudden, violent death that fell out of the sky or burst from the ground, killing in an explosion of blood. The sort of death that he'd prefer for himself, given the choice.

Thorpe closed his eyes against the pain in his chest, against the sights that he saw in the deep shadows among the trees and the tumbled rocks on the slopes of the quarry.

'Oh shit, oh shit,' he said.

He wished he could spit out the permanent bitter taste at the back of his mouth as easily as he could spit out the cement dust. But the taste of violence had soaked into his glands, and now it seeped into his mouth with every trickle of saliva.

Thorpe's hands were trembling. He knew the trembling was caused by hunger, not fear. In fact, he had never been afraid, not even in the worst times, when his mates had been blasted to bits alongside him, when the blood had splattered his face mask so thickly that he could no longer see the enemy. He knew that other men were afraid when they went into action, but somehow it had never bothered him, the knowledge that he might die at any moment. In fact, he wasn't afraid of death at all. It was living that caused him pain.

Thorpe smiled, feeling several days' stubble move on his face. You learned to develop the right instincts, because they might be all that kept your mates and yourself alive. Your senses evolved so that you knew precisely where the members of your own unit were positioned and could see an area of ground as if it were magnified on a TV screen, with any movement immediately apparent. That was what he sensed now – a movement somewhere in the hills. Something coming this way.

There was no sense in giving away his own position. He'd seen men who'd made stupid mistakes and given themselves away. Those men didn't survive long. Worse, they put their mates at risk.

The loud squealing of the vehicle working high on the quarry edge echoed over the cement works like the voice of a desert demon. A huge dumper truck had come over the ridge and was descending the banking. Thorpe couldn't see it yet, but he could feel the vibration in the ground long before it reached him.

4

DI Hitchens poked a strip of paper into his desk fan. The whirling blades chewed it with a noise like a high-speed power drill.

'Her name was Carol Proctor,' he said. 'Quite a good-looking woman when she was alive.'

Diane Fry stared out of the window of the DI's office, wondering what her sister Angie was doing now. Probably she'd gone back to bed, and was rolled up tight in her duvet with a mug of coffee going cold on the floor by the settee. Or maybe she was in the bedroom, trying on her sister's clothes. With a bit of luck, none of them would fit her. But that was ungracious. And unlikely.

'I hope that was noted in her file,' said Fry. 'It would make her relatives feel so much better.'

Hitchens looked up at her sharply from his fan, but she kept her back turned. She didn't really want to get into an argument with her boss about detectives whose first response at a murder scene was to comment on the sexual attractiveness of the victim. Not just now, anyway.

'This was in 1990,' said Hitchens.

'Oh, I see.'

'Carol Proctor was married to one of Mansell Quinn's

closest friends. But Quinn had been knocking her off for years.'

'He was married himself?'

'Oh, yes. The Quinns were doing quite well for themselves, and had bought a nice little detached house in Castleton. He was in the building trade – but he was bright, you know, not some dim brickie with a sunburnt arse. In fact, he'd recently started his own contracting business, if I remember rightly. Small-scale, but doing OK, by all accounts. There's always plenty of work in that area – extensions and modernizations, you know the sort of thing.'

'You said they bought the house in Castleton, though,' said Fry. 'He didn't build it himself.'

'No, the cobbler's wife and all that. This place was new, and nicely done out. I wouldn't have minded somewhere like that myself, but you can't get houses in Castleton these days.'

Fry turned away from the window, irritated by the sound of another strip of paper being fed into the fan. The grinding was making her think of her last visit to the dentist's.

'Were there any children, sir?'

'The Quinns had two, one of each. Sounds like the perfect happy family, doesn't it?'

'But this Carol Proctor . . . ?'

'Yes, that's where the pretty picture falls apart. The other woman.'

'It sounds rather predictable.'

'Maybe. Unfortunately, we were never able to establish why Carol Proctor had gone to the Quinn house that day. She only lived down the road, so maybe it was just an impulse, or she had something to say to Quinn that wouldn't wait. We couldn't find out why they'd argued, either. Quinn himself was notably unhelpful.'

'And his affair had been going on for some time, regardless of the nice new house, two children and a dog?'

'There wasn't a dog,' said Hitchens.

'I meant it figuratively.'

Hitchens watched her as she moved away from the window and found a chair.

'Are you all right, Fry?' he said. 'You seem to be in a strange mood this morning.'

Fry gave herself a mental shake. 'I'm fine. Sorry.'

'Good. Anyway, yes. Quinn's affair was long standing. I was amazed at the time. I mean, how do you keep up a lie to a person you've lived with for so long, and not get caught out? You'd be bound to slip up in some way, wouldn't you?'

'I wouldn't know, sir,' said Fry.

'No?'

'I've lived alone, mostly.'

'Oh, yes.'

Fry had lived alone for a long time, as the DI knew perfectly well. But she'd become hardened to it. She'd been able to hold back the tide of loneliness, until now. Having someone else around made it difficult to deal with things in her own way.

Since the middle of June, she'd been constantly aware that there was another person in the flat. She'd started to notice the grubbiness of the carpets and the damp stains on the walls, as if she were ashamed of the way she lived.

'I think being single can be an advantage sometimes,' said Hitchens thoughtfully. 'I mean, for the job. You're ambitious, aren't you, Fry? Want to get promoted further?'

'Of course.'

'With fast-track procedures, you can rise to superintendent in seven years now. The pressure's immense, and the chances of failure are enormous. But it's possible. That's what I wanted to do, you know. But life gets in the way.'

'Yes, sir.'

If he was appealing for her sympathy, he was wasting his time. Fry remembered the way she'd been thinking when she first transferred to Derbyshire Constabulary. There had been very little on her mind except how quickly she could progress up the promotion ladder, the best way to make an impression on her senior officers, and who among her new colleagues might be of most use in her ambitions. But at this distance, she could see that she'd been trying hard to fill her mind with work, to keep out the things she didn't want to think about.

There had been only one exception to her self-imposed rule then, just one subject that had occupied her thoughts when she was away from the office: her sister.

Yet that first time Angie had visited Grosvenor Avenue, when Diane had driven her back from the Dark Peak village of Withens in a daze, her sister had barely glanced at the flat, commenting. 'This place is OK, I suppose.' She'd shown no interest in seeing the kitchen or the bedroom, let alone any inclination to disapprove of the clutter, or the dirty clothes left on the bathroom floor. So why should her presence have made Fry feel suddenly so defensive about the mess?

'It suits me,' she'd heard herself say.

And it was true, of course. She had no need of a home any more, no desire for a place that she might learn to care about.

'Who are the people in the other flats?' Angie had asked.
'Students.'
'God, students. They're a pain in the arse.'

And the conversation had stumbled into of those awkward pauses again, as if Angie were some total stranger she had nothing in common with, instead of being her sister.

Diane had found herself standing like an idiot in the middle of the sitting-room carpet, shuffling from one foot to the other while she tried to think of something else to say.

Angie had flopped down on the old settee and stretched her legs with a sigh, staring at the toes of her trainers, which were still damp from the rain in Withens.

'Well, aren't you going to offer me a coffee or something, Sis? Even Ben offered me a coffee, when I was at his place.'

Fry didn't move. Even her shuffling stopped. She waited for her sister to meet her eye, but Angie wouldn't look up.

'You went to Ben Cooper's house?'

Angie smiled at her toes in a conspiratorial way, as if they'd done something quite clever.

'I only stayed there the one night,' she said.

Fry clenched her fingers until her nails dug into her palms. 'I don't think I want to know this.'

Angie shrugged. 'It's not important. Ask me about it when you feel a bit more interested.'

Fry opened her mouth, shifted her feet again, and noticed the pain in the palms of her hands.

'How do you take your coffee?' she said.

For some reason, Angie was still smiling. But now she looked up at her younger sister with a knowing look in her eyes.

'We've got a lot to learn about each other,' she said. 'Haven't we, Sis?'

Diane Fry left the DI's office aware that she'd absorbed only part of what he'd been telling her. And that wasn't like her at all. She prided herself on a good memory for details when she was on the job. At home, life might pass in a haze some of the time, but not when she was at work. She was sharp, on the ball, a cut above the rest of them in CID. Well, usually she was. Maybe she was sickening for something.

It was remembering that day in Withens that had distracted her. She still felt the shock of the moment that she'd turned to see Ben Cooper walking away and her sister standing there in the road instead, as if fifteen years had vanished in a blink of an eye. Since that day, she hadn't been able to think of her sister without thinking of Cooper, too. The bastard had intruded himself into her private life like a splinter under her fingernail. She would have to find out the truth from him one day. Until she had an explanation of his involvement, there was a missing connection. And without it, the presence of her sister in her life again just didn't add up.

Pausing in the corridor, Fry pulled out her phone and dialled Cooper's number again before she could stop to reconsider. But all she got was the recorded voice telling her his number was still unobtainable.

She thrust the phone back into her pocket and kept walking. That was the problem with feelings – they could be so ambiguous. It didn't make any sense at all to feel disappointed and relieved at the same time.

'The Devil's Arse,' said the older of the two girls, with conviction. 'We want to go up the Devil's Arse.'

Ben Cooper smiled at an old lady who turned to stare at them. He tried to get a sort of tolerant amusement into the smile, mingled with embarrassed apology. The old lady lowered her head and leaned to whisper something to a friend supporting herself on a walking frame. Cooper flushed, imagining the worst possible thing she could be saying.

They're not mine, he'd wanted to tell her, but he couldn't.

Although it was a Monday, the streets of Edendale were packed. The summer holiday season had started in the Peak District. It was sunny enough for the old ladies to stroll from their excursion coach to the tea rooms, as well as for younger visitors to shed some of their clothes and sprawl on the grass near the river. Cooper found it too humid in town when the weather was warm. He preferred to be on higher ground, where he could feel a bit of cool breeze coming over the moors.

In the pedestrianized area of Clappergate, they weaved their way between the benches and stone flowerbeds, wrought-iron lampposts and bicycle racks. A little way ahead was the Vine Inn and the brass plaque outside it that he knew so well: *In memory of Sergeant Joseph Cooper of the Derbyshire Constabulary, who died in the course of his duty near here.*

41

Cooper tried walking a bit more quickly. Perhaps if he could get away from the crowds, he'd feel a bit easier.

'That's rude,' said Josie. 'I don't say rude words.'

'"The Devil's Arse" is what they call it,' said Amy. 'So it can't be rude.'

'It is.'

'It's not. Just you ask Uncle Ben.'

Cooper stopped. 'Tomorrow,' he said brightly.

'Why can't we ask you now?' said Amy.

'No, I mean we're going there tomorrow.'

'Peak Cavern,' said Josie. 'That's what it's called properly. We'll go to Peak Cavern.'

Cooper was sweating. And it wasn't just the humidity either. Talking to his nieces was like walking through a minefield these days. He didn't want Matt and Kate accusing him of teaching the girls to say 'arse'. But he could already hear them saying it when they went home to the farm tonight. *Uncle Ben says we can say 'arse', Dad*. Just great.

'It's your day off *today*,' said Amy, who was the older of the two and knew CID shift patterns and duty rosters better than he did himself.

'I've got two days off this time,' he said. 'So we can go tomorrow.'

'But . . .'

'Yes?'

'But what if you get phoned up?'

Cooper sighed. He felt a surge of sympathy for all the family men on E Division. This must be what it was like for them all the time. The constant cries of: 'Why weren't you there, Dad?', 'It's supposed to be your day off,' and 'What if you get *phoned up*?'

'If I get phoned up,' said Cooper, 'we'll go some other time. I promise.'

He could almost hear the girls weighing up the value of his promise, and judging its reliability. They were far too wise to trust any promise that an adult made, but they wanted to believe him. He opened his mouth to add: *I've never let you down before, have I?* But he knew it wouldn't be true.

A party of hikers went by. Their clothes were dazzling, and their walking poles the latest anti-shock design. Getting kitted up for a day on the Derbyshire hills was becoming an exercise in fashion awareness, and all the accessories had to be exactly right. Soon, people would be choosing their rucksacks to match the colour of their eyes.

A white-haired man walked towards them on the pedestrianized area. The first thing Cooper noticed was his comb-over. Every time he saw one, Ben prayed that he'd have enough sense not to do it himself when he was losing his hair. Be bald, wear a hat — anything but a comb-over.'

The man was wearing a silver-grey sports jacket and a blue silk shirt that hung outside his trousers. He had dazzling white trainers and a white toothbrush moustache that was probably the height of fashion when it had been black. His hair was long, too, even allowing for the requirements of his comb-over. He looked like an ageing British character actor playing the role of a faded gigolo.

Cooper was so distracted by the shopper that at first he didn't notice a man in a security company uniform gesturing to him from the doorway of W.H. Smith's. He was a retired police officer who had moved into the expanding private security business, so now he got a better uniform to wear.

'I think there's a couple of those Hanson brothers just been in here,' he said. 'Right toe-rags, they are. There's a warrant out for both of them. I don't know them myself, but it looked like them from the pictures.'

Cooper stopped. 'I know them, but . . .'

'You might want to keep an eye out for them. They're probably somewhere down near the High Street.'

Amy and Josie were looking at the man and listening with interest.

'Look, I'm off duty,' said Cooper.

The security man noticed the girls for the first time. 'Oh, right. You've got your kids with you.'

'They're not mine, actually.'

'I see.'

'They're my nieces. My brother's children.'

Cooper had realized before he even stopped to speak to him that the ex-bobby was just the right age to have worked with his father. He found himself fidgeting immediately, anxious to move on before the reminiscences began, the stories of late turns together as young PCs. Because they would be followed very quickly by the assurances of how much everyone had respected and loved Sergeant Joe Cooper, and how devastated they'd all been when *it* happened.

It wasn't so much of a problem at the West Street station in Edendale these days, but the retired coppers were the worst. These were the blokes who had been counting the days and hours until they could collect their full pensions after thirty years' service. Yet now you would think they'd been forced to leave behind the happiest days of their lives.

'Must get on,' said Cooper. 'Nice to see you.'

'Hey, these must be Joe Cooper's grandchildren, then.'

But Cooper just waved and smiled as he put distance between himself and the doorway of Smith's. Josie had to run to catch up with him.

Cooper thought occasionally of his own old age, though it was usually a brief speculation about whether he would live longer than his father had. He didn't feel any great desire to be a dad himself. Not just yet, anyway. But when he was old, when he was as helpless as his own mother was now, who would be there to look after him? At the present rate, there would be no one.

But that day was decades away; not something to worry about now. It was only the approach of his birthday that was making him think about ageing. And it wasn't just any birthday this time, either.

Joe Cooper's birthday had been in July, too. That meant they shared the star sign of Cancer, the crab in its shell. An astrologer would probably have been delighted that it had taken Cooper so long to move out of Bridge End Farm for a place of his own. A reluctance to leave the family home, a need to cling on to his shell. He would be thirty years old on Saturday, for heaven's sake.

As for his job, Cooper was sure he'd be asked one day soon to undergo a bit of lateral development and say goodbye to CID for a while. Somebody was going to turn up with a sharp knife to prise him out of his shell.

'You should have introduced us to that man,' said Amy. 'He knew Granddad.'

'I thought you wanted your lunch?'

'It wasn't very polite.'

'You're not polite either,' said Josie to her sister. 'You say "arse".'

Cooper wondered for a moment if he was being selfish. He hadn't wanted to hear a retired bobby's stories about his father. In fact, he'd been worried that this ex-copper might have been one of those called to the scene of Sergeant Joe Cooper's death, and would therefore be carrying a picture in his head of the body lying in its pool of blood. He definitely didn't want to go there.

But Amy and Josie might *want* to talk about their grandfather with someone who'd known him, someone other than a member of their own family. It might help them understand what had happened.

Cooper shook his head. That was something else he wasn't going to take responsibility for. Matt could negotiate that minefield himself.

At the corner of High Street and Clappergate, a few yards short of McDonald's, Cooper saw two of the Hanson brothers across the road. He recognized them without any problem. He'd arrested them himself before now, and in fact had been to school with their oldest brother. These two had failed to answer to bail given them by a lenient magistrates' bench and had been rumoured to have left Derbyshire altogether, for fear of ending up back inside. Cooper reached automatically for his mobile phone, only now realizing that he had forgotten to switch it back on after the cave rescue exercise.

Then he noticed Amy watching him with the sort of expression that only a child could manage, an expression that came from her natural occupation of the moral high ground when dealing with adults.

'You're off duty,' she said. 'You're not supposed to be finding criminals today.'

Cooper looked at her, pausing with his finger on the first button. He was supposed to take the girls to McDonald's and buy them a Happy Meal before he took them home to Bridge End Farm, preferably safe and uncorrupted.

'Yes, I know,' he said. 'But sometimes they seem to find me. That's just the way it is.' And he continued to dial.

5

The bus from Ashbourne to Edendale was almost empty. Mansell Quinn took a seat near a back window, where other passengers couldn't see him. He watched the scenery gradually change to the familiar White Peak pattern of fields and drystone walls, until a rash of limestone quarries erupted from the landscape near the A6. They were so noticeable on the edge of the national park that Quinn was surprised they were still working.

In Edendale, he went to find the well in Spa Lane. The water still ran from its brass pipe, and people were queuing with plastic containers. A man with a tray of two-litre bottles was collecting gallons of it. Quinn waited until they'd all gone, then bent to take a drink in his cupped hands. He'd expected the water to be cold, like a natural stream. But it was strangely tepid and had a faint mineral tang – not as he'd remembered it at all.

All the way from Sudbury, he'd been building up courage to enter a shop. He'd passed several charity shops on the way to the well, and had noticed that all the assistants were women. As were most of the customers. He was worried that women tended to notice too much.

Then he saw a couple heading towards the door of the

Oxfam shop in Clappergate, and he walked in behind them, almost hanging on to their coat-tails to help him over the threshold. He bought a faded check shirt for two pounds fifty. Encouraged, he moved on, and found a pair of jeans the right size for him in Scope a few doors away.

But he had to choose a coat carefully. He wanted something that was light but rainproof, one with a hood. He'd be outdoors a lot, but he didn't want to be weighed down by anything too heavy in the hot weather. Quinn had a momentary panic when he realized that the same women he'd followed into Oxfam were also in Help the Aged. But they took no notice of him, and he guessed there must be some kind of circuit that people did of the charity shops. Everyone liked a routine.

In Cancer Research, by the delivery entrance to the Clappergate shopping centre, he found exactly the right thing. It was a black Wynnster stowaway smock, waterproof and breathable, but light enough to roll up and carry. It had a peaked hood and a velcro fastening at the back, a storm flap that buttoned up to his face and a drawstring to pull the hood tight. It must have cost about thirty or forty pounds new. This one had a slight rip down one side and the lining was worn inside the collar, but that wouldn't bother him. It smelled faintly of oil, as if someone had worn it while working on a car engine. That didn't worry him either.

And then, at the back of the shop, he came across a small rucksack. It was a dark khaki, not the useless garish colours that he'd seen in the shop windows. This one might have been army surplus stock at some time. It looked as though it dated from the 1950s, but it was well made, sound enough for the use he had in mind.

'It's a bit warm for hiking, isn't it?'

'What?'

Quinn had his cash ready in his hand, having worked out the total amount before he went to the till. He expected to

48

be able to hand over the money, take his purchases and go, without giving the woman behind the counter anything to remember him by.

'Hiking,' she said. 'Your rucksack and waterproof – I assume you're going hiking?'

The woman was folding the smock and finding a plastic bag to put it in. She was only making small talk, and Quinn knew there ought to be an answer he could give that she'd think was normal.

'Yes,' he said. 'But not here.'

She looked up at him then, and smiled. Quinn felt she was forcing him to fill the silence.

'Wales,' he said.

It was the first place that had come into his head. But he knew immediately it had been the wrong thing to say. If there were reports about him in the newspapers, they might mention he was from Wales.

'We went there last year,' said the woman. 'Aberystwyth. I wouldn't go hiking in Wales, though. There are far too many mountains for my liking. I'm getting too old for all that.'

She gave him a quizzical look. Quinn knew she was trying to assess his age, and soon she'd be wondering why he was going hiking on his own with an ancient rucksack and a ripped waterproof.

He could feel himself getting angry. The tremors were starting in his hands, his temples throbbed, and he could hear the hissing inside his head – the sound of blood rushing to his brain.

'Are you going to take the money?' he said.

He put his notes on the counter and picked up the carrier bag.

'Wait. You need some change,' she said.

'It doesn't matter.'

Quinn paused outside the shop to check his purchases,

afraid that he might have left something behind. Instinct made him look back through the plate-glass window, where the woman who'd served him was standing at her counter. She was watching him. Her look made him feel as if someone had seen straight through him and knew exactly what he was planning to do.

He walked quickly away from the shop. She probably wasn't even looking at him at all – she was more than likely staring at something behind him across the street, or admiring her own reflection in the window. Then Quinn remembered that it didn't really matter anyway. By the time he was a hundred yards away, he had calmed down; he began to walk more slowly.

The Vine Inn was still here, anyway. He'd drunk in the pub a time or two, but it was done up now to attract a better class of customer. It had been re-painted, and the chalk boards outside offered specials from a food menu.

Then Quinn noticed the brass plaque fixed to one of the stone flowerbeds outside the pub, and the lettering caught his eye. *In memory of Sergeant Joseph Cooper.* He stared at the wording, reading it over to himself several times before he looked up and remembered where he was. *In memory of Sergeant Joseph Cooper.*

At least he could get out of the town now. The last few items on his list wouldn't be found in any charity shop, so he'd have to go elsewhere. But he had to move on. There were things he had to do. And there wasn't much time.

On the last leg of his journey, Quinn closed his eyes and tried to rest. By the time he looked out of the window again, he was already in the Hope Valley. The familiar hills gathered close around him, welcoming, drawing him in.

The familiarity of it caught at Quinn's throat as he got off the bus and walked through a field towards a line of trees. Tiny flies rose from the seedheads of the long grass as he brushed through it. He broke off one of the heads and put

50

it in his mouth to chew. It tasted nutty, but reminded him of oats, too. He thought of a bowl of muesli, and then of sitting at the kitchen table in the morning, pouring milk, smelling coffee, listening to the children getting ready for school.

And then somewhere he heard a gate creak. He was supposed to have fixed the gate. More than fourteen years ago, he'd promised to oil the hinges. That sound alone was enough to take him back to 1990, to wipe away the intervening years as if they'd never existed. The side gate creaked, and here was Mansell Quinn standing listening to it, expecting at any moment to hear his wife's voice reminding him that he'd promised to attend to it.

Quinn experienced a moment of confusion. He could see himself opening the door of the garage, sighing with exasperation because he'd been distracted from doing something more important. He could picture lifting a can of WD40 from the shelf, coughing at the dust as he moved a box of tools, brushing off an old spider's web, and noticing the spare set of spark plugs he'd been looking for. He could even remember the texture of the breeze-block wall behind the shelf, and see its colour – pale blue, because they had some paint left over when the kitchen was decorated. He recalled spraying WD40 on the hinges of the gate, and watching the rusted metal darken as the liquid soaked in and began to run. He could smell the alcohol fumes as the spray drifted back into his face.

He'd fixed the gate. Yet still he could hear the creak. It was as if his life had re-started – not from the moment the police came to the house and arrested him, on his last day of freedom, but earlier than that. It was as though he'd walked back into his own life at a point before everything had started to go wrong.

After a few minutes, Quinn straightened up. It wasn't the same house, or the same gate. His memories had confused him about what was in the past and what was right here in the present.

But there was one memory he knew was real – the one that hadn't left his mind for the past fourteen years. This one was no mere trick of déjà vu. It was the memory of blood – blood pooling and streaming on a golden field.

It had begun to rain. He hadn't noticed the clouds gathering, hadn't even thought to look at the sky. He put on the smock and pulled up the hood. But his face was already wet, and more water dripped on him from the trees.

Quinn had started making his plans two years ago – on the day they told him he'd be making his final move. It had been a morning in early April, a day when the beech trees visible from the exercise yard at Gartree were starting to change their shape and colour, the outline of their naked branches blurring with the suggestion of spring.

'You're being transferred to an open prison,' his wing governor had told him. 'HMP Sudbury. It's in Derbyshire. That will be a lot closer to your home, Quinn. It will make it much easier for your family to visit you.'

Quinn had stared at the man as if he were speaking a foreign language. He might as well have been, for all the sense he was making. Quinn waited for the translation, but none came. The governor looked at the file on his desk, but failed to see that Quinn had never received any family visits at Gartree, not once in eight years.

'Well, aren't you pleased, Quinn?'

'Oh. Yes, sir.'

'You'll be glad to be out of this place. I know things haven't always been easy for you here. You went through a bit of a rough patch, didn't you?' The governor flicked over a page of the file in front of him. He wasn't attempting to read it. Not even pretending to. He was just flicking it with his long, white fingers, as if he could consign Quinn's memories to the past by turning a page, closing a file, sliding it into a drawer of a cabinet. Was it all there, on that one page of his file, summed up in a few paragraphs typed by a Prison Service secretary?

'A bit of a rough patch. Yes, sir.'

The governor looked at Quinn doubtfully, but relaxed when he saw the prisoner's calmness.

'You'll find life an awful lot easier at HMP Sudbury. And, of course, it's a step closer to your release.'

He smiled hopefully. But something was happening inside Quinn. His body seemed to be filling with a cloud of poisonous gas that rose from somewhere deep in his guts and coiled through his intestines. It flooded his lungs and seeped into his brain. He waited, terrified, for the cloud to dissipate before he could speak.

'Thank you, sir.'

Another smile now, different. An ironic smile. 'That's provided you're on your best behaviour, Quinn. You don't want to end up back here, do you?'

The governor waited a few seconds for a response, then began to get uncomfortable. He closed the file with a little swish and a click. 'Perhaps it's something that will take a while to sink in. I understand that, Quinn. If you want to talk to anybody about it, just let Mr Jeavons know, and it can be arranged. You know there are counsellors available. A chaplain, perhaps . . .'

Quinn tried to shake his head, but the muscles in his neck would hardly move. He felt as though his face had swollen to a monstrous size and was swinging from side to side against the walls of the office, like a hot-air balloon. His skin was on fire and a curtain had dropped in front of his eyes, preventing him from seeing the governor clearly. Yet Quinn remained motionless in his chair, his hands resting on his thighs, as he listened to the sound of the man's voice.

'Well, your transfer is set for next week. You can let your family know where you'll be, so they can visit.'

The voice was distant, like a voice in one of his dreams, the words muffled but menacing.

'Are you all right, Quinn?'

'Yes, sir. Thank you, sir.'

'That's it, then. You can go now.'

And Quinn had walked back to his cell, hardly aware of the prison officer at his elbow and the doors that closed behind him, or the familiar noises of his block and the voices of prisoners echoing on the landings, like the calls of animals in a distant jungle.

He heard none of them, because his mind was too fully occupied. Quinn had been thinking of all the people who were connected to that time in his past, the people who'd inhabited his dreams for so many years. And he had already been deciding which of them should die.

Rebecca Lowe had taken a breath to scream, but it was too late. The air had been punched from her lungs. She felt as if massive fists were squeezing her chest and emptying her of air like a disused plastic bag.

For a few moments, the shock froze Rebecca's muscles. Deep in her belly, she could feel her diaphragm twitching helplessly, like a part of her body that had been amputated but refused to die until its nerve endings stopped spasming. The interruption to her oxygen supply made her start to feel light-headed, and she tried to blink away the dark shadows that formed in front of her eyes. A sound came from the back of her throat – a moan that rolled inside her head but failed to reach the air.

Then suddenly she felt her diaphragm muscles spring back into place. They loosened their grip on her lungs, and a draught of air rushed into her chest. The sound it made was like a death rattle, that one last breath before you died. But you never heard your own last breath.

Rebecca Lowe opened her eyes. She realized she was lying

on the floor of her kitchen. She could feel the tiles under her back and the dampness soaking through her clothes. She'd washed the floor only an hour before, and the smell of detergent was overpowering. Tentatively, she moved a hand and heard one of her rings click against the tiles. But her hand seemed to be a long way from her face, and she couldn't understand why her arm should be thrown out at such an awkward angle.

Then she became aware of how much her head hurt. It was as though the oxygen drawn into her lungs had finally reached her head and activated the pain switch, alerting the nerve cells to the message of the impact on the floor, and now they were shrilling like fire alarms. Waves of agony rolled from the back of her head to the front and burst inside her eyes, forcing her to squeeze her eyelids shut against the light.

Rebecca knew that moving her head would only make the pain worse. So she tried to move a leg instead. It seemed to be the furthest and safest part of her body. At first, she couldn't tell which leg she was moving, because they both were tangled together. But then one leg fell away from the other, flopping on to the floor. It was only when she felt the dampness on her foot that she realized she'd lost one of her shoes. She'd been wearing her flip-flops – a mistake on a damp floor, because their soles were too smooth and slippery.

Automatically, Rebecca began to lift her head to look for the flip-flop. She screamed, and continued to scream as the pain smashed into her brain, bouncing off her skull and surging along her body, ripping through every muscle and nerve. Her head fell back on to the floor, setting off the tide of agony all over again. Her fingers clawed and scrabbled on the tiles, making random patterns in the damp surface. Her stomach heaved and sent streams of bile into her throat. Tears filled her eyes and ran down her cheeks.

Rebecca found that her breathing was ragged and gasping, and she tried to steady it. Somehow, she had to work out what to do. She knew she was badly hurt, and alone in the house. She could call for help, but no louder than she'd already screamed from the pain. She could hear her own scream still echoing in her ears.

The house was nearly airtight and well insulated. No one would hear her unless they were standing right outside her double-glazed window. And the nearest neighbours were three hundred yards away. Rebecca listened for a car on the road, but the only sounds she heard were the wind and the rain.

She knew her one chance was to make it to a phone. But the mere thought of it made her wince in agony. She had no hope of reaching the next room without passing out from the pain and perhaps doing herself more damage. If only she had her mobile phone in her pocket. But she knew it was where she'd left it earlier – in her handbag, on the dining-room table.

Just trying to think made her head hurt. Her tears flowed faster as she realized she might have to wait until somebody came to the house and found her. But she expected to be alone all night, and all day tomorrow.

Slowly, Rebecca became aware that something else was wrong. She thought about her dog, Milly, who had been asleep in the utility room. Milly ought to have woken or reacted in some way to her scream. If she could just have touched the dog, felt her presence nearby, it would have provided a small scrap of reassurance, the company of another living creature.

But there was a silence in the house that didn't feel right. In the midst of her pain, Rebecca felt that silence nudging her towards some small thing that had been dislodged from her memory by her fall – something she couldn't quite grasp, because her mind would no longer concentrate properly.

Then she remembered the sound she'd heard just before she fell. It had been the soft cough of the back door opening.

6

There were no lights on at Parson's Croft when Dawn Cottrill drove up to the house. Not even the security lights, which should have come on when the sensors caught the movement of her car on the drive. That alone was enough to tell her that something was wrong.

Dawn had been trying to phone her sister for the past hour, ever since Andrea had called from London, already in a panic and imagining the worst. Rebecca wasn't answering either the house number or her mobile. Of course, Andrea had wanted to contact the police straight away, but Dawn had managed to talk her out of it. And now she was regretting it. It was a little too dark up here in Aston, where there was no street lighting and all the houses were screened from the neighbours by trees. Rebecca never forgot to switch on the outside lights at night.

Dawn was well prepared, though. She fumbled in her glove compartment for the torch she always kept in case of breakdowns. It was a pity Jeff was at that conference in Birmingham tonight, because she would have preferred him to be with her. But she ought to be able to do some things on her own, and checking on her sister was one.

Carefully locking the car, she went to the back door of the

house. It was the door she always used when she visited her sister, and besides she had a spare key so she could water the plants or feed the dog when Rebecca was away.

Dawn could think of only two possibilities. Most likely, her sister had gone out somewhere and forgotten to take her mobile phone. The garage door was closed, so she couldn't tell whether Rebecca's car was there or not. Everyone forgot their mobile now and then. It was even possible to forget your mobile and not remember to switch on the outside lights when you left the house.

There was also a chance that Rebecca was ill. She suffered from migraines sometimes, and she might have taken her tablets and gone to bed to sleep it off. Probably she wouldn't have heard the phone that way. Dawn imagined her sister lying in her bedroom upstairs, and felt slightly reassured. It was something that could be dealt with.

Even as she tried the key in the lock, Dawn knocked on the back door, knowing it was a useless thing to do. Obviously, Rebecca wouldn't be sitting in the house with all the lights out.

But the key wouldn't turn. Dawn pulled it out, looked at it with the torch to make sure she had the right one, and tried again. She rattled it backwards and forwards, and found it turned to the left quite easily, then back again. The door hadn't been locked.

With a sense of dread, Dawn turned the handle and pushed the door, jumping a little at the soft tearing sound as the seal parted. It was only then that it occurred to her she ought to have gone in through the front door, where the controls for the burglar alarm were located. But she knew with a cold certainty by now that the alarm wouldn't go off.

Sure enough, the house was completely silent. Dawn called her sister's name, listening to the waver in her own voice. She called again, a bit louder, trying to sound confident.

'Rebecca? Are you home?'

Rebecca could have forgotten to lock the back door too, she thought. If she was in a bad state with one of her migraines, all that sort of thing could have gone out of her head. Andrea would be very cross with her mum when she found out.

But Andrea's worries kept going through Dawn's mind. Though she knew there was no logic to it, she had to pluck up courage to switch on the light inside the house. She had come into the utility room, and the fluorescent light flickered and gleamed suddenly on the innocuous shapes of a couple of chest freezers, an automatic washing machine and a tumble drier. Through the door at the far end was the kitchen, still in darkness, and past that the hallway and the stairs. She could hear one of the freezers humming, perhaps a faint trickle of fluid. The house was very warm and airless, warmer than Dawn would choose to have her own home.

She crossed the utility room to the kitchen doorway and reached for the light switch. But she stopped. The hum of the freezer wasn't all she could hear. There was another sound, quite close by. It was just a slight movement, nothing but the tiniest scratch of something hard against the tiles.

'Rebecca? Are you there?'

She was answered by a noise that chilled her skin, despite the warmth of the central heating. It was a whimper. A small, pitiful whimper, so quiet that if she hadn't been standing still she might not have heard it at all. It was no more than a tiny sob, an involuntary release of sound into the silence of the house. Even now, Dawn might have convinced herself that she'd imagined it. But then it came again. And the noise wasn't ahead of her, in the darkened kitchen. It was behind her.

Dawn spun round, staring at the bright, white surfaces of the utility room and at the back door, which she now realized she had left open.

'Who's there?' she said, finding a strength and authority she hadn't known she possessed.

She shone her torch at the back door, but it made no impression on the darkness outside. She listened carefully, holding her breath. And gradually, her attention focused on one of the freezers.

The unit stood a few inches away from the wall. Dawn thought it had always been like that, but she wasn't absolutely sure. It was quite a large one, too, because Rebecca liked to buy organic meat in bulk from a local farm shop. It would take some strength to move it when it was full. So probably there had always been that slight gap between the freezer and the wall.

Dawn looked at the back door and decided to leave it open. She glanced around for a weapon, but could see nothing. Instead, she took a firmer grip on her torch and walked towards the freezer. She was about to open the lid when she heard the noise again. A soft brush against the wall, a scratch on the tiles. Something was behind the freezer.

She leaned over and shone her torch into the gap. Dust had gathered on the back of the freezer, although it hadn't been in place all that long. In among the pipes and cables she saw what at first appeared to be an old-fashioned fur muff jammed into the narrow space. It was brown and white, it smelled of urine, and it trembled when the light hit it.

'Oh, my God. Milly.'

It took Dawn a couple of minutes to prise the elderly Shih Tzu from behind the freezer, where she had crammed herself into an impossibly tiny ball. The dog's claws scratched frantically on the tiles and wall in an effort to prevent herself from being dragged into the light.

'Milly, you poor old thing. What happened to you?'

As far as she could tell, the dog seemed physically unharmed. But when she saw how terrified the animal was, Dawn hardly needed to look any further. She knew without a doubt that her sister must be dead.

*   *   *

60

On the way back from Castleton, Ben Cooper drove past the Hope cement works and over Pindale to reach the Eden Valley. A tiny hamlet lay at the foot of Pindale, with a restored mine building and a camp site. But few people took this route – the road was single track, and too steep and narrow to make for comfortable driving if you didn't know it well.

Further on, he crossed the Roman road, Batham Gate, and joined the B6049 south of Bradwell. After a few more miles, he crested the final hill and looked down on Edendale.

The Eden Valley lay at a sort of geological collision point where the two halves of the Peak District met. On one side were the limestone plateaux and wooded gorges of the White Peak, with its patchwork of fields and quiet villages. Enclosing them on three sides like the fingers of a hand were the higher slopes of the Dark Peak. Its barren peat moors were scattered with gritstone outcrops, eroded into the grotesque and sinister shapes that had created so many folk legends.

For Cooper, the White Peak and Dark Peak carried an irresistible symbolism – they represented light and dark, good and evil. Because of Edendale's location, he sometimes got the idea that he was literally walking the line between good and evil as he moved about the landscape. But the line wasn't so clear-cut as it might at first appear. Those dark outcrops of twisted rock had a tendency to erupt in places you didn't expect them. There was always a kind of darkness lurking just below the surface, ready to thrust its way into the daylight.

Cooper drove into the centre of town and reached his flat in Welbeck Street. He could see thunder clouds approaching in the west. They seemed to hang on the horizon for a while until they amassed a large enough bulk, and then they moved to blot out the sky. When he got out of the car, he could feel the air already becoming heavier and more humid. People would be going around saying 'It's going to break' with a note of relief in their voices.

With no tenant upstairs since the departure of his American neighbour, the house was strangely silent. Cooper still hadn't got used to coming home every night to an empty flat, with the post still lying on the doormat and an unwashed coffee mug standing in the sink from breakfast. He hadn't brought much with him from Bridge End Farm either, only his PC and a few prints, and of course the framed photograph over the fireplace – the one showing rows of police officers lined up in their uniforms, with Sergeant Joe Cooper standing in the second row. It had been taken at some formal occasion a few years before his father's death.

Living alone had many advantages. On his days off, it hardly seemed necessary to Cooper to get dressed or have a shave. He could slop around in an old T-shirt and a pair of tracksuit bottoms for as long as he liked. He could sit at the kitchen table and drink coffee and eat toast all morning, if he wanted to. And living on your own was nothing unusual these days. Soon, nearly half the country would be living alone.

Still, he couldn't help the rush of pleasure when the first thing he saw as he entered the flat was a black cat coming towards him from the kitchen, its fur warm and its yellow eyes gleaming expectantly. Randy had changed into his summer coat, and now he was sleek and dark, and obviously not as big a cat as he'd have everyone believe.

The rumbles Cooper could hear now weren't really a storm, more of a warning that the rain was coming. And come it did, within a few seconds. Instantly, the downpour was so heavy that it sounded as if the river had burst its banks and was surging across the gardens, threatening to flood the houses at the bottom end of the road.

In the kitchen, the noise of the rain was deafening as it fell on the glass roof of the conservatory. Above the sound, he heard the wooden frames of the windows cracking as they cooled and contracted. Cooper fed Randy and walked back into the sitting room. After the cat, the second thing he saw in his flat that night was the green light flashing on his answering machine. It was blinking at him in a way that could mean only one thing. Yet again, a small piece of darkness was about to thrust its way into the daylight.

Raymond Proctor arrived home late that night. Before he locked up the house, he took a look around the caravan park. He prayed there wouldn't be any last-minute arrivals tonight. Or if there were, that they'd find a temporary pitch without bothering him, and without making too much noise about it either. Let the buggers sort themselves out for once.

Proctor wanted to walk down to the pond and check the area round the old 'vans again. But not in the dark. The main lights only covered the central area of the site, around the office and shop. They made the log-cabin effect look grotesque and crumbling, like the set of a cheap horror film. Outside that pool of light, he could see only the glowing rectangles of curtained windows, where families were shut up in their little boxes for the night.

A car had come in through the main gate. It looked like the white Audi that belonged to the young family occupying one of the lodges. As it turned on to the gravel road, the car's headlights caught the outline of a figure moving across the grass near the water taps. Proctor squinted at the figure, but the headlights had passed long before he could make out who it was. Male, he was sure. Probably one of the group of French teachers who were staying on the site for a couple of nights on their way to Scotland. On the other hand, it could have been anybody.

Proctor limped into the house and checked all the bolts on the doors and windows. He left a light on in the hallway and the outside light over the back door. Connie was in the sitting room watching TV. He could hear the noise of gunfire and screeching tyres as soon as he entered the house.

63

'Turn it down,' he called from the hallway.

'What's the problem?'

'Nothing. Just turn it down.'

Connie came out into the hall, which wasn't what he'd intended. She was ready for bed, in her dressing gown and the slippers with blue fur round the edges. She stared at him and sniffed suspiciously.

'Who have you been drinking with?'

'Nobody.'

'Rubbish.'

'I only had a couple.'

'You're sweating, Ray. You can hardly keep still. I know when you've had too much to drink.'

'For God's sake, get back to your telly. I'm sick of your yacking.' A crashing noise made him jump. It was like a door being broken down, kicked in by boots. 'And turn that TV down, will you?'

She pointed a finger at him, jabbing it towards his face. 'If you speak to me like that again, Raymond Proctor, you'll regret it. You know I wanted us all to be together for dinner tonight, but you had to go out boozing. Then Jason started playing me up again and now he's sulking in his room.'

Proctor thought the idea of having family meals together was lunacy. He remembered that Alan had behaved exactly the same when he was about Jason's age. Funnily enough, it had been harder to tolerate from his own son. It must have been something to do with the guilt.

'I just want us to be a real family,' said Connie. 'Doing things together, getting on with each other.'

'I've got news for you, Connie. Real families *don't* get on with each other.'

She glared at him with sudden venom. 'And you should know. You've already lost one family. A wife and son – that was careless, wasn't it, Ray?'

'Leave me alone,' said Proctor.

She was right that he was sweating. The house felt ridiculously hot, but there was no way he was going outside again tonight.

'And take my advice,' said Connie as she turned to go back to her film. 'Be more careful who you drink with. You've never had a head for beer. It always gets you into trouble.'

Raymond Proctor stood in the hallway of his house for a few minutes longer. He was watching the play of light and shadow on the glass panels of the front door. He was familiar with the effect, which was caused by the movement of trees in front of the lights on the main drive. But tonight, there seemed to be more shadow than light on Wingate Lees.

Ye Olde Cheshire Cheese stood on the main street in Castleton, close to the Peak Hotel. It was late when Mansell Quinn arrived there, not much more than an hour before closing time. But he managed to get a room overlooking the street, with a view into the car park – though he wasn't worried about anyone coming to find him tonight.

Quinn felt so confident that he sat in the bar for a while and bought a tonic water. It was the first non-alcoholic drink that came into his mind, and he wanted to keep a clear head. The sweet smell of the beer was tempting, though.

'On holiday, are you?' the barman said, putting his drink down on the counter.

'Yes, I suppose so.'

'Doing a bit of walking?'

'Yes.'

The barman was middle-aged – about the same age as himself, Quinn realized. He stared at the man for a minute, experiencing a sudden, terrifying urge to talk to him, to tell him everything that was in his mind. He threw some money on the counter, leaving the barman to gather the coins together, and retreated to a corner of the bar.

Quinn hid his hands under the table until they'd stopped

shaking. He was angry again, but angry with himself. He looked around the bar, seeking something to distract him. There were so many things he didn't remember. He wasn't sure whether the place had changed or if it was just his memory at fault, a failure to reach back into the world he'd left behind fourteen years ago.

For a start, he couldn't recall seeing the prints of ancient photographs on the wall, showing that the Cheshire Cheese had once been a busy coaching inn. But in the days of horse-drawn coaches the sign had just read Cheshire Cheese'. So 'Ye Olde' must have been a twentieth-century addition.

Over there, at the back of the room, was where he'd often sat with Ray Proctor and Will Thorpe. They'd been sitting there on that day nearly fourteen years ago, though the table and chairs had surely been replaced by now. Had there been four places at the table then? Quinn was amazed how hazy his memory was of that time. The events ought to be imprinted on his mind, but even now there were gaps in his recollection that he couldn't fill. Some of it had come back to him almost randomly in the days and weeks following his arrest, with a sudden, sharp detail hacked out of his memory by a question from the police or a snatch of music in the next room. But not everything. A few of the triggers he needed were still missing, and he didn't know where to find them.

Quinn eyed the barman to see if he was watching and took a drink of his tonic water, which tasted sharp and bitter, like acid. After a while, he regained his composure and noticed the smells of food drifting from the kitchen. He'd eaten nothing since breakfast at the prison that morning, before his eight thirty release. He found a menu on the table, and ordered scampi and chips.

'Don't panic,' said the barman, when he brought the food. 'But do you want tartare sauce?'

As closing time approached at eleven o'clock, Quinn finished his drink and went to his room. He paused in the passage to listen to the sound of staff chatting and clattering their cooking equipment in the kitchen, wondering if they were talking about him. On the landing, he walked under the lens of a security camera that pointed towards his room. He would pass it again tomorrow on the way out.

He'd started thinking about cameras in Edendale, when he noticed the CCTV system covering the shopping area. He had watched the cameras swivelling on their tall poles, and had pictured the operators in a room somewhere – a bit like the control room at Gartree, where they'd watched every move he made when he was out of his cell. But in Edendale they were watching everyone. And nobody seemed to mind.

Quinn counted the number of licence conditions he'd already broken. He hadn't kept his appointment at the probation office, he wasn't living where he was supposed to, and he hadn't told his probation officer where he was going. There were people he wasn't supposed to get in contact with, too. But what was the saying about a sheep and a lamb?

All the money he had was a bit of cash he'd earned working on the farm unit and his discharge grant. The grant was equivalent to a week's benefit, and was supposed to cover him until he received Income Support or Jobseeker's Allowance. At least he didn't have to worry about gate arrest, as so many prisoners did when they were due for release. The police had shown no interest in him.

His room at the Cheshire Cheese was almost filled by a double bed. A shower cubicle stood in one corner, and a couple of steps led down to an alcove containing a toilet and washbasin. A small TV screen perched high up on a bracket near the ceiling. Quinn paced the room for a while. It was dark outside by now, so he drew the curtains. On the window ledge he found a small teddy bear sitting in a spindle chair with a black-and-white cat on its knee.

He played with a touch lamp on the bedside table, then he lay on the bed and pressed buttons on the TV remote. A game show appeared and he left it on, not listening to the voices but watching the faces of the contestants. They seemed to be family groups – mother, father, a couple of teenage kids. They smiled and laughed at the compere's jokes. But Quinn knew there would be arguments in the car on the way home. Tears, accusations, the old resentments and insults dragged out and rehearsed all over again.

Soon, he began to feel tired. Anger tended to drain all the energy from him. He peeled off his charity-shop clothes and took a shower, knowing it might be the last he'd have for a while. The hot water felt good on his skin.

When Quinn got into bed, he could still taste the bitterness of the tonic water in his mouth, and the spiciness of the tartare sauce. The two flavours mingled in his thoughts as he drifted into sleep. Spice and bitterness, bitterness and spice. The taste of blood and kisses.

7

No matter how many dead bodies he'd seen, Ben Cooper
would never forget the first. He'd been thirteen years old at
the time, a pubescent youth in baggy jeans. Until then, he'd
been protected from most of the unpleasantness of the world.
He was oblivious to the grubby human realities that were
waiting to jostle him with their sharp elbows and breathe
their stale breath into his face. He'd thought he was immor-
tal then. He'd thought that everyone around him would live
forever, too. But most of the things he'd believed were wrong.

It was shortly before Christmas, and the pavements in
Edendale had been cold and wet. Ben and his mother had
been shopping for last-minute presents and the vast amount
of food involved in celebrating a family Christmas at Bridge
End Farm. The young Ben had been tired and bad tempered,
and he was sulking about being dragged round the shops. It
was already dark by late afternoon and illuminated Santas
hung from the lamp posts, while plastic trees twinkled in
every shop window.

'Mum, can we go home yet?' he'd been saying, without
any hope.

And then they had turned the corner of Bargate and walked

into a small crowd of people on the pavement between the Unicorn pub and Marks and Spencers. They were arguing with a policeman and each other as they waited for an ambulance to arrive.

In the middle of the crowd, a man had been lying on the floor, covered with a sheet that someone had brought out from the pub. Only the soles of his boots were showing, tilted at an unnatural angle. The wet pavement around him had reflected the Christmas lights, breaking up their colours into fragments of rainbow, as if the man had been lying in the middle of an oil slick.

That was all Ben could take in before his mother hurried him away. There had been no blood to see, no injuries, no staring eyes or offensive bodily fluids. It had been the boots and the angle of them, impossible in life, which had told him the man was dead.

And now, in Rebecca Lowe's home, it was the small things again that conveyed the story of violent death. Not the blood or the stains on the kitchen floor, or even the distinctive smell. It was the way her head had tipped too far back and lay at an angle that would make it difficult for her to breathe if she were alive. It was the position of her right hand, still curled in a spasm as it clutched at the floor, the fingers digging so hard into the tiles that her nails had splintered and broken, and the pale varnish lay around them in flakes of glittering dust. And it was the single blue sandal, turned the wrong way up, lying on the floor a few inches from the victim's foot. Her toes were pointing towards it, as if she had been reaching to retrieve her sandal in her last moments, but had failed.

Some of the team had been allowed into the house, entering via the integral garage into a passage where they could access the lounge and dining room, and reach the stairs. Cooper had been waiting in the garage for ten minutes with other officers until the door had been opened, and there hadn't

70

been enough oxygen in there for them to share. He'd have given anything for a bit of fresh air right now.

Inside the house, Cooper paused in the hallway and looked into the lounge. Fitted carpet lapped from wall to wall, and from doorway to doorway, flowing out into the hall in an unbroken sea of Wilton. Thick curtains covered the windows – in fact, not just the windows, but the whole wall from floor to ceiling, a great blanket of brown velvet designed to shut off the room from the outside, as if the double glazing wasn't enough to do the job on its own.

He imagined that everything in the house had been sealed: the fireplace would have no chimney, the doors would be insulated, and no doubt the roof space was layered with fibreglass. Parson's Croft felt like a warm cocoon.

To Cooper, it seemed unnatural to think about hiding away from the outside world to such an extent. If you were going to cut yourself off from the sun and fresh air like this, you might as well be in prison. And in any case, when a killer had come looking for Rebecca Lowe, her house had given her no protection at all.

An hour earlier, Cooper had found Diane Fry at the rendezvous point on the outer cordon, outside the front gate of Parson's Croft.

'Ah, Ben,' she'd said. 'How nice to see you. Well, this is what is technically known as a crime scene. There's usually at least one involved in a major enquiry, such as the murder case we're currently investigating.'

'I'm here, aren't I?'

'I tried to call you this morning. Your phone was off.'

'This morning? I was in a cave,' protested Cooper.

'Now, why doesn't that surprise me?'

Cooper looked at the house. All the windows on the ground floor were lit, and the front door stood open. A safe pathway had been marked out by the scenes of crime officers,

71

who he could see moving around inside the house in their white, hooded scene suits.

'The body is in the kitchen, at the back of the house,' said Fry.

'Do we have an ID?'

Fry checked her notebook. 'The victim's name is Rebecca Lowe, aged forty-nine. She lived alone. Her assailant seems to have gained access to the house via the back door, which leads into the utility room, next to the kitchen.'

'An intruder? Was it a burglary gone wrong?'

'We can't tell at the moment. There's no sign of a forced entry. The back door was unlocked when the victim's sister arrived at the house.'

'Who's SIO?'

'Mr Kessen, of course.'

Cooper could see Detective Chief Inspector Oliver Kessen sitting in the back of the scenes of crime van, studying a video. Some senior investigating officers would want a clean sweep at this stage. In fact, one or two SIOs would pack up the entire room where the victim had died and send it back to the lab. They had a nagging fear that something would be missed at the crime scene. But DCI Kessen was said to be more focused. By watching the initial video of the scene, he'd be hoping to build up an early hypothesis, so that the number of forensic tests could be limited.

They stood aside to let a group of officers go past, including a SOCO in a scene suit carrying an aluminium step ladder.

'What's the ladder for?' asked Cooper.

'To reach the kitchen ceiling.'

'Sorry?'

'The ceiling,' said Fry. 'Blood splatter on the ceiling. Wake up, Ben.'

'Right.'

A flutter of tape by the open front door marked the inner cordon preserving the scene itself. Contamination was the big fear, so everyone was being kept at arm's length for now, including surplus detectives.

'Blood splatter,' said Cooper. 'So what are we looking at as a weapon?'

'Kitchen knife, probably.'

'They're much too handy.'

'Apparently, Mrs Lowe had an entire block full of them,' said Fry. 'But now they're scattered all over her kitchen floor.'

Cooper watched the Crime Scene Manager enter the van to talk to Mr Kessen. As far as the forensic team were concerned, contamination was something that occurred only after the scene had been preserved. Before that, anything else that went on should have been 'normal procedures' – the desperate attempts to save an injured person's life, the anxious search for the body of another victim or for a violent assailant who might still be on the premises. Normal procedures.

He turned to Fry again.

'When did we get the call-out?'

'Eleven thirty-eight.'

'I was long since out of Peak Cavern by then. You should have got through to me.'

'No, it was earlier that I tried to phone you.'

'Earlier? But –'

'Not now, Ben.'

And then she was away, striding across the edge of the garden towards a bustle of activity around the crime scene van. Cooper watched her, puzzled. But then, he was always puzzled by Diane Fry.

DC Gavin Murfin appeared at Cooper's elbow. A faint aroma of warm pastry drifted from Murfin's clothes, and Cooper imagined the pockets of his coat stuffed with pies. Or perhaps the smell was simply impregnated into the fabric by now. No wonder Murfin was hungry all the time. There was no scent better guaranteed to make the saliva run.

Murfin nudged Cooper and nodded his head at Fry as she

reached the van and was immediately in conference with some of the senior officers.

'Hey, Ben, is it true what they're saying – her sister's moved in with her?'

'Who's saying that, Gavin?'

Murfin shrugged. 'Everybody. You know what it's like.'

'I don't understand how anyone can possibly know that. Diane doesn't talk about her private life at all.'

'Except to you, maybe,' said Murfin, raising an eyebrow. 'Or so they say.'

Cooper shuffled uneasily but said nothing.

'In fact, I heard that the sister turning up was no coincidence,' said Murfin. 'They say you had a bit of a hand in it – arranged the meeting and everything, behind Miss's back. Can't be true, can it?'

'Yes, I'm afraid so. It's a bit of a long story, though. And a bit, well . . . complicated.'

'I don't doubt it.'

'I'm sorry, but I can't tell you any more, Gavin. It's personal. For Diane, I mean.'

'No, no. Do spare me the sordid details. But what I don't understand, Ben, is why you got involved in the first place. I mean, it's a bit like poking a bad-tempered grizzly bear with a sharp stick, if you ask me.'

'I don't know,' said Cooper. 'It seemed the right thing to do at the time.'

'Famous last words, mate. You'll be uttering them as they cart your body away to the mortuary.'

'It's too late now, anyway.'

'Mmm? If it were me, I'd be making sure I got a transfer damn quick, before Miss decides how she's going to get her revenge. Preferably somewhere far away. I believe the Shetland Islands can be nice. They even get a bit of daylight at this time of year.'

Cooper sighed. Why *had* he got involved? It was the

question he'd been asking himself for weeks. But if he could go back and have the time again, would he do things differently? He supposed he ought to have turned Angie Fry away the night she turned up on his doorstep. But Diane had wanted to find her sister, hadn't she? How could he have sent Angie away, knowing that? Somewhere along the route he'd followed, there might have been a moment when he could have found a better, more sensible thing to do. But there was no guarantee he'd have taken the chance just because it was the sensible thing.

'Anyway, what do you reckon about this job?' said Murfin, indicating Parson's Croft with a more vigorous nod of his head. 'Any overtime in it for us? Only, my credit-card bill is up to its limit this month. I'll be paying off that holiday in Turkey for the next ten years.'

'I don't know,' said Cooper. 'We'll have to wait and see what they come up with from the video recording.'

'No doubt Miss will have her own ideas.'

'She's right a lot of the time,' said Cooper.

Murfin looked at him suspiciously.

'Ben, you don't actually *like* her, do you?'

'Well . . . no.'

'Are you sure?'

'Not exactly.'

'I knew it! What on earth do you find to like about her?'

'Gavin, I haven't said that I do.'

'I can tell when somebody is avoiding the question, you know. I've watched Jeremy Paxman in action. So, answer the question, Minister. What do you like about her?'

'Look, I just think Diane Fry is a bit misunderstood by most people around here.'

'Oh, my God.' Murfin raised his eyes to the sky in horror. 'You're not going to make her into one of your causes? You're going to start a "Let's All Love DS Fry" campaign, aren't you?'

'Give over, Gavin.'

'Well, she's not my cup of poison. And I know about poisons. You've met my wife, have you?'

Diane Fry had seen DI Hitchens arriving at the scene. He had to park his car outside in the lane because the driveway was already full of vehicles. As Hitchens headed towards the crime scene van, he looked worried. But he noticed Fry and signalled her over. Then Mr Kessen climbed stiffly out of the van.

'What is it, Paul?'

'I think we have a suspect, sir,' said Hitchens.

'Already? How come?'

Fry watched the DI run a hand across his face. Tonight he was looking tired, even before the enquiry had got properly under way.

'You know Mansell Quinn is out,' said Hitchens. 'He was serving a life sentence for a murder in Castleton back in 1990, but he reached his automatic release date and left Sudbury Prison this morning.'

'Yes. So?' said Kessen.

'He hasn't turned up at his accommodation, and he missed an appointment with his local probation officer this morning.'

'So he's broken his licence,' said Kessen. 'It's a stupid thing to do, but so what? A domestic killing fourteen years ago doesn't put him in the frame for anything that's going off in a fifty-mile radius.'

'No. That's not it, exactly.'

'You'd better explain.'

Hitchens took a deep breath and looked at the house across the garden. The helicopter support unit were just beginning a sweep to the north, their thirty-million candlepower search-light probing the open ground behind Aston. It wouldn't achieve much, except to annoy the residents.

'The victim here – Rebecca Lowe,' said Hitchens. 'She's the former Rebecca Quinn. At the time of the Proctor killing in 1990, she was married to Mansell Quinn.'

8

In Hathersage, it was Gala Week. The village's main street was decorated with bunting, and a caravan parked on the pavement had been covered in posters advertising the week's events. Cooper quite liked village galas. He saw that they'd missed the brass band concert, but if they waited until Saturday they could go to a ceilidh and watch the fell racing.

'We're looking for Moorland Avenue,' said Diane Fry from the back seat of the car. 'I thought you knew your way around every town and village in this area, Ben.'

'If we can pull in somewhere, I'll check the map.'

For some reason, Gavin Murfin was driving this morning. He wasn't the best driver in the world, having a tendency to brake suddenly whenever he saw a chip shop. But maybe it was Fry's strategy to stop him eating in the car while they travelled.

Murfin drew the car into the kerb. A few yards away, dozens of white-haired ladies were getting off a coach opposite the George Hotel. Hathersage was mostly a tourist stop on the way up the Hope Valley these days, and the village centre seemed to consist mostly of outdoor sports specialists, tea rooms and craft shops. Cooper wound down the window to get some air, only to let in the scent of candles and aromatherapy oils. And, strangely, the smell of fish.

'Remember, when we see old Mrs Quinn, she'll probably need sensitive handling,' said Fry. 'Every mother thinks her beloved son can do no wrong.'

'In this case, her beloved son is a convicted killer,' said Murfin, tilting his head to see her in the rear-view mirror.

'It makes no difference, Gavin. She'll be the only person in the world who thinks the bastard's innocent.'

Looking around for the road they needed, Cooper noticed various forms of what he supposed would be called community art. A bus shelter had been converted into the 'Hathersage Travel Machine', decorated with wheels and photographs of exotic locations. Across the road, cut-out figures had been lined up against a garden wall. They made him think of targets at the police shooting range. Then he saw that some of the people near the bus shelter were actually queuing at a fish van. A bowl under its tailgate was catching the run-off from thawing ice that had kept the fish fresh on its way from the East Coast docks at Grimsby.

'Wind up the window, Ben,' said Fry. 'There's a stink of haddock.'

'Sorry. I've got it now.'

Food was a dangerous topic with Gavin Murfin around. Cooper had already noticed the balti restaurant across the road. He fancied a Chicken Dhansah, but he kept the idea to himself.

'OK, I've got it,' he said. 'You'll have to turn round, Gavin.'

Enid Quinn lived in a small estate off Mill Lane. The old mill itself was still largely intact, though elder saplings were growing out of its chimney. Cooper recalled that Hathersage had once been a centre for the needle-and-pin industry, with local people working at grindstones that filled their lungs with steel dust. The industry was remembered now only because conditions in the mills had led to legislation against children being employed as grinders.

The original Mill Cottage stood among stone troughs full of geraniums, with climbing roses hanging from its walls, and pink and yellow petals drifting on to a stone-flagged path. Ash trees swayed and creaked in the breeze as a string of cement tankers rumbled over a nineteenth-century railway bridge.

And then there was the Moorland estate. The houses weren't particularly new – not built in the last couple of decades, anyway. So the estate had been there most of Cooper's lifetime, without him suspecting its existence. He'd only ever seen what the tourists saw of Hathersage – the historic buildings, the spire of the church, the gritstone edges in the distance.

'It looks as though we're in right-to-buy country,' said Murfin.

'How can you tell?'

'Those first two places had dormer windows. You wouldn't do that in a council house.'

A man in blue overalls was smoking a cigarette in the cab of a pick-up truck with the name of a property management company painted on its cab door. Murfin was right – this must be only partly a council estate these days, if at all. Many of the tenants would have bought their cement-rendered semis when the right-to-buy policy came in during the 1980s.

They parked near a patch of grass on Moorland Avenue, and Murfin stayed by the car as Fry and Cooper walked up the path to number 14. While Cooper rang the bell, Fry looked with amazement at an ornamental pig squatting by the doorstep. She gave it a tentative kick to see what it was made of. It didn't budge.

'Cement,' said Cooper.

Getting no answer to the bell, he knocked. His knock created a hollow sound that echoed through the house.

'It doesn't look as though she's in,' called Murfin, who had been watching the windows.

'Thanks a lot, Gavin,' said Fry. 'We'll take a look round while we're here. Ben, why don't you check out that alley by the side of the house?'

Cooper looked where she was pointing. 'A gennel, we call it.'

The gennel ran alongside the garden of number 14 and past a row of houses set at right angles to it. Money had been spent on some of these properties: porches had been added, and driveways opened up. Satellite dishes sat under the eaves. Over here was an imitation wishing well, and there a few square yards of paving for a caravan to stand on.

Cooper could see into Mrs Quinn's garden from here. The flowerbeds contained more ornamental concrete figures: squirrels, rabbits, a badger, an otter and a giant frog. At the end of the path he came out almost opposite the railway station. He could see Hathersage Booths and Throstle Nest on the long incline towards Surprise View in the east.

He turned to walk back and saw Fry beckoning to him. A patrol car had pulled up and two uniformed officers had stationed themselves outside number 14. They'd be attracting plenty of attention soon.

'Gavin found a neighbour,' said Fry. 'She says Mrs Quinn tends her husband's grave on Tuesday mornings. You two can go up the church to find her. I'm going to talk to the neighbours. I'm presuming you know the way, Ben.'

With Cooper and Murfin out of her hair, Diane Fry left the two PCs at the gate of number 14 and spent some time talking to anyone she could find at home in Moorland Avenue, using her custody suite mugshot of Mansell Quinn to prompt memories.

She found two residents who remembered Quinn because of the 1990 murder case, but both of them assured her confidently that he was in prison and would be there for the rest of his life. It was curious how convinced the law-abiding public were that a life sentence actually meant life. After all these years of double-speak, they still believed that the meaning of a word was the same as what it said in the dictionary. But Fry knew better. In the police service, they'd been living in Orwell's *1984* since . . . well, the 1990s, at least.

Suddenly, she felt a strong urge to know what Angie was doing. She'd left her sister in the flat this morning, talking about going for a walk or catching a bus into town to have a look round. But she'd only been talking about it. Angie had been half-dressed, curled up in an armchair with her knees in the air, painting her toenails. She'd looked drowsy, even content. Of course, that was only because she hadn't been awake very long.

Angie had insisted from the beginning that she'd been through rehab in Sheffield and was clean now. But suspicion was a difficult habit to break. Fry felt guilty every time she caught herself assessing her sister's behaviour for signs of euphoria or drowsiness, slurred speech or inattention, or when she found she couldn't look Angie in the eyes without checking for constricted pupils.

Though she despised the weakness of addiction, Fry was terrified at the thought of seeing her sister suffer the agonies of withdrawal if she missed a fix. The fact that Angie was her own flesh and blood made a difference that defied logic. In a way, Fry would prefer to see the signs of continued use rather than witness her sister in the condition she'd known addicts reduced to. She had seen plenty of them back in Birmingham, and even in the custody suite at West Street. Within a few hours of their arrest, they would decline from restlessness to depression, and the vomiting, diarrhoea and muscle cramps would set in, or the shivering and the sweating. And then they'd begin screaming for the methadone. The relief of the pain without the high.

Fry tried to dial her home number, but eventually her own

voice cut in on the answering machine. That didn't mean Angie wasn't there, just that she wasn't bothering to answer the phone. She ought to have a mobile of her own. For a moment, Fry thought of buying her one – she had a feeling she could add an extra handset to her account quite easily. But that would be like treating her sister as a child.

Like a neurotic mother, Fry found herself imagining the worst: Angie still sitting in the armchair at Grosvenor Avenue, heating white powder on a piece of tin foil and inhaling the fumes through a tube. Chasing the dragon – was that still what they called it? Heroin dealers existed in Edendale, of course, as they did in every market town in England, cutting their product for sale on the street with glucose, flour, chalk or even talcum powder. But in E Division they weren't quite such big business or so well organized as the city operations, where Asian gangs had been moving in recently to compete with the East Europeans.

Clean, Angie might be. But most worrying of all for Fry was the question of where her sister might have been getting a hundred pounds a day or more to feed her habit. And who she'd been scoring the smack from.

Ben Cooper stood over the grave and read the inscription: *Here lies buried . . .* it began. But that's what they all said. In this case, was it true?

'It's ten feet long, if it's an inch,' said Gavin Murfin. 'I don't believe it.'

Old churchyards always filled Cooper with a sense of history. It was the thought of generation upon generation of the same families mouldering together under his feet. According to the memorial stones around him, scores of Eyres and Thorpes, Proctors and Fieldings had been buried here over the centuries. But this churchyard seemed to have mixed history with folklore.

'A thirty-inch thigh bone is impossible anyway,' said Murfin. 'It must have been an elk or something.'

'An elk?'

'A reindeer. A moose. God, I don't know. Something big, anyway. Something that lived around here in the Ice Age.'

The Church of St Michael and All Angels stood high above Hathersage next to an earthwork built by Danish invaders. Transco had dug a hole in the road outside the church gates, and the smell of gas was strong when they got out of the car. But at least mobile phones worked up here. In many areas of the Hope Valley it was impossible to get a signal.

Murfin had produced a ham sandwich from his pocket. He brushed some crumbs on to the grave, as if he were a grieving relative scattering the first handfuls of soil at a funeral, paying tribute to the dead. The plaque on the grave was quite specific: *Here lies buried Little John, the friend and lieutenant of Robin Hood.*

'Is there any *evidence*?' said Murfin. 'I mean, have they done the DNA?'

Among the newer graves to the west of the church, they could see a figure in a red T-shirt, with short blonde hair. She was wearing yellow rubber gloves, and she was dusting a headstone with what looked like a hearth brush. She bent occasionally to pull at a few weeds.

'You definitely think that's her?' said Murfin.

'There's no one else here. And she answers the description the neighbour gave.'

'OK, let's talk to her then.'

'No, we ought to wait until she's finished,' said Cooper.

'Why?'

'She's tending her husband's grave, Gavin.'

'Right. And you don't want to interrupt her while she's enjoying herself. I suppose she'll start singing in a minute, and do a little dance.'

'Gavin . . .'

'Yeah?'

'Are you having trouble with your marriage, by any chance?'

'Trouble? No, everything's going according to plan. I'll be dead in a year or two, and Jean and the kids will get the insurance money. Then everybody will be happy.'

The woman in the red T-shirt straightened up, brushed off her hands and began to walk back through the rows of gravestones. From the front, she looked more her age, which must have been approaching seventy.

'Who's going to take the lead?' said Murfin.

'I suppose I'd better. She might need to be handled sensitively.'

'That's what I thought, too.'

As the woman came nearer, she looked across at the two detectives, probably aware that they'd been watching her. She was only a few paces away, clutching a plastic bag with her gloves and brush in it, when Cooper raised a hand to stop her.

'Excuse me – Mrs Enid Quinn?'

'Can I help you?'

Cooper showed his warrant card. 'Detective Constable Cooper and Detective Constable Murfin, Edendale CID. We really need to talk to you, Mrs Quinn. You haven't been answering your phone.'

She was a slim woman with pale skin like lined parchment. Liver spots freckled her bare arms and thin hands. She looked up at Cooper with a faint smile, ironic and resigned.

'Police? Well, I wonder what you could possibly want to talk to me about,' she said.

Enid Quinn took Ben Cooper and Diane Fry into her sitting room. Inside the house, her red T-shirt made her look even paler. She settled on a sofa and sat very primly, her hands folded on her knees, as she listened to Murfin and the two PCs trampling up her stairs.

'Do I *have* to tell you anything?' she said.

'We're hoping for your co-operation, Mrs Quinn,' said Fry.

84

The woman looked at Cooper's notebook. 'My son isn't here.'

'Where is he, then?'

'I can't tell you. Sorry.'

'When you say you can't tell us . . . ?' said Fry.

'I mean I can't. I don't know where Mansell is.'

'Has he been here?'

Mrs Quinn unfolded her hands and folded them again in the opposite direction. She gazed back at Fry steadily. 'When?'

'In the past twenty-four hours, perhaps?'

'No.'

'He hasn't visited you? Or phoned you?'

'No. I don't know where he is.'

'Nevertheless, we hope you might have some suggestions about where he could be heading. What friends does he have in the area? Is there somewhere he might think of going to stay – a place where he'd feel safe?'

'I don't think there's anywhere safe for him,' said the woman calmly.

Cooper realized that Mrs Quinn had a slight Welsh accent. It wasn't so much the way she pronounced the words as the intonation, the unfamiliar pattern of emphasis in a sentence.

'Do you have any other sons or daughters?' asked Fry.

'No, Mansell is my only child.'

'Any other relatives in the area?'

She shook her head. 'We're not from Derbyshire originally. Both my family and my husband's are from Mid Wales.'

'We know of two friends of your son's,' said Fry. 'Raymond Proctor and William Thorpe.'

'I'm aware of the names,' said Mrs Quinn. 'That's all.'

'Can you name any other friends of his?'

'No. I don't believe he has any remaining friends. Not in this area. I don't know what acquaintances he might have made in prison, of course.'

Cooper wasn't writing very much in his notebook. He

looked at the old lady with her dyed-blonde hair, and thought she seemed out of place. Despite the trellises and patios and dormer windows of the estate outside, Mrs Quinn had a sort of poise that suggested she'd be more at home sitting in a grand drawing room at Chatsworth House or one of the county's other stately homes.

'You were visiting your husband's grave at the church earlier?' he said.

'Certainly. He died many years ago.'

'Before your son went to prison?'

'Yes, thank God. The trial would have killed him.'

Cooper was so thrown by the unconscious irony that he forgot the next question that he'd been planning to ask. But Fry either didn't notice or didn't care about such things, because she stepped in with exactly the right question, as if they'd been thinking along the same lines for once.

'Did you visit your son in prison very often, Mrs Quinn?'

The hands moved again. They stayed unfolded this time, and instead tugged at the hem of her T-shirt. Her neck was slightly red from her exposure to the sun on the hill above the village.

'He got them to send me a visiting order sometimes,' she said. 'I didn't always use it.'

'Why not?'

'I don't think that's any of your business.'

'And what about his wife?' asked Fry.

'Rebecca? What about her?'

'Did she make a good prison visitor?'

'She visited him a few times, but she went less and less often, and eventually stopped going altogether.'

'Why do you think she stopped, Mrs Quinn?'

'At first, Rebecca said it was too difficult getting there by public transport, and she couldn't afford taxi fares and a hotel overnight. But then she gave another version. She said she couldn't keep up the pretence any more once Mansell was inside.'

Cooper looked up and saw Gavin Murfin go past the front window. He waved, shrugged, and signalled that he was going round to the back of the house.

'Pretence? What pretence?' said Fry.

Mrs Quinn shrugged very slightly, as if merely settling her T-shirt more comfortably around her shoulders. 'Well, marriage,' she said. 'You know.'

'I don't think I understand what you mean, Mrs Quinn.'

'I mean that she couldn't be bothered making the effort to keep their marriage together.'

'Ah. Not if it meant putting herself out to visit her husband in the nick?'

'That's right.'

'And then they divorced.'

'She couldn't wait, I imagine. That's the way things go these days. Couples don't stand by each other, not like we used to do in my day. When we made our marriage vows, they counted for something. Now, they're planning the divorce before they've swept up the confetti. It's utter hypocrisy, in my view.'

'You don't think much of your former daughter-in-law?'

'It's not obligatory, is it?'

'Well, no . . .'

'I didn't think she was bringing the children up very well, if you want the truth.'

'That's not an unusual view for grandparents to take,' said Fry.

'That's as may be. But I was convinced it was the reason Simon went off the rails the way he did when the murder happened. If he'd been a more stable, disciplined child, like his sister, it might have been different. But he'd already been allowed to get into bad ways by the time he was fifteen. He was mixing with the wrong company, missing lessons at school. Drinking alcohol, even.'

'None of that was your son's fault, I suppose? He was Simon's father, after all.'

'I have my own views,' said Enid Quinn firmly. 'I know where I put the blame.'

Fry paused. Out of the corner of his eye, Cooper saw her give him a slight nod.

'Mrs Quinn, your son's former wife, Rebecca Lowe, was attacked and killed last night at her home in Aston,' he said.

Enid Quinn could no longer keep her hands still. Unsteadily, she felt in her pocket for a handkerchief, but didn't use it except to twist it in her fingers.

'I know,' she said. 'Andrea called me this morning. That's my granddaughter. She still keeps in touch. But Mansell can't have done that to Rebecca. He wouldn't.'

'Why not?'

She didn't answer, and Fry began to get impatient.

'You realize we have to take this very seriously, Mrs Quinn,' she said. 'It's no use protesting that your son is innocent. He was convicted by a court and served his sentence. And now we think he's a danger to more people. We need to find him.'

Mrs Quinn seemed to gain a little more dignity.

'I was not going to protest Mansell's innocence,' she said. 'On the contrary, I'm quite sure that he was guilty of murdering Carol Proctor.'

'You are?'

'Yes. But you see, whatever I think, it won't stop my son from seeking what he wants.'

'And what's that, Mrs Quinn?' said Fry.

'Retribution.'

9

Adopting his best manner with grieving members of the public, DI Hitchens turned to the Lowes. 'Are you ready?'

Simon Lowe nodded. From Andrea, there was no visible response. But they seemed to take a step closer together, and then began to move towards the viewing window.

Andrea Lowe wore blue denims and a pearl-grey sweat-shirt, with her dark hair tied back in a ponytail. She seemed very calm and self-contained. But Diane Fry had seen her almost step out into the traffic as she crossed the car park to get to the mortuary.

Her brother seemed the most distressed. He clung to Andrea's hand, looking almost like an older version of her, but slightly lighter in his colouring and several inches taller. At first, Fry thought he seemed to have no strength in him for the task of identifying his mother, yet it was Simon who spoke.

'Yes, it's her. That's our mother.'

'Thank you, sir.'

Simon's voice was very low, and he hardly moved his mouth when he spoke, as if all the energy had been drained out of him. His sister said nothing, but leaned closer to the glass, as close as she could get. She dropped her brother's hand and pressed her fingers against the window, like a small child peering into a toy shop. Her breath condensed on the glass, and she touched the patch of moisture with her forehead.

Through the window, the mortuary attendant hovered uncertainly, not sure if an identification had been made and he should now replace the sheet, or whether the bereaved relatives should be allowed a last, lingering look at the deceased.

'Miss Lowe, are you all right?' said Fry.

Andrea nodded, but Simon pulled her hand away from the glass and gripped it. Hitchens shuffled his feet and looked around for the family liaison officer, who was trained to deal with grieving relatives.

'You know we're looking for your father,' said Hitchens. 'He was released from prison yesterday.'

Then a strange thing happened. Simon Lowe changed colour. Fry had seen this happen to family members identifying their loved ones – but usually they turned white, or worse, an unnerving shade of green. But Simon had flushed a deep red, almost purple. Blood suffused his face and neck until he reminded Fry of the corpse of a strangulation victim who had lain on the same slab as Rebecca Lowe not many months ago.

'If you mean Mansell Quinn,' said Simon, 'he's not my father.'

'Oh, but I thought –'

Andrea turned away from the glass at last and threw her arms round her brother, becoming the little sister in a moment. Simon took a deep breath that shuddered through air passages swollen with emotion.

'He *was* my father. But not any more. He hasn't been my father for fourteen years.'

'I see,' said Hitchens.

'Do you?'

'I think I understand how you feel. So if you should

90

happen to have any idea where your . . . I mean, where Mr Quinn is at the moment, you would be sure to let us know?'

'Of course we would,' said Simon.

'And you, madam?'

Hitchens waited politely for Andrea to reply.

'I spoke to Mum, you know. Not long before it happened. I spoke to her on the phone, and I told her to make sure she was safe. I didn't think she was taking the situation seriously enough. But that was Mum – she preferred to enjoy life than to worry about things all the time.'

'We'll want a statement from you,' said Hitchens. 'If you feel up to it.'

'I'll do it today,' she said.

'In the meantime . . .'

'We'll tell you anything we can think of that might help, Inspector.'

Fry noticed that it was Simon who had taken over again. Rebecca Lowe's children clung together as though they were inseparable.

The cattle market that used to stand on the main road in Hope had been demolished. Perhaps it had lost too much business during the foot and mouth outbreak in 2001, when all livestock markets had been closed for a year. Now the site had been re-developed for housing.

'Mansell Quinn was given a twenty-year sentence,' said Ben Cooper. 'If he was refused parole, his automatic release date must have been two-thirds of the way through his sentence. That's, er . . .'

'Thirteen years and four months.'

Diane Fry looked up briefly as Cooper slowed to avoid a squirrel that darted across the road. But, as usual, she showed little interest in the scenery.

'Why do you think he changed his story about the Carol

Proctor murder?' said Cooper. 'All it meant was that they refused him parole and he got knocked back.'

'There are all kinds of factors the parole board would have taken into consideration,' said Fry. 'They'd want to know about his plans when he got out. And he had some issues to deal with – anger problems.'

'Right.'

Hope village lay in the centre of the valley, dominated on one side by Lose Hill and Win Hill, and on the other by the cement works. Going up the valley, the chimney of the works had been visible from as far away as the Rising Sun Inn. Its curious tower-like structure resembled the ruins of a castle, with gaping holes like empty windows in a high battlement. Behind it was the long white scar of the quarries driven deep into Bradwell Moor.

Cooper had looked at Mansell Quinn's mugshots earlier. For a long time in prison, Quinn must have been like a man holding his breath under water. Worse, he would have had no idea how long he needed to hold it for. There would have been a time when he hoped to get parole and be out of prison at the ten-year mark. But he'd been branded unsuitable for release. Many men might have given up then, stopped holding their breath and let the despair rush in. But Quinn had waited.

'I suppose his home circumstances didn't meet the requirements. Not suitable for assisting his rehabilitation.'

'It's not a sensible option to change your mind about whether you're guilty,' said Fry. 'You're branding yourself a liar. Most men who change their stories in prison do it the other way round, though. Remorse being more important than innocence, they express remorse and get their parole.'

Cooper had to drive more carefully through Hope, where a constant stream of lorries rumbled backwards and forwards over the bridge to reach the cement works.

He had seen men leaving prison after their release, setting off along the roadside in the direction of the nearest town, their entire belongings in one bag and only the vaguest idea where they were going. He'd often wondered whether they made it any further than the nearest pub, following the first sniff of freedom that drifted through a bar-room window.

'If it were me, I'd do anything to get out, including lying through my teeth. I mean, if I was actually innocent, I'd know I was – even if no one else did. So it wouldn't be on my conscience . . .' Cooper paused. 'Quinn won't be planning to go back inside again, that's for sure.'

'That's what I thought, too,' said Fry.

A few minutes later, Cooper and Fry stood at the bottom of Rebecca Lowe's garden at Parson's Croft. A stiff breeze had sprung up, and Cooper watched it bustling through the trees on the slopes of Win Hill.

The SOCOs were still working on the house, and a group of officers were on their hands and knees searching the garden and driveway, seeking traces of the killer on his route to the house. Cooper noticed a garden ornament here, too – not a squirrel or a rabbit, but a concrete heron standing on one leg in the middle of the lawn, as if waiting for a pond to arrive.

'They think he may have waited under the trees for a while before he approached the house,' said Fry, who'd been speaking to the crime scene manger. 'Probably he wanted to be sure she was alone.'

'Here?' said Cooper.

'A few yards along the fence. See the markers? He must have watched the place for a while before he entered. This is the best spot to remain unnoticed, yet have a clear view of the house.'

Cooper looked up at the tree above his head. Most of its leaves were dark green, with the distinctive pointed tip of the lime. But many of the branches had thinner, paler foliage. With a slight stretch he was able to reach up, take hold of a branch and give it a shake. A shower of water droplets fell from the surface of the leaves, followed by a small cloud of brown specks that landed in Fry's hair and on her shoulders, and clung to the sleeves of Cooper's shirt.

'What do you think you're doing?' said Fry.

Cooper picked one of the specks off his shirt and looked at it. It was a tiny round floret on a short piece of dried stem.

'This lime tree is seeding,' he said. 'There are thousands of these things up there. If the killer stood here, even for a few minutes, he'll have them on his clothes, like us.'

'And in his hair,' said Fry, brushing the top of her head. 'OK, if we find Quinn, they'll still be on him. I don't suppose he's changing his clothes very much.'

'We ought to suggest to the SOCOs that they look for seeds in the material they bagged from inside the house.'

'It wouldn't really prove anything. Rebecca Lowe could have carried seeds into the house herself. They could have been taken in by the dog, or anyone.'

'Yes, you're right.'

Fry stared at him. She wasn't used to being told that she was right. But Cooper had a picture in his mind. He was imagining the killer standing here, under the lime tree, watching the house. He hadn't approached the house straight away, but had stood for some time, waiting. Waiting for what, though?

'It was already dark, wasn't it?' said Cooper. 'It had been for an hour or so.'

'Yes, of course it was dark.'

She watched him in amazement as he reached up and shook the nearest branch of the tree again. This time he tugged a bit harder, and the bough dipped. More water fell around them. Fry got a spatter of it in her face and wiped it away with her fingers as she stared at Cooper.

'I wonder,' he said, 'if it had already started to rain.'

'I've no idea, Ben.'

Cooper looked at the ground. He saw a ripe seedhead from a stem of grass that had been chewed by mice or something. Nearby were a series of markers placed on the damp soil by the SOCOs.

'Footprints,' said Cooper.

'Boots, by the look of them. Nice, clear impressions.'

'Useful.'

Between the lime trees and the house stretched two gently sloping lawns edged by flower borders and divided by a brick-paved path. The path meandered a little before ending at a sundial on a stone plinth. Cooper could see no more white markers, and the SOCOs were already progressing towards the drive and garage.

'There are no impressions between here and the house, though. Yet the grass is fairly long, not recently cut.'

Fry shrugged. 'He must have walked on the path.'

'Oh, right. He was worried about damaging the grass with his big boots. And what about the six-foot leap to the sundial?'

'Ben, the grass just didn't retain any impressions, that's all.'

'But it would do,' said Cooper, 'if it was wet.'

He watched Gavin Murfin scouting around the side of the house, peering over the dense hedge into the neighbours' property. Cooper realized this was the first time that he'd been alone with Diane Fry for months, without Murfin or anybody else being on hand to overhear what they were saying or butt in. For once, Fry wasn't trying to get away from him. In fact, she seemed to be absorbed with her own thoughts.

'Diane . . .' he said.

'What?'

Fry looked at him suspiciously, already alerted by a change in the tone of his voice. Cooper wished he were a better actor sometimes.

'I know it's none of my business,' he said, and paused

while she rolled her eyes in exasperation, though she still didn't move away. 'But I heard that Angie is staying with you.'

'Been gossiping round the coffee machine, have you?'

'Is it true, Diane?'

'Like you said, Ben: it's none of your business.'

'I was involved, in a way –'

'In a way? *Too* bloody involved, if you ask me.'

'Yes, I know, I know. But is Angie just visiting or has she moved in? I mean, are you sure you're doing the right thing, Diane?'

'Ben, would you like me to break your neck now, or do you want to annoy me for a bit longer?'

Fry began to walk across the garden, her shoulders stiff. Cooper had seen her walk away from him like that too often before. He shook his head, spraying more water and brown specks from his hair. Then he hurried after Fry, falling into step alongside her.

'Have you seen anything of Rebecca Lowe's children?' he said.

'They came in earlier today for identification of the body,' said Fry. 'They already knew Mansell Quinn was coming out of prison, of course. Andrea said she'd tried to get her mother to take extra precautions.'

'Andrea and . . . Simon?'

'That's right.'

'Any children from the second marriage?'

'She was too old by then, Ben.'

'I meant, did the second husband have any children? Step-children for Mrs Lowe.'

'No.'

'A woman living alone, then.'

'That's right.'

'But if Mansell Quinn came looking for revenge,' said Cooper, 'why his ex-wife? What did she do?'

'We don't know. And there's another thing we don't know: who else he might be looking for.'

'What?'

'What I mean, Ben, is – who's next?'

Will Thorpe had taken to watching other people breathe. It was effortless and automatic for most of them. They weren't even aware they were doing it. He liked to watch their chests gently rise and fall, and imagine the smooth flow of air in and out of their lungs. He stared at their mouths as they talked or ate, trying to recollect a time in his past when it had been possible to talk and breathe at the same time, as these people did. He cocked his head to listen to them, but he couldn't hear them breathing.

There were some, of course, who gave themselves away. Now and then, he heard a wheeze or a cough, and he'd turn around to find where it had come from. They must know the reality – or if not, they soon would. But others he watched so long that he began to believe they didn't breathe at all. Maybe they absorbed oxygen through their pores, or drew it in with the sunlight, like trees did through their leaves.

These people didn't understand what breathing was. It was the most important thing in the world, a privilege that had to be fought for every minute of the day and night. Especially the night.

Thorpe was sitting in a small grassy hollow overlooking the entrance to Cavedale. Below him was a series of worn limestone shelves that he'd climbed to reach his vantage point. It had taken him a few minutes, frequently pausing to get his breath, fighting to control the pain in his chest.

From here, he was looking down on people entering the dale through the narrow cleft in the limestone at the Castleton end. Behind him, a clump of elms and sycamores screened the roofs of the tea rooms and B & Bs near Cavedale Cottages. If he kept still, even the walkers coming down the dale wouldn't notice him in his hollow. Once they'd passed below the keep of the castle, they didn't look up any more but kept their eyes on the ground to avoid stumbling on loose stones.

After a few minutes, Thorpe lit a cigarette. Two young boys entered the dale, chattering loudly, oblivious to the fact they were being watched. They were probably part of the group he'd seen in the village carrying their worksheets, ticking off the things they were supposed to find.

These two had found Cavedale, but they weren't satisfied with simply ticking it off. They scrambled up the rock across the dale from Thorpe and stood at the mouth of one of the small caves in the limestone cliff. It looked dark and mysterious, but Thorpe knew that it ended after only a few feet. Though the hill was honeycombed by the Peak Cavern and Speedwell system, there was no entrance to it from Cavedale.

The two boys looked around and noticed him. Perhaps it was the whiff of his cigarette smoke that had alerted them to his presence.

'Excuse me, is this cave safe?' called one of the boys.

Thorpe was impressed by polite children. They always took him by surprise.

'Safe?'

'Are there bats – or anything?'

'No, I don't there'll be any bats. Or bears.'

'Thank you. We're going in to explore.'

'If you're not out in an hour, I'll call cave rescue,' said Thorpe.

The boys disappeared. Thorpe laughed to himself, coughing and taking a drag on his cigarette. The hollow was quite a little sun trap, and the warmth felt good on his skin. He'd forgotten that it was possible to feel like this. Temporarily, he could even ignore the constant struggle to draw in air. Once he'd got this burden off his mind, he'd be able to breathe properly at last. No dust or poisons would break down his lungs, no holes would erupt into his chest cavity. He'd take a breath with ease, as everyone else did. That was all he wanted.

'Did you know it was so small?' called a voice.

Thorpe looked up. The two youngsters were out of the cave, looking disappointed. There had been no bats, then. Only a couple of yards of damp sandy floor and a graffiti-covered rock face.

'No, I didn't. Sorry.'

The boys looked as though they didn't believe him. But Thorpe reckoned you had to find things out for yourself in this life. You had to learn from your disappointments. There would be bigger ones to come later on.

He watched the youngsters clamber down the rocky path and head back into Castleton. What was next on the work-sheet? Church, youth hostel, school?

In the distance, Thorpe could hear a hammer tapping on stone, a whistle blowing for a football game, and kids chattering in the market square. He lay back on the grass, letting a cloud of blue smoke drift away into the sky, and closed his eyes. In the warmth of the sun, he began to relax, and was almost asleep by the time Mansell Quinn found him.

10

In the incident room at Edendale, officers found themselves in a reversal of the normal routine – they were drawing up a list of potential victims rather than suspects.

For a few minutes, DCI Oliver Kessen watched Hitchens organizing the enquiry teams.

'And once we have a list of names, what do we do?' said Kessen.

'We warn them of the risk, sir.'

'Look, we have to be careful here. If the press gets hold of the idea that there might be more murders, it could lead to a general panic.'

'That goes without saying.'

'Does it?'

'Yes, sir.'

Ben Cooper hadn't quite got used to DCI Kessen. He was too quiet by far. In fact, he was so quiet as he moved around West Street that his officers often turned around to find him standing in the doorway, watching them. And they wouldn't know how long he'd been there, or what he was thinking.

'All right, so who have we got?' said Kessen.

'There are the two children from the Quinns' marriage,' said Hitchens. 'The daughter, Andrea, is twenty-six. I don't suppose she'll remember all that much of her father. But the son, Simon, is twenty-eight now. He'd have been about fifteen years old when his father was sent down. He'll remember.'

'I should think he damn well would.'

'But I don't think we're looking at the children as potential victims. He's still their father, after all.'

Kessen shrugged. 'Unfortunately, fathers have been known to kill their children. Do we have any evidence as to how Quinn viewed his two?'

He watched Hitchens shake his head. 'No.'

'Get somebody on to the prison authorities. They have personal officers for prisoners on each wing these days. They also have counsellors, and all that business. Someone will have talked to Quinn about his family. Or tried to, at least. Let's see what we can get out of them. Any insight into how his mind might be working would be useful.'

'Yes, sir.'

'Where do Quinn's family live?'

'The daughter is working in London. But the son, Simon – he has a job in Development Control with the district council. He recently bought a house right here in Edendale.'

'He was lucky,' said Gavin Murfin. 'There isn't much property for first-time buyers around here.'

'No, you're right. I wonder how he managed the mortgage.' Hitchens sighed. 'There's an awful lot of stuff to work on, sir.'

'Information is what we need,' said Kessen. 'If we can establish what sort of people we're dealing with and what terms they're on with Quinn, we might be able to work out his intentions.'

'I suppose so. But we can't begin to take measures to protect all these people, can we?'

'We can warn them that they might be at risk. Who else do we have?'

'There are two friends of Mansell Quinn. Or former friends,

at least. The three of them were very close at the time of the murder. Both were called to give evidence at the trial, and both declined to give him an alibi. That was pretty much the clincher.'

'Who needs enemies, eh?'

'Number one, we have Raymond Proctor, aged fifty, married. He runs a caravan park near Hope.'

'Family?'

'Married, as I said. Two teenage children. Hang on, no – one grown-up son. The teenagers are step-children, from his wife's previous marriage. Poor bugger.'

Kessen regarded him coolly. 'Proctor, you say?'

'Yes, this is the guy whose first wife was killed by Quinn – he'd been having an affair with her. So we can't expect much love lost there, I suppose.'

'Friend number two?'

'Number two is William Edward Thorpe, aged forty-five, single. Thorpe was a soldier, spent quite a lot of his time serving overseas. He was with the local regiment, the Worcestershire and Sherwood Foresters, but he was discharged last year.'

'Current whereabouts?'

'Unknown.'

'His regiment should have records.'

'We've tried them,' said Hitchens. 'On discharge, Thorpe went to Derby for a while. He was staying with one of his old army buddies who'd finished his stint a few months earlier. But the friend says Thorpe walked out after a few days, and he doesn't know where he went after that. The computer throws up a drunk-and-disorderly charge for a William Edward Thorpe in Ashbourne a couple of months ago, but his address was given as "no fixed abode".'

'We need to find him. Quinn has a motive for looking him up.'

'So much work,' said Hitchens.

DCI Kessen waved away the comment.

'Sudbury's an open prison, right?' said Murfin.

'Yes.'

'Didn't we have one who escaped from there recently?'

'If you can call it escaping. He was on an unsupervised work party on the prison farm, and never went back to his cell at the end of the day.'

'I don't know why they bother doing it. I mean, those open prisons are a cushy number. And he'll only get sent back to somewhere worse when he's caught.'

'If he's caught.'

'Come on, sir. When did we not catch someone who'd walked out of Sudbury? These blokes always go straight home. The poor sods don't know what else to do.'

Cooper put his hand up. 'Gavin has a point, sir. Mansell Quinn didn't escape, but his thinking could be the same. He might just have been going home.'

'Damn right. He turned up at his wife's house and killed her.'

Cooper shook his head. 'That wasn't his home. He never lived there.'

'No, you're right. His previous address was in Castleton. But somebody else lives there now. Complete strangers, I assume. Check on it, would you, Murfin.'

'Quinn's mother lives in Hathersage,' said Cooper. 'That will be the place he thinks of as home.'

'We've talked to her, haven't we? DS Fry?'

'Yes, sir. But I don't think she was being entirely open with us.'

'Put a bit of pressure on, then. Get some officers into the area to talk to all the neighbours. See if we can get a sighting of Quinn. OK, Paul?'

Hitchens had no choice but to nod.

'Somebody look into public transport,' said Kessen. 'Is there a railway station near Sudbury?'

'We'll check, sir.'

'He might have hired a car,' said someone. 'Or stolen one.'

'We should look into it,' said Hitchens. 'Right.'

'If Quinn does have a car,' pointed out Kessen, 'it's going to make it much less difficult for us. A known vehicle will be easier to locate than an individual who may or may not be on foot, and who has the whole of the Peak District to wander around in.'

'We hope for the easy option, then,' said Hitchens.

'Obviously. So we want sightings of vehicles in Aston, near the victim's home.'

'And appeals, sir?'

'The press office are already on to that. They're fixing up a press conference later this afternoon. We aim to get Quinn's photograph on the local TV news tonight. We need as many members of the public looking out for him as possible.'

'I got chatting with some of Mrs Lowe's neighbours at Aston this morning,' said Murfin. 'They said they were just passing, but of course they'd come for a nosy around to see what was going on.'

'The next-door neighbours?'

'No, further up the village. They didn't see anything last night, but they volunteered Mansell Quinn's name themselves. They'd heard he was due out.'

'Where did they hear that from?'

'They seemed to think it was something everybody knew.'

'The Carol Proctor killing is a case everyone in that area will remember,' said Hitchens. 'At least, everyone who was living around there in 1990. But we have to reach the others as well – the newcomers, and all those thousands of visitors, too.'

'If necessary, we'll spend some money on distributing posters. Anything else, Paul?'

'I think that's it for now, sir.'

But Cooper raised a hand. 'Sir, if Quinn is looking for revenge for some perceived injustice at his trial, I wonder if he might also go after the professionals involved. For example, the judge, the lawyers –'

'– or the police officers,' said Kessen. 'Yes. Specifically, the officers who worked on the Carol Proctor case and put the evidence together that got him sent down.'

The DCI looked at Hitchens. 'You'd better add looking up the investigating officers to your list of tasks, Paul,' he said.

Hitchens looked more uncomfortable than ever. 'No, sir.'

'Why not?'

'I don't need anyone to look them up.'

Kessen smiled at him. 'Perhaps you'd better tell us why, DI Hitchens. I think some of us here don't know.'

'Well, one of those officers,' said Hitchens, 'was me.'

Rebecca Lowe might have lived alone, but she had an active enough life. Analysing her diary, address books and other material that had been taken from her house, the incident room staff had already begun to piece together her movements, her regular activities and closest contacts. Later, her phone records would be gone through, her letters and bank statements read in the hope of tracing connections that might point to a motive, a suspect, or a possible witness.

Along with the forensic examination and the postmortem, it was all part of the routine that had to be observed to demonstrate that things were being done properly. But everyone knew that a separate operation was going on at the same time – the effort to find the man already identified as the prime suspect: Mansell Quinn.

Ben Cooper found himself with an interview to do almost immediately. At least once a week, Rebecca Lowe had attended a gym located on an industrial estate in Edendale. Her sister Dawn said that she'd been talking about joining a new fitness centre at Hathersage instead, because it was nearer. But changing your gym was a bit like converting from one religion to another. You risked being told that everything you'd done so far in your life was wrong. Perhaps Rebecca had been a bit set in her ways, after all. She'd stayed at the Edendale gym.

'One of our more mature ladies,' said the trainer at Valley Fitness. 'But she was in better shape than most. In fact, she could outlast a lot of the younger women on the bikes. Also, she wasn't afraid to try new things. She'd put her name down for a trial Pilates class.'

'Did she ever talk about her ex-husband?'

'Wait a minute – he died, didn't he?'

'Sorry, I mean the husband before that.'

'An earlier ex? No, I didn't know she had one. She'd lived a bit then, had she, Rebecca? Seen off two husbands, but still kept herself in condition? Well, good for her.'

'When did you last see her?'

'Monday morning. She always comes in for a session on Monday morning. Never misses.'

That checked with the photocopy Cooper had of a page from Rebecca Lowe's week-to-view diary.

'And she was definitely there yesterday morning?'

'Yes, ten o'clock to eleven. She made a joke about working off the excesses of the weekend. She liked a bottle of wine now and then, I think.'

Cooper looked at the entries for the previous two days. Lunch with her sister on Saturday. A dinner party with some friends on Sunday night.

'And did Mrs Lowe seem her normal self?'

'How do you mean?'

'Did she seem worried about anything? Did she mention anything that was bothering her?'

'I didn't talk to her that much, but she seemed perfectly happy. Just as usual. Wait a minute, though . . .'

'Yes?'

The phone was silent for a moment. Cooper could hear a series of strange noises in the background, and imagined the running and stretching and pedalling that must be going on while they spoke. The thought of it made him feel tired.

'There was a man who was due out of prison about now,' said the trainer. 'Is that right? Somebody that Rebecca knew very well.'

'Yes, that's right. Did Mrs Lowe tell you that?'

'No, I don't think so.'

'Oh.'

'Somebody else must have mentioned it. An old murder case, wasn't it? Or maybe it's just a bit of gossip. I might be able to remember his name, if you give me a minute.'

'Never mind. I expect it was Quinn.'

'That's it! So is it right? Is he out?'

'Yes, I'm afraid so.'

As Cooper put the phone down, he was handed a photograph. It was a recent shot of Rebecca Lowe, the one they'd be issuing with the press releases. She was dressed for the outdoors, in a green body warmer and jeans, and she had a dog at her heels – a small thing with a plumed tail and a screwed-up face. Rebecca had rather a narrow face, with lines around her eyes but enviable cheekbones. Her hair was blonde, though surely it must be dyed at forty-nine.

The trainer at the fitness club was right – Rebecca Lowe looked in good condition. But seen off two husbands? It looked as though one of them had come back again.

For a while, Cooper found himself waiting for someone to tell him what to do next. A major murder enquiry was a rigid bureaucracy, with clearly defined responsibilities and not much chance for anyone to work outside the system. As a divisional detective, he'd be allocated to the Outside Enquiry Team. Somebody had to do the physical part of the investigation, even if the SIO opted for HOLMES.

Of course, Cooper regretted that he'd have to let Amy and

Josie down and skip the visit to the caverns. But they would understand – they always did.

Finally, he saw Diane Fry walking between the desks in the CID room.

'You're supposed to be on a rest day, aren't you, Ben?' she said.

'Yes, but –'

'You might as well take what's left of it off.'

'Don't you need me?' said Cooper, hearing his own voice rising a pitch in surprise. And sensing, perhaps, that sinking feeling of disappointment.

'Not today. It looks like a self-solver. We just need to get some leads on where Mansell Quinn is and catch up with him.'

'Are you sure, Diane?'

'That's what they're saying further up.'

'Well, I don't mind, because I've got things planned. It just doesn't feel right, that's all.'

Fry shrugged. 'We just do what we're told, don't we?'

It felt strange to Cooper to be leaving the office and going home when a major enquiry might be about to start. But, if he stayed, he'd become eligible for overtime. Somebody was making tough budget decisions in an office upstairs, gambling on an early conclusion.

Before Cooper could escape from the building, DI Hitchens put his head round the door and caught his eye.

'DC Cooper.'

'Yes, sir?'

'Have you got a few minutes? Just before you go.'

Hitchens inclined his head to his office, and Cooper followed him in.

'Shut the door.'

Hitchens looked serious – more serious than Cooper could remember seeing him for a long time, not since the DI had failed his interview for a chief inspector's job. He also seemed a little uncomfortable, hesitating at his desk as if about to sit down, but then remaining where he was at the window. Apart from the football ground, there was nothing for him to look at outside, only the roofs of houses in the streets that ran downhill towards the centre of Edendale.

Cooper waited until the DI pulled his thoughts together.

'I thought I'd tell you this privately first, Ben,' he said, 'rather than during a team briefing.'

Now it was Cooper who was starting to feel uneasy. He could sense bad news coming. Was he going to be reprimanded for something? Had he committed a serious enough offence to face a disciplinary enquiry – or worse? Cooper swallowed. He knew that he had. But time had passed, and he'd become convinced that he was safe. There was only one person who might have shopped him.

He studied the DI's face to try to gauge how serious it was. Hitchens hadn't even bothered to use the positive-negative-positive technique that was taught to managers. He ought to have praised Cooper for something first before he tackled the difficult subject, so as not to destroy his morale. Maybe that meant it was something else. A transfer, perhaps. Cooper had a few years of his tenure in CID to go yet, but that didn't mean they couldn't dispense with his services sooner.

'It's the Mansell Quinn case,' said Hitchens, taking Cooper by surprise. 'I mean, the murder of Carol Proctor.'

'Yes, sir?'

'It's funny that you should be the one to raise the point about the professionals involved in the case being at risk. I'm thinking about the police officers particularly.'

'You were one of the officers involved, sir.'

'Yes, I was, Cooper.'

'But how does that affect me? Is there something you want me to do?'

Hitchens smiled.

'You think I might be asking you to protect me? That's very good of you, Ben. But I'll take my chances.'

Then the DI sat down at last and folded his hands on the desk, intertwining his long fingers nervously.

'This is a bit difficult, Cooper,' he said. 'But, first of all, you've got to remember that the Carol Proctor killing was nearly fourteen years ago. I was a divisional DC then, much like yourself. A bit younger, in fact, but every bit as keen. Anyway, it was my first murder case, so I remember it well. I made notes of everything. Of course, things were done a bit differently in those days.'

Cooper nodded. He had run out of things to say.

'All the senior officers on the case have long since retired,' said Hitchens. 'The SIO died three years ago. Heart attack.'

'I'm sorry. Was he a good detective, sir?'

Cooper knew that the first Senior Investigating Officer you worked for on a major enquiry could make a lasting impression, like an influential school teacher. He still thought fondly of DCI Tailby, who he'd worked for a couple of times.

'A good detective? Not particularly,' said Hitchens. 'He was an old school dick – some of them were still around in the early nineties. He had his own ideas about how things were done. Well, he wasn't the only one, of course.'

'No, sir.'

'My old DS is still around, but he's a training officer at Bramshill now,' Hitchens continued. 'That only leaves me from the main enquiry team that put Mansell Quinn away. However, the actual arrest wasn't made by CID but by uniforms. The suspect was still at the scene when the first officers arrived and so the FOAs arrested him. They found the knife, too. Obviously, Quinn hadn't given any thought to concocting a story before the patrol turned up.'

Cooper shook his head. 'I still don't understand, sir.'

Hitchens sighed. 'I know how much the death of your

father meant to you, Ben. I think it still bothers you a lot, am I right?'

'Yes, sir.' The words hardly came out, because Cooper's mouth felt numb. His mind had latched on to the acronym FOA – first officers to arrive. A uniformed patrol responding to a 999 call. He had a sinking certainty that he knew what the DI was going to say next. 'So in the Mansell Quinn case . . . ?'

Hitchens nodded. 'Yes. After Carol Proctor was murdered,' he said, 'the arresting officer was Sergeant Joe Cooper.'

11

Another enquiry team had been assigned the action on Mansell Quinn's friend, William Thorpe. And good luck to them. According to the initial intelligence, he was living on the streets, as so many ex-soldiers did.

To Diane Fry, 'living on the street' meant one of the big cities – Sheffield or Manchester, maybe even Derby. Edendale didn't have many homeless people. Those who hung around the town were too much of a nuisance to the tourists to be tolerated for long. If Thorpe had been surviving locally, he'd have been picked up by a patrol, but there was no record of it. The only leads were his drunk-and-disorderly charge in Ashbourne, thirty miles to the south, and the existence of an ex-wife, long since divorced. So that action was likely to tie up two unlucky DCs for a good while.

Fry was on victim's background. The only trouble was, she'd been teamed up with Gavin Murfin. Their first task was a visit to Dawn Cottrill, Rebecca Lowe's sister, who had found the body.

Mrs Cottrill lived at the end of a modern cul-de-sac in Castleton. It was what the designers called a 'hammerhead' close, opening out into two stubby arms at the top. Fry understood this to be something that the planners insisted on to provide room for fire appliances to turn round. Otherwise, the whole point of these modern developments was to allow people to feel they were out of the way of the passing hoi polloi, while still being handy for the shops.

As they drove into the road, two young men in dark suits and white shirts were walking up the drive of one of the houses. They had short hair and carried leather satchels.

'Watch out,' said Murfin. 'Jehovah's.'

'What?'

'Jehovah's Witnesses. Don't stand still when you're out in the open, or they'll get you.'

'Just concentrate on the job, Gavin.'

By the time they'd found somewhere to park the car, the two young men had disappeared – maybe somebody had actually let them in. As Fry looked around the cul-de-sac, she realized it must have been one of the last developments built in Castleton before the national park planning regulations were tightened. To stem the influx of affluent outsiders, the only planning permissions given now were to affordable homes for people who'd lived in the village for at least ten years or had strong family ties with the area.

'Well, I'm not local enough,' said Murfin when she mentioned it. 'And I'm damn sure you're not. They probably lynch Brummies around here.'

'I'm from the Black Country.'

'You *sound* like a Brummie, though. Maybe you'd better let me do the talking, Diane.'

'What does Dawn Cottrill do?' asked Fry.

'She's a lecturer at High Peak College. Economic history.'

'Educated, then.'

'Well, obviously.'

'Maybe you'd better let *me* do the talking in that case, Gavin.'

Dawn Cottrill had iron-grey hair in a bob. Her face was pale, and her cheekbones seemed very prominent. Fry could almost have believed that her hair had turned grey overnight since her sister's death, that her face had been sharpened by the pain.

'It seems impossible to believe that something like this could happen again,' said Mrs Cottrill. 'But this time . . .'

'Yes, I understand,' said Fry. 'When you think something is a long way in your past, it's very shocking.'

They had been ushered through the house on to a sort of wooden veranda overlooking the garden. The decking had been partly covered with rugs and set out with a table, on which stood glasses and a jug filled with fruit juice and ice. Fry and Murfin sat on a settee with a blue blanket thrown over it and cushions scattered everywhere.

Dawn Cottrill sat with her back to the sun, perhaps to avoid having the light in her face as she talked. With a steady hand, she poured them a drink. Fry was impressed by the woman's composure, a reassuring sign when her job was to ask difficult questions.

'Mrs Cottrill, do you happen to know when your sister last saw her ex-husband, Mansell Quinn?'

'It would be the final visit Rebecca made to him in prison. Not the open prison at Sudbury, but about two before that. I'm sorry, but they seemed to keep moving him from one prison to another. I think this one was somewhere in Lancashire.'

'And that last visit was several years ago, I think?'

'Oh, yes. I can't remember how long exactly, I'm afraid. But Andrea was still quite young.'

'Before the divorce and her new marriage, though?'

'Of course. Rebecca was only married to Maurice Lowe for eighteen months before he died. He had a heart attack, you know. He'd been playing squash. I always thought it was too energetic a game for a man of his age.'

Mrs Cottrill's voice faltered. She brushed a non-existent strand of hair from her forehead. Her hand was very slender, too – the veins and tendons showed clearly through the skin.

'I'm sorry,' she said. 'It's been such a difficult time. Thank goodness the children are old enough to cope with it better. They were both worried, you know, about their father coming out of prison. More worried than Rebecca was herself. She was obviously much too trusting.'

'Did Mrs Lowe say why she stopped visiting Mansell Quinn in prison?' said Fry, sticking to her line of questions.

'Why? It was understandable, wasn't it? The divorce was going through. She had her own life to lead.'

'But the children – Simon and Andrea. He was their father, after all. It meant he didn't see them again.'

'They were teenagers,' said Mrs Cottrill. 'Old enough to make up their own minds. They could have gone to visit their father, if they'd wanted to. But they never did, not since then. You couldn't expect Rebecca to force them to go, if they were frightened.'

'Frightened?'

Dawn Cottrill looked at her. Fry realized that the woman hadn't really been focusing on her until now. Her gaze had been fixed somewhere over Fry's head, at the trellising on the wall of the house.

'I imagine you've been inside a prison,' she said. 'In *your* job.'

Fry felt suitably put down. Mrs Cottrill's tone of voice suggested that her job made her almost as bad as the prison inmates.

'Yes, I have,' she said. 'It isn't pleasant for visitors. Especially for children. But, as you say, Simon and Andrea were teenagers by then. They were old enough to know what was going on.'

Mrs Cottrill considered for a moment. She looked at Gavin Murfin, who had sensibly chosen to remain silent, taking notes. He took a drink of the fruit juice, which Fry hadn't tasted. She saw him look around the table, as if hoping for some home-made cake to go with it.

'Rebecca once said that Mansell had started to be rather strange when they visited him.'

'Strange in what way, Mrs Cottrill?' said Fry.

'He used to grab at the kids, wanted to hold on to them too tightly, tugged at their hair even. Well, Simon in particular. He was always especially fond of Simon, and I suggested to Rebecca that it was just the frustration of not being able to hold his own children, you know, that made him a bit rough. The lack of physical contact. Anyway, the children didn't like it, and they were frightened.'

'I see.'

'I said they were teenagers, but I recall now that Andrea must have been about twelve at the time. She's nearly three years younger than Simon. You can't imagine what might be going through a child's mind at that age.'

'Would you have said Mansell Quinn was a violent man generally?'

'Actually, no I wouldn't. No one was more surprised than I was when he committed that dreadful act. I didn't know Mrs Proctor, so I can't say what their relationship had been to have provoked that kind of outburst from him.'

'And now?'

'This? I can't explain it. I have no explanation for it at all.'

Fry detected a slight break in the woman's voice. She might not have much longer before the interview began to slip away from her.

'It's Simon I'm mostly worried about now,' said Mrs Cottrill.

'Why?'

'I had Rebecca and both the children to stay in my house for a while after it happened. I mean, the first time. They were dreadfully shocked and upset, of course. We all were. But Simon went completely in on himself. Rebecca took him to see a counsellor at one stage, when he was having problems at school. I don't know what this will do to him now.'

'We will need to talk to him, I'm afraid,' said Fry.

116

'I suppose so. But you'll get more out of Andrea. She spoke with her mother on the phone shortly before it happened. She might be able to give you an idea of what Rebecca was thinking in the last hour or so of her life.'

'Let's hope so,' said Fry.

'You know, I've thought about Mansell Quinn quite a bit over the years,' said Dawn. 'We have to make an attempt to understand what goes on in the mind of someone like that – especially if we've become their target. We always want to know "why", don't we?'

'Sometimes you can ask "why" for as long as you like,' said Fry, 'but there's never going to be an answer.'

She pushed herself out of the settee and left her drink sitting on the table on the warm veranda.

At Wingate Lees caravan park, Diane Fry and Gavin Murfin found that the Proctors lived in a large house that stood a little way back from the site itself, sheltered by a line of dark conifers. Leylandii, in fact. They had grown fast, and would soon be so big that they'd block off the light from the windows of the house.

Thanks to the Victim's Charter, a probation officer should have contacted the Proctors to let them know when Mansell Quinn was being moved to an open prison, and when he came due for release. Maybe Raymond Proctor had even been allowed to give his views to the parole board when Quinn's review came up. At least it ought to mean that their news wouldn't come as too much of a shock.

The man who answered the door looked suspicious, though – even more suspicious than most citizens would on finding Diane Fry and Gavin Murfin standing on their doorstep. He was reluctant to open his door fully and peered at them in irritation.

'Don't worry, sir, we're not more of those flamin' Jehovah's Witnesses,' said Murfin cheerfully.

117

Instead of seeming relieved, the man looked at him even more sourly.

'I am,' he said.

'Sorry? You're what?'

'A Jehovah's Witness.'

'Oh.'

For once, Murfin was lost for words. Fry grimaced and tried to edge him aside.

'Mr Proctor? We're police – Detective Sergeant Fry and Detective Constable Murfin.'

'Bloody hell.'

'You *are* Mr Raymond Proctor?'

'Of course I am. What do you want? Is it one of my guests?'

'Who?'

'The guests. My customers. The buggers staying in my caravans. There's that bunch from Glasgow in one of the cabins. Two youths, and two girls with them – that's always a recipe for trouble. I wouldn't have let them rent a cabin if I'd realized how old they were.'

'It isn't about any of your customers,' said Fry. 'It's about an old friend of yours: Mansell Quinn. Can we come in?'

Proctor's face changed, but Fry wasn't sure if he was surprised or not.

'I suppose so,' he said.

They followed him down a passage into an extension at the side of the house, where a room had been equipped as an office, with filing cabinets, a phone and a wooden desk on which stood a PC with a blank screen. Three oak cupboards were lined up against the back wall, and dozens of keys hung on orderly rows of hooks, neatly tagged and labelled. Despite its business use, the place had a general air of untidiness, making the neatness of the keys look out of place.

'Are you really a Jehovah's Witness?' said Murfin as he passed Proctor in the doorway.

118

'Am I buggery. I said that so you'd go away.'

'It didn't work.'

'More's the pity.'

'Mr Proctor, are you aware that Mansell Quinn is out of prison?'

'No. Is he? Well, I suppose it had to be around this time. I haven't been keeping track exactly.'

'Did you know when he was moved to an open prison?'

'No. Why should I?'

'You have the right to information like that under the Victim's Charter. A probation officer should have contacted you to let you know what your rights are.'

'Oh, I recollect that someone came to see me a couple of months after Quinn was sent down. Perhaps that was a probation officer. He asked if I wanted to know about Quinn's progress. He mentioned parole boards, and all that stuff. But why would I want to know? I'd rather forget about him.'

'A lot of people would have wanted to know when he was due for release. It can come as a shock to see someone walking down the street when you thought they were safely inside. That's the whole purpose of the Victim's Charter.'

Proctor shrugged. 'I didn't want to know. I'm married again now, got a new family. What happened is all in the past, as far as I'm concerned. And Quinn wouldn't come back here, anyway. Would he?'

'Actually, we think there may be a threat to your safety, sir,' said Fry.

'What?'

'Mansell Quinn was released from prison on Monday morning, but has since gone missing. We have reason to believe he may be in this area.'

'No kidding?'

'Also, we think he might already have attacked one person. We don't know what his intentions are, but we're very concerned.'

'Attacked one person? Who?'

'Well, it'll soon be in the news. His former wife was murdered last night.'

Proctor stared at her, almost glassy-eyed. 'Rebecca? So what has that to do with me? Why are you here instead of out there looking for Quinn?'

'If he's planning more violent attacks, it's possible he might have you in mind as a potential victim, sir.'

'What a load of rubbish,' said Proctor. 'Somebody's over-reacting here, aren't they? What did you say your name was?'

'Fry. Detective Sergeant Fry.'

'Is this all your idea?'

Fry began to get rankled. He seemed to be suggesting she was some kind of neurotic female, worrying about nothing.

'No, sir. There's concern at senior level. We've come to advise you –'

'I mean, Mansell Quinn . . . well, it was all over and done with fourteen years ago. Why should Quinn care about *me*? I never did anything wrong. In fact, it was *me* that was done wrong to. If Quinn comes here, it'll be to apologize.'

Fry took a deep breath. 'We'd advise you to take what-ever precautions you can, Mr Proctor. Keep your doors and windows locked, don't open the door to anyone you can't identify, make sure someone knows where you are at all times, and keep in touch.'

'I don't think that'll be necessary.'

'We hope not, sir. But it's better to be safe than sorry. We can give you a number to phone if you're worried. Of course, it would be even better if you left the area for a while. Perhaps you could take your family on holiday or stay with friends?'

'You *are* kidding, aren't you?' said Proctor. 'Have you seen this place? Who do you think runs it? This is our busiest time of the year. If I'm away from the site for a couple of hours, the whole thing starts to grind to a halt.'

'Well, what about your family? They could go away some-where.'

'Connie and her kids? Chance would be a fine thing.'

'Just until the situation is resolved.'

'Until you've caught Mansell Quinn, you mean? Well, I'm not holding my breath.'

'What do you mean?'

'I'm sorry, Sergeant, but I don't think it's very likely that you'll catch him. I know your lot – you couldn't catch a cold in winter. In my opinion, if Quinn's gone walkabout, he won't be caught until he wants to be.'

Fry hesitated, still concerned that Raymond Proctor hadn't grasped the seriousness of the situation, or the immediacy of the danger he was in.

'What sort of security arrangements do you have here, sir?'

Proctor simply laughed in her face. 'Are you thinking in terms of razor wire and searchlights? You think I should get a dog? Perhaps a couple of Rottweilers to patrol the garden? Or a few man-traps and CCTV cameras?' He stared out of the window, and for the first time Fry thought she saw a trace of uncertainty in the man's eyes. 'None of them would mean anything to Quinn.'

'We can't offer protection, I'm afraid, sir,' she said.

'I don't expect it. Believe me, I don't. What, some goon of a bobby hanging around my gate? It wouldn't achieve anything, except to scare my customers off.'

'We can ask patrols to come by at regular intervals.'

'Oh, if you like. Now, have you finished?'

Proctor assumed an expression of indifference. It was the sort of expression worn by teenagers who wanted to look cool. Raymond Proctor had obviously practised it to perfec-tion over the years, and had even added a little curl of the lip that hinted at contempt. Fry expected him to shrug and say: 'Yeah. Whatever.'

Then she lost patience. Before she turned to leave, Fry leaned forward towards Proctor, pointing a finger in his face.

'Just remember this,' she said. 'Every day and every night, somebody could be coming here to kill you.'

Will Thorpe lit another cigarette. He had moved back from the hollow into the trees, where he could look across the rooftops of the houses on the southern edge of Castleton.

'I don't suppose you've got any fags on you?' he said.

'No.'

Mansell Quinn wouldn't sit down or relax. He stood among the trees, staring down into the gardens of the houses, running his eyes across the back windows, watching anyone who came in view.

'You must have smoked inside,' said Thorpe.

Quinn didn't answer.

'Suit yourself, then.'

'My house is just up the road from here,' said Quinn.

'Pindale Road? It *was* your house.'

Quinn turned quickly and covered the few feet between them in a second. Thorpe flinched and doubled over in a spasm of coughing. But Quinn simply stood over him. He looked up at the keep of the castle, where it hung over the sheer side of Cavedale.

'See those bits sticking out of the wall of the tower?' he said.

Thorpe wheezed and tried to control his breathing. He wiped some saliva from his mouth.

'What are you on about, Mansell?'

'Can you see them?'

'Yeah, all right. I can.'

'They called those *oubliettes*,' said Quinn. 'It's where they used to tip their shit out of the castle. Those folk down there in the dale would have been wading through it.'

'Oh, very nice.'

122

'But even then, they knew that you have to get rid of your shit. You can't have it fouling up your own home. So you offload it on to someone else. Isn't that right, Will?'

Thorpe coughed again. 'Get on with it, then, Mansell.'

'Just one more thing, and then I'll leave you alone.'

Quinn continued to stare at the castle, watching the distant figures moving about on the walls. Two young girls ran up the spiral stairs into the keep and appeared in an arched window further up, laughing. Their voices reached across the dale.

With the back of his hand, Quinn wiped away the sweat and the flies that had settled on him as he stood among the trees. But his voice was cold, like a sudden draught of air from the caves below the limestone dale.

'I want the other addresses,' he said.

'Mansell, are you sure –?'

Quinn turned then and looked down at Thorpe. 'Have you got them or not? Did Rebecca give them to you?'

'Yes, but . . . I'm not sure it's right.'

'What?'

Thorpe squinted up at him. 'He has a new life now, Mansell. Why rake it all up again after so long?'

Quinn lashed out almost blindly. He ripped a branch from the nearest sycamore, snapped it in his hands and shredded the bark into strips, exposing the white flesh underneath. The wood tore under his fingers with a sound like a faint scream.

'Everyone thinks they can just get on with their lives as if nothing happened, don't they?' he said. 'They're about to find out how wrong they are.'

12

The red stains of ferrous oxide showed through white limestone and a coating of green algae, and water ran continuously down the face of the multi-coloured rock. The stream
bed where it left Peak Cavern was almost dry at this time of
the year, but the flow reappeared down the gorge, spurting
from a gash at the foot of the cliff.

Ben Cooper and his nieces watched the jackdaws chattering continuously overhead.

'Do the birds nest on the cliff ledges?' asked Amy, who
was taking an interest in wildlife at the moment.

'Yes, I think so,' said Cooper, looking anxiously for ducklings planning to take a suicidal dive.

Inside the cavern entrance, they found themselves on a
series of wide terraces cut out of the rock. Families of ropemakers had set up their workshops here centuries ago,
building their houses into the floor and knocking out tiny
doors and windows, so that the rope walks they worked on
were also the roofs of their homes. The rock walls were
stained black from the soot of their fires.

On the top terrace, a small crowd was watching a guide
stretch hemp twine from winders to pulley-poles and twist it
into rope using a sledge and a jack with rotating hooks.

Amy and Josie ran down the dirt slope to a reconstruction of a ropemaker's house. The roof was hinged up, so that visitors could look down into the living space, otherwise it would have been too dark to see anything. Inside, there was just enough room for a fireplace, a couple of chairs and some beds covered in straw, built into the wall like shelves. Suddenly, the girls laughed nervously.

'Who's *he*?'

'A ropemaker, I suppose,' said Cooper.

A stuffed figure was propped in one of the chairs near the fireplace. He was dressed in black and had a pale, shapeless face, with crudely defined eyes that stared blankly into a dim corner.

'He's a bit scary,' said Amy.

'It's only like a Guy Fawkes.'

'They should burn him, then.'

Cooper blinked as he watched Amy go back to join the crowd at the demonstration. Josie stayed with him, staring into the house. She was the more thoughtful of the two, and he guessed she was trying to imagine what life would have been like for the ropemakers' families. Or at least, he hoped she was. For all he knew, her mind might be absorbed in some fantasy of flames and immolation, too. He didn't really understand children.

He sniffed, inhaling the scent of the hemp as it moved through the guide's hands. It smelled like wet horses' tails.

It occurred to Cooper that earlier visitors would have been able to smell this place long before they reached it. The ropemakers had kept animals in here – pack horses, cattle, goats, and even pigs for their tallow. The effluent must have gone into the stream flowing out of the cave, along with human waste. It would have been quite a culture shock for the genteel visitors of the eighteenth and nineteenth centuries.

'Welcome to the Devil's Arse,' said Alistair Page, coming to stand alongside him on the terrace. 'We'll be able to go through the show cave in a moment. We had to wait for a party to come back out, so thank you for being patient.'

Page had a verbal mannerism that had caught Ben Cooper's attention even when they'd been underground during the rescue exercise. On occasional words he emphasized a final 't' with a click of his tongue against his teeth. It was audible in 'moment' and in 'patient'. Cooper found it distracting and began to listen more carefully, to see if he could discern a pattern. He soon noticed that it only happened when the word fell at the end of a sentence. It produced an exaggerated emphasis, like a full stop pronounced out loud. Each time he heard it, he imagined Page spitting out an exclamation mark, ejecting it like an apple pip that had stuck between his teeth.

Cooper called the girls, and they followed the path along the wall, above the terraces. The change from warm outside air to the cooler atmosphere of the cave was noticeable as they descended wide steps into a chamber called Bell House. Of course, it was a constant nine degrees Celsius down here. Mist hung in the chamber, and steam rose from the lights where water dripped from fissures in the roof.

They entered Lumbago Walk, a low tunnel blasted from the rock. Alistair Page explained that it had been created for a visit by the young Queen Victoria. Previous visitors had been forced to enter the cavern lying flat on their backs in a shallow boat, clutching candles to their chests. The adults had had to bend double to avoid knocking themselves senseless on the roof.

As they hunched over, Page leaned towards Cooper and whispered to him. 'Quinn's out of prison, isn't he?'

Cooper stared at Page, surprised by the question.

'Who?'

'Mansell Quinn.'

'Do you know Quinn, Alistair?'

'I've lived in Castleton all my life.'

They emerged from the tunnel into the Great Cave, where bands of blue fluorite ran across the ceiling. Page pointed out the fossils in the rock, the remains of sea creatures that had died in the reef. He showed them a flowstone formation called Mother-in-law's Tongue and an imitation boulder left by the BBC while filming *The Chronicles of Narnia*.

'So you were in Castleton back when Carol Proctor was murdered?' said Cooper.

'Of course. In fact, at the time I lived very near where it happened.'

'In Pindale Road? So your family were neighbours of the Quinns?'

'Well, very close.'

Page pointed to crystal-clear water lying in a rock pool, with tiny blind shrimps flickering across the surface.

'Apart from the shrimps, there isn't much natural life in a cave like this,' he said. 'But it's amazing how things can find a way to survive.'

He showed them moss growing in the walls near the fibre-optic lights, and the empty webs left by spiders that had died because they found no flies to feed on. With his lamp, he pointed out the shapes formed in the walls – Father Christmas, Bambi, an alligator's head, and the dog from *Tintin*, whose name none of them could remember.

'And here –' he began, as they entered the Orchestra Gallery.

But then he stopped. Cooper looked at him, puzzled by the change in his manner. It was almost as if he'd frightened himself with his own stories.

'There – in the light from the Great Cave – can you see the shadow on the wall?'

Cooper followed the beam of his light. The outline of a head and shoulders was visible in a shadow picked out by the lights of the chamber they'd just passed through. He could even see two stubby horns protruding from the head.

'It's the Devil himself,' he said.

'Yes,' said Page. 'That's who it is.'

'Are you all right?'

'Fine.'

Cooper looked up at the gallery again. But without a light, the shadow had disappeared.

'You see, the effect of the light is a bit funny in here,' said Page. 'You not only imagine shapes – sometimes you even think you can see them moving.'

Diane Fry and Gavin Murfin had called at West Street on the way to their next call, which was all the way down the county in Sudbury.

'I want to know how they're getting on with tracking down William Thorpe,' said Fry.

'If he's anything like Proctor, they shouldn't bother,' said Murfin.

Fry was struggling to put Raymond Proctor out of her mind. She couldn't stand people who pushed her so far that she lost control, even for a moment. Instead of thinking about Proctor, she ought to be more concerned about Dawn Cottrill. Dawn had been the one to find her sister murdered. She might have had a right to be upset, to react badly to the police. But she hadn't.

In the incident room she was met with shaken heads when she asked about Thorpe.

'And I suppose it's too soon for the postmortem report on Rebecca Lowe?' Fry said.

'Sorry.'

'Any sign of the weapon? Have they finished searching the scene yet?'

'No sign.'

'DNA?'

'You're joking.'

'You didn't ask whether Quinn had been found,' said Murfin, following her as she stamped out.

'Not much hope of that,' said Fry. 'If we can't find Thorpe, what chance do we have of locating Quinn?'

Deeper into the cavern, they entered Roger Rain's House, where a perpetual cascade of water poured through the roof from the floor of Cave Dale. Cooper remembered it from the day before, when the water had spattered his face as he lay in the rescue stretcher. But it was only now that Page decided to mention the water had been found to contain sheep's urine.

'Oh, great,' said Cooper, trying to remember whether he'd kept his mouth closed.

They passed through the Devil's Dining Room and reached a barrier at the top of a slope where the muddy remnants of a flight of steps and a wooden chute ran down into the darkness. They could hear the distant sound of rushing water.

'This is the Devil's Staircase. You can hear the River Styx from here,' said Page, standing at the top of the chute. 'Which is a good thing. As long we can hear it, we're safe. If the noise stops, it means the water on the lower level has reached the roof and the cavern is about to flood. Then we have four minutes and thirty seconds to get out.'

'What's beyond here?' asked Cooper.

'Another twelve miles or so of passages, chambers, crawls and sumps. That's what we know of, anyway – there may be hundreds of miles more that haven't been discovered yet. But this is as far as we go today.'

Cooper gazed down the Devil's Staircase towards the noise of water. Even the girls were quiet as Page reeled off the names of the caverns deep in the hill: Fingernail Chamber, the Vortex, Surprise View. Many of them conjured up images of a fairyland waiting to be explored. But Cooper knew there was no fairyland, only darkness down there.

When they walked back into the Devil's Dining Room, Cooper noticed Page flashing his light into the corners and running it along the ledges where the shadows lay thickest.

In the roof of the chamber were black spikes of stalactite, like meat hooks.

'Those are called the Devil's Hooks,' said Page. 'In fact, there's a nice little story about this chamber. It's where they used to hold the Beggars' Banquet.'

'The what?'

Page seemed not to hear Cooper's question, but continued his story with a distracted air.

'For hundreds of years, Peak Cavern was used for an annual gathering of gypsies or tinkers. It was called the Beggars' Banquet, and it was held right here in the Devil's Dining Room every August – by royal permission, no less. It was said to be a celebration of the pagan festival, Lughnasa.'

It might have been the echo effect of the chamber, but Page's voice sounded unnaturally loud, as if he were addressing a more distant audience than the small group around him. He turned as he spoke, performing a complete circuit of the Devil's Dining Room with his lamp. The stalactite spikes glittered and winked in the ceiling.

Cooper was momentarily reminded of his panic in the narrow tunnel during the rescue exercise. He was conscious again of the massive weight of rock above him, and pictured the spiked roof gradually descending. Even from here, it seemed a very long way to the exit.

'The bands of tinkers were led by a famous outlaw called Cock Lorrel, "the most notorious knave that ever lived",' said Page. 'Cock Lorrel was the King of the Beggars, and it was said that he invited the Devil to his banquet in Peak Cavern to prove he was afraid of no one. Hence the Devil's Dining Room.'

He paused. As his voice died away, they could hear the sound of running water, the strange and unidentifiable noises made by the crevices in the rock, the inexplicable rattle of small stones.

Page turned his head back towards where they had come

from. Back towards the Devil's Staircase and the endless web of passages deep in the darkness of the hill.

'The festival went on for two weeks,' he said, 'so we can only imagine the condition of this place by the end of it. But what we do know is that they were pretty blood-soaked affairs. The guests at the Beggars' Banquet were cannibals.'

Amy and Josie laughed, thinking the story was over. Still bursting with energy, they went ahead up the wide steps through the Orchestra Gallery. Cooper saw their faces glowing in the light from the pool where the tiny, blind shrimps lived.

'He is, isn't he?' said Page.

'What?'

'Quinn – he's out of prison?'

'It seems to be general knowledge,' said Cooper. 'But you must have been only a youngster in 1990, Alistair.'

'I was fifteen.'

Page fiddled with the cord of his lamp, giving his full attention to it for no apparent reason, as if to discourage Cooper from probing any further. Even though his father had dealt with violence in his job, Ben knew how deeply he himself would have been affected if, at the age of fifteen, he'd learned of a murder near to his home. Close to home, it was a different matter. He wanted to ask Page what he'd thought of Mansell Quinn, but decided to leave it. It was doubtful what value there might be in the memories of a fifteen-year-old boy

They caught up with the girls in the Great Cave. Amy and Josie were gazing up into the roof sixty feet above them, awed by the swirl holes made by the waters of the prehistoric river. And they were looking for the rock that had made the shape of the Devil in the next chamber.

'The poet Ben Jonson wrote about Cock Lorrel and the Beggars' Banquet,' said Page cheerfully, spitting out the 't' in 'banquet' so hard that it ricocheted off the walls like a bullet.

'Back in the seventeenth century, that was. It's in his poem *The Gypsies Metamorphosed*. It's a bit gruesome, though. He says that the dishes eaten at the banquet were made from all the people Cock Lorrel and his followers didn't like – they broke open their heads and ate their brains.'

Page looked at the two girls doubtfully, but Cooper knew they wouldn't be bothered by anything gruesome. Amy and Josie had been raised on a livestock farm. They'd seen more birth and death in their short lives than most adults ever did.

Feeling the change of air as they passed through the Bell Chamber, Cooper realized he was nearly outside again. His mind went back to the conversation he'd had with DI Hitchens before he left West Street that morning. There seemed to be a short gap in his memory of what the DI had been saying, just after he'd told Cooper that his father had been the arresting officer in the Mansell Quinn case. But then Hitchens' voice had drifted in again, like a radio station coming back on to its wavelength.

'Joe Cooper and a PC were the crew of the car that responded to the 999 call when Carol Proctor was killed. Your father knew Mansell Quinn, of course.'

'He knew everybody,' Cooper had said automatically.

'Yes, I think he probably did.'

Then Hitchens had deliberately let a silence develop. Cooper had felt he was being watched for a reaction, much as the DI might watch a suspect in the interview room. Almost everyone showed physical signs of their state of mind, no matter how hard they tried to conceal them. And Cooper knew he was no exception.

'Sir, does this mean that you think . . . ?'

'I don't know,' said Hitchens. 'I don't know what Mansell Quinn has in mind. He might come looking for me, but I doubt it. I was only a junior DC – he probably wouldn't even have known my name. I didn't get any publicity, or any of the credit. You don't, as a detective constable. I'm sure you know that, too.'

Hitchens smiled, but Cooper found he couldn't work his face muscles sufficiently to respond.

'Yes, sir.'

'Obviously, I've had to mention this to DCI Kessen,' said Hitchens. 'In case it's relevant to the current enquiry in any way.'

'I understand.'

'Quinn had been in trouble prior to the murder, you know. In fact, your father had arrested him twice before – once for receiving stolen goods at a building site he was working on, and the second time for an assault in a pub. There was a general punch-up, and both Quinn and Thorpe were involved.'

'Will Thorpe was there, too?'

'They were good friends, don't forget.'

'Right.'

'Quinn was charged with assaulting a police officer, among other things. Do you want to guess who the officer was?'

'I remember it,' said Cooper. 'Dad had a black eye and a foul temper for weeks afterwards.'

'But he didn't take even a day off work, which the defence made use of at the trial, in an attempt to minimize the injuries.'

'He could have lost an eye. Quinn used the thick end of a pool cue.'

'That was denied by the accused, and there were no eye witnesses willing to confirm it. In fact, it was never really clear whether Quinn or Thorpe was nearest to Joe Cooper at the time. The court had no choice but to acquit Quinn on that charge.'

'And then there was the Carol Proctor case.'

'Yes. I always thought it was a bit lucky myself, the way Quinn's case fell apart before it even came to a trial. But we were more than happy to get a conviction, of course.'

'In what way did you think it was lucky, sir?'

'The whole alibi business. Raymond Proctor and William Thorpe alibi'd each other, and Quinn's wife was at work. So the only person without an alibi was Mansell Quinn himself.'

'Right. The obvious suspect – the one found at the scene.'

'The clincher, though, was the knife. It had Quinn's fingerprints on it, and Carol Proctor's blood. Also, the blade matched several of the wounds on her body. According to the postmortem report, some of the wounds couldn't be conclusively matched to the knife, but some were definites. Quinn said he had never touched the knife, hadn't touched the body, hadn't walked in the blood.'

'He might have been in a state of shock and not aware of what he was doing.'

'That one was tried by the defence.'

'It's possible, sir.'

'They only tried it out of desperation. They could see their client was going down for life.'

Hitchens passed across a file. 'I've dug out the interview transcripts. Why not read them, Cooper, and see what you think?'

Cooper took the file reluctantly. 'But this was in 1990,' he said.

'Yes, 1990. You won't remember those days, Cooper – you haven't been in the force long enough. PACE and tape recorders were still quite a new thing then, and some officers regarded them as a nuisance. But it's much better the way it is now. All open and above board, and no chance for some clever defence lawyer to claim you tricked his client into confessing to something he didn't do.'

'Are you saying –? Was there anything wrong with Quinn's conviction?'

'God, no.' The DI shook his head. 'I'm not saying that at all. Nobody doubted it.'

'Except Mansell Quinn.'

'Well, that's the point.'

Hitchens sat back in his chair and swivelled towards the window. Looking past his shoulder, Cooper could see mould on the roof of the football stand. It seemed to symbolize the stagnation of Edendale FC, permanently stranded in the lower division of one of the pyramid leagues, forced to sell off their best players to pay their debts, with no money to buy new ones and match-day attendances dwindling to hundreds. Or maybe it just symbolized the damp weather.

'Quinn's opinion wouldn't matter ordinarily,' said Hitchens. 'At the time, he was just another violent thug caught bang to rights. And now he's another embittered old lag. But in view of what happened to his wife, it looks as though he could be an extremely dangerous old lag. You get my meaning?'

'He claimed he was innocent at first, but put in a guilty plea,' said Cooper. 'Then he changed his story again in prison.'

'Can you think of any reason for that?' said the DI carefully.

Cooper tried to let that sink in. 'Sir, are you saying Mansell Quinn could have been innocent all along?'

'I think Mansell Quinn might *believe* he was innocent. And that's all that matters.'

'Is it?'

'I think so, in the circumstances. Don't you, Ben?'

Hitchens smiled, as if inviting Cooper to join with him in a small conspiracy. But Cooper felt unable to respond. Something inside him seemed to be inhibiting his reactions. He was afraid he was missing something, or that he wasn't going to ask the right question. Or maybe that he would blurt out the right question, and the DI would give him the truth. And then it would be too late.

'Do you think Quinn knows my father is dead?' he asked instead.

'I have no idea,' said Hitchens with a small sigh of relief.

'I suppose it's a question we could ask his probation officer, or his personal officer at Sudbury.'

'We'll be talking to those people anyway, won't we? I mean, about any comments he might have made regarding his family, or his old associates.'

'Yes, we will.'

'So it might not seem too odd to be asking whether he ever talked about Sergeant Joe Cooper.'

'Mmm.' Hitchens sounded doubtful.

'I suppose it might seem odd to the officers tasked with making the enquiry, though,' said Cooper, trying to interpret the DI's hesitation.

'Damned odd, unless we explained the reasons to them. And then the results of their enquiries would have to be put into their report, and that would go back to the receiver in the incident room and be looked over by the analyst, and then entered on to the HOLMES system by one of the operators, and maybe it would generate another action which the allocator would give to a second enquiry team . . .'

'Enough,' said Cooper.

'You see how complicated it is?'

'Yes.'

Hitchens watched him for a moment. 'So, what do you think, Cooper?'

Cooper swallowed painfully. The effort of trying to control his physical reactions was becoming almost too much to bear.

'I'll deal with it.'

Then the DI had nodded and smiled. 'And do you know, Ben – that's exactly what your father would have said.'

As he made his way back across the rope walks, Cooper smelled the hemp again, pungent with the scent of animals. He looked up at the black soot stains on the roof and thought of Alistair Page's tale of Cock Lorrel and the Beggars' Banquet, all the wickedness and blood-soaked horrors imagined by superstitious locals.

But if the people who'd lived in the cavern all those centuries had meant no harm to anyone, they ought not to have become objects of fear and hatred, stigmatized as cannibals and worshippers of the Devil. They ought to have been left alone.

And that's what his father would have said, too.

13

Diane Fry and Gavin Murfin passed through the security checkpoint at the gate lodge. The building nearest to the entrance was the officers' mess, which was surrounded by banks of colourful flowers. Yellow, purple, white and red. Fry thought the purple ones might be pansies, but there were very few flowers whose names she knew. Murfin wouldn't know them either, unless they were something he could eat, so there was no point in asking him.

At the entrance to the visitors' parking area, warnings had been posted of the penalties for helping prisoners to escape or bringing in prohibited items like drugs. They offered the prospect of ten years in prison yourself or a £10,000 fine, which would certainly deter most visitors. But there had been nobody to help Mansell Quinn escape, even if he'd wanted to. Fry had just learned that Quinn had received only one personal visitor during his stay at Sudbury.

'Where are you going?' said Murfin. 'The car's over here.'

'Wait for me, Gavin. I won't be a minute.'

She walked over a set of speed humps towards the steel fence. A few black-and-white cattle grazed beyond the fence, and outside the gates two young prisoners with shaved heads and green waterproofs were picking litter from the grass and filling black bin liners with it. A prison officer stood watching them, glancing occasionally at his watch. Until she noticed the waterproofs, Fry hadn't realized it was raining. It was a gentle rain here, not the downpour of the night before.

Then she saw a pedestrian underpass leading beneath the main road, the A50. When she walked into it, Fry found it smelled of urine and the floor was scattered with rubbish and bits of broken blue plastic. Perhaps the litter team weren't allowed this far from the gates.

The rain had run down the grass slope and pooled in the bottom end of the underpass. Only half the lights were working down here. But it looked like a deliberate policy rather than mere vandalism, because there was a precise alternation – dark and light, dark and light, all the way along to the exit. Half of the fluorescent tubes had either been removed or switched off.

This was something Ben Cooper would do – follow the movements of a suspect, reconstruct his actions, try to get into his mind and understand what he'd been thinking. After an hour inside the prison, Fry believed she had an inkling how Mansell Quinn might have felt on his release. It wasn't the worst institution she'd ever been in, but the atmosphere was oppressive nevertheless.

Sudbury had been built as a hospital to take wounded US airmen during the D-Day landings in 1944, and most of the original single-storey accommodation was still in use – rows and rows of long, cream-coloured huts. By the time she left, Fry's head had been buzzing with positive PR for the prison regime: education and training, pre-release courses, resettlement schemes and community projects. Strictly speaking, Sudbury wasn't even one of Her Majesty's prisons any more, but a facility of the National Offender Management Service.

Entering the underpass, she followed a broad white line that divided the path from a cycle track that ran through on its way to Ashbourne. Traffic buzzed overhead on the A50. Emerging on to the side of a small road, she found a pair of bus shelters facing each other across the carriageway. On this side, the buses to Sudbury and Burton on Trent stopped.

The shelter had all but one of its glass sides knocked out, and it would be pretty miserable in there waiting for a bus. Rain came down the banking from the A50, and spray blew in from the traffic passing towards Sudbury. Instead of a bench, a sort of plastic bar had been fitted for people to perch on, as if they were birds. Signs in the shelter told passengers how to reach the prison through the underpass. Everything was painted a drab, institutional green. Perhaps the colour had been chosen specifically for the people who would use it to get to and from the prison.

Try as she might, Fry couldn't conjure up the image of Mansell Quinn perched in the shelter waiting for a bus to take him to a new life at the end of his sentence. She'd seen photographs of him, but they had lacked the spark of humanity that might have enabled her to form a picture of him as a real, living individual. All she saw in her mind's eye was a dark, amorphous shape passing across her line of vision, not standing still to be pinned down but forever moving on somewhere else.

Fry found herself frustrated by the failure of her imagination. She couldn't work out what had been going on in Mansell Quinn's mind. There were too few dots to be joined up yet.

But there had been another prisoner released at the same time as Quinn: Richard Wakelin, twenty-five, from Derby. The two men had been seen talking as they left the prison gates. Perhaps Wakelin could help her to get a glimpse of what had been in Quinn's head that morning.

Ben Cooper had parked under one of the maple trees in the Castleton car park to get a bit of shade, and he hoped the car wouldn't feel quite so much like a blast furnace when he got back in. One family had removed their shoes and sandals and were paddling in the stream alongside the car park, while a couple with two panting dogs had allowed them to splash in the water to cool off.

Cooper decided they should walk into Castleton to get an ice cream. He had a fancy for a dark chocolate Magnum, and the girls went along to humour him. What he hadn't anticipated was that they would insist on climbing the hill to Peveril Castle.

'It's a long way up,' he said.

'We can't come to Castleton without seeing the castle,' said Amy, as if the logic were obvious. 'Look at all those other people going up. Some of them are even older than you, Uncle Ben.'

By the time they reached the top of the hill, Cooper was sweating. The grass was warm from the sun, and he was glad of the chance to lie down while the girls explored the ruined keep of the castle. At close quarters, the tower looked gaunt and forlorn. One side of it seemed to have crumbled away over the centuries, reduced to a ruin by locals stripping the stone to use as building materials for their homes.

According to the guide books, the castle had originally been built by a bastard son of William the Conqueror to protect his local mining interests and hunting preserves. Cooper hoped the girls didn't ask, in case he had to explain what a bastard was.

When he got his breath back, Cooper walked along the wall and looked down into the dale. A middle-aged couple looked up and waved. Then Cooper noticed two men together in a sheltered spot near the entrance. He couldn't see them clearly, but one of them was wearing a black waterproof with a hood, despite the heat. He watched them for a moment, wishing he weren't so suspicious, but with thoughts of predatory paedophiles going through his mind as he heard the voices of children in the dale.

In fact, the two men seemed harmless, although there was some tension between them, one standing and the other sitting, as if they'd had a disagreement. A gay couple, perhaps – they should have chosen somewhere that wasn't so easily overlooked.

A siren began to wail at the cement quarry. Somewhere in the vast excavations, half a mile behind the works, they were preparing to blast more limestone out of Bradwell Moor. A minute or two after the wailing a sharp boom reverberated in the depths of the hillside like a single stroke of a bass drum. A cloud of white dust drifted over the edge of the quarry.

The Peak Cavern system wasn't far from the hole blasted to feed the cement works. Any passages running south-east would emerge from the face of the quarry. Who knew what undiscovered stalactite-hung chambers might have vanished in the blasting over the years?

Cooper looked round for his nieces and spotted them peering from one of the windows of the tower. It was his temporary responsibility for them that was making him paranoid, he supposed. Maybe this was what being a parent was like.

Passing the prison sign and the officers' mess to return to the car, Diane Fry took one more look at the violently colourful display of bedding plants and sneezed. A few seconds later, she sneezed again. She could feel the membranes inside her nose swelling and her eyes starting to water. Damn. Hay fever.

The pollen count must be up today. She'd been told she should always try to breathe in through her nose instead of her mouth, to filter out the dust and pollutants in the air and prevent them from reaching her airways. Her grass pollen allergy had been worst in her late teens and early twenties, but it still hit her now and then, forcing her to resort to sunglasses to reduce the irritation to her eyes – even if it meant having to put up with cracks from the station wits about her having deserted E Division for the LAPD.

She got back into the car with Murfin, and they were soon heading towards Ashbourne on the A515. As they passed a tractor dealer's, Fry looked across the fields to the rows of cream-coloured huts that formed the prison, with several large greenhouses lined up behind them. She thought of how hot it would be inside those glass buildings among the plants. Stifling.

'Get anything useful?' said Murfin, unsettled by her silence.

'Yeah. Everything I could possibly want.'

Andrea Lowe stopped her brother at the door, her hand on his arm enough to communicate her concern.

'Stay here,' she said.

Simon shook his head. 'No, I can't.'

'Why not?' she said.

'Jackie will be worried sick.'

'I suppose so.'

'Anyway, there are things to do at home. The plumber is coming first thing in the morning, and if I'm not there to let him in he might not be available again for weeks. And I have to let them know at work what's happening.'

Andrea was staying at their aunt's house in Castleton. She was the sort of person who needed company for reassurance, so being constantly under Dawn's eye would suit her.

'You can't go back to work, Simon,' she said.

'No, of course not. There are just a few things to sort out – jobs I was in the middle of yesterday when they called me. You know what I mean. I'll come back here as soon as I can.'

'I don't like you being on your own,' said Andrea. 'Not now, Simon. If Mum hadn't been on her own yesterday . . .'

Simon squeezed her shoulder and smiled. 'I'll be fine. Stop worrying.'

'You should tell the police, shouldn't you?'

'Don't be silly.'

Andrea held the door and stood on the step, still reluctant to let him go. He could see her studying the houses in the close, as if afraid that they were being watched from behind the curtains at any one of half a dozen windows. Simon thought she was probably right. It was one of the reasons he had to get away.

'Well, take care, then,' she said. 'Simon, take care.'

Simon nodded and walked quickly to his car. The whole day had been spent indoors, most of it in unfamiliar surroundings, among unsettling sounds and smells. A bit of fresh air was what he needed, and a chance to get things straight in his own head, before he had to go over it all again with his fiancée back in Edendale. Everything that had happened during the day, all the questions the police had asked him, every emotion he'd felt in the past few hours – Jackie would want to know the lot.

He drove down into the centre of Castleton and parked in the market square, intending to take a walk by the river. But when he saw the pubs in Castle Street, Simon realized that what he really needed was a drink. Or perhaps a couple. If the police stopped him driving home later on, then it was just tough. After a day like today, he didn't really care.

Simon chose the George, for no other reason than it was the nearest pub, just a short walk through the quiet church-yard from the market square. He'd never been inside it before, but he liked the look of its whitewashed frontage with clematis growing up the walls. It looked a safe and reassuring place.

But once he'd set his mind on a drink, Simon forgot all about his promise to his sister to take care. And he forgot that it would be dark by the time he left the pub to walk back through the churchyard to his car.

14

Ben Cooper bumped his Toyota down the rough track to Bridge End Farm, twisting the wheel at the familiar points along the way to avoid the worst of the potholes. The girls were curled up together in the back of the car as it rattled over the cattle grid and into the yard past the tractor shed. Only the big John Deere stood in the shed now, because Matt had sold the old grey Fergie that he used to tinker with. He'd said it was no good to him any more, and other people might be able to afford an expensive hobby better than he could.

Bridge End was still good land. Their maternal grandfather had cared for it well, tottering about the place in his shiny black suit with baling twine round his trouser bottoms. Their father had never been interested in running the place, though occasionally he'd roll up his sleeves to help.

Like all the family, Joe Cooper had been a tall man, with well-muscled forearms and big hands. He'd been such an archetype of integrity and moral principles that it was impossible to imagine him bending the rules. Even among his family, rules were made to be kept.

'Home,' called Cooper, turning off the engine.

Amy and Josie clambered out and ran across the yard to the house, being immediately surrounded by a flurry of dogs.

Cooper heard his sister-in-law, Kate, greet them from the kitchen and send them to wash their hands. There was a clatter of feet on tiles and excited voices.

He followed the girls in, taking his time. He had too much on his mind to be able to cope with the memories that leaped out at him from the corners of the house.

The kitchen was the room they'd always used most at Bridge End, and these days it seemed to smell of herbs whenever he entered it. Kate made him a coffee, and he told her about his day. His sister-in-law was easy to talk to, and he was happy to get a chance to chat to her alone now and again.

'I hope you're ready for the party on Saturday,' she said. 'Amazingly, we seem to have got everything organized and under control.'

'You've worked miracles, Kate. I just wish you'd let me do more for myself.'

Kate cocked her head, listening to the sound of raised voices at the back of the house. For a moment it sounded as though an argument was developing, but the children quietened down again, apart from a bit of thumping and pounding of feet, which was perfectly normal. Kate went back to what she had been doing.

'We thought of making it a surprise,' she said.

'The party? Why? Were you worried I wouldn't come if I knew about it?'

'What?' She looked at him with concern, but decided he was joking. 'Anyway, we've arranged for Isabel to have a day out of the Old School so she can come, and we knew she'd mention it you.'

'If she remembers,' said Cooper, and instantly regretted sounding churlish.

He could hear the voices of his nieces coming towards them through the house. In another moment, their mother would be swept up by their demands, and she'd have no more time for Ben. But right now, she could sense that something was wrong. Sometimes, Cooper thought he must walk around with a traffic light on his head, because his moods seemed to be so transparent to the women in his life.

'Are you worried about her, Ben?'

'No, Kate. Like you say, Mum's doing well.'

'But there's something –'

And then it was too late, as the girls burst through the door of the kitchen, talking nineteen to the dozen. Their voices rose a few decibels, and Ben had to give each of them a hug.

So the moment passed, and he didn't have to think of something to say. But he knew what the problem was – he didn't want to see his mother back in her old house. It was an unkind reaction, but he feared that seeing his mother back at Bridge End Farm would bring home to him, as nothing else had until now, the extent to which she'd deteriorated.

Finally, Cooper tore himself away from the warm kitchen and went back to his car. After only a few months living in town, he knew he'd started to lose touch with his family. On the farm, he'd regarded the landscape as a place to make a living. The most important things were the fertility of the land, the quality of the drainage, the stability of the walls that kept the cattle and sheep on their grazing. But as he drove around the Peak District now, he found himself admiring the shape of a hill or noticing the way a quarry spoiled the view, as if it was all some kind of scenic backdrop.

Cooper saw his brother coming towards the house, still in his working overalls. Matt was bulking up as he got older, and was looking more like their father every year.

Matt nodded. 'Ben. Had a good day?'

'I think the girls enjoyed themselves.'

'Good. I hope they used up some of their energy. They tire me out when they're at home.'

While they stood in the yard, it began to rain. Neither of

them made a move to go inside. Cooper tried to see what stock was in the sheds or grazing on the in-by land.

'Will there be some calves going to market soon?' he asked.

Matt looked at him in surprise. 'The only batch of calves I had went in last week. Colin Sidebotham came over to give me a hand.'

'That was good of him.'

'Well, I helped him get his hay in a week or two back. He cut it just before the forecast turned bad.'

'That's the way it works.'

'It's how it *used* to work. Some of the miserable buggers I see at the mart wouldn't give me the time of day any more. It's every man for himself. They're all worried about going under next season, or the one after. I reckon they don't want anyone coming down to their place, just in case.'

'In case what?'

'In case we see them laying out a new golf course, or ripping up their fields to make fishing lakes.'

Cooper knew his brother had moody fantasies these days in which every livestock farm in the valley sold off its stock and diversified, each becoming a little tourist attraction – a nature trail here, a tea room there, a craft centre across the lane. Matt had once muttered that he'd stick out to be the last farm still operating, then he could call his place a museum and coin in money from the tourists.

Kate had emerged from the house again and was watching them. The rain was getting heavier, and Cooper could feel it soaking his shirt.

'About Saturday,' said Matt. 'I'll pick Mum up from Old School a couple of hours before the party starts.'

'No, I'll pick her up myself – if that's all right with you.'

'No problem,' said Matt, frowning a bit. 'If you're sure, Ben.'

'Just a few minutes together would be nice.'

'Yes, of course,' said Matt. 'She'll be chuffed with that.'

Cooper found himself exchanging a nod with his older brother. It was a gesture they'd developed between themselves as teenagers, a means to avoid having to put their feelings into words. A nod had communicated anything they wanted it to.

Sharing that gesture now seemed to remove all the distance that Cooper had begun to sense between Matt and himself. It brought a sudden rush of affection, like making up with someone after an argument. But he didn't know quite how to express the feeling. So he hesitated for a moment. And then he gave Matt another nod.

Diane Fry walked towards the sitting room from her kitchen, where she'd been sorting the ironing into separate piles – outfits for the office, casual stuff, clothes for special occasions. The difference in the size of the piles had started to depress her, and she'd given up.

Angie was watching TV, a hospital drama in which a doctor was spending all his time trying to reunite a dying woman with her estranged son. She'd also found a box of chocolates from somewhere. Fry had forgotten she had them in the flat, so the box must have been hidden away in a safe place. Another comfort resource.

'Hey, Sis, don't you ever go out?' said Angie.

Fry stopped. 'Out?'

'Yeah. O-U-T. Out.'

'Out where?'

'I don't know. Just out of here –' Angie waved a hand lazily around the room.

'I go out every day,' said Fry. 'I'm not a hermit. I have a job.'

'I don't mean go out to work. I mean go out to enjoy yourself. Jesus, Di.'

Fry didn't answer. She didn't like being forced to justify her private life, even to her sister. She had grown accustomed to not having to justify herself to anybody.

'Surely you must need to get out of this place occasionally?' said Angie. 'I mean, look at it.'

'What's wrong with it?'

'It's so depressing. Jesus.'

'You said that.'

'Well, it is. Come on, Di, couldn't you do a bit better for yourself than this on a detective sergeant's salary?'

'Maybe. But there's not much choice around here. Property is so expensive.'

'And you don't even have a bloke,' said Angie. 'Or do you?'

'Not at the moment.'

'Not even nice Constable Cooper?'

'You're joking.'

Angie sucked some chocolate off a praline. 'Hey, Di, you're not gay, are you?'

'What?'

'Just asking. You said yourself we had a lot to learn about each other.'

Fry smoothed her hands on the T-shirt she was carrying. 'Tell you what, Angie, let's go out together.'

'Tonight?'

'Well, tomorrow – are you up for it?'

'Damn right,' said Angie. 'Let's hit the high spots of Edendale. Let's get totally rat-arsed!'

'We can go out for a meal.'

'What?'

'We can have dinner at a restaurant. A couple of glasses of wine, perhaps. Then we can relax a bit.'

'It takes more than a couple of glasses of wine to help me relax,' said Angie.

Fry felt her face harden and her jawline tighten. She tried to control her expression, but knew she wasn't succeeding.

'The restaurants shouldn't be busy at this time of the week,' she said. 'We can get somewhere quiet, relax and talk.'

150

'Are you sure there's nowhere we can go clubbing?'

'You're too old to go clubbing.'

Angie laughed. 'Too old? You cow.'

She chose another chocolate, got bored with the doctor and clicked the remote to find something more interesting.

When Ben Cooper finally got home that night, he decided he must be so exhausted that he was hallucinating. In the reflection of the fluorescent light in the kitchen, he thought he saw a single eye pressed up against the rain-soaked window. It was a hard, grey eye surrounded by a patch of wrinkled skin, crumpled against the wet glass, with water trickling around it in two small streams.

He froze with his finger on the light switch. His first instinct had been to turn it off again so that he could see what was outside, instead of being distracted by the reflection of himself standing in his own kitchen, his mouth hanging open like an idiot. But he waited until everything came properly into focus and his brain began to work again. Halfway up his kitchen window, there was a snail.

He supposed it had been following the stream of rain-water – though what it hoped to find on his window, he couldn't imagine. Its antennae waggled left and right, as if it couldn't quite figure out where it was.

Cooper tilted his head to see the creature better. Its underside looked like the pursed lips of a long-dead corpse.

'You're going the wrong way,' he said.

He watched it for a moment longer, then looked at his watch, remembering the appeal for sightings of Mansell Quinn was due on the local TV news. He drew the blind, and turned to find Randy smiling at him from the floor, eyes half-closed and his front paws paddling on the tiles.

'Yes, I was talking to you, obviously,' said Cooper. 'Who else would I be talking to?'

He began to relax, shrugging off the uneasy feeling he'd

experienced when he entered the flat. It was just a wet, lost creature that had been watching him from the night, after all.

The blow came out of the darkness like a stab of lightning. It caught Simon Lowe in the back of the head and half-stunned him. He staggered for a few seconds on the edge of a grave, his brain bouncing painfully against his skull, unable to make sense of what had happened. He knew the wall of the church was only a few yards away, but he couldn't see it. He saw only blurred streaks of light shooting across his vision. He knew there must be someone behind him in the churchyard, but his muscles had lost the power to turn his body or lift his head. There were other people, too, dozens of them laughing and shouting, back there in the warmth of the pub. But he couldn't hear their voices. Simon heard only a faint whistling in the air, a sound which seemed to go on almost for ever, until the second blow fell.

15

Wednesday, 14 July

The incident room staff at West Street had been maintaining a sequence chart. It showed what was believed to be the order of events leading up to the murder of Rebecca Lowe, and following it. It also revealed the gaps which the enquiry team's efforts had so far failed to fill.

Some time during the morning, the analyst had removed two items from the chart and replaced them with additional information. Each entry had a time, a description of the information and its source.

'I can't help worrying that we're relying too much on doubtful intelligence to dictate the direction of the enquiry,' said Ben Cooper, running his eye over the chart. 'There ought to be some trace and interview tasks for us to handle, at least.'

Diane Fry didn't even glance at the chart. No doubt she'd checked the new information already, before anyone else came into the office.

'It's a resources decision, Ben,' she said. 'Why should we commit staff to needless T/Is and chasing down witness statements when a ready-made suspect presents himself on a plate? It's manpower on the ground that's vital now. Quinn can't be far away.'

Cooper shook his head. 'We'll just end up doing the work later on.'

'Let's hope not.'

'DCI Tailby wouldn't have done it this way. He'd have made sure all the possibilities were covered.'

'Yes, but that approach fills up the system with vast amounts of irrelevant data. There's a lot to be said for being more focused.'

'Provided you're focusing on the right things,' said Cooper.

'Well, we'll see who's right, won't we?'

To be fair, plenty of intelligence was available this morning – calls were flooding in from members of the public responding to the local TV news bulletins. A decision had been taken to release Mansell Quinn's name as a person being sought to help with enquiries, and all the usual phrases. The broadcast of his mugshot had netted a shoal of potential sightings, even before the attack on Simon Lowe in Castleton last night.

'Any news from the hospital?' said Cooper.

'He'll be all right,' said Fry. 'A few cuts and bruises, that's all. He's lucky the people in that area take an interest in each other's welfare. In a lot of places, he would have been left to bleed.'

'I don't suppose he saw anything?'

'No. He was attacked from behind, in the dark. And it seems the resident who heard the disturbance and found him made a big performance of putting all his lights on and creating a lot of noise before he came out of his house, so the assailant was well away before he got near.'

'Sensible.'

'But not helpful to us, in the circumstances. Lowe's attacker could have been anyone – an opportunist mugger, or just some drunk who thought Lowe looked at him a bit funny in the pub. Who knows?'

Cooper looked at the map again. 'But the temptation is to chalk it up to Quinn, right?'

Fry shrugged. 'Scenes of crime are there, but I don't think we should hold our breath for anything useful. If it was Quinn, he'll be off to the next place by now. He vanishes too easily for my liking.'

'He knows the area well,' said Cooper. 'But why would he attack his own son?'

But Fry had turned her attention to a call from a lady living on Moorland Avenue, Hathersage.

'Near Mansell Quinn's mother?' she asked the actions allocator in the incident room.

'That's right. She's lived there for a long time and knows Quinn by sight. But she wasn't sure until she saw his photo on the news last night. Now she says she saw him in the street near his mother's house on Monday afternoon.'

'I knew old Mrs Quinn was lying,' said Fry. 'I just knew it.'

Cooper felt uncomfortable at the tone of her voice. He didn't like being lied to himself, but it went with the territory. Some people lied to him automatically, simply because he was a police officer, and all he could hope for was an opportunity to expose the lie. Fry's reaction sounded too much like gloating.

'You'll get a chance to ask her to explain herself, anyway,' he said.

'Damn right.'

A large-scale map of the Hope Valley had also been pinned to the wall of the incident room. Rebecca Lowe's house in Aston was marked in red on the slopes of Win Hill, halfway along the valley, as was Castle Street, where a local resident had found Simon Lowe lying unconscious in the churchyard.

Blue stickers flagged Raymond Proctor's caravan park outside Hope and Mrs Quinn's home on the estate at Hathersage. A third blue sticker had been reserved for when they located William Thorpe. The bottom of the map reached as far south as Bradwell and Hazlebadge, and right up to the

Camphill gliding club on Abney Moor. Just off the map was Bridge End Farm.

'Damn it, the quickest and easiest way for him to get from Hathersage to Aston would be on the train,' said DI Hitchens. 'We need to talk to the station staff at both ends and see if they remember him.'

The railway line from Sheffield to Manchester, passing through Totley Tunnel and up the valley, with stations at Hathersage and Hope. The Sheffield stretch was also used by cement trains from the works. But what Hitchens had noticed was that Hathersage railway station lay right behind the estate where Mansell Quinn's mother lived, while the stop at Hope was only a mile from the marker indicating Rebecca Lowe's house at Aston. The red blobs made the connection obvious.

'I think they're both unmanned stops,' said Cooper. 'He'd have to buy a ticket from the guard on the train.'

'Is that how it works? Well, check it out, Cooper. See if you can map his route to Rebecca Lowe's house. Any sightings of him. You know the routine.'

'Yes, sir.'

'This is all very well,' said DCI Kessen, settling the team down again. 'But we're only establishing where Quinn has been, not where he is now. Or at least where he might be heading next.'

'With respect, sir, the key to his intentions surely lies in the past,' said Fry. 'Either with the circumstances of the Carol Proctor case fourteen years ago, or with what happened while he was in prison.'

'I quite agree, DS Fry. So what about while he was inside? Any interactions with his family or other contacts that might cast light on his intentions?'

'Well, his mother doesn't seem to have visited him very often,' said Fry. 'She was cagey about it when we spoke to her, but her name doesn't appear in the visitor records at

Sudbury for the two years he was there. We've haven't checked back any further than that, but if we need to . . .'

'No, that's enough.'

'And the victim, Quinn's ex-wife, hadn't visited him for ten years. Though I got two different versions of why that was – one from his mother, and one from her sister, who both might be considered biased, I suppose.'

'These two close friends of Quinn's –'

'*Former* close friends,' said Hitchens. 'I think that's how I described them.'

'Don't tell me – they were so close they couldn't be bothered to visit him in prison?'

'It's true he doesn't seem to have had many visitors to speak of.'

'OK, the two friends . . . ?'

'Raymond Proctor and William Thorpe. Proctor, of course, was the husband of Quinn's first victim.'

'I'll grant you, that's enough to damage a friendship. Your best mate kills your wife, it puts a bit of a dent in the old camaraderie.'

'Not necessarily.'

Cooper turned to stare in amazement at Murfin. It was unlike him to offer constructive comments during a briefing. He was more the sarcastic muttering under his breath sort of man.

'What do you mean, DC Murfin?'

'Well, it depends on what sort of relationship you have with your wife. The state of your marriage, like. Some folk would be glad to get rid of their better halves. Grateful to the bloke who did her in, even.'

DCI Kessen looked at him silently for a moment, his mind almost visibly ticking over. Cooper reflected that this was one of the differences between working for Mr Kessen and their former DCI, Stewart Tailby. Cooper had liked Tailby, but he'd have put Murfin down within seconds.

'Was this possibility looked into at the time?' asked Kessen, looking towards Hitchens.

Hitchens hesitated. 'I can't remember, sir.'

'Only, you never know whether it might have been a conspiracy between the two of them,' said Murfin, sensing he was the man of the moment. 'Proctor might have set Quinn up to do the business on his missus, but then backed out of the deal, like.'

'Yes, I think we understood what you were suggesting,' said Kessen.

'Or something might have gone wrong. Maybe Proctor cocked up the alibi somehow. Hey, Thorpe could have been the spanner in the works – what do you think? He wasn't supposed to turn up when he did, and Proctor couldn't get rid of him. If Proctor had alibi'd Quinn then, Thorpe would have been able to scupper the whole deal.'

Fry looked from one to the other. Cooper could see her putting two and two together, and suspecting there was something she hadn't been told.

Hitchens fidgeted. 'We'll check it out.'

'All right,' said Kessen. 'What else do we have on the victim? It seems she had no visitors on Monday that we're aware of?'

Heads were shaken, but Cooper raised a hand. He reported that he'd visited Rebecca Lowe's near-neighbours that morning – the only house that was within sight and sound of hers, owned by a family called Newbold. The Newbolds had invited friends to their house on the night that their neighbour had been killed. After the heat of the day was over, they had spent a couple of hours in the garden, drinking wine and playing croquet on the lawn.

'Croquet?' said Fry. 'You're kidding.'

'It's quite a fashionable game in some circles these days.'

Fry nodded tiredly, as if she didn't believe him but couldn't find the energy to argue. 'What time did they play croquet until?'

158

'They say half past nine, which is probably about right. At this time of year, it's still daylight at nine fifteen, but getting dusk half an hour later. They would have been complaining that bad light was affecting play by half past.'

'OK. So they packed up the hoops and put away the flamingos at about half past nine. And after that? Did they stay outside drinking more wine and admiring the sunset?'

Cooper smiled, noticing her effortless reference to Lewis Carroll, surprising in someone who claimed not to read books. 'They went indoors.'

'So they'd have seen nothing outside after nine thirty, when the croquet finished.'

'Well, not until one in the morning, when the first guests started to leave.'

'That's too late.'

'I know,' said Cooper. 'By the way, the Newbolds did report seeing a tramp in the area.'

'A tramp?' said Kessen.

'Well, a vagrant they called him. They saw him on the road between their house and Parson's Croft.'

'No, no,' said Kessen. 'A passing vagrant as a murder suspect? That's just too Agatha Christie.'

'Actually, it was a couple of weeks before Mrs Lowe was killed that they saw him,' said Cooper. 'They just thought it was worth mentioning.'

'We did check out her phone calls,' said Murfin. 'Mrs Lowe seemed to spend a lot of time on the phone to family and friends. She did that generally, but on Monday in particular.'

'Perhaps she needed to hear friendly voices for reassurance,' suggested Fry.

'She told her daughter she didn't need reassurance. In fact, she could have had somebody with her if she was worried.'

'Gavin, it's perfectly possible to want your independence and still need reassurance.'

'Well, if you say so.'

'Yes, I do.'

'No unusual calls then, Murfin?' asked Kessen.

'Family and friends, like I say. Everyone you might expect – her sister, Andrea and Simon, a friend from the gym she goes to, the Proctors –'

'The Proctors?' said Fry. 'Was she still in touch with them?'

'She'd known Raymond Proctor for years.'

Fry nodded. 'Of course she had. So that call was probably *mutual* reassurance, despite what Mr Proctor tries to pretend.'

'But there was no phone call that could possibly have come from Quinn himself,' said Kessen. 'So it seems reasonable to deduce that Mrs Lowe wasn't expecting a visit from him that night.'

A few moments of silence followed. Kessen waited, but saw there was nothing else forthcoming.

'OK, so until we have a clearer picture of Quinn's intentions, we're continuing to warn the relevant individuals of the potential risk.'

'Is that all?' said Cooper.

'We're offering security advice and alarms, too, if they want them. No one would expect us to provide full protection at this level of threat. We don't have the resources. But there *will* be more uniforms on the streets in that area. Division is drafting in some extra bodies for visible reassurance.'

'And, who knows, they might even stumble over Mansell Quinn,' said Hitchens. 'We've got lucky before.'

Diane Fry marched up to DI Hitchens as soon as the briefing meeting broke up. He looked as though he might have liked to escape to his office, but she was too quick for him.

'Sir? A word?'

'Yes, Diane?'

'I'd be interested in going over the case notes from the original Carol Proctor enquiry, if you'd like somebody to take a look who wasn't involved.'

'Why, thank you, DS Fry. Tell you what, you handle it with DC Cooper.'

'Ben Cooper?'

Hitchens smiled bitterly. 'Yes. Let's see what the two of you make of it together.'

A few minutes later, Fry and Cooper were both sitting in the DI's office, looking at a heap of old files. Witness statements, forensic reports, crime scene photographs. Bits and pieces of the case that had put Mansell Quinn away for a life sentence. There would be a lot more documentation somewhere, dusty stacks of it, accumulated by all sides during the pre-trial stages of the investigation.

Fry looked at Cooper. Of the three of them, he seemed the most ill at ease. It was strange that every time something seemed to be going on behind her back, Ben Cooper was involved. She hadn't yet got to the bottom of the connection between him and her sister, how he'd managed to find Angie when Fry had been looking for her for years. But since Angie was being evasive, the only way to discover the truth would be to talk to him, which Fry baulked at.

'Mansell Quinn wasn't considered ready for parole,' said Hitchens, 'because the prison authorities were concerned about the lack of family support. Quinn was a man on his own. And therefore a potential risk.'

Fry saw Cooper blink and open his mouth to speak. But the moment passed.

'Of course, Mansell Quinn's initial story was that he came home, went into the house and found the body on the floor,' said Hitchens. 'He said he thought at first that it was his wife who'd injured herself – cut herself with a carving knife or something like that. He didn't even seem to recognize that the clothes she was wearing weren't his wife's.'

'That's no surprise.'

'Right, Fry. Well, the first thing he said he did was to turn the body over.'

'Getting blood on his hands in the process, of course.'

'And on his clothes, and on his shoes. He said he touched her where she was injured, to try to help her. He said it didn't occur to him at first that she was dying. But when he turned her over, the biggest surprise for him was that she wasn't his wife.'

'He recognized his mistress, though, I suppose.'

'Oh, yes. But apparently not the fact that she was on the point of death. He started to pull at her clothes to get at the injuries, thinking that he could stop the bleeding.'

'Hold on, what was Carol Proctor doing at the Quinns' house?'

'We couldn't be sure. Quinn insisted there was no prior arrangement to meet. But he admitted they'd been having an affair for some time. Off and on, he said. We can only surmise that they'd argued, that she went up there to continue the argument, or perhaps to tell him something that made him angry.'

'That she was ending the affair?'

'Possibly, Fry. We don't know.'

'So he lashed out.'

'And he didn't stop until she was dead.'

Fry hesitated. 'Exactly how much blood was there?'

'A lot,' said Hitchens. 'There are photos, if you want to see them.'

Fry didn't really want to look at them but supposed she had to. Every photograph of a murder scene she'd ever seen seemed seedy and depressing. Maybe it was a result of the photographic techniques the SOCOs used, or the quality of the lighting. Or perhaps it was something to do with the nature of the crime itself – as if photographs could capture a shameful residue left in the air, or a thin layer of dirt lying on the carpet and coating the pathetic, scattered possessions of the victim.

Cooper picked up the photos first, but didn't look at them himself. Instead, he passed them to Fry. Surely he wasn't

162

squeamish about them? Cooper didn't know the woman; he had no connection to the case at all, as far as she could see. So why should he even be involved?

Sure enough, the shots of Carol Proctor's body in situ looked like something out of a third-rate horror movie: her limbs were bent at unnatural angles, while dark red stains were daubed on her face and arms, and soaking through her clothes. A sea of red stained the carpet. The blood had surged and splashed outwards in a ragged pattern, as if the woman had tripped and spilled a five-litre can of crimson gloss.

'There are footprints,' said Fry. 'Both sides of the body.'

She would never have spotted them, except that the SOCOs attending the scene had indicated the location of each print with a white marker. At first glance, they were nothing more than irregularities in the spread of the blood. But she turned to the next photo and found a close-up of a print, with a heel mark now clearly visible in the drying stain.

'Mansell Quinn's prints,' said Hitchens. 'He was wearing the same boots when he was arrested. They got a perfect match.'

'Blood on the soles of his boots, or on the uppers?'

'Both.'

'And no other impressions?'

'None in the blood.'

Then Cooper chipped in for the first time.

'It could just mean that anyone who was present at the scene earlier took more care than Quinn not to step in the blood,' he said.

Hitchens nodded. 'That's what the defence said. But there was no evidence to put anyone else at the scene. Everything fit Quinn. The scenario the enquiry team constructed had him picking up the knife and stabbing Carol Proctor repeatedly, thereby getting blood on his shoes and his clothes. She fell to the floor, and he bent down to stab her again. He

163

walked around the body a couple of times, not sure what to do. He moved her to see if she was dead. Then he dialled 999.'

'Where's the phone?' asked Fry.

'Just by the door. There should be a photo.'

'Oh, yes.'

'See the trail of blood?'

'Quinn's footprints?'

'Exactly. His fingerprints were in the blood on the hand-set of the phone, and in the smears on the dial. Having made the emergency call, he walked back to the body, then across to the other side of the room and sat down in the armchair. He said in his statement he felt faint, a bit sick. He said he was in shock.'

'I suppose that's possible,' said Fry.

'And that was where the uniformed patrol found him when they arrived,' said Hitchens. 'In the armchair.'

Fry caught a fleeting moment of communication as Hitchens looked towards Cooper and met his eye. She felt a surge of anger. Somehow this was a test, and she wasn't going to let them get away with their little secrets. She concentrated on the photographs, flicking them over one after another. Was there something she ought to be able to see, some factor they thought she would miss?

'Wait a minute – was the front door open?'

'Yes,' said Hitchens.

'Why would that be?'

'I don't know. But don't forget that Quinn phoned the emergency services himself. He probably opened the door so they'd be able to get into the house when they arrived.'

'Did he say that was what he did?'

'As far as I recall, he couldn't remember.'

'Shock again?' said Fry. 'It can be quite convenient some-times, don't you think?'

She felt Cooper watching her, too, now.

'Were there bloody footprints in the hallway?' she said.

'Mmm. Not sure. But it doesn't make any difference. Everything was tied up.'

'The weapon?'

'It was in the kitchen. It looked as though he'd been trying to wash the blood off it. Quinn was arrested right there at the scene. It was a self-solver. And, after he'd been interviewed, Quinn changed his story anyway. He pleaded guilty. So, no problem.'

'The similarities with the Rebecca Lowe killing are obvious,' said Fry, 'apart from the absence of the suspect from the premises. I suppose he just learned his lesson the first time.'

'In the Carol Proctor case, there was some question of an alibi,' said Cooper.

'In the early stages, yes. Quinn tried to give us a story about the time he left the pub where he'd been drinking with Raymond Proctor and William Thorpe. Ye Olde Cheshire Cheese, it was, in Castleton.'

'I know the place. It's hardly any distance from the Quinns' house in Pindale Road.'

'And that was a relevant point, Cooper. Quinn maintained that it took him only five minutes to drive home from the Cheshire Cheese, so he couldn't have left the pub before three fifteen – about ten minutes before he dialled 999.'

'Three fifteen would have been chucking-out time. There was no all-day opening in 1990.'

'Yes. And Quinn's argument was that he couldn't possibly have had time to drive home, unload his tools from the car, go into the house, get into an argument with Carol Proctor, stab her several times, and then make the call. Not in ten minutes.'

'I think I'd agree,' said Fry.

'Indeed. But Quinn's two pals failed to support that version of events. When we interviewed Proctor and Thorpe, they both said their friend had left the pub earlier, before three o'clock. Quinn couldn't account for the rest of the time.'

'How long had they been drinking that day?' asked Cooper.

'Since before one o'clock. And they were all heavy drinkers, by their own admission.'

'Five, six pints of beer? More?'

'Their statements don't quite agree on the amounts,' said Hitchens.

'But Quinn wouldn't have been sober.'

'Far from it, Cooper. In fact, he was asleep when the first officers arrived at Pindale Road.'

Fry sucked in her breath. 'Asleep? With a woman lying dead on the floor in front of him, soaked in her own blood? What sort of man is that?'

She watched both Hitchens and Cooper drop their eyes and avoid the question.

'And after that,' said the DI, 'Quinn could only say that his memory was hazy.'

'I damn well hope the vivid details came back to him eventually,' said Fry.

16

The sound of Carol Proctor's last breath still haunted him. Sometimes, when he lay in bed in his cell at night, he'd imagined all those hundreds of thousands of branching tubes, and all the millions of tiny sacs that had made up her lungs. He tried to picture the membrane that covered them. It was a fraction of the thickness of tissue paper, they said – but a hundred square yards of it, bigger than a tennis court. It seemed impossible that it should fail to draw in a breath. Just one more breath.

Mansell Quinn closed his eyes and tried to feel Carol's lungs as if they were his own, receiving all the blood from her heart with every beat, feeding oxygen into her arteries, supplying her brain and her heart and the other organs of her body. And then he imagined the whole system stopping, like a clock winding down. Her chest rising and falling more slowly, until the final breath had been forced through the slackened muscles of her throat with that dry rattle, the scrape of escaping air that he'd heard and still remembered.

The memory of that sound only made him more angry. So angry that he wanted to smash something.

Quinn breathed deeply for a few minutes to regain control, then sat up slowly. Sudden movements were much more likely to be noticed, even here among the trees, with a cover of deep bracken. But the only people he could see were the same two anglers on the banks of one of the fishing lakes, so motionless with their nets and tackle boxes that they might be asleep.

The sight of the cement works chimney across the other side of the lakes reminded him of Will Thorpe. There was some place near here that Will had talked about using as a doss, but Quinn didn't plan to turn up anywhere that he might be expected to.

Talking to Will had been surprisingly difficult. For the last fourteen years, Quinn had talked to no one about his past. For all his fellow prisoners and his personal officer knew, he had no memories to speak about. Perhaps they thought he wanted to start his life afresh and put everything behind him.

But Quinn's memories were still there. They lay in his heart, cold and heavy. He thought of them as being like the shapes in the petrifying wells at Matlock Bath, which his father had taken him to see as a child. Some of them were ordinary household objects, hardly recognizable for what they'd once been, the accumulated layers of lime rendering them useless drip by drip, but preserving them for ever in their grotesque forms. They'd been turned to stone.

His father had talked about a petrified bird's nest that had belonged to his grandmother. It had been a gift from a relative who'd spent a holiday in the Peak District – and the only connection the Quinn family had had with Derbyshire until they moved there. Like the other souvenirs sold in the shops at Matlock Bath, it had been left in one of the petrifying wells until it had covered over with lime and attained the peculiar appearance that visitors prized so much. Quinn had never seen the nest, though he'd pictured it in his imagination. The detail that had impressed him most was that the nest had been complete with eggs.

'Four of them,' his father had said. And he would hold up

four stubby fingers, pitted with blue scars, as if his son couldn't count. 'Real eggs, turned to stone. Imagine the little chicks inside them.'

'Were the chicks turned to stone, too?'

'I don't know, boy. We never opened the eggs to look.'

The thought had repelled Quinn but fascinated him at the same time. They told him at school that eggs were supposed to represent new life. But here, life had been snuffed out at the moment of birth, turned to stone for the amusement of day trippers. It had symbolized the Peak District for him then – a place where his spirit had been stifled, forcing him to fight his way out into the world all over again. He felt crushed by the weight of the stone he could see in the hills all around him.

'What sort of bird made the nest?' he would ask his father, needing the specifics to make sense of the story.

But there was only one answer he ever got: 'Well, *I* don't know, do I?'

'A blackbird, Dad? A starling? Something bigger?'

'I've no idea. What does it matter, for goodness sake?'

'What did Grandma have the nest for?'

'She just *had* it, that's all.'

Then his father would get irritated and go back to his newspaper, or he'd walk out into the garden to look at his vegetables. And next time he told the story, it would be exactly the same. He never saw his son's need for explanation.

Quinn thought there ought to be ways of making sense of his petrified memories, of forcing them out into the open and letting the sun pierce the calcified layers to find the original shapes underneath.

But memories seemed to become attached to personal possessions, and he had very few of those. For years, his life had been measured by prison service regulations. The possessions he'd been allowed in his cell had been subject to what they called 'volumetric controls', which meant everything he possessed had to fit into two boxes. At intervals, his cell was inspected to make sure he hadn't broken regulations and created a private life for himself beyond his battery radio and his statutory three books and six newspapers.

Many of the permitted items held no relevance for him anyway. Diaries and calendars had seemed like self-inflicted torture, and he had no family photos for his locker.

After a while, Quinn became aware that his lack of personal items might reflect badly on his suitability for parole. He'd placed a subscription for *Peak District* magazine and *Birdwatching*, and he'd asked the library for more books on natural history and geology. One of his magazines came with a calendar featuring scenic views of Derbyshire, which he taped to the wall of his cell. One day, an officer on lock-up had pointed out that he hadn't turned over the page, even though the old month had finished six days ago. But the old month had been January. It showed a snow scene over Castleton to the slopes of Win Hill.

A movement caught his attention. A couple of golfers were walking across a green on the golf course to the north of the fishing lakes, but they were too far away to see him. Quinn scanned the anglers again, then lay back down in the bracken.

It had been in *Peak District* magazine that Quinn had found the article about the Castleton caves. He'd read about cave breathing, the movement of air in and out of a cave entrance. It could draw in small creatures, leading them away from their natural environment into the depths, from where they never returned. Accidentals, they were called. Creatures drawn in by cave breathing.

Mansell Quinn liked that idea. He thought he could be called an accidental himself. He had been drawn into the darkness. But he was on his way out now. He'd learned to control the breathing.

17

Standing outside 14 Moorland Avenue, Ben Cooper noticed that Millstone Edge was visible from the estate, too. He'd done a bit of rock climbing up there a couple of years ago. The long cliff face lay partly in shadow, producing a corrugated effect like the edge of a pie crust. The ancestors of men who lived in Hathersage now would have worked up there on the gritstone faces, cutting the millstones the area had become famous for – the same millstones which now lay abandoned in heaps on the slopes.

Not bothering with the bell this time, Fry pounded on the door of Enid Quinn's house with the knocker. It sounded hollower and more echoey than ever. But now Cooper knew it was due to the bare walls of the empty hallway.

'I suppose my neighbours have been sticking their noses into things that aren't their business,' said Mrs Quinn, when she let them in. 'They tend to be like that around here.'

'One of your neighbours saw your son near here on Monday afternoon.'

'Oh?'

Mrs Quinn settled herself down on the settee in the same position she'd occupied last time they visited her. She had her back to the window, her fair hair framed by the light. Rather than stand over her, Fry sat in one of the armchairs and motioned Cooper to do the same. He saw she'd assessed Mrs Quinn as someone who couldn't be intimidated.

'Mansell came here, didn't he?'

'I suppose there's no point in denying it now.'

'Not now that he's got well away.'

Enid Quinn waited impassively. Fry had not asked her a question, and she wasn't going to be tempted into volunteering information.

'Why didn't you tell us before, Mrs Quinn? Why did you lie to us?'

'As I said yesterday, people of my generation don't walk away from things as easily as they do these days.'

'You were talking about marriage.'

'Perhaps I was. But there are other commitments, other kinds of ties to those we love. Obligations we can't ignore.'

'Yet you believe your son was guilty of murder.'

Again Mrs Quinn sat quietly for a moment, her hands motionless in her lap. She gave every impression of being a calm woman, untroubled by conscience.

'Yes, I do believe that,' she said. 'But it has nothing to do with whether I love my son, or whether I'm willing to open my door to him when he calls.'

Fry and Cooper exchanged glances. Clearly, Mrs Quinn wasn't going to concede anything she didn't want to.

'What did your son want?' asked Cooper.

'He wanted nothing from me. Nothing except some human contact. I couldn't refuse him that, could I?'

'Did he tell you what he was planning to do?'

'No, he didn't.'

'Nothing at all? Did he say where he was heading from Hathersage?'

'No.'

'Did he talk about his ex-wife?'

'He made no suggestion to me that he intended to go and see Rebecca.'

'And his son, Simon?'

Enid Quinn flushed. 'I know about that, of course. Well, Mansell certainly didn't attack Simon. It's nonsense to suggest it. That's the very last thing he would do.'

'OK. So, how did your son seem when you talked to him?' asked Cooper. 'What state of mind was he in?'

'State of mind?'

'Did he seem distressed? Angry? Frightened? Or was he just his usual self?'

Mrs Quinn smiled tremulously. 'I don't know what Mansell's usual self is any more. And I couldn't say what his state of mind was, I'm afraid. I didn't feel I could read his mood as I used to be able to.'

'But you're his mother,' said Cooper, who didn't find her claim believable.

And Enid Quinn took his point. She thought about it further. 'I should say that he was none of those things you mentioned. He was absorbed. Distracted.'

'Something on his mind?'

'Yes.'

'But what?'

'I can't help you.'

'Mrs Quinn, when we were here yesterday, you told us you thought your son was seeking retribution. That was the word you used. What did he tell you to make you think that?'

'Nothing.'

'So why did you say it? Why that word – *retribution*?'

Mrs Quinn shook her head. 'It just seemed to me that's what he'd want. Mansell was angry. He's been angry for a long time.'

'But retribution against who?'

'I have no idea.'

'Did he want any information from you? Names and addresses?'

'No.'

'Money? Food?'

'Mansell didn't ask me for money. But I made him a meal. Of course I did. I couldn't refuse him that.'

'What time did he leave here?'

'Oh, I suppose it must have been about half past eight.'

'It was still light?'

'Yes.'

'Did he have transport? A car?'

'I couldn't tell you. He was on foot when he left here.'

Cooper sighed, and gave Fry a small shrug.

'Mrs Quinn, we have to ask you again,' said Fry. 'Where was your son heading?'

'I don't know.'

'We must find him, Mrs Quinn. You can see that, can't you? You wouldn't want anything to happen to somebody else, no matter how you feel about your son. Would you?'

She shook her head jerkily. 'I don't know where he was going.'

'Mrs Quinn, if you're not telling us the truth –'

'Look, Sergeant, the truth is that I'm not sure I'd tell you anything that would help you find my son, even if I could. But I don't have to make that judgement, because I asked him not to tell me what he intended to do or where he was going. And he didn't. So I can't help you.'

Fry's jaw clenched. But she stood up, and Cooper followed suit.

'It's very likely that we'll be back to ask you more questions,' said Fry.

'I'm usually here. I don't suppose I'll be going out much for a while. Now that my neighbours are watching every move I make.'

Fry managed to call in to the incident room when they were back on the A625 out of Hathersage. Cooper could tell she had some news by the way she sat up straight and listened without interrupting.

'What is it?' he said, when she ended the call.

'The nerve of the man is unbelievable.'

'Who?'

'Mansell Quinn, of course. Enid's golden boy. Last night's TV appeal has brought another result. Quinn spent Monday night in a hotel in Castleton – the Cheshire Cheese.'

'The hotel recognized him from the photos?'

'They didn't need to. He registered under his own name.'

'Mmm. That *was* pretty cool.'

'Quinn knew we wouldn't be looking for him at that stage. And he was gone from the hotel in the morning.'

'I suppose his room has been cleaned since then.'

'Twice. But Forensics might get something, I suppose. And the staff are being interviewed.'

'I don't suppose that will help much. He won't have talked to anybody.'

They had crossed the point where the River Noe flowed into the Derwent and were passing the weir at Lumble Pool. Rebecca Lowe's home lay to the north, on the lower slopes of Win Hill.

'The Cheshire Cheese,' said Cooper. 'It's the pub Quinn was drinking in with his friends on the day Carol Proctor was killed.'

'A coincidence, do you think, Ben?'

'I doubt it. Quinn obviously has something on his mind. I wish we knew what it was.'

'There's one more thing: the PM results on Rebecca Lowe have come through.'

'And?'

'She was killed not more than an hour or two before her body was found. Cause of death was a punctured lung. Most of her other injuries were post mortem.'

'Nasty.'

'Yes. Somebody definitely wanted Rebecca Lowe dead. As dead as Carol Proctor was.'

'Where are we going next?' said Cooper.

'This Raymond Proctor,' said Fry. 'Mansell Quinn's old friend, the husband of his first victim; Gavin and I visited him yesterday, but we couldn't seem to get through to him He refused to believe he's at risk from Quinn. We have this guy who's a convicted killer, on the loose right in this area, yet Proctor doesn't seem in the least concerned at the prospect of being his next victim. Why would that be?'

Cooper said nothing, but concentrated on driving for a while, trying to keep his distance from the tourist traffic. After a few moments, Fry noticed his lack of response.

'Ben, do *you* have any idea why he wouldn't be worried about Mansell Quinn?'

'None at all,' said Cooper. 'I haven't even met the man.'

'Well, I think maybe *you* should talk to Proctor. You could be on the same wavelength.'

'I will, if you like.'

'Besides, it won't do any harm for him to have another visit from us. It might make him realize we're serious.'

At temporary lights near Bradwell, they came up behind a silver Vauxhall Omega with three men inside it. Cooper saw a Derbyshire Constabulary crest on the back and realized they were officers undergoing advanced driver training. At the moment, they were being trained in stopping at temporary lights and crawling in traffic at fifteen miles an hour.

'What impression did you get of the Proctors' caravan park?' asked Cooper. 'Did it seem to be doing well?'

'Not according to Raymond Proctor. But we could have a look round while we're there, if you like. We could say we're checking his security.'

'Which would be a good idea anyway, if Quinn is planning a visit.'

176

'Yes, you're right. I should have been thinking more of his family. The man himself annoyed me too much.'

Cooper already felt a little sorry for Raymond Proctor. It didn't do to annoy Diane Fry, especially not on first meeting. She would never forget it.

'I was wondering if Mr Proctor has had financial problems,' he said. 'Business might not be too good.'

'I couldn't tell you that,' said Fry. 'There were quite a few people around.'

'It's a very seasonal business. If a caravan park isn't full at this time of year, it never will be.'

Cooper found it impossible not to have some sympathy for people involved in the tourism trade – their livelihood was so unpredictable. Fewer retired people took trips to the Peak District since their savings and investments income had plummeted. Sixty per cent of visitors came only for a day and spent enough for a visit to a show cavern and an ice cream, or for a couple of hours' parking and a Bakewell pudding to take home.

'You know,' said Cooper, 'I wonder if Quinn understood why his wife stopped visiting him. The thing that often tips a prisoner over the edge is the belief that their wife or partner isn't waiting at home for them to come out, but has met somebody else. It's the most common reason for escapes. They get the idea into their minds that if they can just get home for a while they'll be able to sort things out.'

'Quinn's wife got a divorce ten years ago, while he was inside,' said Fry. 'Besides, he waited out his full sentence. Or until his automatic release date, which is the same thing.'

'Maybe he's just the patient type?'

'Possibly.'

Cooper thought about Quinn's thirteen years and four months in prison. Many Category A prisoners were visited once by their families, and never again. The willingness of their wives and children to visit them didn't survive the humiliation of the first strip search. Some children grew up being told their father was a monster, and learning to believe it. They developed the habit of concealing their identity, evading questions about their parents, escaping the shame.

And for a prisoner like Quinn, thirteen years was a long time to let the imagination work on why you came to be on your own. Much too long. In that time, a man could develop a vivid fantasy of what was going on in the outside world, and in his own home. Perhaps in his own bed. He might build a convincing conspiracy theory. He could certainly create enemies for himself in his mind – enemies that had to be destroyed.

But even worse was the idea that Quinn had waited patiently, nurturing his fantasy, waiting for the opportunity to take his revenge. Or *retribution*, as Mrs Quinn had called it. It was more than patience, though. It seemed like the single-mindedness of a hunter, prepared to wait as long as necessary for prey to come within reach.

Cooper shuddered. He always found the slow, deliberate killers more frightening than those who killed in a sudden rage. They were a less understandable type of killer.

'I've got to say, it sounds as if everyone was against Quinn,' he said. 'His wife, his friends – none of them did a good job of standing up for him.'

'Maybe they were all glad to get him out of the way,' said Fry. 'I think I would be, in their place. But no doubt Quinn thinks everything that's happened to him has been somebody else's fault. I bet he has a list of people to blame.'

'So do you think he's following a plan?'

'There must be a reason he's staying in this area. If it were me, I'd get as far away as possible.'

'There are ties to a place like this that are difficult to break.'

'Not family ties, in his case. Those have been thoroughly broken.'

'But he's not unique there,' said Cooper. 'Nearly half of prisoners lose contact with their families during their sentence..

178

The prison population is what, seventy thousand? And mostly men. Yet they say a stable family life is the factor most likely to keep a prisoner from re-offending. So if they don't have families waiting to be reunited with them, where do all those men go?'

'There's a system to deal with all that, Ben.'

'The system is overloaded. Some of those men are just going to drop off the radar. A few might manage to get a job and settle down, perhaps even make new relationships. But the others . . . well, who knows?'

'Does it matter?'

'Yes, I think it does.'

'Ben, I saw a social worker's job being advertised last week. Maybe you should apply for it.'

Cooper flushed. 'I'm just saying there could be a lot of Mansell Quinns around the country that we don't even know about. It's an inevitable outcome of the whole process.'

Fry seemed to be digesting what he'd said, but Cooper suspected she was merely filing away the statistics. Or was she actually relating them to an individual, the person who was somewhere out there in the Hope Valley, alone and possibly desperate.

'Ben, could you put your foot down a bit?' she said. 'We don't have all day.'

Cooper sighed. 'No problem.'

Further on, he saw the Omega crew again, still training. Now they were practising parking at the kerb near the off-licence in Hope.

'I know one thing anyway,' said Fry suddenly.

'What's that?'

'We treated Enid Quinn too damn sensitively the first time.'

Going north from the village, they crossed over Killhill Bridge and turned past the cemetery into the valley of the River Noe. Cooper had to slow down to negotiate the unmade road, which must make the touring caravans bounce a little. Once they were clear of the railway bridge, he could see a number of mobile homes huddled close together, painted in shades of lime green and cream, with little chimneys and carriage lamps.

He parked on the grass and they walked up towards the house, past a chemical toilet disposal point. They found Raymond Proctor inside one of the mobile homes. According to the sign, it was a Westmorland 2000 two-bedroom model, a twenty-eight footer. Proctor was lying on the floor with his head in a cupboard under the sink unit, tinkering with the connection on a plastic water pipe.

'You lot again,' he said when he saw them. 'Still fretting about my health?'

'We wondered what steps you've taken to improve your security, Mr Proctor,' said Fry. 'And whether you might benefit from some more advice.'

Proctor snorted, banged a spanner into his toolbox and shoved his head back under the sink. He didn't notice his wife, who appeared around the corner of the caravan, breathing a bit hard as if she'd run down from the house when she saw the car arrive.

'Are we going to get police protection?' she said.

Fry opened her mouth to give her all the reasons why it was impossible, but before she could say anything, Proctor interrupted. 'We don't need police protection, thanks very much.'

His wife didn't even look at him. 'There are the children to think about. I'm not having them put in danger. And *he's* no use looking after us. He goes out drinking every night and staggers home late. I mean, what good is that? He's been doing it since Monday, no matter how much he tries to tell you he's not scared.'

Proctor sat up and heaved himself out of the door of the caravan. 'Did you hear what I said?'

'Yes, I heard,' said Connie, stony-faced.

'I'm afraid it wouldn't be possible anyway,' said Fry. 'We

can advise you on precautions and safety measures. If you're worried, Mrs Proctor, you might want to consider taking the children away somewhere for a short while.'

'Surely, if you think Quinn will come to the caravan park, you should have somebody here watching for him,' said Connie.

'If we had the resources . . .'

Proctor pushed his way in front of his wife. He stood only a few inches from Fry and repeated: 'We don't need police protection. Got it?'

Cooper thought Proctor was probably taking his life in his hands doing that. Fry was perfectly capable of reducing three Raymond Proctors to a quivering heap. But she didn't move a muscle. He thought he ought to divert attention, all the same.

'Don't you think you should worry about Mansell Quinn being in the area, Mr Proctor?' he said.

'No, it's rubbish. Why should I worry about Quinn?'

'Rebecca Lowe was murdered on Monday night. If Mansell Quinn calls here, it might not be to say "hello" to an old friend.'

'Why me? There's no reason for him to come here.'

'At his trial –'

Proctor snorted. 'That was fourteen years ago. We've all forgotten about that now.'

'Have you?'

'Look, it was a bad time, I won't deny that. But I put all that behind me. I've got a new wife now, and a new family. There's no point dwelling on the past – it doesn't do a bit of good.'

'Do you think you might be able to convince Quinn of that?'

Proctor glowered. 'If necessary. But you're barking up the wrong tree. Now, if you don't mind, I've got this unit booked out to some German tourists, and the water supply had better be working when they arrive. My maintenance man should be doing this, but he's bloody useless with water.'

Cooper looked in through the window of the mobile home

181

Proctor had emerged from. It was well equipped, with a kitchen about the same size as his own back at Welbeck Street, plus a toilet and shower, and a separate bedroom at the far end.

'Quinn expected you to give him an alibi for the time of the murder, Mr Proctor,' he said. 'The main plank of his defence was that he'd been with you and William Thorpe until nearly a quarter past three, so couldn't possibly have been home by the time your wife was killed.'

'But it wasn't true,' said Proctor. 'He'd left the pub half an hour before that. I think Mansell expected me to lie for him. But why should I lie for somebody who'd just – well . . .'

'Murdered your wife?'

'Exactly.'

Cooper watched Raymond Proctor for signs that he really had put the death of his first wife behind him so completely. He would have liked the opportunity to test Proctor's statement to see if his version of events stood up to questioning after nearly fourteen years. Lies were difficult to sustain under proper probing – and it was even more difficult when you might have forgotten the lies you told the first time round.

But he wouldn't get the chance. Diane Fry was already giving him a warning look that told him he was straying into forbidden territory.

'It was all gone through at the trial,' said Proctor. 'I don't see how it matters now.'

'But it matters to Mansell Quinn.'

'Ben, thank you,' said Fry. 'Perhaps you could go and wait in the car. We've nearly finished here.'

Reluctantly, Cooper went back to the car. It was parked in the area reserved for touring caravans entering the site at night – three or four pitches with separate points for services, so that late arrivals didn't disturb the rest of the residents. Beyond the gravelled area was a patch of grass where four older static caravans stood.

Cooper glanced over his shoulder. He could see Proctor

trying to get back into the Westmorland to carry on with his work, while Fry continued to lecture him. A few yards away, an old man in overalls was raking the gravel, but taking a keen interest in what was being said. The maintenance man who was useless with water, presumably.

Out of curiosity, Cooper strolled towards the old caravans. They all looked a little battered round the edges and not so clean or well cared for as the mobile homes on the main part of the site. They'd been parked too near the trees, and their white panels were green with mould, their roofs spattered with bird droppings.

The window of the nearest one was badly cracked, too. He couldn't imagine Raymond Proctor managing to rent these out to his German tourists. They must have been old stock, now obsolete and beyond restoration. But if so, why hadn't they been scrapped and removed from the site?

Cooper approached the nearest one and peered through the cracked window. He was trying the second one when Fry came up behind him.

'Ben, what the hell do you think you're doing?'

'What do you mean?'

'Those questions you were asking about the murder of Carol Proctor. You seem to have forgotten which enquiry you're on. That case was dealt with years ago.'

'Yes, I'm sorry.'

'There was a trial and a conviction. The man has served his sentence, for God's sake.'

'I said I'm sorry, Diane.'

She narrowed her eyes at him.

'I don't know what you're up to, Ben. But I always know when you're up to something.'

'Diane, aren't Raymond Proctor and William Thorpe old friends?'

'Yes. The three of them were very close – Quinn, Proctor and Thorpe. Why?'

'I wonder if Proctor and Thorpe stayed good friends. If you had spare accommodation like this that you didn't need, wouldn't you put up an old friend who had no home of his own?'

Fry smiled. 'You're right.'

To their surprise, Raymond Proctor admitted it straight away when they asked him. 'Yes, Will stayed for the winter,' he said.

'And then he left?'

'Look, he can survive perfectly well on the streets in the summer. In winter, it's a different matter. A winter spent outside would kill him for sure. That's why I let him come and stay in one of the 'vans. I didn't want that on my conscience as well.'

'As well as what?'

Proctor shook his head. 'Nothing you need to know about.'

'It's good to know you have a conscience, though, sir. Not everyone would have done something like that for a homeless person. Most people would just have said it wasn't their responsibility and sent him packing.'

'He's an old mate,' said Proctor. 'That's all there is to it.'

'So where did Mr Thorpe go?'

'I don't know.'

'You just kicked him out without any idea where he would go, or whether he had somewhere else to live?'

'I'm not running a homeless hostel.'

'There's a limit to your friendship, then?'

'I gave Will a place to doss for six months while he sorted himself out. That was the agreement. It was understood that he'd leave at the end of April. If he couldn't find himself somewhere else to live, it's not my problem. Will called in a favour for old time's sake, and I paid up. But now we're quits. I'm not obliged to be his keeper for ever more.'

'I see.'

'I needed the caravan. That's how I make my living.'

'But there's no one in it.'

'Not now. But there might be. Things could pick up any time.'

'Mr Proctor, are you sure you have no idea where William Thorpe might have gone when he left here?'

Proctor shrugged. 'Not my business.'

He locked the Westmorland and began to walk back towards the house. Cooper followed him, making a show of examining the security lights. He noticed there was only one vehicle parked outside the Proctors' house – a bright red Renault panel van with white lettering on the side. A business vehicle, presumably. But no car?

'You should think seriously about your security, sir,' he said. 'Don't just hope for the best. Think about your family.'

Proctor cut across him with weary insistence. 'I am not,' he said, 'frightened of Mansell Quinn.'

'You realize we're giving you advice entirely in your own interests?'

'Oh, really? Well, thanks and all that.'

Proctor reached the door of his house. He took hold of the Yale lock and fiddled with it restlessly, rattling the latch in its barrel.

'Mr Proctor?'

'What?'

'Take care, sir.'

Cooper turned to walk away from the house. He passed the maintenance man, who had stopped raking the gravel and was giving a cursory wipe to the windows on one of the Westmorlands, well within earshot of the house. He met Cooper's eye for a second, smiled, then went back to his work. Perhaps the opportunities for entertainment were rare when you were employed by Raymond Proctor.

18

'Anger-management training,' said Diane Fry. 'It's a bit of an American idea, isn't it? It seems to go with botox and pre-nuptial agreements.'

Ben Cooper looked up and noticed her sniffing and rubbing her eyes, which seemed a bit red today. He had been getting ready to go out of the office again when she came to his desk. She was carrying a file, too, but he couldn't quite see what it was.

'I don't know,' he said. 'Maybe it works for some people.'

'Not in Mansell Quinn's case, obviously.'

'I imagine Quinn to be quite an intelligent man,' said Cooper.

'Why?'

'Well, you'd need to have some power of concentration to stay angry for so long. When most people get angry, they just flare up for a short while, and then it's all over. A few minutes later, they can hardly remember what they were angry about.'

'I know what you mean. The blessings of a short attention span.'

'But to stay angry for thirteen or fourteen years – that's quite some achievement.'

'Yeah.'

Fry sneezed and pulled out a tissue from a pocket. Cooper noticed her eyes were not only red but watering.

'Hay fever?' he said.

'Full marks. I'll probably be like this for weeks. Should give you a good laugh, anyway.'

She pulled the file from under her arm and looked for a place to put it on his desk, which was crammed with overdue paperwork as usual.

'Well, I hope you feel better soon.'

'Don't worry, I won't be going off sick and leaving you to your own devices. That's much too risky.'

'I didn't mean that, Diane. I –'

Fry ignored him. 'Anyway, if we can get back to the business in hand; I don't think what Mansell Quinn is doing right now is the behaviour of an intelligent man, do you?'

'I'm not sure I agree,' said Cooper. 'I think he's an otherwise intelligent person doing something extremely stupid. Like we all do sometimes in our lives.'

With an exasperated sigh, Fry snatched up the report again. 'Point taken.'

'Hold on,' said Cooper. 'I didn't mean anything.'

'No?'

'Diane, wait. I was just wondering what sort of books Quinn reads. Did you check with the prison library what he was interested in?'

'*Books*?' said Fry, as if he'd suggested checking the sewers for evidence of what Quinn had been eating.

Cooper couldn't help smiling. 'You don't read many books, do you, Diane?'

'I'm a graduate, damn it,' she said. 'I've read more books than you've ever dreamed of. I just don't bother with fiction – I can't see the point.'

But Cooper still smiled. He wasn't impressed by this graduate business. All right, he'd never gone to university himself, but he knew plenty of people with degrees. And he'd noticed that it was possible to be a graduate and still be ignorant.

'What was the last book you remember reading?' he said. 'I mean, really *remember*. The last book that changed your life.'

'No book has ever changed my life,' said Fry. 'People have messed up my life for me often enough. But not books.'

'That wasn't quite I meant,' said Cooper. He already knew he was going to regret mentioning the subject. Everything he said to Fry these days seemed to be taken as an intrusion into her private life. But when he asked her what book had changed her life, he'd assumed there must have been one that changed it for the better.

He looked at Fry hopefully. Did she understand at all? What subject had she taken her degree in, anyway? It wasn't something she talked about very much, and he'd never thought to ask her. It would have to be some kind of legal subject, he guessed. Criminal Justice, perhaps? Something that focused on rules and procedures and didn't involve dealing with real people.

'There *is* one book I remember,' said Fry.

'Really?' Cooper looked at her hard, suspecting she was about to make some cutting remark.

'I can't say it changed my life, though.'

'No – but you remember how it made you feel?' he said.

'Yes. It made me feel filthy.'

'Sorry?'

'The author's thoughts were in my head, and I didn't want them there.'

'Diane, that wasn't what I meant either.'

'So I burned it.'

'What? You burned a book?' Cooper was shocked. He wanted to ask her what book it was, but he was worried he might be even more shocked if she told him.

'You're right, though,' said Fry. 'I'll check with the prison library what Quinn liked to read when he was inside. Maybe he let some kind of poison into his mind.'

'Yeah.'

'So what are you doing this afternoon, Ben?'

'We had a call from an outdoor equipment shop in Hathersage. One of the staff remembers serving someone who answers Quinn's description. Then I'm going to drop by the railway station up there, on the chance someone might have seen him catching a train when he left his mother's.'

'Are you taking Gavin with you?'

'Unless you need him.'

'No, that's fine.' Fry tapped the file, which Cooper had almost forgotten. 'Well, I thought you might want to see this before you go. Then you can't say I don't keep you up to date.'

'What is it?'

'The postmortem report on Rebecca Lowe. Mrs van Doon estimates that the victim had died between an hour and two hours before she was found by her sister at eleven thirty that night. She was killed by multiple knife wounds, as we know. The problem is the weapon.'

'Not a kitchen knife, then?'

'Oh, yes. But not one that we've found in the house.' Fry slipped a photograph out of the file. 'You remember me mentioning the knives at the scene?'

'Mrs Lowe had a whole block full of them in her kitchen.'

'Yes. Decent stuff, too. Henckels Professional S range, according to one of the suppliers in town. Stainless-steel blades. Kept in good condition, they're as sharp as hell. And these were almost new.'

Cooper looked at the photo. Taken by one of the SOCOs, it showed a section of the floor in Rebecca Lowe's kitchen at Parson's Croft. The victim's left leg and hip were just visible on the edge of the picture, and the blood spatter spread most of the way from her body to the kitchen units. Lying on the tiles were several items that Cooper hadn't noticed when he was in the house, because he'd been too busy looking at the body and the blood.

'The wooden block itself is here, on the floor near the end unit,' said Fry. 'Dawn Cottrill says it usually stood on the work surface there, or on the window ledge behind it, depending on whether Rebecca had been using the knives. It would have been near enough to the door of the utility room for somebody to make a quick grab at it as he came through.'

Cooper could see five or six black-handled knives of various sizes lying on the floor. They were all neatly labelled by the crime scene examiners, and all of them had traces of blood visible on their stainless-steel blades.

'So we reckon he grabbed one knife from the block, sending the rest flying in his hurry,' said Cooper.

'The position of the block and the knives is consistent with that theory.' Fry sniffed again and tried to clear her throat. 'There's a close-up of the block here.'

'It still has a knife in it.'

'It's a ten-centimetre paring knife – the smallest and lightest item in the set. It wasn't thrown clear of the block, as the others were.'

'How many pieces in the set?'

'Seven.' Fry pointed at the main picture again. 'Here's a twenty-centimetre cook's knife, and near it a bread knife the same length. There's a smaller sandwich knife over here, a sharpening steel under the edge of one of the units. And just by the victim's foot, where you can hardly make it out, there's a pair of kitchen scissors. As you can see, they all have blood-stains on them, except the paring knife.'

'So which of them was the murder weapon?' asked Cooper.

'None of them. At the PM, they tried all the blades to get a match with the victim's wounds. There was no fit.'

Cooper looked up. 'One piece of the set is missing, of course.'

'Ah. So you did arithmetic at school, as well as reading.'

'That means he took the murder weapon away with him.'

'It would be the sensible thing to do, especially if he wasn't wearing gloves when he grabbed it.' Fry consulted the report again. 'The seventh item in a set of this kind would be a slicing knife. The same length as the bread knife and the cook's knife, but with the perfect blade for the job, I guess.'

'In fact, it's the one you'd choose if you knew what you were going for, rather than just grabbing the first thing that came to hand.'

Fry wiped her nose again. 'Good point, Ben. I suppose you're thinking that he must have known what he was doing and planned which knife he was going to use in advance. Then he knocked the rest over to make it look like an impulse grab. Clever, eh?'

Cooper was starting to feel he should have made more of an effort to escape from the office before she cornered him.

'Even though I didn't say that, I suppose you're going to tell me I'm wrong,' he said.

Fry didn't smile. She didn't smile often enough at the best of times. But this afternoon she looked as though she just didn't have the energy.

'One of our people had the idea of obtaining a twenty-centimetre slicing knife out of the Henckels Professional S range from one of the stores in town. That didn't match the victim's wounds either. It *almost* matched, but not quite. Not enough to satisfy our meticulous pathologist.'

'So what's the conclusion? Unknown weapon?'

'Somebody was sent to see Dawn Cottrill,' said Fry. 'And they asked her to rack her brains about her sister's kitchen equipment.'

Cooper was starting to feel sorry for Mrs Cottrill. She was an intelligent, and no doubt imaginative, woman. Though the officers who'd spoken to her would have been discreet, she could certainly have worked out for herself what they were doing with all the knives.

'Poor woman,' he said.

'Who?' said Fry vaguely.

'Never mind.'

'She got us a result, anyway. She remembered that when Rebecca was equipping the kitchen in her new house, she wanted something a bit longer for slicing. Apparently, she used to buy large joints of meat from some organic place and had to cut them up into smaller portions for herself.'

'So Rebecca had the knife in the set replaced with a longer one,' said Cooper.

'Correct.'

'And I think you were about to tell me why the killer didn't necessarily know what he was doing when he chose that particular knife?'

'So I was. Well, Ben, imagine a block full of knives with their handles pointing towards you. If you're going to grab at one of the handles, which would be the nearest to you?'

'The longest one,' said Cooper.

'Correct again. The handle of the longest knife would be sticking out of the block furthest, yes? And the item we have missing from the crime scene is a twenty-six centimetre Henckel slicing knife. Twenty-six centimetres. That's over ten inches long.'

'Nasty.'

Fry sneezed and dabbed at her eyes with a tissue. 'Nasty is right. It looks as though Mansell Quinn could turn out to be a very dangerous man indeed. When we find him.'

As Fry drove her Peugeot out of the E Division car park, she was still thinking about that book. She didn't know why she let Ben Cooper do it to her. As soon as he started one of his conversations, she knew that he'd be sticking some kind of pin into her that she wouldn't be able to pull out for days.

It had been years since she'd thought about that book. She'd been in Birmingham, studying for her degree back then; deluded into thinking of herself as educated and literate, just because she went every day to a place that called itself a university. In those days she could still read books for escape, letting her mind drift off into somebody else's world without her subconscious throwing up horrific flashbacks. Since then, events had taken place that had changed her life in ways a book never could – they had altered it permanently and painfully.

The book in question had been so vile that it hadn't been enough to pick it up and throw it at the wall. That was the fate of the merely bad books, the ones that irritated or annoyed her. This one had been different. This one she'd felt obliged to remove completely from her life. Normally, her unwanted books would have gone to a charity shop or into the recycling bank. But this particular book had been different. She hadn't been able to bear the thought that someone else would pick the thing up. Besides, she had needed some small act of protest against the author's unpleasant thoughts being forced into her own.

So she'd started a fire in the garden incinerator with some dead branches. Then she'd torn as many pages as she could from the book and burned them. She had finally dropped the mutilated cover into the flames and watched the glue of its binding melt on to the boards before it caught light and the author's name had blackened and charred, letter by letter.

Simon Lowe was being allowed home from hospital this afternoon. Overnight observation following a blow to the head – that was all you got these days.

'I didn't see a thing, to be honest,' he said, fiddling with the plaster on a cut to his hand. 'The first blow stunned me. And it was dark, anyway.'

'Did your assailant say anything?' asked Fry.

'Not a word.'

'Did you notice any other details? A sound, a smell?'

Simon shook his head. 'I wish I could think of something.'

'A car parked nearby, perhaps?'

'There were cars parked on the street near the church, but I didn't take any notice of them. It was dark.'

'Yes, you said. And you spoke to no one in the pub, apart from the landlord?'

'No one.' Simon looked at her. 'Do you think I might have lost my memory? Did I get into an argument with someone in the George?'

Fry sighed. 'No. The landlord confirms that you spoke to no one, and there was no sign of any trouble.'

'So that means . . . ?'

'That means you're going to take much more care from now on, aren't you, Mr Lowe? Don't go out on your own at night again. Take sensible precautions.'

She said the words without much hope. Nobody seemed to heed her warnings.

Simon Lowe nodded, then winced at the pain of the bruise that Fry could see on the back of his head.

'But I'll be safe back home in Edendale, won't I?' he said, looking at her sharply.

'Well . . .'

'Because he's still in the Hope Valley, isn't he?'

Fry stood up. 'Yes, sir. We think he's still in the Hope Valley.'

19

Out and About was one of the newer outdoor equipment shops on the main street in Hathersage. After speaking to a member of staff, Ben Cooper and Gavin Murfin collected a tape from their security system. The visit didn't take long, and left them plenty of time to take a look at Hathersage station. Cooper remembered where it was, having seen the approach road from the back of the Moorland estate, where Mrs Quinn lived.

The station car park looked full, so he pulled up at the side of the road near a row of bungalows. He was surprised by the extent of the development that had been taking place here – Hathersage Park, it was called. He could see a long row of new business units stretching past the station itself, many of them already in use.

'Where are we going?' asked Murfin.

'I want to have a look at the station, in case there's any way Quinn might have been seen on the platform.'

'I think I'll stay here with the car, then.'

Cooper looked around. There was nowhere selling food, so it was probably safe.

'OK, Gavin.'

He walked through a tunnel and up a ramp to the

Manchester line. Not only was the station unmanned, but there wasn't much station to speak of – just two platforms, with a small concrete shelter on each side. First North Western had provided a payphone on the Sheffield side, but that was about it. It was bad luck there were no CCTV cameras covering the platforms, but he supposed crime was more likely to happen down in the car park.

Cooper examined the train timetables. Judging by the time of the sighting of Mansell Quinn, he must have left his mother's house in Moorland Avenue by seven fifteen. It was only a short walk to the station, and there was a train towards Manchester at seven thirty-three, so Quinn must have waited for a quarter of an hour, perhaps on the platform.

But when had he left Rebecca Lowe's house? And did he leave the area by train? There were two services in either direction that he could have caught, but the times of the later trains meant Quinn would have had to stay in the house for some time with the body – or found somewhere else to be out of sight.

Turning, Cooper looked across the car park to the new development. At the far end was a complex of apartments and penthouses. They looked perfect for affluent commuters, who could reach the centre of Sheffield by train in twenty minutes or so, yet still enjoy a rural view. Next to them were business units, and across from the corner of the car park, a health and fitness centre. Its front wall consisted mostly of glass on the upper storey, with two big, arched windows reaching from floor to ceiling.

Cooper felt a sudden surge of interest. He could see a woman in a black sweatshirt and leggings exercising on a treadmill. She was striding out vigorously on the moving surface, doing a good five miles an hour he reckoned. There was a console in front of her that probably displayed her time, speed, distance, calories, pulse and maybe even her heart rate. It

196

was one of a row of machines lined up in the window – and they were all facing outwards.

He jogged back down the ramp, and found Murfin starting to doze in the car.

'Gavin, you might want to visit the fitness centre over there.'

'Visit a fitness centre? Me?'

'Look – see the woman on the treadmill up there?'

Murfin looked up. 'Oh, yeah. She's not bad. Well spotted, Ben.'

'She has a great view of the platform – or she would have, if she took her eyes off her console. And anyone using those machines on Monday evening would have been able to see Mansell Quinn boarding the train.'

'So you want me to go and talk to a load of women in leotards and tight shorts?'

'If you can manage that.'

'Manage it? It's what God made me for. But what are *you* going to do?'

'Take a little train ride.'

'A what?'

'I can't stop to explain, Gavin – there's a Manchester train due in two minutes. I'll be back in not much above an hour.'

When a pair of diesel units appeared around a curve in the track, Cooper was the only passenger waiting to get on. Realizing he ought to let Diane Fry know what he was doing, he checked his mobile. No signal. And the payphone was on the other side of the track – no time to get across and back before the train came. Oh, well. He could explain later.

On the train, a guard wearing a uniform of shirt, tie and checked jacket in three different shades of blue charged him a couple of pounds, then had to tap a lot of buttons on the metal box strapped round his neck to produce a ticket. At Bamford, Cooper watched him operate the doors and step out on to the platform to see passengers on and off before signalling the driver.

The train crossed the River Derwent on a bridge of steel girders just before it slowed to enter Hope station. Cooper looked at his watch. The journey from Hathersage to Hope had taken just seven minutes. DI Hitchens had been right so far – it would have been ridiculously easy for Mansell Quinn to get here from his mother's house in Moorland Avenue.

To cross the tracks at Hope, Cooper had to climb a set of wooden steps on to an iron footbridge where two men with cameras were standing. They must be waiting for express trains to come through, because they didn't look interested in the diesel units that had just pulled away.

He soon found a path that led into trees and through a kissing gate before heading up the hill to Aston. A stone barn with a corrugated-iron roof stood in the middle of a field, adjoining an old cattle shelter full of spray tanks. An ideal place to loiter unseen, if you needed to.

By the time he reached the village, Cooper was breathing hard. But the walk hadn't been taxing, just short of twelve minutes from the station. And he hadn't seen a soul, apart from the trainspotters on the footbridge and a few sheep. In another minute or two he would pass right by Rebecca Lowe's driveway at Parson's Croft.

A woman came towards him with a Labrador trailing at her heels. She gave him a close look before saying 'hello'. Cooper knew he didn't look like the average hiker. If she was a resident, the woman had probably been interviewed already and would be suspicious of strangers.

At Parson's Croft, a liveried police car was parked on the driveway and a uniformed female officer stood near the front door, but otherwise it was quiet. The press had gone away, moving on to the next news story as soon as the SOCOs and detectives had dispersed.

Rebecca Lowe's killer wouldn't have needed to approach the house via the main gate. The hedge around the property was five feet high, but ragged. It consisted largely of elm saplings, which would die before they reached maturity as the beetles that spread Dutch Elm Disease got under their bark. Cooper could have forced his way through in several places. Had the Crime Scene Manager worked on the assumption that the killer had arrived via the obvious route? Or had the weak points in the hedge been examined for fibres left on the branches by someone pushing their way through?

What Cooper really wanted to do was explore the garden, but his presence would have been recorded. In any case, he ought to get back to the station if he was going to catch the train back to Hathersage.

He reached Hope station with five minutes to spare and stood with a group of hikers on the Sheffield platform, listening to an announcement about a delay. Cooper looked round. Nobody seemed to be surprised.

With a shriek and a whine, an express train thundered through. A plate on the locomotive said it was the 'City of Aberdeen'. The two photographers ran from one side of the bridge to the other to get shots of the train. When it had disappeared around the bend, they began to pack their cameras away. Perhaps they were going for lunch in one of the pubs in Hope.

Cooper gazed around the station. Unlike Hathersage, the platforms here weren't overlooked. It was well out of the village, and the only vantage point was from the footbridge. On an impulse, he ran up the wooden steps and explained to the photographers what he wanted. He wasn't very hopeful, but it made sense to cover all the bases while he was here.

'When did you say?' asked one.

'Monday. Between seven thirty and nine in the evening.'

The photographer shook his head and zipped up his bag. But the other man hesitated, reluctant to get involved, or perhaps keen to get started on his lunch.

'I was here,' he said.

'You were?'

'I live just down the road in Bradwell, and I noticed the light was interesting that night. There were some thunderclouds moving in from the west. Cumulonimbus.'

'Right.'

'It made for some nice lighting effects. I knew a Manchester express was due, so I chucked the bag in the car and came down.'

'You were here, on the bridge?'

'Yes, of course.'

'What time would you have been in position?'

'About seven thirty, I suppose. I did a bit of setting up, checked the light meter, put a high-speed film in, and took a few trial shots.'

'Did you notice anyone on either of the platforms?'

'On the platforms?' The photographer looked down from the bridge, as if seeing the platforms for the first time. 'But they're waiting for the local trains, aren't they?'

Cooper sighed, recognizing the fact that the photographer wouldn't have noticed another human being unless they were there on the footbridge with him, comparing the sizes of their zoom lenses.

'Have you had the film developed?' he asked.

'No, it's still here in my bag.'

'Would you let me borrow it? I'll give you a receipt, and you'll get free prints from it.'

Cooper heard the first rattle of the approaching Sheffield train, the one that would take him back to Hathersage. He braced himself for an argument that he didn't have time for.

'Will it help?' said the photographer.

'It might do. I can't say until we have a look at it.'

The friend was fidgeting impatiently in the background, tapping the iron railing of the bridge. The photographer looked over his shoulder at him. And Cooper saw with relief that he, too, didn't have time to get into a long argument.

'Here, you can have it,' he said. 'I don't think they'll come out too well, anyway. The sun was at the wrong angle.'

Diane Fry had more driving to do this afternoon. Just her luck, when she felt so bad and all she wanted to do was stay indoors, away from the pollen. She'd have to leave her car windows closed all the way. Her doctor had told her to avoid freshly-cut grass, but from May onwards the stuff was all around her in the Peak District. First there were silage trailers blocking the roads, and then vast loads of hay bales filling the air with dust. Try keeping that lot out of your car.

Fry had two more people to interview this afternoon – first, Mansell Quinn's probation officer, and then a convicted burglar called Richard Wakelin, aged twenty-five, who lived in Allestree, on the outskirts of Derby. Wakelin had been the last person to speak to Quinn on his release from HMP Sudbury. She didn't think that Quinn would have said anything to either of them that would hint at his intentions or where he was heading. But the long shots had to be covered. At the moment, they had no other leads.

On her way through Ashbourne, Fry pulled in at a chemist's and bought herself some Zirtek antihistamine tablets. She ought to have had pollen-extract injections before the summer started. The tablets would be nowhere near as effective, but at least they'd make life more tolerable.

On the train back to Hathersage, Ben Cooper showed his return ticket to the guard, who simply nodded, making no effort to clip a hole in it or tear it to show the return portion had been used. It didn't seem quite right to Cooper. It meant he could use the same ticket again later in the day, if he felt like it. That sort of thinking must come from mixing with too many criminals.

He took a closer look at his ticket. It showed the date and time he'd bought it, as well as his starting point and destination. In addition, there was a long serial number – seventeen figures in total. Before he got off at Hathersage, Cooper asked the guard what happened to his ticket machine when he finished his shift.

'I just hand it in at the office with the money, and collect a new one when I clock on again the next morning.'

'Thanks.'

Cooper watched him go through his routine, checking passengers on and off the train, closing the doors, giving the driver his signal. A small crowd had got on at Bamford, and the guard hadn't managed to issue tickets to them all by the time the train arrived in Hathersage.

If the train had been full on the evening that Mansell Quinn had travelled on it, the guard might not have reached him by Bamford, or even Hope. There must be people who managed to take short journeys without ever buying a ticket. It wasn't likely that the guard would remember one individual who'd ridden two stops on a busy evening run, unless that passenger drew attention to himself.

And a man planning to commit murder wasn't going to do anything to draw attention to himself, was he?

As Cooper walked back down the ramp to the car park at Hathersage, the smell of garlic was wafting from one of the bungalows. Someone had tied a bouquet of flowers to the station fence as a funeral tribute to a train service that had been cancelled. The flowers themselves were long since dead.

'How did you get on with the lycra ladies?' he asked Murfin, who was waiting in the car.

'They're a bit self-obsessed.'

'They didn't notice anything?'

'Nope. And, worse than that, they weren't interested in *me*. Still, I got a coffee out of it. No cake, obviously. What about you, Ben?'

'I met a trainspotter.'

'Well, the afternoon wasn't entirely wasted, then. Did you get his autograph?'

'Better – I got a film.'

'You're hoping to get evidence that Quinn was at Hope? A bit of a long shot, isn't it?'

Yes, of course it was. And it still wouldn't answer the big question: where did Quinn go after he left Rebecca Lowe's house at Aston? Back to the station? If so, he might have retraced his route and returned to his mother's home in Hathersage. Alternatively, he could have stayed on the train and travelled as far as Sheffield, or crossed the tracks and been in Manchester within an hour.

In either case, it would be difficult to track him down. No known associates of Quinn's lived in either city, so there was nowhere to start. DCI Kessen could ask for Quinn's details to be circulated to all the B&Bs, hostels and cheap hotels – but there must be hundreds of them, possibly thousands. And what about the railway and coach stations? The airports, even? How much money did Quinn have with him, anyway? Might his mother have subbed him, handed over her life savings to help him get clear? Could she have found enough for an airline ticket? Nearly two days had passed since Rebecca Lowe had been killed. In theory, Mansell Quinn could be anywhere in the world by now.

Cooper shook his head. There was only one consolation. Any one of these scenarios might make Quinn more difficult to find – but at least it would mean he was out of Derbyshire for a while, and therefore not a threat to anyone else he might have on his list. But in his heart, Cooper felt that Quinn was still around.

He looked at the Ordnance Survey map he kept in the car, locating Aston and then the railway station half a mile away down the slopes of Win Hill. The station was a long way out of Hope village. That was because instead of continuing up the Hope Valley, the line took a shallow curve to follow the course of the River Noe and crossed a series of small bridges before it met the cement works spur. Trains had to pass over three unmade roads leading to farms or isolated homes. He could see some of the names on the map – Farfield Farm, Birchfield Park, the Homestead.

And there, just a little way to the north of Hope station, less than a mile west of Rebecca Lowe's house, was the track that led to Wingate Lees. The Proctors' caravan park.

Cooper shivered, though he wasn't cold. Thunder flies had coated the windscreen of his car, dying slowly in their dozens on the hot glass. He tried to clear them away, but his wipers smeared them into a sticky mess, leaving greasy swirls embedded with black specks. It took several minutes before he could see clearly enough to drive back through Hathersage.

20

Before she got ready to go out that night, Diane Fry spent ten minutes running through some exercises, winding down from the day, flexing her muscles and stretching her limbs until her body tingled comfortably.

It had been a frustrating afternoon. Neither the probation officer nor the released prisoner, Richard Wakelin, had been able to offer her any insights into Mansell Quinn's mind. It looked as though Quinn had been playing his cards pretty close to his chest for some time, as if he knew that somebody like her would come along asking questions.

In the middle of a bend, Fry found herself looking at a patch of wallpaper, noticing where the edge had starting peeling away from the wall. She'd never really noticed it before. She always felt she'd been lucky to find the flat in Grosvenor Avenue when she came to Edendale. It was depressing, but in a tangible sort of way. It contained no painful memories or associations, no significant possessions from her old life – she'd thrown them all away.

But Angie's arrival had changed that. The flat was no longer empty of feeling. It was starting to fill up with random recollections, incidents from her childhood that she'd long since forgotten or buried in her subconscious. They were reappearing now in the sound of a half-familiar phrase of Angie's, or in the tone of her voice, or a gesture of her hand that hadn't changed since she was a teenager. They were creeping into the corners of the rooms and hanging in the air – small things in themselves, but capable of catching her off guard with a jolt of remembrance. Some of the memories made her smile, but others took her breath away with the pain they caused.

She closed the window of the sitting room to keep out the pollen, had a shower and washed her hair, hoping for an allergy-free atmosphere for a while. But still she sneezed and her eyes ached. She used tissue after tissue, screwing them up and throwing them in the bin. Sometimes, she screwed one up just for the sake of it, because it made her feel a bit better.

'God, is it that bad?' said Angie, after watching her sister for a while.

'Yes.'

'Can't you have a jab for it or something?'

'It's too late for that. I've got some tablets, which might help. But otherwise, you'll just have to watch me suffer.'

'You can still eat, can't you?'

'If I don't try to breathe at the same time.'

'Because we're going out tonight, you know.'

'I hadn't forgotten. It's all booked.'

Angie watched her throw another tissue towards the bin and miss. Fry remembered that there was a genetic link to hay fever. Allergies ran in families.

'Angie, did you ever have hay fever as a teenager?' she said.

'Nope. Why?'

'I just wondered. It was one of those things I couldn't remember.'

'You didn't catch it from me, if that's what you're suggesting.'

'I couldn't have caught from you. It's an allergy.'

'Well, there you go. I never had an allergy in my life.'

Fry sniffled. 'Something else we don't have in common, then.'

After he'd delivered the tape and film to the incident room at West Street, Ben Cooper realized it was time for him to go off duty. No overtime today.

His face felt itchy, and he brushed at his cheeks and forehead, suspecting they were covered in thunder flies, attracted by his sweat. There always seemed to be one week of the year, in the middle of July, when the flies moved in from the fields and invaded the town in swarms. Walking down Clappergate and the High Street became an ordeal; it was a mistake to leave any parts of your skin bare outdoors. Even in the office, they were impossible to avoid. They were attracted to computer screens, and he often found them sitting among the black letters as he typed, like stray commas. No matter how many he squashed under his thumb, another would appear in a different part of the text.

Closing the windows failed to keep the flies out. There were too many of them, and they were too small. Every draught of air through an open door brought more in, and anybody entering from outside carried dozens of them on their clothes and in their hair. By the end of the working day, all Cooper wanted to do was get home and have a shower, in the hope that he could get rid of the itchiness.

He went into the men's toilets and splashed cold water on his face. Drying himself with a paper towel, he looked in the mirror, seeking the black specks he'd imagined were crawling in his hairline and sitting in the folds behind his ears. But he could see nothing.

As soon as he entered his flat, Cooper heard the bang made by Randy coming in through the cat flap. But instead of marching straight into the sitting room, the cat stayed in the kitchen. It was an unusual enough break in routine for Cooper to go to see if he was all right.

The cat was sitting quietly near his bowls, but he wasn't eating. His long, black fur was gummed up on one flank. Randy kept himself very clean usually, and was never happy when he couldn't untangle his coat.

'Blimey, you're a bit of a mess,' said Cooper. He put his hand to the patch of fur, and it felt sticky. It also glistened strangely in the kitchen lights.

Cats might be intelligent, but they hadn't learned the basic rule of forensic science: Locard's Principle, the fact that every contact left a trace. A snail had left its slime on Randy, and no doubt had taken away a few cat hairs sticking to its mucus. If it was dead, its murderer could be identified by the traces they'd left on each other.

As he cleaned the cat, Cooper's thoughts turned to DNA, the holy grail of trace evidence. The national DNA database had gone live in 1995 and every week now the Forensic Science Service laboratory in Birmingham matched more than a thousand profiles taken from crime scenes, solving crimes up to thirty years old. Soon, the database would hit its target of three million profiles.

Like many police officers he knew, Cooper was in two minds about the development of such a vast database. There was no doubt it was a valuable tool for catching criminals, but it was too easy to believe that DNA evidence was foolproof. The larger the database, the greater the chance of somebody being wrongly linked to a crime. And for Cooper, it felt a little too much like the beginnings of a Big Brother society he didn't really want to be part of.

He gave Randy a quick rub with an old towel and let him go. The cat looked clean, but he probably still carried minute traces of snail, if anyone cared to look closely enough. The lab needed only tiny amounts these days.

Cooper wondered what it had been like in 1990, before

the DNA database was created. Frustratingly, the practice of routinely taking buccal swabs from charged suspects hadn't been adopted until 1995, so Mansell Quinn hadn't been sampled when he was charged with Carol Proctor's murder. Even a recent Home Office 'sweep' to collect samples from convicted prisoners had come too late. It had never reached Quinn as he waited for release in his cell in HMP Sudbury.

Whatever the value of the national database, it didn't help in this case. Mansell Quinn's profile wasn't on it.

Back in his sitting room, Cooper stood in front of the photograph over the fireplace. He was familiar with every face in the neat rows, even with the texture of the wall behind them and the concrete yard beneath their boots. Without looking, he could have described the way each man held his arms, which of them was smiling, who looked suspicious of the photographer, and who hadn't fastened his tie properly that morning. He also knew the exact feel of the mahogany frame in his hands, the smoothness of the edges, the slight scratch in the glass that was almost hidden by the shadow of the chair one of the sergeants was sitting in on the front row. If you turned the picture towards the light, the scratch became obvious. He couldn't remember how it had happened. Somehow, it had always been there.

Diane Fry had chosen the Italian restaurant on Eyre Street, Caesar's. She had never been inside it before, but from standing on the outside, looking through the window and reading the menu, she'd assessed it as smart and interesting, without being too up-market. Now that she was sitting at a table in the far corner, with her confit of duck on its way at any moment, she thought she'd been right.

Even so, Fry felt uncomfortable. It was true that she didn't go out often, but at least she'd made an effort. She was wearing her cord blazer over a hand-knitted alpaca cotton top that she'd bought in Bakewell and never worn before. Angie had made do with the usual jeans and vest; and when she reached for the butter to spread on her bread roll, Fry noticed that her fingernails were none too clean. She hoped the waiter didn't look too closely.

The waiter was making his way from the kitchen now. Fry didn't think he was Italian, more East European – perhaps an Albanian. But then, confit of duck wasn't an Italian dish either, was it?

'You never really want to talk,' said Angie, after they had been served.

Fry paused with a forkful of duck on the way to her mouth. 'Talk? We've talked a lot. Ever since you came to stay, we've done nothing but talk.'

'Do you think so, Diane?'

'I've told everything I've done since I saw you last.'

'Yes, I suppose that's true, in a way.'

'In a way? I've given you all fifteen years of it. I've told you what I did at school, how I managed to get my "A" levels and scraped a place at university to do my degree.'

'I liked the bit about you getting drunk at a student party and being sick into somebody's window box. I can't imagine you doing that, Sis.'

'I didn't do it often.'

'No, I bet you were a real hard worker. Studious.'

'I wanted to get an education.'

'This steak is nice,' said Angie. 'A bit underdone in the middle, but I don't mind a bit of blood. How's the duck?'

'Wonderful,' said Fry, putting her fork down. '*And* I told you about our parents coming to the graduation ceremony.'

'Our foster parents.'

'And how they got lost in Birmingham, so they arrived late.'

'And you didn't think anyone was coming, I know. If the duck's wonderful, why aren't you eating it?'

'Then I went back to Warley and joined the police.'

'Which is where you lose me a bit. You really *did* change somewhere along the way, didn't you, Sis?'

'It's an interesting job,' said Fry. 'Challenging.'

Angie nodded. She poured two more glasses of wine, but Diane ignored hers.

'And I told you about the incident – I mean, what happened to me in Birmingham . . .'

'Incident? That's a mealy-mouthed police word for it, if ever I heard one. You mean the rape.'

Fry looked around the restaurant. The other tables were a little too close for her liking. But the restaurant wasn't full on a Wednesday night, and there were no shocked expressions to deal with.

'Yes, I know all that,' said Angie. 'You told me.'

'Don't minimize the things that have happened in my life,' said Fry. 'Just don't.'

'I wouldn't.'

Angie took a drink of her wine. She smiled at a man a couple of tables away, causing his wife to glower back.

Fry hesitated, watching her sister, reminded again how much of a stranger she'd become. As children they had been so close that she felt she always knew what her sister was thinking. But not now.

'Is there something else you wanted to tell me about yourself?' she asked.

'Such as?'

'I don't know.' Fry speared the piece of duck again with her fork. She cut it into two, then cut it again into smaller pieces. 'I know about the heroin, of course.'

'I'm off it now. I had treatment. It's not an experience I recommend.'

'I'm pleased to hear it.'

'I'm sure you are.'

'And there was a man?'

Angie shrugged. 'Quite a few men. They come, and they go. There's always somebody else.'

Fry put her fork down with a clatter, tired of pretending to eat. Even the small piece of roast duck felt like dust in her mouth, and she had to force herself to swallow.

'So what then?' she said. 'What do you mean we haven't talked? I've told you everything. And you say you've told *me* everything – at least, everything that matters.'

Fry regretted sounding so abrupt. She could hear the tone of her voice echoing in the corner of the restaurant – the tone she used when she was irritated by one of her colleagues at work, when Ben Cooper or Gavin Murfin had been particularly annoying.

Angie's eyes clouded and she began to sit back in her chair as if withdrawing from contact with her sister, deliberately distancing herself from the moment. Diane leaned forward, reaching to touch her sister's hand, to prevent her from pulling away too far.

'Sis? What is it?'

But Angie was reluctant to speak now – afraid, perhaps, of people overhearing her, after all.

'We haven't talked about *before*,' she said.

Fry felt a chill go through her. For a moment, it was as if someone had opened a freezer cabinet door just behind her, loosing an icy draught that penetrated her shirt and raised goose pimples on her skin.

'Before?' she said. But she knew what Angie meant.

'What happened before I left home,' Angie said. 'What happened to me – and to you.'

Raymond Proctor opened the door to his office, and stopped. At first he thought one of the visitors from the caravan park had walked in of their own accord, taking liberties because he wasn't there to deal with them. What a bloody cheek, he thought. Here's some oik with a short

212

haircut sitting at my desk, bold as brass, as if he owns the place.

'What the hell –' he started to say.

Then his mouth hung open in mid-sentence as the figure at his desk turned, and he recognized the profile of a man he'd hoped never to see again.

'Hello, Ray.'

Mansell Quinn's face was wet. He'd come straight in from the rain, taking the trouble only to throw the hood of his waterproof back from his head. Water was running off him and gathering on the carpet around the chair he was sitting in. Proctor could see the drips from Quinn's sleeve landing on the polished mahogany of his desk.

'Aren't you going to say hello to an old friend?' said Quinn.

'Mansell –'

'Not going to ask how I am? Don't you want to know what I've been doing with myself all these years?'

Quinn smiled. Proctor felt a cold shudder go down his spine.

'You shouldn't be here,' he said feebly.

'Oh, and where should I be, Ray? Back inside?'

Proctor shut the door behind him nervously. He walked across the office and opened the inner door, which led into a short passage between the back door and the kitchen. He looked up and down the passage, listened for any noises, and closed the door again quietly.

He turned to find his visitor watching him with that same chilling smile.

'Why don't you make an effort, Ray?' he said. 'Why don't you tell me that I haven't changed much since you saw me last?'

'You haven't changed all that much,' said Proctor.

'Good. Because you've changed, Ray. I can see that you're not the man you were fourteen years ago. I wonder why that is?'

Proctor tried to speak, but found his mouth too dry. He went round his desk and fumbled in a bottom drawer. He produced half a bottle of malt whisky and a glass.

'Hospitality at last,' said Quinn. 'I take it you can run to two glasses?'

'Not without going to the kitchen.'

'And you don't want what's-her-name . . .'

'Connie.'

'And you don't want Connie to know you have a visitor? Pity. You looked as though you could have done with a drink.'

Proctor poured some whisky. His eyes met Quinn's and tried to hold his stare. Finally, he passed the glass across the desk, splashing the liquid on to the mahogany in his haste to get rid of it.

'You've got a bit nervy in your old age,' said Quinn, running a finger through the spilled whisky, creating a pattern on the polished surface with an air of concentration, as if it were the most important thing in the world. Proctor watched him, keeping the open bottle still in his hand, trying to gather the courage to speak. He noticed that Quinn was chewing something, his jaw muscles clenching as he bit on it with his back teeth.

'I don't want you here,' said Proctor. 'It's not right.'

Quinn stopped moving the amber drops of whisky and looked up. 'Not right, Ray?'

'It's not fair. We've got children in the house, you know.'

'Yes, I know. Not *your* children, though, Ray. They're what's-her-name's children.'

'Connie's. From a previous marriage. Two teenagers, Jason and Kelly.'

'From a previous marriage. Yes.'

'Mansell –'

'I used your bathroom, Ray. I hope you don't mind. I needed a wash and a shave, and there aren't many places I can get them.'

'God, how long have you been here?' said Proctor.

'A few minutes, that's all. The door was open.'

'Connie is bound to have heard you. But she probably thought it was me.'

'I didn't see her,' said Quinn. 'Pity. I don't get to talk to many people.'

Quinn smiled, and Proctor saw bits of brown seed stuck between his teeth.

'I used to be an outgoing sort of bloke,' said Quinn. 'Do you remember, Ray?'

'Yes.'

'Not now. Not any more. And you know something else, Ray? When you're in prison, you can't help thinking you'll be able to come out and go back to your life, and things will be exactly the same as they were before. No matter how many years have gone by in between, that's what you believe. It's something to hold on to, if nothing else.'

'Yes.'

'So I come back here, and Castleton looks pretty much the same. Except somebody else is living in my house. A complete stranger. It's bloody weird, Ray.'

'It must be.'

'And you. You married again.'

Proctor nodded. 'Yes.'

'Still trying to pass your genes on to a son then, Ray?'

Then Proctor heard an intake of breath. He turned to see Connie standing in the passage, staring through the doorway at Mansell Quinn. He was amazed that he hadn't heard the door open.

But Quinn didn't seem worried to see her. He even smiled as he raised the whisky to his lips.

'Who's he?' said Connie.

And Proctor remembered that she'd never seen Quinn before, that the man had never featured in her life the way he had in his. She would have seen the press photographs at the time of Carol's death, but Mansell Quinn had changed since then.

'I'm an old friend,' said Quinn.

Connie was no fool. She put two and two together quickly enough.

'Get rid of him, Ray,' she said. 'Then call the police.'

'That's not very hospitable,' said Quinn. 'You must be Connie.'

'Ray –'

But Proctor didn't move. He felt transfixed between the two of them.

'I'll phone the police myself,' said Connie, and began to turn to go back across the passage.

'No,' said Proctor. 'Leave it to me.'

'I won't have him in the house,' she said.

'Don't worry. He's just about to leave.'

Quinn raised an eyebrow, but he wasn't as self-confident since Connie appeared. He got up, letting more water drip from his smock where it had gathered in the creases. Connie continued to stare at him, as if trying to drive him towards the door with the strength of her will.

'Mansell, what are you going to do?' asked Proctor.

Quinn put his glass back on the desk. Proctor was surprised to see that his hand was shaking.

'Later, Ray,' said Quinn. 'I'll be seeing you later.'

'I don't want to talk about it,' said Diane Fry again as they came through the door of the flat.

'But, Di –'

'Angie, I don't want to talk about it. Not now. Maybe not ever.'

'But you must *think* about it sometimes? You can't wipe out memories completely.'

'I can try.'

Angie slumped on the settee while Diane hung her jacket carefully in the wardrobe.

'Is that why you're so obsessed with your job, so you

can keep the memories away?' called Angie from the sitting room.

'Me? I'm not obsessed with anything.'

Fry took off the alpaca top as well and folded it away. She found a T-shirt thrown over a chair and pulled that on instead. She immediately felt more comfortable, more ready to defend herself.

'Because I can relate to that, you know, Sis,' said Angie. 'That's what an addiction is all about, in the end.'

'What do you mean?'

'Like heroin. When you start using, it's all about the buzz you get at first. But after a while, you're using it to take the pain away.'

'I don't want to know this,' said Fry.

'The point is – that doesn't make a heroin user much different from anyone else, does it? We all need something to take the pain away now and then. Some of us need it more often than others, that's all.'

'There are better ways. Positive things that don't damage your body.'

Angie laughed. 'I bet you've never taken anything in your life, have you, Sis? Not even a puff of cannabis?'

Fry shook her head stiffly.

'God, I can't believe how straight you are.' said Angie. 'My little sister. It's a scream.'

'I'm glad you think I'm so funny.'

Angie's mood changed suddenly. 'Look, there's no need for you to get all snotty about it. I'm off the stuff, all right? I told you, I went through the whole detox business. Besides, don't you know that in hospitals they use heroin as a painkiller? Only they call it diamorphine, which makes it all right because it has a posh medical name. They even give it to mothers in childbirth. Hey, Sis, you could hang around the maternity ward and nick a few new mums. Earn yourself another promotion, why not?'

Fry stood. The conversation was making her too restless. She couldn't bear to sit still and listen to what her sister had to say.

'I'll make some coffee,' she said.

'Besides, it doesn't do the body much harm,' said Angie. 'Provided you're careful and don't do anything stupid like overdosing. You probably lose a bit of weight, you get a bit of a tendency to infections and stuff, that's all.'

Angie looked sideways at her sister, and Fry became conscious of her running nose and itching eyes. She popped a couple of tablets of Zirtek from their package.

'In your case, Cetirizine takes it away,' said Angie.

'Mmm?'

Fry went to the kitchen to make the coffee. She drank a glass of water and wiped her face on a piece of kitchen roll. Ceti-what? She looked at the box that her antihistamine tablets had come in. She had never read the ingredients before – why should she? But Angie was right. The active constituent of Zirtek was something called Cetirizine hydrochloride.

'So if it really doesn't do you any harm, why did you stop?' she said from the kitchen doorway.

Angie looked up. For a moment, she'd seemed to be about to fall asleep. But Fry couldn't let the subject go just yet.

'When you're single, skint, homeless and begging on the street, then you know it's time to stop,' said Angie. 'If you still have any sense left, that is. Then there's the wait for rehab. Nine months it was for me, even after I got the money together.'

'But you found a way to do it?'

'Sometimes, you'll do anything to find a way out. Anything.'

Late that night, Diane Fry woke with a jolt, sweating. She had been dreaming of the sound of a footstep on a creaking floorboard, a door opening in the darkness. Opening and

218

closing continually, but nothing coming through. She had been dreaming that she was frightened, yet had no clear focus for her fear. She heard the footstep, and the door opening, saw shadows sliding across the wall. Still nobody came in. She woke with a wail in her throat and the smell of shaving foam in her nostrils – a smell that always made her nauseous, even now.

It was the presence of her sister in the house that had caused the nightmare, and Angie's insistence on talking about their childhood. It had been a big risk, she knew. Just one sound, a single movement or a smell, could trigger the train of memory that stimulated her fear.

Angie herself had changed a lot in fifteen years, yet there was still the familiar rhythm in her speech, the faint buzz of a Black Country accent under the studied flatness from her time in Sheffield. And Fry couldn't avoid noticing a characteristic gesture, a tense lifting of the shoulders that she knew very well because she was aware of doing it herself.

Fry turned over and tried to go back to sleep. She heard the sound of voices on the street outside, two men arguing loudly, a girl shouting, but she ignored them. When she was off duty, she didn't feel any obligation to concern herself about the dangerous private lives of her neighbours.

When it had quietened down, all she could hear was the rain. It beat against her window in fat drops, hard and persistent. But her window was closed against the intrusion of pollen. So the rain couldn't get into her room, and not even the poisonous air could reach her.

21

Thursday, 15 July

At 15.40 hours on Monday, 9 October 1990 I attended an incident at number 82 Pindale Road, Castleton, following an emergency 999 call. At the time of the incident, I was on Uniformed Patrol with Constable 4623 Netherton in a liveried police vehicle.

I parked the vehicle in the entrance to the driveway of the property and PC Netherton and I went to the front door, which we found to be unlocked and partly open. I pushed the door open fully. I saw a hallway with four doorways leading from it. Two of the doors were open, but the hallway was empty. I shouted: 'Police! Who's in here?' There was no response. I moved further into the hallway and called again: 'Police! Is there anyone here?' An unidentified person said, 'In here.' I determined that the person was speaking from the second room on the right, where the door was open. I indicated to PC Netherton that he should wait in the hallway and I proceeded to enter the room, which transpired to be a sitting room. Inside, I saw a man who I knew to be the Defendant,

Mansell Quinn. He was in an armchair near the fireplace, about ten feet away on my left. He was sitting in a relaxed posture, slumped in the chair. I gained the impression that he had been asleep until woken by our arrival, and I could smell alcohol on his breath. Although I could not see a weapon in his possession, I knew it was possible that he was concealing one, either in the upholstery of the chair or under his clothing. Also, I noticed several heavy items within the Defendant's reach that might be employed as a weapon, including an iron poker which was in the fireplace. There were no other exits from the room apart from the doorway I was standing in.

When he saw me enter the room, the Defendant said, 'I don't know what the hell's happened here.'

Lying on the floor of the room was the body of a woman I now know to be Mrs Carol Proctor. There was a considerable quantity of blood around the body, and I noted a knife on the floor nearby. It was a large kitchen knife with a serrated edge. I formed the initial impression that Mrs Proctor was dead.

I summoned PC Netherton, who entered the room. I instructed him to observe the Defendant while I approached the body of Mrs Proctor and checked for signs of life. There were none. I then used my radio to summon assistance, whereupon the Defendant rose from his chair, as if to attempt to leave the room. I told him that I was placing him under arrest and I cautioned him, to which he made no reply. PC Netherton assisted me in handcuffing the Defendant, who offered no resistance.

PC Netherton then placed the Defendant in our vehicle, while I secured the scene and waited the arrival of Specialist Officers.

Signed: Police Sergeant 285 Cooper

221

Ben Cooper closed the file, and shuddered. It was as if the words on the page still carried the breath of the man who'd spoken them.

The file had been lying on his desk for almost two days, since DI Hitchens gave it to him on Tuesday. But his reluctance to read it had been justified. Even from a quick scan, it was clear that Sergeant Joe Cooper must have been alone at the scene of Carol Proctor's murder for a short time. There would have been a crucial gap, if only for a few minutes, between the prisoner being escorted to the police vehicle and the arrival of CID, scenes of crime officers, a medical examiner, and the whole paraphernalia.

Cooper knew from experience that once the mob descended on a murder scene, it could be chaos for a while. A lot depended on the officer who had taken responsibility for securing the scene. Any contamination that happened before that point couldn't be helped. But once the scene was secured, precautions were foremost in everyone's mind.

Though DNA would not have been foremost in the minds of the officers at a crime scene back in 1990, it would have been even less significant to the perpetrators. Back then, fingerprints would have been the main worry. Offenders wouldn't have thought twice about leaving other traces of themselves. Hence the high detection rate for cold cases – crimes that had lain on the files for years. It came as a shock to many criminals to find they could be connected to an offence they committed fifteen years ago.

Cooper looked again at the photographs of the Quinns' sitting room. If Quinn had maintained his innocence and persuaded somebody to take up his case, perhaps to pursue it as far as the Criminal Cases Review Commission, then evidence might have turned up to throw doubt on his conviction. Traces might have been found on the knife, on the victim's clothes, or on the Coke bottle standing on the table.

In fact, those traces might be found even now, if the evidence had been stored in the right conditions. But there had been no reason for anyone to doubt Quinn's conviction.

Cooper paused, and looked a bit more closely at the bottle. Who had been drinking from it? Had it been Mansell Quinn, who had allegedly had arrived home only a few minutes before becoming involved in a violent argument with the murder victim? Or Carol Proctor, who wasn't even in her own home but had let herself in with a spare key to surprise her lover?

Flicking through the files again, Cooper found an interview with Raymond Proctor. He'd answered questions the way a bereaved husband might be expected to: he seemed shocked, uncomprehending. He had no explanation for what had happened. He hadn't been aware that his wife had been conducting an affair with Mansell Quinn, though he admitted their marriage had been going through a rocky patch. Proctor told the interviewers he'd known Quinn for twenty years. They'd started work as labourers for a local building firm at the same time, straight from leaving school. The two had become close friends, drinking together regularly in the local pubs – no doubt before they were of legal age, though that went unsaid. Carol had been 'one of the crowd', a girl they'd both known but whom Raymond Proctor had later married. Quinn had agreed to be his best man, just as he had for William Thorpe.

Cooper skipped through the transcript to the afternoon of Carol Proctor's death. According to Proctor, he'd arranged to go for a drink in the Cheshire Cheese with Mansell Quinn and Will Thorpe, who was home on leave from the army. They'd drunk several pints of beer – Proctor couldn't remember how many rounds, but it was Thorpe they'd both been trying to keep up with. At some stage, Quinn had switched to single-malt whiskies.

It was difficult now to imagine the three men as they

would have been in their thirties. But Cooper suspected there might have been some tension in the group – perhaps between the experienced soldier, Will Thorpe, who had seen action in Northern Ireland by then, and the two older men, who had barely been outside Derbyshire. Usually, male friends drifted apart when their lives diverged to such an extent. Cooper wondered whether they'd have had much to talk about, or if there had been some kind of ritual element to the meeting, just something they'd always done and were still doing after twenty years. Maybe they'd been drinking quickly to numb the embarrassment, to overcome the feeling that they had nothing to say to each another.

Cooper wanted to know who had suggested the meeting, but it seemed that nobody in the interview room at West Street in 1990 had thought to ask Raymond Proctor. Of course, the interview had been approaching the crucial question by then. The times had been important, and the two detectives had probably spent a good deal of effort manoeuvring Raymond Proctor towards a statement that was as precise as it could be. Proctor claimed that Mansell Quinn had left the Cheshire Cheese first, at about ten to three, leaving Proctor and Thorpe together until chucking-out time – which meant they'd staggered out of the pub at around three-twenty, this being a Monday afternoon.

Cooper put the transcript down and picked up Thorpe's statement. It was a shorter document, referring mostly to the drinking session in the pub. Again, the interviewee had been questioned carefully on the time of Quinn's departure. Thorpe's story coincided with Raymond Proctor's to within a couple of minutes.

Despondent now, Cooper checked the statement list for an independent witness. The landlord of the Cheshire Cheese had been interviewed. He remembered all three of the men being in the bar that afternoon, but was unsure about the exact time they left, because the place had been busy. The only other thing he recalled was that the last round of drinks had been bought just before closing time by Raymond Proctor, and had consisted of two pints of beer. No malt whisky for Mansell Quinn, then.

Cooper sucked at his teeth. As evidence, it wasn't just peripheral but orbiting somewhere beyond Pluto. Quinn might still have been there, but falling behind his friends' consumption of alcohol. Besides, Proctor and Thorpe were the only sources for the claim that it was Quinn who'd been drinking whisky.

If the two men had conspired to concoct a story undermining Quinn's alibi, they'd been taking a big risk. The landlord might have remembered seeing Quinn, and so might some of the other customers. Assuming the enquiry team had taken the trouble to ask them, of course. But Quinn had presented himself as the obvious suspect. Why bother to put in unnecessary work on the case?

Cooper went back to Proctor's statement. The final thing to strike him was a question about the Quinns' house. Whatever the interview rules, detectives could still use a bit of misdirection – they could seem to be seeking information or assistance when actually they were considering someone as suspect. This seemed to be an example of that technique.

'Have you ever been inside the scene?' one of the interviewers had asked.

'The scene?' said Proctor.

'The house. Have you ever been inside the Quinns' house?'

'No, I haven't.'

And the line of questioning was left there. It was a straightforward enough question, but Cooper thought he could see what had been going on. Probably Proctor had been asked to give his fingerprints at a later stage, so that there seemed to be no direct link with the question. If his prints had matched any found at the scene, it would have proved him to be a liar and given the police a lever to use against him.

In this case, Cooper would have preferred the line of questioning to have been pursued, for the sake of preserving Proctor's answers for posterity – or at least, for the benefit of a detective constable thumbing over the files fourteen years later. It seemed unlikely that Proctor had never visited his old friend Mansell Quinn in his own home. The Quinns had been in the house on Pindale Road for five years, and the Proctors lived close by. Quinn and Proctor had been regular drinking partners throughout that time. If Proctor had really never been in the Quinns' house, then why not? Was it something to do with Rebecca Quinn? Cooper wondered if she might have had some objection to Quinn's friends. Maybe she'd already been aspiring to better things.

In any case, Cooper had to assume that Proctor's prints had not been found at the scene, because nothing more had been made of his claim.

Cooper put down the file with a sigh. There was no sense in looking for reasons to cast doubt on Mansell Quinn's guilt. Everyone else accepted it. In fact, it had been assumed from the start.

But then, Cooper had to keep reminding himself of one of the things that his father had told him: You should never assume. Never assume anything.

Diane Fry stared at the strip of orange-and-green paper that Ben Cooper was showing her. It was a train ticket. Anyone could see that.

'This is a Sportis travel ticket,' said Ben Cooper. 'Issued by First North Western on the Sheffield to Manchester line.'

'And the significance of it is . . . ?'

'See the code number? It splits down into sections. The first four numbers tally how many tickets a guard has sold, so they can calculate the takings at the end of a shift. The next set of numbers record where a customer went from and to. Look, these four numbers are the station code for the where the ticket is valid from – in this case, 2826 is Hathersage.'

'Right.'

'The next four numbers are the station code for where the ticket is valid *to*. This is 2828 – Hope. There's two numbers difference, you see – that's because there's only one station in between, Bamford.'

'And all the zeros at the end?'

'The routing code. Five zeros means any permitted route.'

'So can we tell whether he got a single or return?'

'First North Western say they can make an accurate guess.'

'Not good enough.'

'No, I know.'

'Would it make a difference?'

'Not really. It might have been one indicator of where he was heading afterwards, though.'

'Possibly.'

Cooper sighed. 'These people,' he said. 'They're a strange combination.'

'How so?'

'Rebecca Lowe and her family all seem a bit . . . well, middle class. It's hard to picture them in the same circles as the Proctors and the Thorpes.'

'People change. She may have moved on since Quinn was sent down. She got half of the proceeds of the sale of the business and the house. And her new husband was a part-ner in an estate agency. More than thirteen years, remem-ber – she probably has nothing in common with the Thorpes and Proctors any more. Except a past.'

'I phoned William Thorpe's father,' said Cooper. 'He lives at a farm over the Winnats Pass from Castleton. In the Peak Forest parish.'

Fry had been trying to write up a report on their visit to the Proctors' caravan park at Wingate Lees. She had a box of tissues open at her elbow, and her voice came out in a wheeze when she spoke.

'What did he say?'

'Not very much,' said Cooper.

'I take it his son isn't there with him?'

'Mr Thorpe says not. In fact, he was quite vehement about it. "I wouldn't have the bugger in my house" were the words he used. He says William isn't welcome there.'

'And he doesn't know where he might be?'

'No.'

Fry looked up. 'Did you believe him, Ben?'

'Yes, I did,' said Cooper without hesitation.

'OK. He might still be worth a visit. A surprise visit. Especially if he thinks he's convinced you.'

'Right.'

It was easy for Fry to suggest that old Jim Thorpe could have been lying. She hadn't been the one to speak to him. Cooper had flinched at the undisguised venom in the old man's voice when he talked about his son. 'I wouldn't have the bugger in my house' was only the half of it.

'What about the prison end, Diane?'

'Well, the most interesting interview I had was with Richard Wakelin. Or Rick, he prefers to be called. He's a convicted burglar, released from HMP Sudbury at the same time as Mansell Quinn. They walked out of the gate together. They were supposed to catch the bus together to Burton on Trent.'

'Supposed to? That sounds like the crucial phrase.'

'Quinn didn't get on the bus. But we figured that out, didn't we? The thing is, the two of them had never met before, but they did talk a bit on the way to the bus stop. Wakelin says that Quinn was in "a strange mood". Not as happy as you might expect someone to be who'd just been let out after a life sentence.'

Fry remembered how depressed she'd felt after her visit to the prison, and her walk through the smelly underpass to the bus shelter with the broken glass. Perhaps, after all, she *had* managed to catch a bit of what had been going through Quinn's mind.

'What about Quinn's visitors? Did he have any?'

'Official visitors,' said Fry. 'His probation officer, a solicitor.'

'No journalists, no campaigners for miscarriages of justice?'

'Not in Mansell Quinn's case. He wasn't of any interest to them.'

'Maybe he didn't want to be.'

Fry nodded. 'In fact, he had only one other visitor in the last couple of years while he was in Sudbury. But that one is of interest to us.'

'Someone we know?'

'Someone whose name we know, anyway: William Edward Thorpe.'

'Now, that *is* interesting.'

'Quinn managed to get in contact with Thorpe via their old regiment. Thorpe was still living with his friends in Derby at the time.'

'But he went AWOL shortly afterwards, didn't he?'

'Yes. Remember Thorpe's drunk-and-disorderly charge in Ashbourne? I pulled up the date, and it turns out the offence was committed on the same day as a visit to Quinn in Sudbury.'

'Even more interesting.'

'Oh, and I checked with the prison library,' said Fry.

'You did?' Cooper looked at her in surprise. 'That was my idea.'

'Yes. And it was a good idea, Ben.'

'Thank you.'

'Has your ego been massaged enough now? Would you like to know what I found out?'

'Sure.'

'It seems Quinn favoured books about caving, particularly the Castleton system.'

'Peak Cavern?'

'I guess so. His number one favourite was a book called *Death Underground*. Sounds like a barrel of laughs, doesn't it?'

'Have we found a copy?'

'Not yet. But we just had a call from a Mr Henry Marrison. Know him?'

'Never heard of him.'

'He works at Wingate Lees, the Proctors' caravan park.'

'Oh, the maintenance man?'

'That's him. He seems to have overheard some of what Mr Proctor told us yesterday.'

'I'll bet he did,' said Cooper.

'He says Will Thorpe was staying at the site much more recently than April. Up to last week, in fact. So that gives us another excuse to visit Mr Proctor, doesn't it?'

'I'm sure he'll be thrilled.'

They joined the rest of the team to watch the tape from the security camera at Out and About. Most of the officers watched in silence, squinting at the jerky footage.

When it was finished, Cooper asked for the tape to be rewound and played over again. He watched the assistant behind the counter look up and smile as a dark figure approached from the right of the camera. The time stamp showed that it had been 15.32. It must have been raining at the time, because Mansell Quinn was wearing a black slicker that glittered with drops of water in the grainy light. Cooper had seen plenty like it on sale in Out and About, but Quinn could have bought it in any one of a dozen places.

Cooper had no doubt that it was Quinn, even though they had only a profile view of him as he waited patiently for the assistant to run his purchases through the bar-code reader and ring up a sale on the till. Quinn had changed in appearance from the photographs they had of him, even the most recent. He was leaner and fitter, the planes of his face narrowing from his cheekbones to a strong jawline. He had short-cropped hair, grey at the temples now.

Even so, a side view of him on a poor-quality CCTV film might not have been enough for a positive ID. Cooper was waiting for the moment when Quinn paid with a couple of ten-pound notes, took his purchases and began to turn away from the counter. Then he paused fractionally and tilted his head in the direction of the camera. His eyes became visible then, just for a second. He wasn't looking straight at the lens, but slightly to the side, like a man gazing into the distance at a view that had just caught his attention. Then Quinn walked to the door of the shop, and was gone.

'Freeze that and print it,' said DI Hitchens. 'It's him.'

'No doubt about it,' said Diane Fry. 'The eyes are very distinctive.'

'What did he buy, Cooper?' said Hitchens. 'Do we know?'

'A self-inflating mattress in a stuff sack, and a bundle of light sticks.'

Hitchens stared at him. The DI wasn't the outdoors type, and some of the technical details baffled him.

'What does that mean?' he said.

'He's planning on sleeping rough somewhere.'

'No more nights at the Cheshire Cheese, then. Pity.'

'No. But I wonder how well Mansell Quinn knows the outdoor equipment shops in Hathersage,' said Cooper.

'Why?'

'Well, there are four or five of them. I'm wondering why he chose this one.'

'It was probably just the nearest. Or the biggest and busiest, so that he'd be less likely to be remembered.'

'But it was also one with a camera covering the till.'

'He just didn't notice the camera, that's all,' said Fry. 'Most people don't.'

Cooper froze the tape and played back the short section where Quinn took his purchases and turned away from the counter. There was that slight tilt of the head towards the screen, only a subtle gesture, almost unnoticeable. To

231

Cooper, it seemed like the nod of an actor acknowledging his audience.

But that could have been just his imagination. It could have been because Cooper thought he'd seen Mansell Quinn before. Less than two days ago.

22

At fifty, Raymond Proctor was older than either Quinn or Thorpe. And Ben Cooper found himself thinking of the caravan park owner as the most tired and demoralized of the three men. He wasn't sure why this was – Proctor was happily married, and the big trauma in his life had happened fourteen years ago. He ought to have put it all behind him by now.

'Mr Proctor, with your permission, we'd like to have a look inside some of your caravans,' said Diane Fry when they found him in the office at Wingate Lees.

Proctor stood up, immediately aggressive.

'You can't do that,' he said. 'They're occupied. I've got visitors in them. I can't let the police go ferreting around in their property while they're out. What do you think it would do to my business? And what are you looking for, anyway?'

'We're looking for your old friend William Thorpe,' said Fry. 'And we don't want to look in the occupied units, just the old 'vans down at the far end.'

'Those? They're empty.'

'We'd like to check, if you don't mind.'

Proctor sighed heavily, and made a great performance of opening and shutting drawers, then sorting out the right keys from the neat rows of hooks on the wall behind his desk.

'I'll have to come with you.'

'Fine.'

They followed him through the site, past the trees and the pond.

'Do they *look* occupied?' said Proctor, gesturing at the caravans.

'No, they don't. That's the point.'

'Oh, so you think it's all a clever plot to fool you, do you? What do you reckon I'm doing – running an international drugs operation from a two-berth caravan?'

'Stranger things have been known.'

'Not in the Hope Valley, they haven't.'

Proctor poked a key into the door of the first caravan, rattled it without any result, and had to try another one before he got the door open. He cursed continuously as he did it.

Fry and Cooper exchanged a glance. Proctor was making far more noise than necessary. Was it merely a gesture of irritation, a bit of reassurance for himself? Or a warning to someone?

'Look – there's nobody in them,' said Proctor, flinging open the door.

Fry peered in. 'Nobody in this one, perhaps.'

'What?'

'We'd like to see inside them all.'

'You're joking.'

She pointed at the next 'van. 'Mr Proctor, if you don't mind . . .'

'For God's sake. What a waste of time.'

The interior of the second caravan smelled mouldy and stale. A bad leak in a corner of the roof had stained the ceiling brown and one of the panels was peeling away.

'Who lives here?' asked Cooper.

'No one. Well, no one at the moment.'

'Someone has been living here recently. There's used bedding, and some cutlery in the sink.'

234

'They were Iraqi refugees.'

'What happened to them?'

'As far as I know, they went back to Iraq.'

'They left some of their belongings behind,' said Cooper, looking at a pair of old shoes and a portable TV set.

'Probably they didn't want to cart the stuff all the way to Baghdad.'

'Really?'

Cooper looked at Proctor. His story was almost possible. Refugees and asylum seekers turned up in the most surprising places.

'Mr Proctor, you told us that William Thorpe left the caravan site at the end of April, because you needed the caravan for the tourist season.'

'Yes.'

'But that wasn't right, was it? We believe that William Thorpe was still living here much later than the end of April.'

Proctor shrugged. 'All right, I felt for sorry for him. Like you said, he didn't have anywhere to go. He asked me for a few more weeks.'

'And you didn't have any bookings?'

'Bookings have been a bit quiet this season. They were quiet last season, too. They've been bloody quiet ever since the foot and mouth thing.'

'So it wasn't a problem for you to have Thorpe staying in the caravan a bit longer?'

'I wouldn't say that. Will got to be a nuisance after a while. I had the paying customers to think of. Business is bad enough, without having someone like Will around the place, scaring them off.'

'Why didn't you tell us this before, sir?'

'I thought he might be in trouble.'

'Perhaps he is.'

'Well, there's the question of loyalty, you know.'

'Oh, suddenly there's a question of loyalty, is there?'

Proctor glowered and began to turn away.

'Was there some particular incident that brought matters to a head?' asked Fry.

'Yes, there was. It was the last straw. I told him, "Will, I've done what I can for you, but I can't do any more. You're going to have to go."'

'What happened exactly?'

'Some fool gave him money. I don't know whether Will had been in the village begging from the tourists, or if he'd nicked it, but he used the money to buy booze and he got himself totally pissed. He was going round banging on all the caravan doors wanting people to let him in so they could have a party. I've never had so many complaints as I did that night. We had kids crying, and half the men threatening to punch his lights out. There were two women staying in one of the Westmorlands. They never said a word at the time, but they upped and left first thing next morning. Good customers lost.'

It was the longest speech they'd heard from Raymond Proctor. He had become a bit red in the face as he spoke, and his voice had grown louder.

'I'm sure you can't afford to lose business,' said Cooper.

'Damn right I can't. Do you know how difficult it is to make enough profit in this business to keep that lot in the house in food and clothes, let alone the bills I have to pay? And I'm here at every silly bugger's beck and call, all hours of the day and night. It's a mug's game, mate.'

'All right, Mr Proctor. Calm down.'

Proctor glared at him. 'Somebody else should be looking after Will Thorpe, not me. By rights, he should be in hospital. But he's such an awkward bugger, he'd never agree to that. That's why he steers clear of Social Services and all those kind of folk. He's terrified they'll put him away in a hospital and he'll never come out again. Will has set his mind on dying in the open air, and that's what he'll do, no doubt. It won't take much longer, either. Another bad winter, and that'll be the end of him.'

'What exactly is wrong with Mr Thorpe?'

'He has emphysema. It was diagnosed while he was still in the army. Too many cigarettes from too young an age, I suppose.'

'Nobody can do anything to help him unless we find him,' said Fry.

Proctor shrugged. 'Try near the cement works. God knows why, but he hangs out up there.'

Fry nodded to Cooper, and they turned to go. Proctor watched them, clearing his throat and rattling his keys nervously. He caught Fry's eye for a second.

'I hope you haven't forgotten our advice about taking precautions,' said Fry.

'I told you, I'm not frightened,' said Proctor. 'Not of Mansell Quinn. I'm ready for anyone.'

'You don't happen to have any unauthorized weapons on the premises, do you, sir?'

Proctor instantly looked capable of being belligerent again.

'Oh, this is a different tune now,' he said. 'Well, don't worry your head about that. I know all about what happens to people who try to defend themselves. Don't we all?'

As they reached the car, Cooper looked up at the railway bridge and the embankment rising over the caravan park. The bridge had stones missing here and there, and thick clumps of weed grew on the parapet. It would be impossible to see if anyone was up there, unless they wanted to be seen. Cooper suddenly felt very vulnerable standing under such a perfect vantage point.

Fry followed his gaze. 'Personally, I don't think Quinn will still be in this area. He's miles away by now. He has a head start on us.'

'Where would he be going?'

237

'I've no idea. But he'd want to get some distance away from here, wouldn't he?'

'Only if he'd done what he came to do.'

'Which he has, hasn't he?'

Cooper felt the back of his neck prickle. He turned away from the viaduct. Trees and dense undergrowth climbed the banking behind the Proctors' house. It was dark in there, even in the middle of the day. No sunlight penetrated the canopy. The ground would be dry and covered in dead leaves, an ideal place to lie in the shade, unseen, and watch what was going on down in the caravan park. But surely it must only be his imagination that made him feel as though he was being watched?

When Ben Cooper drove to the gate of the cement works, he was seeing it up close for the first time. The entire place was the colour of cement – pale, like a desert landscape. The girders and aerial conveyor belts, towers and silos, hangars and concrete tanks all blended into each other as if camouflaged. Above them rose the tall chimney that was visible from both ends of the valley. To the south, a huge fan of quarries had been blasted into the hillside. On the map, the cement works and its quarries looked as big as Hathersage, Hope and Castleton all lumped together.

He met Diane Fry and Gavin Murfin in a lay-by near the bridge. Another team of officers were on the older part of the site to the east, where exhausted quarries had been landscaped with trees and fishing lakes.

Murfin had been gathering information on William Thorpe, and he seemed to have brought it all with him. Thorpe had served in the local regiment, the First Battalion of the Worcestershire and Sherwood Foresters Regiment, referred to in the army documents as 1WFR.

'Join the army and see the world,' said Murfin. 'According to the Regimental HQ in Nottingham, this battalion has spent the last few years serving everywhere from the Falkland Islands to Sierra Leone and Brunei. Me, I joined the police, and all I've seen is a selection of the worst shit-holes in Derbyshire.'

'They wouldn't have taken you in the army,' said Fry.

'You're right. I had too many GCSEs. It seems you're over-qualified for the infantry if you can spell your name on the application form.'

'So where's the battalion now?' said Cooper.

'Back in their barracks after a spell in Northern Ireland. Did you know the squaddies get nine weeks leave and four long weekends a year? And the army pays to get them home, too.'

'Nine weeks? So where did William Thorpe go all those times when he was on leave? He didn't come home to Derbyshire – not to his dad's place, anyway.'

'Are you thinking of a change in career, Gavin?' asked Fry hopefully, looking at Murfin's copy of the army recruitment booklet.

'I'm just amazed,' he said. 'Amazed how easy it is to get into the army. You don't need any educational qualifications at all. You take an entrance test, but they give you a practice book beforehand, and you can have three goes at passing it. How difficult can that be?'

'Well, I suppose you don't have to be a genius to be a soldier. As long as you can fire an automatic weapon in the right direction.'

'It says here Thorpe was in a mortar platoon.'

Cooper picked up Thorpe's file and looked at the photos of him. The ex-soldier wasn't a big man physically – only five feet six inches tall. As a recruit to the Worcestershire and Sherwood Foresters, he must have been one of those soldiers who looked out of place marching in the ranks, with the peak of his cap a few inches below those of the men on either side.

But a photograph of him in a T-shirt suggested he must have spent time working out in the gym to make up for his lack of size. He would already have been in his forties when the photo

239

was taken, but the muscles in his shoulders and upper arms were still firm, though the flesh was receding a little from his cheekbones, giving his face a sharp look, like an old dog fox.

In the picture, Thorpe wore a black beret at a jaunty angle, and his face was tanned. The narrowing of his eyes as he stared at the camera hinted at hostility. Cooper thought it might simply be a result of living outdoors, a physical reaction against exposure to wind and sunlight, or an effort to keep out the fine, hot sand that filled the desert air. But there could also have been a trace of ingrained suspicion, a need to be aware of dangers approaching from a distance.

Cooper passed the photograph back. 'When was he discharged, Gavin?'

'Nine months ago. The army says he was a good soldier. A sound record, and all that.'

'He served in several hotspots, I see.'

'That's not so unusual these days,' said Fry. 'The time is long past when British soldiers could look forward to spending their service careers idling around in Germany or Cyprus. They have to go out and get shot at on peacekeeping missions.'

'You're just trying to put me off,' said Murfin.

'He was in Northern Ireland in the eighties. Kuwait and Iraq during the first Gulf War; Bosnia, too. Did he see much action?' asked Cooper.

'I don't know. They won't give us that sort of information.'

'I was just thinking a few survival skills would help him.'

Fry shook her head. 'Lots of people claim to have been in the SAS, but very few actually were. Even fewer ever talk about it, and the ones that do tend to write books. But we'll check, anyway.'

A railway engine went past on the cement works spur, pulling a line of dirty white tankers over the bridge.

Fry gazed at the works. 'This place is pretty big,' she said. 'What's it doing here? How come the environment lobby didn't stop it?'

240

'It was here before the national park,' said Cooper. 'Besides, it employs a lot of local people.'

'A bit of the real world, eh?'

Cooper was sent to follow the public footpath that ran alongside the works fence and skirted the hillside hollowed out by quarrying operations. The whole scene was coloured a drab cement grey, but for red doors among the buildings and the occasional worker in orange overalls.

Against a continuous background roar and rumble, he heard the squeal of some kind of machinery operating on the spoil heap at the edge of the quarry. Down in the centre of the works, he saw a slowly rotating metal tube about two hundred yards long, its end disappearing into one of the buildings. Cement several inches thick lay encrusted on pipes, like ice formed on the masts of an Arctic exploration ship. Sirens sounded now and then, but not the one like an air-raid warning he'd heard from Peveril Castle.

The path crossed the tracks to the quarry itself, and conveyor belts rattled through a runway over his head. A vast hunk of machinery passed him on one of the tracks. He had to step aside and cling precariously to the banking in order to avoid its tyres, which only just fit into the width of the track.

Then he found an abandoned concrete building. Its walls were broken and its steel reinforcements were exposed. It lay half-buried in a mountain of limestone chippings, like a bombed bunker.

After only a few minutes in the vicinity of the cement works, Cooper's mouth was starting to feel dry. His tongue was coated with dust, and he could taste nothing but limestone. Soon, he was having difficulty swallowing.

Cooper looked down at the ground. The bottom inch of his boots had turned white with cement dust. When he stamped his feet, the dust flew off them in clouds.

Diane Fry was standing on the grass in the middle of the

241

works compound while a worker in orange overalls and a white helmet pointed out where he'd seen Thorpe. The strange structure of the pre-heater building towered above them, and the long metal tube of the kiln rumbled behind them as it rotated slowly.

A marked police car pulled into the works entrance. Back-up. If Thorpe was around here and saw that, he'd be away.

Cooper came to a point where three dirt tracks met just beyond the fence, and he stopped underneath the runway of the conveyor belt and a cement-encrusted pipe. Two uniformed officers were making their way up the path from the road, puffing a bit on the steeper stretches.

'Some of these buildings near the fence are empty,' said Fry. 'They don't look as though they're used for anything. And there isn't even a door on this one – anybody could walk in.'

'We'll have to check them, I suppose.'

Cooper recalled the abandoned building outside the fence, half buried in waste limestone. No one could be desperate enough to try living rough in something that looked like a bombed-out bunker. But as a temporary refuge, it would do fine.

While Fry directed the two PCs, Cooper walked a few yards further along the path. He thought the building had been under the gantries carrying the conveyor-belt mechanism, where the limestone came down from the rock crushers. At first, he couldn't see it. His eyes had become too used to seeing everything in the same shade of cement grey. But the broken walls and exposed steel reinforcements gradually emerged from the dusty background.

Cooper stepped on to the unstable heap of limestone chippings, his boots crunching as if he was walking on a shingle beach. He stopped, and looked back to see where Fry had got to. She was still some way down the track, and he ought to wait for her to catch him up.

The continuous roar and rumble from the works and the

242

squeal of machinery above him on the edge of the quarry made it difficult for Cooper to hear much else. But he heard the cough quite clearly.

He peered through an empty and broken window into the darkness of the building, squinting to adjust his vision from the glare of the sun on the limestone. He felt as though he was staring deep into the hillside, though the building couldn't have been more than a few yards across. It was a wheeze of breath that gave him a fix on what he was looking for, and a pair of startled eyes came suddenly into focus.

Then somebody was running. A figure had burst out of the doorway of the building, ten feet up the right-hand track. Cooper tried to turn too quickly, and found himself slithering on the heap of limestone, with his feet sinking in as he threw out an arm to support himself, sending up a cloud of white dust.

'Diane!' he called. 'Up here!'

But Fry had already seen what was happening.

'Don't let him get away,' she shouted.

Cooper slid to the bottom of the limestone, scraping his hand on a protruding piece of reinforced concrete, and began to run up the track. The figure ahead of him was dressed in a dirty khaki anorak and baggy blue jeans, with greying hair that hung over his collar. Cooper felt sure it was William Thorpe. And this time, Thorpe wasn't going to get very far. He had chosen to escape along the dirt track that led uphill towards the edge of the quarry, and he clearly wasn't a fit man. Within seconds, he was starting to flag. Instead of running on his toes, he was kicking clouds of dust into Cooper's face with his heels.

In another moment, Cooper would have caught up with him. But then the ground began to shake, and a rumbling noise hit them as a dump truck came round a bend of the track and started to descend the slope towards them.

Thorpe stumbled and froze. He looked tiny and helpless

as he stood outlined against the massive snout of the truck. Its tyres came almost to head height, and it left barely two inches of clearance on either side of the track – nowhere near enough to fit a human body. If Thorpe tried to go to the side, the wheels would crush him against the dirt wall. And a thing that size wasn't going to stop too quickly coming down a steep slope.

Then Cooper had reached Thorpe. Grabbing his anorak from behind, he pulled him to the side and began to drag him bodily up the banking into the trees. Thorpe was lighter than he looked, but Cooper was unable to keep his footing and had to lie down in the dusty earth and brace himself against the root of a tree to get Thorpe clear.

He became aware of the dump truck grinding to halt, and saw Fry standing in front of it on the track, waving her arms like a traffic policeman. Thankfully, Thorpe was lying still. He was breathing with difficulty and felt like a dead weight.

Cooper's mouth was full of dust. It blocked his saliva glands and stuck to the back of his throat like a coating of pebble dash. He was having real difficulty swallowing now. In fact, he didn't *want* to swallow for fear of layering his stomach with an indigestible skin of limestone.

Fry helped him to get Thorpe down from the banking.

'Come along, sir,' she said. 'All we want to do is talk to you.'

Back on the ground, Cooper looked down at himself. Earlier, the bottom inch of his boots had been white with cement dust. Now, his trousers were covered with it right up to his belt. No doubt it was on his back, too. He brushed at himself, but only added more dust to the air around him. He wondered if he could manage not to breathe until he got back to the car.

23

Mansell Quinn leaned his head against the wall and stared at the ceiling. He was sitting in one of the cubicles at the men's toilets in the main Castleton car park. He'd managed to get a wash, and had even shaved himself as he sat in the cubicle, using the safety razor and mirror he'd brought with him from prison. Looking grubby would draw too much attention.

The car park had two blocks of toilets, so there were plenty of cubicles for the people he could hear coming in and out. No one would trouble him for some time, unless a cleaner came by later in the day. He'd seen police walking the streets in Castleton, mingling with the visitors, wanting to be noticed in their yellow reflective jackets. For now, the car park was the safest place for him to be. Though it was right in the centre of Castleton, the only people around were tourists. They'd stay in town for a few hours, thinking of nothing but visiting the caverns, or the castle or the gift shops, and having lunch in one of the pubs. And then they would leave again, off to their homes miles away. They wouldn't know Mansell Quinn, or even be familiar with the name. As far as they were concerned, he was just one more person with a rucksack among hundreds.

But Quinn had picked up a copy of a Sheffield newspaper that somebody had left in the bin outside. When he unfolded it, his own photograph had jumped out at him. He'd known it would happen, and that wasn't a problem. It was the picture of Rebecca that had hit him hardest. He hardly dared to read the story that went with it.

The door of the toilets banged open, and he heard the voices of two or three boys entering and using the urinals. Quinn thrust his hands into the pockets of his waterproof and kept quite still. His fingers found some of the seedheads he'd pulled from the long grass growing near the river. He waited until he heard the taps running and the hand driers blowing before he took one out and chewed it. He'd found it gave him a bit of comfort. It produced a little surge of satisfaction as his teeth bit down on the hard kernel, cracking it with a tiny explosion in his jaw.

Quinn was trying to hold in the rage, the way he'd been taught on the anger-management course. He knew that if he let it out, it would burst from his mouth like fire. With an effort, he forced it to disperse through his body. He could feel it seething in his guts and seeping out through the pores of his skin, until it seemed to shimmer around him in the cubicle like an aura. By the time the anger had died down, he was hot and sweating, and his palms left wet marks on the walls when he steadied himself to stand up. Finally, he dared to release a breath.

There had been times in the last thirteen years when illogical things had made Quinn angry. Before Sudbury, he had been in HMP Gartree in Leicestershire, a place that reminded him of a 1960s comprehensive school. There hadn't even been any bus services; a prison minivan ran visitors from the railway station at weekends, but not during the week, and taxis were far too expensive. Not that he had any visitors by then. Quinn had already seen the last of his children.

But there had been a visitor centre located by the main

gate at Gartree, with a play area and baby-changing facilities. Two afternoons a week, volunteers had run a children's corner there. Perhaps it made some of the lifers feel better, but for Quinn the thought of children playing near the main gate made everything seem so much worse.

He listened carefully, checking that the toilets were empty, then came out of his cubicle. He spat out the stalk from the grass seed, and took a last look at himself in the mirror over the washbasin.

Quinn had learned more from the anger management course than the prison authorities would ever realize. He'd learned to recognize anger and channel it. He'd learned that it could be used. And he'd discovered that anger could give you strength.

With a shrug, Quinn shook out his waterproof smock and put it back on. And then he went out into the rain that he could hear falling on Castleton.

24

William Thorpe sat in one of the interview rooms at West Street with his elbows on the table and his head drooping, as if his neck didn't have the strength to hold it up.

'You've no reason to keep me here,' he said.

'We just want to ask you a few questions, sir.'

'I've done nothing.'

Diane Fry consulted the file she had on William Edward Thorpe. She took a few moments over it, frowning a little, before she looked at Thorpe again. Watching her, Ben Cooper wondered if Fry had considered getting herself a pair of half-moon glasses, which would have completed the effect of a disapproving headmistress.

'You're here voluntarily, sir,' said Fry. 'You're free to leave at any time. But if we don't clear up a few things now, we may have to talk to you again in the near future. And if the matter becomes more urgent, we might not have time for all the courtesies.'

Thorpe was thinking about it. For a moment, Cooper thought he was going to get up and walk out. Fry wasn't even watching him, but had dropped her head to read the papers in front of her, as if it was of no concern to her whether Thorpe stayed or left, since she had plenty of other things to do. But Thorpe had understood what she was saying. He was free to leave now because he was co-operating voluntarily. If they had to pick him up a second time, it might not be so voluntary.

'I'm not sure what you want to know,' he said.

Fry looked up, as if slightly surprised that Thorpe was still there. She smiled.

'Well, let's see what we can do about that, sir.'

Cooper thought that Thorpe's eyes had the pale, watery look of someone who never slept enough. They were deep in their sockets, and looked even deeper because of the dark shadows that lay on his cheekbones and underneath his eyebrows. His cheeks were covered in grey stubble that accentuated their sunkenness.

'Mr Thorpe, you were discharged from the Worcestershire and Sherwood Foresters Regiment nearly a year ago,' said Fry.

'That's right.'

'A medical problem, I gather.'

'My time was almost up,' said Thorpe.

'Even so, you left the army before your discharge date.'

'A few months, that's all.'

'They don't tell us what the medical problem was,' said Fry, raising her eyebrows and turning over a page as if to look for a medical report she knew wasn't there.

Thorpe said nothing.

'Nothing to be ashamed of it, is it?' asked Fry.

'I was diagnosed with emphysema.'

'Oh, I'm sorry.'

'My lungs are shit.'

'So you left your regiment a few months early. And you went to live at an address in Derby, according to your regimental office.'

'That's right. With a friend.'

'You didn't come home to this area straight away?'

249

'I had no reason to, did I?' Thorpe shook his head. 'I still don't know what you want from me.'

'Let's come forward a bit, then. You left the address in Derby. After that, your life is something of a mystery. Your regiment has no further record of you. No one seems to know where you were . . .'

'Well . . .'

'Except,' said Fry, 'for a drunk and disorderly charge in Ashbourne in May this year.'

'Oh, that.'

'What were you doing in Ashbourne, sir?'

'Getting pissed,' said Thorpe. 'Obviously.'

'Do you have more friends in that area?'

'I might have.'

'Staying with them, were you? I mean, I know old friends look after each other – especially army mates. They're the sort of people you can call on when you need help, aren't they?'

'Yes, they are.'

'So, were you staying with a friend in Ashbourne?'

'I'm not telling you about any of my friends.'

'Well, if you were,' said Fry, checking her file, 'it's odd that you were listed as "no fixed abode" when you appeared in the magistrates court there for your drunk and disorderly. Was that a lie?'

'I've spent some time on the streets,' said Thorpe. 'I'm not ashamed of it. It just happened. Sometimes, your circumstances change, you know.'

'What circumstances would those be?'

'Look, I stayed with some mates in Derby when I came out of the army, you know that. The doctors had told me I was a mess. I felt really pissed off that I'd spent all that time to reach my discharge date, and then suddenly there was no future for me.'

'Had you planned a future after the army? I presume you must have. You knew your discharge was approaching.'

'I thought of setting up a little business,' said Thorpe. 'A shop.'

'Anything in particular?'

'Weapons. Only legal stuff, obviously. Air rifles, slingshots, crossbows, samurai swords. That sort of stuff.'

'Samurai swords?'

'There's a lot of demand. And I know about weapons.'

'Do you, indeed?'

'It was my main interest,' said Thorpe. 'In the army, I mean.'

'But according to your regiment, you spent most of your time as a mortar man.'

'I was an infantryman in the beginning, same as everyone else. Then I got into a mortar unit. You have to know about weapons. I mean, that's what it's all about.'

'I don't know much about mortars,' said Fry. 'But I've a feeling they're a bit different from Samurai swords. A bit more twenty-first century.'

'I can learn. I knew blokes who collected stuff like that. Two of my friends in Derby were going to come into the business with me. We were going to use the money we'd saved to start up a shop.'

'So what went wrong, Mr Thorpe?'

'Like I told you, it was the illness. It knocked the stuffing out of me at first and I couldn't see the future any more. There just didn't seem any point in putting all that work into starting a business. I'd never have seen any of the profit. That's the way it looked at the time.'

'I understand.'

Thorpe sneered. 'Do you?'

Cooper could see that Thorpe was gaining more confidence as he talked. But that wasn't a bad thing – at least he was talking. It was a sign that he felt on safe ground.

'So you parted ways with your friends in Derby?'

Thorpe hesitated. 'Yeah.'

'Was there some kind of problem?'

'No.'

'It would be understandable if they were unhappy with your decision. Did they go ahead on the shop idea without you?'

'I don't know.'

'Mr Thorpe, we do have the address you gave in Derby at the time, so we can always go and ask them.'

Thorpe shook his head. 'I left, that was all. I got on a bus and came back here. I knew there'd be plenty of places I could sleep and not be worried about people getting up close to me like they did in the city.'

'OK. And then what?'

'And then nothing,' said Thorpe. 'That's pretty much my life. I'm just hanging around waiting for it to finish. I'll be glad when it's over, to be honest.'

'Where were you sleeping rough before Raymond Proctor let you use one of his caravans?'

'Bus shelters are a good place. No one uses them after the buses stop running at night. And around here, field barns. A lot of them are abandoned now.'

'But you did decide to look up other old friends, didn't you?' said Fry.

'What?'

'I'm sure that's what I would do, in the circumstances.'

Now Thorpe had started to look uncomfortable. 'What old friends?'

'There must be some that you'd like to tell us about.'

Thorpe could sense that they had reached dangerous ground. His eyes flickered to the door of the interview room.

Fry didn't need to look at her file for the next question.

'For example,' she said, 'in April you visited your old friend Mansell Quinn. Twice.'

'Oh.'

'Now, that might be something that you would forget about, Mr Thorpe, given the exciting and varied life that

252

you've led. But I imagine those two visits were very memorable indeed to your friend Quinn. After all, you were the first person to visit him in years.'

'That's what people do,' said Thorpe. 'Visit old friends. If you're really nice to me, I'll even visit *you* in prison, when you get sent down for harassing innocent citizens.'

'That's very kind of you. I'm sure it would make it all worthwhile. If I ever found an innocent citizen to harass.'

'Ha, ha.'

'Mansell Quinn,' said Cooper, 'what was the purpose of your visit to him in prison?'

'To say "hi". To see how he was keeping. To take him a birthday present. For God's sake, I hadn't seen the bloke for years.'

'OK,' said Fry. 'You went the first time to say "hi". You saw how he was. So what about the second visit? Was his birthday present the wrong size? Maybe he wanted you to change it for him?'

'Get lost.'

'You see, Mr Thorpe, we think that your friend Mansell Quinn asked you to do something for him.'

Thorpe began to cough, and suddenly looked weaker.

'And what if he did?'

'We think that you gave him some addresses.'

'There was no harm in that.'

'No harm?'

'Well, no.'

Cooper looked at Fry, who raised her shoulders in a gesture that said: 'He's nuts' or possibly, 'Don't ask me, I can't make sense of this either.'

Thorpe was watching their faces. He was starting to look puzzled, too.

'It was only some addresses, so that Mansell could get ready for coming out. He said the prison and the probation wouldn't give him any information.'

'Mr Thorpe, where have you been living for the past few days?'

'What's that got to do with it?'

He was even more confused now. Cautiously, Thorpe looked from Fry to Cooper, sensing that there was something he didn't know. Something bad. The anxiety was plain on his face. And they could hear the wheezing in his chest as his breathing grew laboured.

'I told him,' he said. 'I told Mansell that people who've made a new life should be left alone and allowed to get on with it.'

'He didn't take much notice, then.'

'What's happened?' said Thorpe.

Fry didn't answer the question directly. 'Mr Thorpe, did you give Mansell Quinn his wife's new address?'

'OK, I did.'

'And are you telling us that you don't know why Quinn wanted her address?'

Thorpe stared at Fry, slowly trying to work out the implications. 'Rebecca? What's happened to her?'

'Rebecca Lowe is dead, Mr Thorpe. She was killed.'

Thorpe shook his head, denying the conclusion he'd come to.

'Who killed her?'

But no one answered that. And the question hung in the air of the interview room like the sound of William Thorpe's breathing as he gasped to force oxygen into his damaged lungs.

Several drunks had been brought into the custody suite an hour before. They were waiting for the doctor to examine them for any medical problems, or for injuries they might have sustained while being arrested. A pool of urine was running under the door of one of the cells into the passage. One of the drunks either couldn't find the lavatory, or was doing it deliberately.

'I'll have to translate for the doctor when she arrives, too,' said the custody sergeant.

254

'Why? Are the drunks foreign?'

'No, but the doctor we have on duty today is a bit middle-aged and middle class, if you know what I mean. If a prisoner is under twenty-five, she has no idea what they're on about, even when they're sober. Especially if they start telling her the street names for the drugs they're on.'

Cooper could hear the doctor now, talking to a prisoner. Her voice was loud enough to carry down the passage.

'Are you injecting? Which part of your body are you using?'

'Here.'

'Your groin. That's your groin you're pointing at. Well, I can see why you're not using your arms any more. There's nothing left of them, is there?'

The custody sergeant gave a despairing shrug that involved his whole body.

'We haven't been able to find any accommodation for your Mr Thorpe,' he said. 'There aren't many places round here, as you know, and they're all full.'

'We can't just turn him out on to the streets again,' said Cooper.

'We can't keep him here either. Unless you're thinking of charging him with something.'

'No.'

'Well, we're running out of options. I wanted to get the doctor to take a look at him, because he's obviously ill. But Thorpe won't have it, and I can't force him. He knows perfectly well he'd end up in a hospital.'

'Wait a minute,' said Cooper. 'I know someone who might take Mr Thorpe in for a while.'

'Do you? He says his only relative is his father, who doesn't want to know him.'

'No, not his father. A friend who's taken him in before.'

'I'll leave it with you for a bit, then,' said the sergeant. 'But he'll have to be out of here before long, mind.'

* * *

255

Cooper held the phone to his ear with one hand while he tried to sort out the paperwork on his desk with the other. He had a system of wire trays that were supposed to help him keep order. But he didn't really need the 'in' and 'out' trays. Just one very large one marked 'pending' would have been enough.

'No,' said the voice at the other end of the line.

'Mr Proctor, I hope you'll reconsider,' said Cooper. 'You said you couldn't let Will Thorpe stay there in the summer because the site fills up with paying customers, but those old caravans are just standing empty. What would be the problem in letting Mr Thorpe stay in one of those for a while longer?'

'I don't see why I should,' said Proctor. 'He's not my responsibility.'

'He has nowhere else to go. He'll be out on the streets again very soon, and he might be at risk.'

'You know he caused trouble with my customers when he was here before?'

'Yes, but this will only be for a night or two, until we can find somewhere more permanent.'

Proctor was silent for a moment. 'Does Will know about Mansell Quinn and all that?'

'Yes, we've told him exactly what we told you.'

'Are you sure there's nowhere else he can go? There must be hostels.'

'They're full at the moment.'

'Or there's his father. He lives just over the pass, in Peak Forest.'

'His father won't have anything to do with him. Apparently, they haven't spoken for years.'

'The old man's a miserable bugger. I met him once.'

'So . . . ?'

Proctor sighed. 'I suppose I'll have to come and fetch him myself, too?'

'We'll be happy to deliver him to your door, sir.'

'Well, that's something.'

'Thank you for your assistance, Mr Proctor. I'm sure Mr Thorpe will appreciate it.'

'Oh, yes,' said Proctor. 'I'm sure he will.'

Cooper waited with William Thorpe while a car was arranged to take him back to Wingate Lees. The death of Rebecca Lowe had clearly come as a shock to him. He, for one, hadn't been reading the papers or catching the news on TV. Mansell Quinn might be relying on there being more people like Thorpe, who weren't watching out for him in the Hope Valley.

'Mr Thorpe, how well did you know Carol Proctor?' asked Cooper.

'Carol? Not as well as Mansell did.'

'How would you describe her marriage to Raymond Proctor?'

Thorpe coughed. 'I think she found Ray a bit boring. She was much more adventurous than he was. If you ask me, it was one of those marriages where they only found out what a bad match they were when it was too late.'

'Adventurous?' said Cooper.

'Yeah. From what people used to say about her, anyway. She had a reputation from being a teenager, and I don't suppose she changed very much.'

'Would you care to expand on that a bit?'

'Let's just say,' said Thorpe, 'that she didn't care for the same diet all the time. She liked to try out spicier food now and then. If you know what I mean.'

'Like Mansell Quinn?'

'Mansell? I suppose you might call him spicy.'

Thorpe laughed his rattling laugh, but soon became breathless.

'Are you sure we can't get a doctor to look at you while you're here?' said Cooper.

'No,' said Thorpe firmly. 'Just bring this car and let me get away from here. That's all I want to do.'

257

Cooper went to the door to look for the car. He noticed the cement dust still on the knees of his trousers, and brushed it off. He thought about the curious relationship between the three men – Mansell Quinn, William Thorpe and Raymond Proctor. The army provided a link between Quinn and Thorpe, and that might go some way towards explaining their bond. For whatever reason, Thorpe had felt an obligation to Quinn and had done him a favour when he was approaching the end of his prison term.

Of course, Raymond Proctor had felt some obligation to William Thorpe, in his turn. He'd put Thorpe up at his caravan park for a while when he needed somewhere to stay. And Proctor hadn't been in the army, so it couldn't have been due to comradeship among ex-soldiers. Did the origins of the obligation go back to the events of 1990, or beyond?

Cooper turned to look at Thorpe. The most interesting fact in this three-cornered relationship was the absence of any similar bond between Quinn and Proctor. It was understandable in the circumstances, he supposed. Proctor believed that Quinn had killed his wife, after years of carrying on an affair with her.

Curiously, it seemed that Will Thorpe had been the one to feel guilty. But guilt could make people act in strange ways. Thorpe had felt under some obligation to Quinn, certainly. But he feared him, too.

A patrol car pulled up near the door at last, and he signalled to Thorpe. He watched the man get to his feet, looking thin and tired. Cooper knew that fear and anger were simple emotions, easy to understand. Guilt was far more difficult.

25

Somebody had managed to open one of the big sash windows in the CID room. No breeze came in, only waves of humidity. But at least when the phones stopped ringing for a while, they could hear the sound of children playing in the gardens on West Street, a snatch of music from somebody's radio, and the tune of an ice-cream van. They were sounds that suggested normal people enjoying themselves, out there in the real world.

Ben Cooper had so far failed to track down a copy of *Death Underground*. The library didn't have it, and the local branch of Ottakar's didn't have it, but had offered to get one on special order within a few weeks. It was a shame that the only worthwhile secondhand bookshop in town had closed a few months ago when its owner died; the place had been a treasure trove of hard-to-find books on specialized subjects.

Thinking about specialists, he decided to phone the company that ran Peak and Speedwell Caverns. They told him that Alistair Page was his best bet, and promised to give him a message. Within half an hour, Page rang back.

'Yes, I've got a copy of that at home,' he said. 'It's fairly old, though. I can suggest something much more up to date.'

'No, that's the one I want. Can I borrow it?' said Cooper.

'Of course. But it'll be a day or two before I can get into Edendale.'

'Don't worry about that, I'll pick it up. Will you be home tonight?'

'Yes, that's fine. You know where it is, don't you? Rock Cottage.'

Cooper put the phone down. At least that was something achieved today.

'Ben, did Will Thorpe get away all right?' called Diane Fry, without lifting her head from her desk.

'Yes, Diane.'

'It's a pity we couldn't keep him in custody.'

'He hasn't done anything,' said Cooper.

Fry looked sceptical. 'I'm convinced he knows a lot more about Mansell Quinn than he's telling. If that's the case, we could have him on a charge of withholding information.'

'That won't worry Thorpe very much.'

'Well, at least we know where he is now. We can have another go at him tomorrow – it'll give us time to put a strategy together.'

'A strategy?'

'An interview strategy. We need something to use against him, some detail from his background that would make him open up.'

A large red-and-black butterfly came in through the open window. It flapped madly across the office ceiling, found itself caught in the draught from Fry's fan, and came down again suddenly. It fluttered so close to Cooper's face that he could feel the waft of its wings and hear its quiet flapping. Then it left him and headed back to Fry's desk, perhaps mistaking the movement of the fan for the outside air. Fry picked up a file and swatted at it, missing by a mile.

'What are you doing?' said Cooper. 'It won't harm you. It's only a Red Admiral.'

'It should get back to the sea, then,' said Fry.

Cooper got up from his desk and followed the butterfly around the room until it came within reach. He cupped his hands around it gently, feeling its wing-tips tickling his fingers for a moment before became still.

'Hey up, Ben's made an arrest,' said Gavin Murfin. 'Do you want the handcuffs, Ben?'

'Have you nothing better to do?' said Fry, without looking up.

'It won't take a minute.'

'Ben doesn't like killing anything,' said Murfin. 'This is the man who rescues wasps and puts them out of the window.'

'You're joking? Wasps are on pretty high on my extermination list.'

'That's quite a long list, I bet.'

'Could be. Do you want to know where you come on there, Gavin?'

'As long as it's below wasps, I'm happy.'

Fry didn't say anything.

'Or at least, not too many places above them,' said Murfin.

Before he could get to the window to release the butterfly, Cooper's phone rang.

'Damn.'

'Don't worry, I'll get it,' said Murfin. 'You're on prisoner duty.'

Cooper nodded his thanks, and edged his way around the desks while Murfin reached over for his phone. He was careful not to bring his palms any closer together, for fear of wiping the golden dust from the insect's wings. His grandfather had told him that wiping the dust off a butterfly's wings prevented it from flying.

As he arrived at the window, he was half-listening to Murfin's voice and smiling at his colleague's telephone manner, which Murfin claimed charmed the old ladies who rang up to complain.

Cooper reached out of the window before opening his

cupped hands. He watched the Red Admiral hesitate for a moment, resting on his palms. But then it unfolded its wings, flashed its red-and-black pattern in the sunlight, and fluttered away into the warm air.

Satisfied, Cooper turned back to the office and became aware of the silence. Murfin was standing waiting for him, holding the phone out with his hand over the mouthpiece.

'It's Mr Thorpe,' he said. 'William Thorpe's father.'

Cooper took the phone. Fry went to the window and closed the sash with a thud that hurt his ears.

To reach Rakelow House, Cooper had climbed the 1:4 gradient of Winnats Pass out of Castleton, crawling behind a couple of cars whose drivers didn't know how to handle the gears on a steep hill.

Like many Pennine farms, Rakelow lay sheltered just below the level of the road, with only its roof line visible to passing motorists. From the roadside, it would be possible to toss a stone down its chimney. A glass porch had been built some years ago to keep the weather from the back door, which of course was the entrance that everyone used. Inside the porch, Cooper could see a tabby cat lying on a shelf among a few pots of cactus.

This was typical hill-farming land – poor, steep and half of it in shade except for a few months of the summer. A large wooden building next to the farmhouse might at one time have doubled as a barn and cattle shed, but it had been allowed to decay beyond repair. The roof was mostly gone, and fallen timbers lay in a heap under the back wall. Wooden buildings weren't worth a lot. They needed too much maintenance, and no one was interested in converting them as long as there were stone barns left to be bought.

It was very warm inside the porch, the glass panels focusing too much sun into the small space. The cat looked listless, and barely roused itself to stare at Cooper when he clicked his tongue at it. Bluebottles buzzed around the plants, and one of them circled Cooper's head as he introduced himself to Jim Thorpe. He swatted it away, but still had the impression that it followed him into the house.

Mr Thorpe was a morose-looking man with a long, bony face like a sheep. His wrists and chest sprouted wiry hair, which burst from the cuffs and collar of his shirt. Raymond Proctor had said he was a miserable bugger, and Cooper had come prepared to find exactly that. Old or middle-aged men living on their own were rarely the most sociable of people. But tea had been offered readily when he arrived, with the instinctive hospitality of a genuine country person.

While Mr Thorpe was out of the room, Cooper bent to take a closer look at the window sill near the door. The sill and the lower edges of the casement were covered in spots of blood. They were smeared on the white paint across a wide area, but not in a consistent pattern – and at the same time too far apart to be caused by a spray of blood from a wound.

'Biscuit?'

Cooper jerked upright, embarrassed to find that Mr Thorpe was watching him, a cup and saucer in one hand and a plate of chocolate-chip cookies in the other. His face registered no curiosity about what his visitor had been doing with his nose pressed into the window sill. But Cooper mentally chided himself for becoming so absorbed that he'd lost his alertness.

'Er, yes – thank you.'

'Take a seat, then.'

He pointed at the table, and Cooper pulled out one of the dining chairs. Mr Thorpe himself sat in the armchair near the window. He had his sleeves rolled up to the elbow, and the sunlight fell on his bare arms, making the forest of fair hairs glint and sparkle. The cat walked into the room and rubbed itself against the old man's legs. Thorpe seemed to ignore the animal at first, but as soon as he'd settled in his chair, the cat jumped on to his lap and began to purr. Thorpe stroked it obediently.

'As you know, I'd like to talk to you about your son, William,' said Cooper.

Now Mr Thorpe became even more morose. His nose seemed to droop towards his moustache, and his expression became puzzled and slightly pained. It was a Swaledale ewe he resembled, thought Cooper.

'Have you seen him?' said the old man.

'Yes, sir. I interviewed him earlier today.'

'What would you call my son, then? A loner, a hermit, an outcast? Maybe a tramp?'

'None of those, sir.'

'Well, that's what you say.' Mr Thorpe took a drink of tea. 'He joined the army, you know. Will was happy in the army. The life suited him down to the ground. There were rules for everything, and somebody to tell him what to do all the time. He never had to make a decision for himself.'

Cooper frowned. 'Your son saw service in a number of hotspots. He must have been in action.'

'Yes.'

'So I imagine he had to make a few tough decisions along the way, don't you?'

Mr Thorpe lifted one hip and pulled out something that had been pushed down the side of the seat cushion. It was a newspaper, but one that had been folded and crushed into a shape about a foot long.

The old man shook his head. 'He was trained how to respond to everything. He was trained when to shoot people, and how. He was trained always to obey orders. He was trained by his mates how to enjoy himself when he was off duty – how many pints of beer he was expected to drink, how often he was supposed to go with a tart, when it was the right time to get in a punch-up. You know.'

'Some people need that kind of structure.'

264

'William needed it. It was no good for him at home. He had no mates here, and no routine. It made him edgy and frustrated. Any time he came home on leave, it was obvious he couldn't wait to get back to his regiment. He'd go out all night and drink himself silly, then sleep all day. It broke his mother's heart. She saw so little of him, and she was always disappointed when he was here.'

Mr Thorpe seemed to have become distracted. He didn't look at Cooper as he spoke, but at something in another part of the room. Suddenly, the old man raised the newspaper and smacked it down hard on the window sill. He lifted it again and inspected the underside: a flattened bluebottle was stuck to the paper. Mr Thorpe flicked the squashed body towards the fireplace.

'Filthy little buggers,' he said.

Even from his chair at the dining table, Cooper could see a new smear of blood on the sill.

'We get a lot of wildlife in here,' said Mr Thorpe. 'You can't keep nature out.'

Cooper nodded. Bridge End Farm was like that in the summer, too. If they left a window open at night, the whole of nature would end up inside the house, one way or another.

'Your son must have had a few mates around here,' he said. 'He didn't go drinking on his own, did he?'

Jim Thorpe looked at him with vague eyes, as if surprised to find somebody sitting at his table, listening to what he was saying. Cooper wondered if he, too, talked to the cat when he was alone.

'Yes.'

'Who were those friends, Mr Thorpe?'

'You know who they were.'

'Mansell Quinn and Raymond Proctor?'

'Aye, those were the two that William drank with most when he was on leave. They'd kept in touch for years. Quinn and William acted as best man for each other when they got married.'

265

'Your son's marriage didn't last, did it?'

'About eighteen months. Compared to some young folk these days, that's a marathon.'

'She didn't like army life?'

'She got bored in no time. She was working as a receptionist at a car showroom when she met William. I always reckoned she only wanted to get married so she could be the centre of attention for a day.'

'Where is she now?'

'Buggered if I know. She found some other bloke quick as you like, and went off with him.'

Cooper examined the biscuits. He was trying to judge which might be the least stale without having to pick them up, which he had been brought up to consider rude. Finally, he chose one from the bottom of the pile, but knew as soon as it was in his fingers that he'd made the wrong choice.

'Why didn't your son come home here after he was discharged from the army?'

The old man began to stroke the cat a little faster, brushing the back of its head too hard, so that the cat growled a low warning. He didn't look at Cooper, but at the phone on the table, as if regretting the call he had made earlier. Surely he must have known he'd be asked questions that might be painful. There always came a time to face up to these things. For a moment, Cooper wondered what had made Jim Thorpe decide to make that call. But it didn't really matter.

'Like I told you, he was always bored here,' said Thorpe. 'And he had some friends in Derby, old army pals. I never met them, but I expect he would have been happier with them.'

'I don't think he was,' said Cooper. 'He went off drinking again in Derby. Only this time, he was on his own.'

'Was he?'

'In the end, he had no friends left.'

Thorpe lowered his head towards the cat, which purred

more loudly. Cooper thought he had seen a faint glitter in the old man's eye for a moment, but he couldn't be sure.

'And you know he's ill? He has emphysema.'

Thorpe nodded.

'But you wouldn't let him come back here to live when he called you, would you?'

Jim Thorpe lifted the cat off his lap and put it down on the floor. He got up and left the room without a word, leaving Cooper chewing the last of a stale biscuit. The cat glared at him, knowing without hesitation whose fault the interruption was. Cooper put his hand out to the cat as a friendly gesture. It opened its mouth in a sharp snarl and lashed out with a paw. A set of claws whistled past the skin on the back of his hand.

'OK, I get the message.'

A few more minutes passed, and Cooper began to feel very uncomfortable. He was about to get up and leave quietly, thinking he had already outstayed his welcome, when he heard footsteps in the next room.

'This is William when he was a youngster, with me and his mum,' said Thorpe.

The family photographs. Cooper groaned inwardly. He wasn't sure what he had said or done to bring on a burst of nostalgia. But perhaps he should have got up and left while he'd had the chance. Now it was going to be more difficult to do it politely.

'Very nice,' he said.

'No. You're not looking properly,' said Thorpe.

Cooper looked at the photograph again. He could recognize Jim Thorpe without any difficulty, though he must have been about forty years younger. The long, bony nose and morose expression were distinctive, even under the flat cap he wore. He was standing in front of the farmhouse with his arm round a dark-haired woman in a flowered dress. She was a well-built, cheerful-looking woman, a woman that his mother would have described as 'bonny'. This was no scrawny receptionist from a Buxton car showroom. She was made to be a farmer's wife. Standing in front of the couple, and looking rather shy at having his photograph taken, was a boy of about six with soft, dark hair falling on to his forehead in a fringe. He was smiling and leaning into his mother with a look of contentment.

'William?' he said, tapping the picture of the boy.

'Of course. We never had any other children.'

There was nothing unusual about the photograph, as far as Cooper could see. They were an ordinary family group – a little old-fashioned for the middle of the 1960s, but that wasn't surprising for a farming family. The latest trends didn't reach Derbyshire hill farms for a decade or two. He could see nothing worth commenting on. Yet Thorpe waited impatiently for him to notice something.

'I'm sorry,' he said. 'I don't know what you're trying to tell me.'

Thorpe jabbed a finger. 'There, look. A cigarette.'

Cooper had to squint to see the faint trail of smoke caught by the camera as it drifted across the sleeve of Thorpe's jacket towards his wife.

'You smoked. But I still don't see . . .'

He looked around the room he was sitting in. It hadn't been decorated for years, yet the paintwork and the ceiling were merely dusty, not stained yellow with nicotine. There was no sign of an ashtray, not even a plant pot with a pile of butts stubbed out in its compost. And Mr Thorpe himself smelled slightly of cat hair and hay, which wasn't particularly unpleasant.

'You don't smoke any more,' said Cooper.

'Not for years. Not since she died.'

'Who? Your wife?'

'She got lung cancer.'

'I'm sorry.'

'Sometimes it's very quick. But it took Sylvia a long time to die.'

'Did she smoke as well?'

'No.'

Thorpe took the photograph from him. He looked at it for a moment, then he drew another from the envelope and passed it over.

This one showed only father and son. Cooper wondered for a moment who had taken the photographs, but guessed it was some visiting relative insisting on a snap of the occasion. It was obvious that this time neither of the subjects had wanted to be photographed. And certainly not together.

William Thorpe might have been in his mid-twenties by then. He was tall and upright, and he looked tough and smart in his soldier's uniform. Perhaps he had just arrived home on leave that afternoon, and his relatives had been so impressed by the uniform that they'd had to get a snap. And, of course, his proud father had to be in the picture, too.

The family resemblance between the two Thorpes was noticeable this time, in a way that it hadn't been when the boy was six years old and smiling. This young man looked as though he didn't know how to smile and had never smiled in his life. He was frowning and serious. No, not serious – angry.

'That was the last time he came here,' said Thorpe.

'He looks very smart,' said Cooper, knowing how inane the comment sounded. But the old man didn't seem to notice.

'She was dead by then.'

'I'm sorry.'

'And William said it was me that killed her.'

Diane Fry reached Derby again by the late afternoon. The address she'd been given by the Worcestershire and Sherwood Foresters regimental office was in an area of Victorian terraced housing close to the city centre. Most of the people on the street were Asian, and an old Methodist church had been converted into a Hindu temple.

The original sandstone lintels and door jambs had been cleaned and brick chimney pots added at some time. But the northern façade of the entire row had been rendered with cement. The render had turned grey and somebody had chipped it off in several places, as if to check what was underneath. A few tufts of grass were pushing their way through cracks at the base of a chimney, where seeds dropped by birds had germinated in the warmth and a thin covering of soot.

'Oh yeah, Will was in a state,' said the friend, Eddie Berrow. 'I mean, the bloke ought to have been able to pull himself together. He was a soldier, for God's sake. He fought in the Balkans. He must have seen some shit go down in his time.'

'It's different when the shit is happening to you,' said Fry.

'Oh, yeah? Know about that, do you?' said Berrow, giving her a sharp stare.

'Why did he leave?' she said. 'Did you kick him out?'

'We didn't have any choice. He lay in bed for the first few days, then went out on a bender. Well, that was OK, we all like a drink and a bit of a laugh. But for Will, the party just went on and on. He didn't want it to end. I reckon he had decided he never wanted to be sober again. He spent his money on booze, drugs, gambling, women – bloody hell, he went through it like water.'

'Women?' Fry hadn't imagined Thorpe forming relationships.

'Prostitutes,' said Berrow. 'But only decent ones.'

'Oh, good.'

'We couldn't stick it any more, Terry and me. So we packed his bag one day and left it out on the doorstep – not that he had much stuff of his own, basically just what he had when he came out of the regiment. Will got the message. I mean, he wasn't paying us rent or anything. And we knew he wasn't coming into the business by then. The fact is, he'd just become a liability. Being an old mate is one thing. Being a right royal pain in the arse is another.'

'He'd changed from when he was in the army?'

'Oh, totally.'

'He didn't have any problems when he was in the regiment? Like the alcohol, I mean.'

'We all drank quite a bit, of course,' said Berrow. 'But no drugs. Soldiers have to go through random compulsory drug testing. A positive test means a discharge.'

'Right, I see.' Fry looked around the interior of the garage. 'Are you the one who's the expert on Samurai swords?'

'No, that's Terry.' Then Berrow looked at Fry more keenly. 'Are you interested in buying?'

'I could probably find a use for one, but not just now.'

'Shame.'

'Business not good, then?'

Berrow shrugged. 'We never did find a location for a shop. Without Will, we didn't have enough money between us for the rent.'

'So he scuppered your business, in effect?'

'No, we do mail order. Are you sure you're not interested?'

Ben Cooper wondered whether he had really learned anything useful from his visit to Rakelow House, except that Jim Thorpe's name might be one they should add to the 'at risk' list.

'I don't know much about it, Mr Thorpe,' he said. 'But there's no way the doctors could say conclusively that your wife's lung cancer was caused by passive smoking, is there? What evidence could there be?'

'Who needs evidence?' said Thorpe. 'It's what you believe that counts. Like religion.'

'I suppose so.'

'William never had any doubts. He was a pig-headed sort of a lad in a lot of ways. Priggish, too.'

Cooper picked up the most recent photograph again. 'How long is it since your wife died, Mr Thorpe?'

'Twenty years, nearly.'

'So this photograph was taken . . . ?'

'On the day of her funeral.'

'And that was the last time he came home?'

'Aye. William got compassionate leave and arrived home a couple of days before the funeral. The night before we buried his mum, we had a blazing row. I was smoking a lot then, as you might imagine – it was a bit of a trying time. But then, I'd always smoked a lot. Had done since I was a kid. We didn't know any better then.'

'And William blamed your smoking for his mother's lung cancer – that's what he meant when he said you'd killed her?'

'Well, yes.'

'But your son was a smoker himself.'

'All his life, practically.'

'So –'

Mr Thorpe shook his head. 'Don't ask me to explain that. Maybe some of it was guilt. But there was something else as well. William was always getting hold of odd ideas, and once they were in his head, they stayed there. Somebody had told him about this gas – radon.'

'Radon? I know it can be a problem in some areas.'

'We're on limestone here, you know,' said Thorpe. 'William said radon can be sucked into houses that are built on limestone. He said that two thousand people a year die from it. And he said that breathing tobacco smoke and radon multiply your chances of getting lung cancer.'

'And that was your fault?'

'Obviously,' said Thorpe. 'If I hadn't made Sylvia live here, and hadn't smoked, she might still be alive. So William was right, wasn't he?'

'Mr Thorpe, I have no idea.'

'It was Mansell Quinn that told him, you know.'

272

'About the radon? Well, Quinn was a builder, so I suppose he'd know about the risks.'

'Just because you know something, it doesn't mean you have to spread it around. A wise man knows when to keep things to himself.' Thorpe made small kissing noises at the cat, which gazed up at him with its eyes half-closed. 'Anyway, on the day of the funeral a lot of things were said on both sides that shouldn't have been said, and Will was packed and ready to go back to his regiment as soon as the service was over. I'm lucky I got that photo – it was one of the aunties that insisted on taking it. She said Will was just like his mother. I could never see it myself.'

'Are you suggesting that Quinn would have told your son about the effects of radon just to cause trouble between you?'

Thorpe shrugged. 'I never liked him, and he never liked me. He was always the one who got the others into bother. There were fights in pubs, sometimes. Trouble with the police.'

'Yes, I know.'

The old man peered at him. 'Yes, I suppose you would. But there, you see – you've learned to keep things to yourself in your job, haven't you? You wouldn't have let on that you knew that, if I hadn't volunteered it.'

'Did you ever meet Mansell Quinn, Mr Thorpe?'

'Yes, once or twice. Before he went to prison.'

'He's out now.'

'Yes, you said.'

'Your son and Quinn stayed friends while he was in prison, didn't they?'

Mr Thorpe moved his jaws thoughtfully – not chewing on anything in particular, except his own saliva. He ought to have produced some cud to munch on.

'Maybe.'

'Yet Mansell Quinn claimed your son as an alibi for the time that Carol Proctor was killed, and William gave a different statement.'

'I suppose he was just telling the truth,' said Thorpe.

'But Quinn might not have seen it like that. It would have seemed like a betrayal to him.'

'I can't help that. It happens.'

Cooper took a drink of his tea. There was no point in trying to rush somebody like Jim Thorpe. He watched the old man gazing out of the window, past the greying net curtains towards Mam Tor. Cooper waited. Mr Thorpe's expression didn't change, but his hand grew still, and he stopped stroking the cat. The animal looked up and met Cooper's eye. He felt as though some communication had passed across the room at last – as if the cat, at least, understood something of the old man's relationship with his son.

'Are you going to be speaking to Will again?' said Mr Thorpe.

'Yes, I'm sure I will be.'

'Tell him, then.'

'Tell him what, sir?'

The old man swallowed convulsively, as though trying to shift something that had got stuck in his throat.

'Tell him if he really wants to . . . he can come back here.'

26

Castleton was one of the cleanest places Ben Cooper knew. The thousands of plastic bottles, aluminium drinks cans and polystyrene cups were actually in the litter bins rather than scattered on the grass or floating in the stream. Even the feral pigeons were more attractive than the dirty grey things on city streets. When he paused near the bridge at Stones Bottom, they flocked around his feet in seconds. Even though it was already dusk, they hadn't given up hope of a tourist with spare bread from his sandwiches to feed them.

Cooper could still taste the dust from the cement works in the back of his throat. It made him unnaturally thirsty, and he'd have preferred to be heading for the Hanging Gate right now for a few pints of beer to wash the coating away. But he didn't have time, if he was going to call on Alistair Page tonight. He knew Diane Fry would have said he'd spent too long at Rakelow House. But she'd wanted background on Will Thorpe, and he'd come away with plenty of that. She might see a reconciliation with his father as exactly what she needed to make Thorpe open up.

Knowing there wasn't time for a proper meal either, Cooper called into a chippy on the hill near the Market Place and bought a jumbo sausage and chips, which he ate in his car. When he'd finished, he jammed the paper and wooden fork into a bin near the visitor centre, and went into one of the toilet blocks to wash the grease off his hands.

Returning to Castleton had reminded him of the two men he'd seen from the castle on Tuesday, when he'd been with Amy and Josie. Watching the tape from the outdoor shop, he'd been convinced that he recognized Mansell Quinn as one of the men who'd been talking in that secluded spot above Cavedale. But a few hours later, the memory was fading and he was less sure. No doubt it had been his imagination leaping into action because of the similarity between the black, slicker-type waterproofs.

Cooper was glad he'd said nothing – it would only have made him look a fool. He supposed it was the idea of Quinn in such close proximity to Amy and Josie that had frightened him beyond rationality.

Turning his hands in the stream of warm air from a drier, he wondered when these toilets were cleaned. Early in the morning perhaps, before the first visitors. Like the bins outside, the one in the toilet block was full. And there was something scattered on the floor near his feet, and on the edge of the washbasin, speckling the stainless steel.

Cooper looked more closely. The specks resembled the seeds that had fallen from the lime tree in Rebecca Lowe's garden at Parson's Croft. Under the waste pipe leading down from the washbasin, he saw a pale leaf lying in a small pool of water, as if it had dropped from someone's clothes.

He felt a prickling in the small of his back, and turned sharply to look at the cubicles. Only one door was closed, down at the far end.

'Paranoid,' he said to himself. 'Paranoid – that's what you are.'

But still he pushed the door open, just in case. The cubicle was empty.

276

Then Cooper looked at the floor. He crouched, felt in his pocket for some latex gloves or a plastic bag, but found nothing because he'd left his jacket in the car. He pulled a few sheets of toilet paper off the roll. It would have to do for now.

Gingerly, he grasped the thing in a fold of paper and held it up to the light. It was the ripe seedhead of a grass stalk, and it had been chewed. And surely by something bigger than a mouse.

The outer door of the toilet block creaked open on its spring. Still crouching, Cooper turned his head. An old man had entered and was unzipping himself at the urinal. He looked at Cooper squatting on the floor of the cubicle, clutching a small brown thing in a wad of toilet paper.

'Pervert,' he said. 'You ought to get out of here before I have the police on you.'

Alistair Page lived in a narrow lane that rose steeply from the cavern approach. The house had recently been renovated, but alterations to the appearance of a property were strictly controlled in this area. The stonework had been cleaned, the new window frames were made of pine, and the front door was a stable-type design to match the nearby cottages. In the hillside above was a house with an arched window, like a chapel.

Page's house sat right into the limestone cliff, with a gap knocked out of the rock big enough to take a small car. A blue Volkswagen was parked there now, but it was a narrow fit – its wing mirror came with an inch or two of a High Peak Council wheelie bin standing against the side door of the house. There was no garden. And the front door, like most of the others, opened directly on to the street.

The view was impressive, though. The first-floor windows looked down on to the cottages in the gorge below, and right into the mouth of Peak Cavern itself.

The sight of the cavern made Ben Cooper pause. The Devil's Arse, they called it. But surely they had the wrong part of the anatomy. To Cooper, the cavern entrance resembled a gaping maw waiting to suck in unwary passers-by, like the business end of a primeval sea creature lying just below the surface, its mouth hung with enticing stalactites and curtains of flowstone to tempt in the curious minnows that it fed on.

And during the daytime, minnows flocked into the mouth in large numbers. Cooper had seen them queuing at the turn-stile to pay their money, and gathering at the top of the ropemakers' terraces to watch the demonstrations before venturing deeper into the cave. More of them had been climb-ing the path into the gorge – scores of them thronging the riverside walk to the car park. The cavern's gaping mouth never went hungry. Not during the tourist season, anyway.

'Come in, come in,' said Alistair Page, appearing at the front door of his cottage in a black T-shirt and jeans. 'I was watch-ing out for you. I don't normally use this door much – I go in and out at the side entrance, so I'm not stepping right into the roadway.'

'Of course.'

'You look hot. You'll find it cooler in here.'

Cooper did feel a bit sticky from the walk. It wasn't the heat that was the problem – the temperatures hadn't got anywhere near last year's record high. It was the humidity that wore him down and made him uncomfortable.

'Sit down,' said Page. 'Drink?'

'Yes. Something cold would be good.'

'Cranberry juice OK?'

'Fine.'

'Sit down, then, while I get the drinks.'

Cooper didn't like to sit down right away, if he could avoid it. Not in a house he'd never visited before. Slumped in one of these low-level imitation leather armchairs, he would miss

278

a lot of the details that gave a house its character and told him so much about its owner.

So instead of accepting Page's invitation, he paced the room a little, then stood in front of the gas fire like a man warming himself at an open hearth. Within those few seconds, he'd taken in the main impressions. There was no sign of a pet of any kind. No children, either. No sign of a partner, in fact. This was a single man's home.

Page's interests were indicated by the caving and hillwalking books that filled the pine shelves in an alcove next to the fireplace, and by the widescreen TV and DVD player with a neatly ordered selection of DVDs, all in their cases and possibly even arranged in alphabetical order. Cooper saw *Blade Runner – Director's Cut* near one end, and *The Sixth Sense* at the other. Science fiction classics and disaster movies, with a smattering of comedies.

And there were stacks of CDs, too – U2, Del Amitri, INXS. You could almost rely on being able to judge someone's age from their CD collection. Many people formed their musical tastes in their teenage years. In Alistair's case, the crucial period had been the late eighties and early nineties. Cooper remembered that time himself – in fact, Del Amitri's 'Nothing Ever Happens' had provided the backing track for a particularly painful spell of teenage angst.

He examined the rest of the room. During renovations to the cottage, an open-plan staircase had been installed. A couple of steps led up into a kitchen extension at the back of the house, where Page was chinking glasses and slamming the door of a fridge. Space must have been very tight, because the back window of the extension looked directly on to a stone wall bordering the next property. The whole place was very small, of course – there wouldn't have been scope to build any bigger in this side of the gorge.

'The houses at this end of town were built pretty randomly,' said Page, coming out of the kitchen and catching Cooper's glance at the back window. 'They were miners' cottages, of course. When a new miner arrived, they used to buy a corner of someone else's yard and put up their own property, which is why the cottages ended up so close together.'

'I suppose you get the problem of tourists gawping through the windows,' said Cooper.

'Well, it's an occupational hazard if you live in Castleton. Aren't you going to take a pew?'

'Thanks.'

'You said on the phone you were interested in a book,' said Page.

'That's right. It's called *Death Underground*.'

'Yes, I've got a copy you can borrow. But what's your interest? Were you really so scared by your experience on Monday?'

'Well, it was pretty scary. But I remembered you mentioning a death in the cavern. A real death. It was unique, but a long time ago, you said.'

'Not many people know that story now,' said Page. He went to the shelves and pulled out a book. '*Death Underground* has a chapter on it. There was a young caver who died.'

'Where did it happen?'

'Some way into the system from the show cave. A place called Moss Chamber.'

'That's an odd name. How could there be moss, when there's no light down there?'

'The chamber is named after the caver. He was called Neil Moss.'

'I see.'

'This was back in the late fifties, when the system was first explored to any extent.'

'Neil Moss was the first to discover this chamber, I suppose, if it was named after him?'

'No, he didn't discover the chamber itself, but a tiny fissure

280

that goes down inside the wall. You can't see it now – only a sort of depression filled with small stones.'

'Who was this man?'

'Neil Moss? He was a philosophy student at Oxford University; about twenty years old at the time. In March 1959 he joined a party exploring beyond the Mucky Ducks. When they saw the opening in the rock, Moss volunteered to try it out, to see how far it went. The thing about this shaft is that it's only about two feet wide. A human body barely fits into it, and it must have been a really tight squeeze for Moss. It also descends at a steep angle, and about eighteen feet down there's a corkscrew twist which he just managed to get round. Moss reached the bottom. But on the way back up, he got stuck.'

'Damn.'

'The shaft was so narrow that he couldn't bend his legs or move his arms. He couldn't do anything to raise himself. Unfortunately, he wasn't belayed – they'd assumed that the shaft was too tight for him to fall through it. It was only when he got stuck that a line was lowered. But it was a light hand-line, not meant for hauling the weight of a human body. They struggled for nearly three days, trying to get Neil Moss out.'

'Three days?'

'If he'd been able to move just a few inches, it would have made all the difference,' said Page. 'But carbon dioxide sinks. And at the level where Neil Moss was trapped, it began to build up, fouling his air. On top of that, his acetylene lamp went out, adding carbide fumes to the mix. Cave rescue techniques weren't as good then as they are now. The party had no oxygen with them – you know lack of oxygen causes brain damage?'

'Of course.'

'Well, Moss became weaker and weaker, until he was unconscious. Eventually, his father sent a message that he didn't want any more people risking their lives trying to save his son. So Neil Moss died down there. He was unable to move or, finally, to breathe.'

Cooper was hardly aware of his surroundings now. Mentally, he'd put himself in the young caver's place and was trapped in a two-foot cleft in the rock, unable to move his arms and legs, with his air almost exhausted.

'You can take the book with you, if you want,' said Page. 'Thanks.'

'It wasn't the best of times for the cave rescue organizations. They took a lot of flak over that lad's death, and it put exploration back for years.'

Cooper picked up the book. It was the sort of thing you'd only find in a secondhand bookshop or a library. Mansell Quinn had found one in the prison library at Sudbury, perhaps donated by some benefactor. What had been his fascination with it?

'Can you explain how far into the cavern it was that Moss died, Alistair?'

'I can do better than that – I can show you.'

Page unfolded a huge map of the Peak–Speedwell cave system and spread it out on the floor, which was the only flat surface big enough. He crouched over it eagerly, like a child showing off a favourite game.

'This shows the whole system, as far as we know. It links up Peak and Speedwell caverns, as you can see.'

'It's vast,' said Cooper. 'Is it possible to get all the way through from one show cave to the other?'

Page poked a finger at a point in the middle of the map. 'Well, for a long time a boulder choke at the end of the Trenches here was the limit from Peak Cavern. But in the eighties some cavers managed to force a way through into a low passage they called Colostomy Crawl. That was the first time non-divers could get into Speedwell.'

Cooper looked for the Peak Cavern entrance. 'Visitors only see a very small part of it on the show cave tour, don't they?'

'Only as far as the top of the Devil's Staircase these days. They used to be taken through Five Arches, but the passage floods completely in wet weather and it gets too muddy. On the exercise, we took you past that. And the party Neil Moss was with went way beyond Five Arches.'

Page continued to move his finger slowly along the route of the wandering passages.

'The Inner Styx is the river at the foot of the Devil's Staircase. You'll have heard it from the show cave. Downstream is a sump – a section that's full of water right up to the roof. The only way past that is by diving. But the other way, through Five Arches, you've got an ascending passage and a short crawl to the Mucky Ducks. The ducks are stoops in deep water. Normally, there's just enough air space, provided you keep your head down.'

'And there's still a long way to go.'

'Yes. There's a boulder passage, and about a hundred and fifty metres from Mucky Ducks you find a tube up in the right-hand wall. That's another crawl you do partly full length, with an awkward bend almost blocked by another sump. Above that is a narrow eyehole that it's just possible to wriggle through, and then you go up a mud slope, wade through a pool and locate a small fissure in the scree. And that's it. That's where Neil Moss died.'

Cooper sat back, feeling exhausted and stunned. 'It sounds like a week's journey to me. Even if you could face all those crawls and ducks.'

'Experienced cavers do it regularly. And there's another ten miles or so of the system beyond that.'

'What happens if there's an emergency down there – if somebody is trapped or injured?'

'At least one member of the party comes out and phones 999. Then the operations room at Ripley and Cave Rescue send a team out. Of course, you're supposed to let someone know where you're going and what time you expect to be back, so the alarm can be raised if you're overdue. Some people don't bother doing that. A lot of our call-outs are false alarms – cavers who get lost or stop to rest, so they take longer than they expected.'

'Is radon a problem down there?'

'Not in the show caves,' said Page. 'There are fans to clear the air, so the radon doesn't settle. Beyond the Devil's Staircase, it's a bit different.'

Cooper got up to stretch his legs, ready to leave. It was dark outside now, and when he looked out of the front window the mouth of Peak Cavern had disappeared completely in the blackness beyond the last few cottages.

'Alistair, what do you remember about Mansell Quinn?' he said.

'Quinn? Well, I wasn't very old at the time of the murder.'

'You must have had a reaction to it, though. Being so close to home and all.'

Page shrugged. 'I was a teenage boy, so I suppose I thought it was kind of exciting. A bit like having a TV programme come to life in your own street. We went out to look at the police cars like they were part of a film set. Murder isn't so exciting really, though, is it? It's very unpleasant and regrettable.'

'Regrettable? Yes, I suppose it is.'

It was an odd word to use, the sort of expression senior police officers used when they were addressing a press conference, choosing their words carefully to avoid sounding too much like a real person with emotions.

'You must have been about the same age as the Quinns' son, Simon,' said Cooper.

'I still am, I suppose.'

Page was folding up the map of the Peak–Speedwell system. He put it away in his bookshelf, sliding it in so that it disappeared completely between the spines of two books. He said nothing more. On Tuesday, Page had been keen to hear

284

about Mansell Quinn, but Cooper seemed to have touched too close to something sensitive.

'A difficult time, was it, Alistair?' he said.

'I knew Simon Quinn very well. That's all I can say, really. You can imagine . . .'

'Simon is still in the area. So is his sister Andrea at the moment. After what happened to their mother, you know. I can pass your phone number on to him, if you'd like me to.'

Page looked startled. 'No, no, that's all right. I'm sure he wouldn't want to come to see me.'

'OK,' said Cooper. 'Well, thanks for the book anyway.'

'You're welcome.'

But in that moment, Alistair Page had given more away about himself than in all the time Cooper had spent talking to him. He had seemed not just startled at the idea of Simon Quinn visiting him but frightened.

On his way back along the waterside walk, Cooper found a jackdaw going ahead of him. It fluttered along for a few yards, landed on the wall and looked back at him with a tilt of its head before moving on again. But then he got too close, and it launched itself into the air and disappeared into the shadows around the bend.

Cooper could feel that the atmosphere had changed. A cloying dampness in the air made him feel more uncomfortable than the heat, and when he looked up he realized the sky had already darkened. He was in danger of getting very wet before he made it to his car.

He had almost reached the bridge when the first drops fell from the sky. They began to hit the ground and splash on the roofs of the houses in a regular pattern, echoing his own footsteps, growing louder and faster, louder and faster, as the storm closed over him.

But there was more than noise in his head. There was the memory of Alistair Page's last words about the trapped caver, Neil Moss. As Cooper had been about to leave the house, his thoughts had come back to it, strengthened by the recollection of is own experience of feeling helpless in the darkness.

'So Neil Moss was dead by the time they got him out,' he said. 'That's terrible.'

Page had paused then, as if deciding whether to tell him the next thing.

'They never got Neil Moss out,' he said. 'In the end, they left him there and sealed up the shaft with stones.'

'What? You mean . . . ?'

'Neil Moss is still in Peak Cavern. He's been there forty-five years.'

There had been an awkward silence between them for a few moments. Cooper hadn't known what to say. The thought of Neil Moss's awful death made his chest tighten. He could almost feel the weight of the rock, the air getting thinner and filling with poison.

But finally Page spoke again.

'So that's why they call it Moss Chamber,' he said. 'I think he's sort of claimed it as his own, don't you?'

'Yes,' said Cooper. 'I think you're right.'

Page had opened the door for him, and Cooper had looked out into the darkness of the gorge, glad that he could no longer see the gaping mouth of the cavern.

'Do you know what the men say who were part of that rescue operation?' said Page. 'While they were working, they could hear Neil Moss breathing. It was very loud, because the shaft acted as a kind of amplifier, and the sound filled the chamber they were in. They said it was the worst thing in the world to be able to hear a man breathing, yet not be able to see him or reach him. Eventually, the breathing stopped. Stopped for ever . . .' Page paused. 'Unless, like some folk, you have too much imagination.'

*   *   *

The thunder woke Cooper at five in the morning. It had been a threatening rumble in the distance for a while, but now it was very close. It crackled in the sky overhead like somebody ripping the clouds apart. He could hear the rain again, slapping on the roof of the conservatory and the flags of the back yard. Soon, it was tumbling from the sky in bucketloads.

Cooper knew he wouldn't be able to go back to sleep while the storm lasted. He was even more certain of it when he heard one of the cats calling plaintively from the kitchen, and knew that he was about to get a ball of wet fur on his bed.

As he tried to avoid Randy's muddy paws, he thought of the people who would be outside just now, perhaps caught in the open by the downpour. Mansell Quinn was out there somewhere – though maybe he would have found himself a shelter from the storm. Quinn was a man who planned his actions carefully, and he'd have been prepared for the storm. He might even have known it was coming.

At least William Thorpe wasn't out there tonight. Thorpe wasn't a man to make long-term plans. If Raymond Proctor hadn't agreed to take him back in, he'd probably have been sleeping rough again by now. The fact the police were interested in him would have driven him from his familiar refuges. He wouldn't have thought to take precautions against drowning in a cloudburst. But for tonight, he was safe and dry. Or dry, at least.

Cooper shivered, imagining himself as wet and cold as the cat's fur under his fingers, but with nowhere to go.

Wide awake now, he got out of bed and went to the window. He pulled back the curtain just in time to see a flash of sheet lightning above the roofs of the houses on Meadow Road. It lit up the slates and chimneys for a second, leaving an imprint on his retinas before the rattle of the thunder followed.

When the rain eased off, he went to check on the cats and

see if there were any leaks in the conservatory. On an impulse, he pulled on a coat, grabbed a torch and stepped outside. He shone his torch on the ground and swung it from side to side. There were dozens of snails – big ones, trailing right across the gravel path from the crevices in the stone wall to the patch of grass that Mrs Shelley called a lawn. Their winding silvery tracks reflected in the torchlight, crossing backwards and forwards over each other in an apparently haphazard fashion.

The picture he'd conjured of Mansell Quinn lying up somewhere safe and dry suddenly seemed unlikely. On the contrary, this was exactly the sort of time Quinn would choose to go out. Cooper imagined him emerging from the black mouth of Peak Cavern, slipping silently through the gorge in the rain like the outlaw Cock Lorrel, bent on murder.

He shuddered, and turned back towards the house. Most police officers couldn't avoid bringing their work home in their heads now and then, especially if they didn't have anybody to talk to. Many of them said it was vital to have another human being around with their own concerns – someone who wanted to talk about shopping or food, or new clothes for the kids. It helped to fill the space in your mind with something else, so you didn't find yourself going over and over the events of the day. Particularly if it had been a bad day. And there could be a lot of bad days.

Cooper had no one at home now, no one waiting with their own concerns. He knew this was why he got obsessed with little things, like snails crawling up his window. It was only to avoid having to think about the alternative – the trails of human slime that sometimes twisted and turned through his head.

27

Friday, 16 July

The next morning, a vast puddle filled the yard behind 8 Welbeck Street. When Cooper went out of the back door to examine the damage, he found Randy and his friend Mrs Macavity sitting on either side of the puddle. Neither of them wanted to get their paws wet, but they couldn't find a way around the water. The cats looked hopefully at Cooper when he appeared, but he wasn't sure which of them he should help across. Besides, he was sure they'd just decide they were on the wrong side of the puddle and demand to be carried back.

'Don't worry, folks,' he said. 'It'll go down in a day or two.' But all he got was a look of contempt in stereo.

Like a man troubled by a nagging toothache, Cooper kept returning to his internal reconstruction of the Carol Proctor murder scene. He worried at it as he drove into town that morning. He had a feeling that something was wrong with his scenario of events at the Quinn house in October 1990, but he couldn't quite put his finger on what it was.

Another thing bothered him, too: the uncomfortable gap between Sergeant Joe Cooper's return to the house and the arrival of what his statement called 'Specialist Officers'.

When Cooper had first joined CID, one of the older detectives had been the type who loved to give advice. He would take any chance to lean confidentially across a desk, the bottom buttons of his shirt popping over his beer belly and his nicotine-stained fingers tapping on Cooper's shoulder. Even now, Cooper could recall the DC's response to a particularly naïve remark about 'the rules'.

'Now, lad, nobody's asking you to break the rules,' he'd said. 'Good detective work isn't about breaking rules. It's about finding ways around the restrictions they put in our way. *Legal* ways, you understand. Nobody would argue with that, would they?'

Cooper still heard similar things even now. And it was strange how there always seemed to be a 'they'.

There were rules for everything, of course, if you chose to follow them. The rules told you what to do when a dead body was found. Whatever the circumstances, the first officers arriving at the scene would check the victim was indeed dead. If a suspected offender was present, they had to make an arrest. They'd collect information and take steps to protect any evidence. Obviously, the chain of command would shift as senior officers were brought in. But in the initial stages the FOAs had a lot of responsibility.

And no scene of sudden death was pretty. The amount of blood could be so overwhelming that it drove everything else out of the mind. Some detectives became bar-room pathologists. They had a detailed knowledge of the biological processes of dying, an expertise gained from attending scenes of death and postmortem examinations, but not one of them could claim that he'd never made a mistake at a crime scene. Mistakes were part of human nature. They were a different thing from deliberately breaking the rules.

Cooper had plenty waiting for his attention when he got to the office. But he reached first for the transcripts of the interviews with Mansell Quinn in October 1990. Two detectives, an inspector and a sergeant, whose names Cooper didn't recognize had conducted most of the sessions with Quinn. DC Hitchens appeared in the transcripts a couple of times, but didn't seem to have asked many questions. He'd have been too junior then, still learning the ropes in a major enquiry.

'You spent some time in the army a few years ago,' the DS had said.

'I signed up in the Foresters with Will Thorpe. He was still a lad, really, and he'd got a bit bored of living in Derbyshire.'

'But what about you? You already had a family by then, didn't you?'

'It was a bad time,' said Quinn. 'The building firm I worked for relied on contracts from the steel works in Sheffield. But the steel industry started to fall apart, and there was no work coming in, so they laid me off. There wasn't much else to do around here.'

'So you joined the army?'

'When Will said he was joining up, it seemed like a good idea. It was a regular wage for a few years, you see. I didn't plan to be a soldier for ever. At the four-year mark I came out, but Will stayed in.'

'That would be in 1986?'

'Just in time for the boom in the building trade. I was lucky. I got myself on my feet pretty quick after that.'

'But you had some trouble while you were in the army, didn't you? Fighting – once in a pub near your barracks, and twice with local youths.'

'A few bits of bother here and there. Nothing major. But they told me I'd be better off employed doing something else.'

'Didn't you like the army?'

'Yeah. It was interesting. And it's a good feeling to have a lot of close mates around you.'

'So why did you keep getting into trouble?'

'Same answer really.'

'How do you mean?'

'I mean there are things you do for your mates,' said Quinn.

'There were others involved when you got into these fights?'

'Look, it's all water under the bridge, that. I don't want to talk about it.'

'Let's talk about something else, then. Let's talk about Carol Proctor . . .'

A packet of photographs landed on Cooper's desk, interrupting his reading. 'Thanks,' he said, without looking up to see who'd brought them. He knew they must be the prints from the trainspotter's film. He slid them out and poked through the pile, pushing aside shots of trains and more trains, locomotives in the distance and in close-up, trains travelling into the sun, trains coming out of the sun.

And there it was. With two First North Western diesel units moving away from him on the Manchester line, and the express coming towards him on the other, Mansell Quinn had been caught on camera at Hope Station, half a mile from his ex-wife's house, within an hour of her murder. It seemed fairly damning.

'Gavin,' he called across the office, waving the packet. 'Photos.'

Murfin looked up in amazement. 'Not the trainspotter?'

'Yes.'

'Judging by your face, he came through with the goods, so to speak.'

'I think so.'

'Bloody lucky.'

Cooper tapped his nose. 'Instinct, Gavin.'

'My missus doesn't like me having instincts. She says it's mucky.'

Cooper held the print closer to study the dark figure on the westbound platform. The most that could be said was that there might be a slight hint of hesitation in Quinn's posture. It wasn't the look of a man with his mind set on impending violence, not the attitude of someone driven by anger. He looked uncertain, as if he wasn't quite sure where he was.

Or so it seemed to Cooper. But he'd been told often enough that he tried too hard to empathize with victims and suspects alike. The moment he felt the first hint of understanding or sympathy for Mansell Quinn, he knew he'd have to keep it to himself. Theoretically, he ought to share his thoughts with Diane Fry, as she was his immediate supervisor. But she would only ridicule them.

Murfin leaned over to look at the photo. 'Mmm. Pity there wasn't a CCTV camera on the platform.'

'Too true.'

A couple of minutes of tape would have told Cooper whether he was imagining the hesitation. If he could see Quinn actually walking along the platform, it might reveal that any uncertainty was merely that of a man who had just been released into the outside world. When would Quinn last have travelled on a train? More than thirteen years and four months, anyway. His transfers between prisons would have been by road. And when would he last have been in Hope? Same again. Under the terms of his licence, he was supposed to live in Burton on Trent until he settled somewhere in south Derbyshire, or back in his old childhood home in Wales.

'This is definitely Quinn?' said Murfin. 'Where are the other pictures of him?'

Cooper pulled out the file of Quinn photographs collected by the enquiry teams. In addition to the old mugshot and a print-out from the security camera at Hathersage, he had an army file picture of Quinn as a young man, some family snaps, and even a wedding photo of him with a smiling Rebecca. Cooper put the new picture alongside the others.

'What do you think, Gavin?' said Cooper.

'A bit of a chameleon, isn't he?'

The photographs Cooper had in his hands could have been of three or four different individuals. Just a few years difference in age seem to produce a different man – the hair slightly longer, or shorter, even a dark moustache in the shot of him in uniform. Quinn's hair colour seemed to change, too, and the even the shade of his skin. But that could be the quality of the photography.

According to his file, Quinn had looked after himself in prison, and had emerged from his sentence strong and fit. It was his friends William Thorpe and Raymond Proctor who had deteriorated over those thirteen years. Thorpe had been eaten away by disease, while Proctor had allowed himself to become overweight, balding and unfit. And Cooper suspected he was also worn down by despair. In a way, Mansell Quinn was already the winner.

'You're sure that's him?'

Diane Fry took the photo from Cooper and examined it.

'Yes, yes, I'm sure. He's wearing the same black waterproof that he had on in Hathersage. It's lucky it had stopped raining by the time this was taken, so he has the hood back.'

'He's carrying a small rucksack, too. Wouldn't you give your eye teeth to know what's in it?'

'I'm betting he has a self-inflating mattress in a stuff sack, and a packet of light sticks,' said Cooper. 'That's what he bought in the Out and About shop at Hathersage before he caught the train.'

'I was more concerned about any weapons he might be carrying.'

'Of course. Diane, isn't there a problem over the time of Mrs Lowe's death?'

'What do you mean?'

'Mrs van Doon estimated that she was killed within an hour or two of her sister finding the body at eleven thirty.'

'You know we can't expect anything more accurate.'

'No – but we have the trainspotter's photo of Quinn, which shows him at Hope station around seven forty. It doesn't take more than twenty minutes to walk up to Parson's Croft, so he'd be there by eight, in daylight. That doesn't square with Mrs Lowe being killed by somebody bursting into the house two hours later.'

'We have the footprints from the garden,' said Fry. 'So we know he waited under the trees.'

'For nearly two hours? In daylight?'

'It was getting dusk. You said so yourself.'

'No, not until nine thirty. Besides, Quinn could have had no idea of the lay-out of the house or garden – the place wasn't even built last time he was in the Hope Valley.'

'Ben, you're just trying to pick holes for the sake of it, and it doesn't work. Physically, the times fit just fine. Quinn was there on Monday night.'

'We don't even know the footprints are his,' said Cooper.

'Well, we'll see, won't we?' Fry looked at the picture again. 'I suppose there's a lot of open country around the Hope Valley for Quinn to vanish into,' she said.

Cooper laughed. So she'd noticed the hills where the railway line disappeared into the distance – the bulk of Mam Tor, and the twin heights of Win Hill and Lose Hill.

'It's almost *all* open country,' he said. 'Take a look at the map. Unless we get really lucky, the only chance we're going to have of catching him is if he decides to go after another victim. Then we have to hope that he makes a mistake, or that someone recognizes him from the TV or newspapers.'

'It comes back to the same question, then,' said Fry. 'Who else might Quinn be going after? Who might he have a grudge against?'

'It would have to be a pretty personal animosity, wouldn't it?'

Fry looked at him curiously for a moment. 'What are you thinking, Ben?'

'Well . . . what about Proctor?'

'If it weren't for his family, I wouldn't be worrying about that one at all.'

'I think Will Thorpe knows a lot more than he's telling. Quinn must have asked him about specific people. We need to find some way of persuading him to talk to us.'

Fry sighed. 'If we pull him in again, he'll just clam up.'

'Yes, you're right. But now he's at Wingate Lees . . . it might be interesting to talk to him and Raymond Proctor together.'

Fry handed him the photograph back. 'That's not a bad idea.'

'There's one other thing,' said Cooper. 'It was something old Mr Thorpe said that made me think of it. You remember Mrs Lowe's neighbours, the Newbolds?'

'The croquet set.'

'That's them. Well, they reported seeing a tramp on the road near Mrs Lowe's house a couple of weeks before she was killed.'

'You think it might have been William Thorpe?' said Fry.

'He'd fit the bill, wouldn't he? But what would he be doing, visiting Rebecca Lowe?'

'We'll both go together,' said Fry. 'Just give me a few minutes.'

While he waited for Fry, Cooper tried to look busy. For a moment, he'd almost blurted out something about his father. That was the animosity he'd been thinking about – the history between Mansell Quinn and Sergeant Joe Cooper. There had been something personal there, no doubt.

He looked at the interview transcript on his desk again. It was one of the earlier interviews, before Quinn had changed his mind and entered a guilty plea. When the detectives first questioned him, Quinn had given the story that he'd come

296

home, found the body on the floor, tried to turn it over. That was how he'd got blood on himself. He hadn't killed Carol, he said. He repeated it, no matter how many times they tried to rephrase the questions.

'So if you didn't kill Carol Proctor, who did?' the DS had asked at last.

'I don't know.'

'Who else could have done it?'

'I don't know.'

'Was anyone else there at the time?'

'No.'

'Well, Mr Quinn, how is it possible that somebody else could have killed Carol Proctor, if no one else was there but you?'

'I don't know. But I didn't kill her.'

'But, Mr Quinn –'

'Somebody else had been there, just before I got home. I could tell somebody else had been there.'

The DI had taken over the questions then. He might have been trying to be fair to Mansell Quinn, to give him a chance to suggest another scenario. That was the way it read in the transcript. But Cooper also knew that a lie was difficult to sustain once it was subjected to detailed questioning. Especially a spontaneous lie. Few people were quick-witted enough to fill in the details on the spur of the moment.

'So, Mr Quinn, you say you could tell someone else had been there? In your house?'

'Yes.'

'How could you tell?'

[Silence]

'Mr Quinn, you said you could tell. How could you tell someone had been in your house?'

'I don't know.'

'Well, let's think about it. Was there anything out of place, for example?'

297

'Out of place?'

'Had anything been moved? Was there anything in the room that shouldn't have been?

'I . . .'

'Yes, Mr Quinn?'

[Silence]

'So you can't remember noticing anything out of place in your house when you got home?'

[Silence]

'Did you hear any noises?'

'There . . .'

'Yes, sir? Would you like to repeat that?'

[Silence]

'Perhaps you heard somebody leaving the house? Was that it?'

'No, I didn't hear that.'

'What, then?'

[Silence]

'Voices? Footsteps running away?'

[Silence]

'Come on, man, I'm giving you a chance. What did you hear?'

[Silence]

'Mr Quinn, you're not helping yourself. I can't believe anything you say.'

[Faintly] 'You, too.'

'Yes, me too. So . . . let's talk about Carol Proctor again, shall we?'

The transcript showed that Quinn had failed to substantiate his assertion. Cooper could almost hear the satisfaction in the voices of the detectives asking the questions. And Quinn must have realized himself that his position was hopeless. From that moment, he'd accepted his guilt.

The Proctors' house at Wingate Lees was the sort of home where the television was never switched off. Ben Cooper saw a second TV mounted on the wall in the kitchen, and he imagined the children would have their own sets in their rooms.

'So where is he, Mr Proctor?' said Diane Fry angrily.

Raymond Proctor shook his head. 'I don't know. When I went out this morning, he'd gone. That's all I can tell you. I couldn't keep him here against his will, could I? What did you expect me to do, lock him in the caravan? If you wanted him locked up, you should have kept him in a cell.'

'Do you know why he went?'

'No. Who knows what goes on his mind? Will's a sick man.'

'What time did you see him last, sir?' asked Cooper.

'I spoke to him about ten o'clock, to see if he needed anything. Those 'vans aren't exactly luxurious, but he said he was OK. He told me he was tired and he was going to sleep.'

'And nobody saw him go?'

'Not so far as I know.'

'Damn it, he could be miles away by now,' said Fry.

'Will doesn't move all that fast,' said Proctor. 'If it helps.'

Cooper turned his back on the TV screen, finding the picture too distracting.

'Did you talk to Mr Thorpe yesterday?' he asked.

'A bit.'

'What about?'

'Why do you want to know that?'

'It might help us to understand why he left.'

A faint crack could be heard behind the Proctors' house, then a slithering somewhere above their heads, like claws sliding down the tiles of the roof. With a small thump, a wood pigeon hit the guttering and flopped over the edge. It hung upside down for a moment, its head rolling drunkenly as if it were trying to see down into the house. Then its weight carried it forward, and it fell past the window with its beak hanging open, the pinion feathers of its wings fluttering.

Proctor seemed glad of the interruption. 'I see Jason got another one,' he said.

'Jason?' said Fry.

'My step-son.'

'Is he shooting them?'

'Aye. They're buggers, those pigeons. They wake us up at three o'clock every bloody morning. They feed on the fields, then they roost up here on our roof. Dirty, they are. Look at the birdshit on the caravans up at this end of the site. It gets on the customers' cars, too, and they don't like it. Pigeons! The only way to get rid of them is to shoot 'em.'

'They're not a protected species, then?'

'Protected?' said Proctor.

Fry put on her most officious voice. 'Well, they're wood pigeons, aren't they? Wild birds, not captive bred. I believe it's an offence under the Wildlife and Countryside Act to intentionally kill or injure any wild bird. Unless you have a licence, sir.'

'Licence?' said Proctor. 'They're bloody pigeons – flying vermin. You don't need a licence to shoot vermin. I've never heard such rubbish.'

But he didn't sound certain. Cooper was pretty sure that Fry didn't know whether you needed a licence to shoot wood pigeons, not without looking it up in her copy of the Police Training Manual. But he wasn't going to say anything.

Fry patted her pockets as if searching for a notebook and stared thoughtfully at the roof for a while longer, until Proctor snorted in disgust. He stamped down the passage to the back yard, and they heard him shouting to somebody. A brief altercation followed, punctuated by swear words on both sides and the word 'police'. Then Proctor slammed a gate and strode back.

After a moment, a youth carrying an air rifle appeared

outside the window. He stared in at Fry as a visitor to a zoo might stare into a cage containing a two-headed buffalo. He looked as if he didn't quite believe that such a creature could exist, and was transfixed by a sort of horrified fascination. In the hand that wasn't holding the air rifle, he dangled two dead wood pigeons. The colours of their plumage were still bright. Cooper could see the pink patches on their breasts and the white under their open wings.

'So,' said Fry, 'why did Mr Thorpe leave?'

'I don't know,' said Proctor.

'What did you say to him?'

'Nothing.'

During a pause they became aware of Connie Proctor standing in the doorway.

'I know what happened,' she said.

'Connie, you can leave this to me,' said her husband.

But Mrs Proctor continued into the room, and she didn't look as though as she was going to take any notice of her husband.

'It was because Ray told him about Quinn. He told him that Quinn had been here.'

'He's been here? When?'

'Wednesday night.'

Fry glared at Proctor. Cooper braced himself to try to restrain her if she decided to throttle him.

'Nothing happened,' said Proctor, taking a step back. 'You said he'd come to kill me. But he didn't.'

'Why didn't you tell us about this?' said Fry quietly.

Proctor was sweating. He withdrew a couple more paces, as if he wanted to be back in his office, hearing nothing but the blare of the TV. His wife glared at him with contempt.

'He's scared to death,' she said. 'Look at him, you can see it. He's scared of you. But he's even more scared of Mansell Quinn.'

'You don't shop a mate,' said Proctor. 'Look, I'm sorry. I know it was wrong of me not to say anything. But you don't shop a mate, whatever he's done.'

'Even when he's killed somebody?'

'Well . . .'

'And what if he kills somebody else?' said Fry. 'Would you have bothered telling us then? Or do other people's lives not matter to you, Mr Proctor?'

Proctor shook his head. 'He wasn't after me, you see. I've done nothing against him. But Will –'

'What about him?'

'I don't know. Will was more worried than me, though. He thought Mansell might be angry with him. He wouldn't tell me what it was all about. I thought he'd done Mansell a favour, but there was something else, too.'

'What did Quinn come here for?' said Fry. 'What did he want?'

'He didn't say. He talked about how things were, what it was like coming out of prison.'

'He just knocked on the door, and you let him in for a chat?'

'Well, not exactly.'

'What, then?'

'I found him waiting in the office when I got back to the house.'

'He just walked in?'

'I don't usually lock the back door, because I'm in and out all the time when I'm on the site. I'm never far away, and it saves me bothering Connie and the kids in the house.'

Fry put her hand to her head. 'After all we said to you about security, you just leave your back door open for a convicted murderer to walk in?'

Proctor laughed nervously. 'I leave the door open completely if there's no one else at home, so I can hear the phone if it rings. You've got to make sure you answer the phone in a business like this, or you can lose bookings. If they don't get an answer, customers just go somewhere else.'

'Of course, I could answer the phone for him, but he doesn't like me coming in the office,' said Connie. 'He doesn't want me to know what he's up to in there.'

'And you've no idea why Quinn came here?' said Fry impatiently. 'Was he looking for Will Thorpe?'

'He didn't say so,' said Proctor. 'I don't really know what he wanted.'

'The funny thing is, Thorpe says he tried to put Quinn off tracking you down. He told Quinn that people who'd made a new life for themselves should be allowed to get on with it.'

Proctor laughed unexpectedly. 'Well, that was good of him.'

'Is there anything missing?' said Cooper.

'Not as far as I can see.'

'Might Quinn have taken money from the office?'

Proctor shook his head. 'The only money on the premises is in the safe. I don't leave *that* open.'

Fry growled. 'I do not believe that Mansell Quinn came here just for a chat about old times. What do *you* say, Mr Proctor?'

'I don't know.'

'Mr Proctor, we're going to ask you to come down to the station later on to make a statement. This is very serious. A senior officer may want to speak to you about your actions.'

At that, Connie Proctor looked triumphant. 'A good thing, too. But it won't make any difference,' she said. 'He's a lost cause.'

She closed the door with a firm click of the lock as they walked away from the house. Her husband came out, but stayed on the path. When they arrived, he'd been unloading some propane gas canisters from the red Renault van, which had a rustic log cabin logo on its side and WINGATE LEES

CARAVAN PARK in large letters, with the address and phone number.

When he looked at his own car, parked inside the entrance to the site, Cooper found he could almost picture Mansell Quinn coming through the gate and moving up the roadway towards him. He saw a Quinn dressed in black and indistinct in outline, his face not quite clear because Cooper had never seen him in the flesh.

As he reached the car, Cooper shuddered. He'd never met Quinn, yet the thought of the man made him apprehensive. Surely he couldn't be the only one who recognized the need to be afraid?

But of course he wasn't. William Thorpe was afraid, too.

Cooper started up the car and let it drift slowly forward, past the end of the nearest caravan, so that they could see the house a hundred yards up the hill. Raymond Proctor was striding towards the back door, moving quickly in spite of his slight limp.

'He couldn't wait for us to leave, in the end,' said Fry.

'I'm certain something occurred to him that he decided not to tell us about.'

'Something that he thought might be missing?'

'Yes. And now it looks as though he's going to check whether that something is still there.'

They watched Proctor enter the house via the back door, where his office was. He didn't bother to shut the door behind him.

'Wasn't there something else you wanted to ask Mr Proctor, Ben?' said Fry.

'Was there?'

'Something you forgot, but you've just remembered. Maybe you wanted to ask him for directions back to Edendale?'

'You're right. I'd better go up to the house and speak to him.'

A moment later, Cooper found Raymond Proctor in the

untidy office, leaning into one of the heavy oak cupboards on the far wall. Cooper couldn't quite see what was in the cupboard because the man's body was in the way.

'Mr Proctor?' he called, knocking hard on the open door.

Proctor dropped the bunch of keys he'd been clutching and jumped back from the cupboard, wincing as he twisted his bad leg.

'What the hell – I thought you'd gone!'

'I just came back to ask –' Cooper began.

And then he noticed Proctor's frightened expression, and a couple of empty wooden shelves behind him.

'What should be in the cupboard?' he said.

Proctor looked at him, dumbfounded. 'I can't believe it, I always have it locked, but the keys were on a hook with the others. I never thought anybody would bother to look in the cupboards.'

'What's missing?'

'But it's gone. He's taken it. Some bolts, too.'

'*What's gone, Mr Proctor?*'

'My crossbow.'

28

And finally, the moment came when they could no longer hear his breathing. It was just one sound missing from the clatter of boots and the murmur of anxious voices, the trickle of water and the clang of oxygen cylinders.

No one pointed out that the breathing had stopped. There was no need. For nearly three days it had been filling the confined space, seeping through the main chamber until it was inseparable from the clinging mud and the scent of fear. The narrow opening of the limestone shaft had been acting as an amplifier, so that no one could escape the sound or fail to recognize the battle for life in every breath.

For most of the rescue party, that sound was all they knew of the trapped caver, and all they would ever know. They had heard his breathing, but they never saw the man. A few feet away, he was pinned upright and dying, slowly being poisoned by the carbon dioxide that oozed into the crevices of the rock and settled around him, fouling his air.

Men cried with frustration as they worked in the chamber. No matter how many lights were brought in from outside, they did little more than cast additional shadows on to the rock walls in every direction, trapping the rescuers in a crushing mesh of light and noise, and dead air.

One rescuer stripped off his survival suit, his sweater and overalls to squeeze into the shaft, and for a few moments he stood with his boots touching the dying man's helmet. It was the last living contact Neil Moss would ever have, though it's doubtful he would have been aware of it. By that time the lack of oxygen had probably caused irreversible brain damage.

When the sound of the breathing stopped, everyone knew that the carbon dioxide had won the battle. As the church clock in Castleton struck eleven, the news was passed back to a hotel in the village. Neil Moss was dead.

It would be another four days before a party began to fill in the shaft with stones from a scree slope, permanently sealing the young caver into his limestone coffin. But it would be much longer before they could forget the sound of his breathing. As they worked for days in the mud at the top of the shaft, they had known what no one dared to say. It had been the sound of a dead man's breath.

Ben Cooper put down the copy of *Death Underground* he'd borrowed from Alistair Page and shuddered. Forty-five years had passed since Neil Moss had died in the cave system beyond Peak Cavern. And he was still there.

In the months leading up to his release, Mansell Quinn had taken this book out of the prison library three times. Cooper wondered why a man who ought to have been looking forward to freedom had instead been contemplating imprisonment for eternity.

'Delta Storm,' said Gavin Murfin. 'Well, I ask you. It sounds like something named by one of those Rambo wannabes.'

Details of the crossbow stolen from Raymond Proctor's house had been distributed, and Ben Cooper had brought back the manufacturer's instruction manual from Wingate Lees. The prospect of Mansell Quinn being in possession of this weapon had changed the mood in the incident room, though there was a certain amount of nervous joking among the team while DCI Kessen went upstairs for a top-level meeting.

DI Hitchens flicked through the handbook. 'Cooper, is Mr Proctor's crossbow black or this camouflage style?'

'Black, he says.'

'Is Quinn experienced with a crossbow?' asked Diane Fry.

Hitchens looked up. 'Where would he have got one to practise with, for heaven's sake? I don't suppose they let him have one in prison, did they?'

'Who knows? He probably got it delivered to his cell by mail order.'

'You don't need a licence, and there's no register either. They're not even classed as firearms. As far as I recollect, the only restriction on them is that they can't be possessed by anyone under the age of seventeen.'

'The Crossbows Act 1987,' said Fry. 'I looked it up. Even those restrictions don't apply to crossbows with a draw weight of less than 1.4 kilos.'

Cooper had no idea how powerful that was in crossbow terms. A bag of sugar weighed a kilo. It didn't sound a lot, but how much force was needed behind an aluminium bolt to kill someone? Not a huge amount, if you hit them in the right place. He checked the details of the Delta Storm again. It had a draw of one hundred and fifty pounds. About sixty-eight kilos.

'He took some hunting bolts, and a bow bag as well,' he said. 'The Delta Storm can be folded up when it's not in use. They call that a "compact". It has fold-down limbs, a tele-scopic stock and a pivoting foot claw, and it weighs only five pounds. When it's in the bag, Mr Proctor says you'd never know what Quinn was carrying.'

'And the bolts he took – aluminium, rather than plastic?'

'Yes.'

'Could an aluminium bolt kill somebody?'

'If fired with enough force,' said Cooper. 'Certainly.'

A draw of one hundred and fifty pounds was more than enough force. And according to the manual, the Delta Storm had a hunting range of forty yards.

DI Hitchens gestured Cooper into his office a few minutes later, and shut the door behind them. More bad news?

'Cooper, DS Fry tells me you've been getting a bit too involved in reviewing the Carol Proctor murder,' he said. 'I know I was the one who suggested that you look at the files, but only because I hoped it would put your mind at rest. The details are no longer relevant to the present situation. You need to be concentrating all your time and effort on finding Mansell Quinn, with the rest of the team.'

'Yes, sir.'

Hitchens looked at him sharply, detecting the uncertainty in his voice.

'Do you have a problem with that?'

'Sir, it just feels as though there was something not quite right with Quinn's conviction.'

Hitchens turned towards the window. Cooper wasn't sure if he actually found any comfort or inspiration from looking at the back of the Edendale FC stand – especially as he was a Chesterfield fan.

'To all intents and purposes, it was a domestic,' said Hitchens. 'Practically a self-solver.'

'Except that Quinn didn't confess.'

'Not right then. But later, he accepted guilt.'

'Why do you think that was?'

'If you ask me, he was just badly advised by his defence team. These days, they'd have made great play of the past history between Quinn and your father. But the judge wouldn't have accepted it then. It wouldn't have been considered relevant to the case.'

Cooper felt guilty that he should be so troubled by that.

Even in fourteen years, the world had become more cynical. And inevitably, the cynicism all around had rubbed off on him, colouring his own reactions.

Hitchens paused, reading Cooper's troubled expression. 'Joe Cooper was very highly regarded as an officer of honesty and integrity. As I'm sure you know, Ben.'

'Yes, of course I do,' said Cooper, flushing at the implied rebuke.

'Mansell Quinn was convicted and sentenced,' said Hitchens. 'There was no appeal, and no attempt to take it to the Criminal Cases Review Commission. So that's the end of that, as far as we're concerned. The important thing is what's going on in Quinn's mind now.'

'Yes, sir.'

'Quinn knew who Joe Cooper was, no doubt about that. And if he put some of the blame for his conviction on your father, then you might have cause for concern. You'd be wise to tread carefully, and take precautions. But the question of whether Quinn had any genuine grounds for resentment is irrelevant now. The risk is the same, whether he's right or wrong. That's what you should be concerning yourself with.'

'Yes.'

'Everybody knows Joe Cooper was as straight as a die. Frankly, Ben, I'm surprised you're even taking any other possibility seriously. If that's what you're doing.'

Cooper didn't reply.

'*Is* that what you're doing, Ben?'

'I don't know, sir.'

'Well, if it is, I'd recommend that you keep your ideas to yourself.'

Hitchens watched him for a reaction.

'You did say you'd deal with it, Ben,' he said. 'And I trust you to do that. Don't let any of this get in the way of you doing your job. Your DS thinks you're getting too distracted, and I'm supporting her on this.'

The DI gave him a moment to think about it. Cooper was about to get up and leave the office, when Hitchens spoke again.

'There's one other thing, Ben.'

'Yes, sir?'

'Despite what you might think, I do pick up on things that are going on around the department. I hear people talking. So I want to give you a word of advice. It's about DS Fry.'

'Sir?'

The DI spun his chair from side to side, betraying a little uncertainty about venturing into personal issues.

'For a start, Ben,' he said, 'you've no idea what a battle Fry has gone through to get this far.'

'Well, I think –'

Hitchens held up a hand. 'Just let me finish. You can do your thinking later.'

'Right.'

'What I'm trying to say, Ben, is that it's a mistake to involve yourself in DS Fry's private life, no matter what your motives are, or how good your intentions. Sorting out her own problems is what keeps her going – it gives her the strength to be the way she is. I don't want anything undermining that. And I don't suppose she'll thank you for it, either. Am I right?'

'Yes, sir.'

'The thing is, you really won't help her by interfering. You'll only make things worse. And you'll make her resent you, too. Do you understand, Ben?'

'Is that it, sir?' said Cooper.

He stood up this time, determined to get out of the room, no matter what.

'Cooper?' said Hitchens. 'Answer me.'

'Yes, sir,' he said. 'I understand.'

In the incident room, the map was starting to show a detailed picture of Mansell Quinn's trail across the Hope Valley.

Hathersage had three red markers: Mrs Quinn's home, the railway station, and the Out and About shop.

There were the same number of locations in the Hope area too. Added to the station and Rebecca Lowe's house in Aston was the third site known to have been visited by Quinn: the Proctors' caravan park. The markers formed another little cluster, a second triangular shape, like the footstep of a giant insect.

The tracks were heading up the valley towards Castleton, where the toilet block in the car park had been marked with a query – a location pending confirmation. The area was being searched right now, but it hardly mattered. Ben Cooper had no doubt that Quinn was already in the Castleton area.

The pattern of markers on the map made Cooper think of the footprints that Quinn had left at crime scenes. He hesitated for a moment, remembering the conversation he'd had with his DI only a few minutes before. Then he got out the forensic reports from the two murder scenes. Fourteen years had passed between the two killings, but there were remarkable similarities.

The two pairs of boots were entirely different, of course. Those that Quinn had been wearing at the time of Carol Proctor's murder had been only a few months old, according to the lab reports. Made in China, a leather safety boot with rubber soles and reinforced toe caps. Despite their newness, they had a number of small damage features on the soles, including a tiny piece of sharp stone embedded in a ridge of the rubber. These were the details that allowed the forensic lab to make a meaningful comparison. Wear alone might not have been enough.

Techniques of crime scene examination had moved on since 1990. In the garden at Parson's Croft, the SOCOs had used a hard-setting plaster to lift the footwear impressions, so that dirt could be washed off the casts. But at the Carol Proctor scene, they'd been relying on plaster of paris, while the bloody footprints themselves had been enhanced by gentian for the photographer.

Cooper moved a desk lamp over and rummaged around in the drawers of his desk.

'Gavin, have you got a magnifying glass?' he said.

Murfin looked up in amazement. 'Who do you think I am? Sherlock Holmes?'

'Well, somebody must have one.'

Cooper opened and shut a few more drawers, and poked at the back among the old mints and bits of crumpled paper. He crossed the office and opened the drawers of a desk that had belonged to a detective who'd retired and not been replaced. Now it was used as a general dumping ground.

'Ah, here we are.'

He pulled a magnifying glass out of a box containing a tangle of paper clips, leaking ballpoint pens and old business cards. He carried it back to his desk and looked more closely at the photographs of the footprints in the Quinns' sitting room. Under magnification, the photos became grainy and the detail unclear. But there was something odd about the edge of one of the impressions – a blurring that was more than just the way the foot had been put down; a sort of halo effect, or a shadow of the footprint's outline.

'Interesting.'

Cooper went to find Liz Petty in the scenes of crime department. The SOCOs occupied a small room that had been converted from some other use a few years ago, and its partition walls gave it an unfinished look. Liz's computer had a row of yellow post-it notes stuck along the bottom edge. A small brown teddy bear wearing a BBC Radio Derby T-shirt sat on top of the monitor alongside a plastic hedgehog that bobbed on a spring with every movement of air.

Though a civilian, like the other SOCOs, Petty was wearing a navy-blue sweater with the Derbyshire Constabulary logo. She looked at the photographs that Cooper had brought with him.

Cooper pointed out the area around the footprint. 'I was wondering what you think of this.'

'Mmm. It's nothing you could draw a firm conclusion from. It could just be a trick of the light. When was this taken?'

'October 1990.'

'Ah. I don't know what techniques they'd have been using at the time, or what light sources they had. No one could prove this was anything other than a shadow, Ben.'

'OK. But what would be your guess?'

'We don't guess in this department.'

'I'm not asking you to put in a written report, Liz. What's your instinct?'

'Well, I'd say there might be an earlier impression that's been almost covered by this one. At least, that's a possibility – but only one possibility. It proves nothing, Ben. Whoever the footprints belonged to might have stepped in the same place twice.'

'Yes, I suppose so. It was just an idea.'

Cooper took the photo back. Yes, Quinn had walked around the body, there was no dispute about that. And at some point he'd stepped in a footprint that had already been there. But whose? His own? Or had Mansell Quinn unwittingly obliterated the one bit of evidence that might have saved him?

'Did you say 1990?' said Petty. 'Is this the Mansell Quinn case?'

'That's right, Liz.'

'No DNA, then. Profiling hadn't come into general use. In fact, the first conviction using DNA evidence was the year before – a case in Leicestershire. A bloke who was sent down for rape. And they got *him* because he persuaded a mate to give a sample for the DNA test in his place, which was a bit of giveaway.'

'I know.'

'So they wouldn't have taken samples from a suspect in 1990, not even after he was convicted.'

'Yes, I know, Liz. But . . .'

She looked up at him. 'But what?'

'I wondered whether there might be some exhibits still in storage from this case that could yield a bit of DNA.'

'In storage? Have you *seen* our storage?' Petty sighed. 'Well, I suppose you might be lucky, depending on what it was and how it was handled. Now and then you can still come across something in an evidence bag attached to a case file.'

'That's the sort of thing.'

'But, Ben, what good would it do? This bloke was sent down for murder, and he served his time. Are you trying to prove that he didn't do it? I mean, what's the point?'

'I know, I know. I understand what you're saying, Liz.'

'You've got a sample from this bloke for comparison, have you?'

'No.'

'No?' Petty handed him the photos back. 'Ben, for heaven's sake, what's wrong with you?'

'Don't worry about it,' he said.

'We can't work miracles, you know.'

'Just forget it, Liz.'

Cooper began to walk away, regretting that he'd raised the subject at all. It had been a ludicrous idea. And worst of all, Liz Petty had asked the one question he didn't know the answer to. What on earth *was* wrong with him?

Back at his desk in the CID room, Cooper saw Diane Fry leaving the DI's office. He tried to catch her eye, but she looked away. He supposed she must have been talking to the boss about him again. But it didn't really trouble him – she regularly told him to his face that he was too easily distracted. It was entirely his own fault, not hers.

'What have you got scheduled, Ben?' said Fry as she passed his desk.

'Old Mr Thorpe – William's father.'

'Don't let it take up too much of your time. And report back, Ben.'

'Of course. Oh, Diane, I got a copy of the book.'

'What book?'

'The one that Quinn was reading in prison – *Death Underground*.'

'Oh, that.'

'There's a story about a young caver who died in Peak Cavern back in 1959. And you won't believe this, but –'

'Ben – 1959?' Fry raised an eyebrow. 'First it's 1990, now 1959. You're burying yourself in the past.'

'But that's exactly what I mean. Let me tell you –'

'No, Ben. You're getting distracted again. You're going to stop this, aren't you?'

'Yes, OK. Sorry.'

As she walked away, Cooper thought of the bloody footprints in the Carol Proctor crime scene photographs. Mansell Quinn would have seen those prints, too – if not as he stood over the body, then later on, in the files of evidence disclosed to the defence before his trial. His own footprints, clearly marked out in Carol Proctor's blood.

Cooper looked at the forensics reports from Parson's Croft. The impressions in the soil in Rebecca Lowe's garden were now pegged out and covered, photographed and cast in plaster. But the SOCOs had failed to establish a route from the lime trees to the house. If Quinn had approached from that direction, he'd been very careful not to leave traces.

He turned to the evidence from inside the house, looking for a mention of seeds in the carpet or on the kitchen tiles. But there had been none. So perhaps Quinn had removed the black waterproof and packed it away in his rucksack, then brushed himself down and combed his hair before approaching the house like a ghost, leaving no trace of his passing. Perhaps.

And then had he slipped as quietly in through the back door? Or had Rebecca opened the door herself and let him in?

Cooper remembering entering Rebecca Lowe's house. Inside, everything had been very quiet. The carpets had been deep enough to muffle footsteps, and heavy curtains had smothered sounds from outside. All the doors had closed quietly, and even the hands of the clock moved silently. In these last few months, Mrs Lowe seemed to have lived in a cocoon, sheltered from the outside world. That was why the atmosphere in the house had made Cooper feel uncomfortable.

Parson's Croft was the sort of home where radon could be a problem, if it was built on limestone. Central heating and insulation could make a building act like a big chimney, the warm air sucking radon out of the soil and into the house through every crack. Like the carbon dioxide that had killed Neil Moss, radon was colourless, odourless and tasteless. Some people had insulated themselves so carefully that they'd increased the risk to themselves.

It would be easy to convince yourself you were safe in a house like Rebecca Lowe's, where the world never seemed to penetrate. But it would be a false illusion. The outside world had a way of getting into your life in ways that you didn't expect. It crept through the tiniest cracks in the foundations. It rose out of the ground, and it seeped into the water. It was as insidious as radon gas. And just as deadly.

29

'The net is closing in,' said DCI Oliver Kessen. 'But we're asking everyone in the area to be vigilant and report any possible sightings of this man.'

Kessen looked sombre. He gazed directly at the camera for a few moments with a determined expression until he was faded out and the newsreader came back on to give the phone number. Watching the performance, Ben Cooper wondered if the DCI had been on a media course recently. He'd got the direct gaze off quite well.

'Well, that was a result,' said DI Hitchens. 'A few tears, a bit of emotion. That should get us on the one o'clock news. They couldn't have done it any better.'

'I take it you mean the Lowes, rather than Mr Kessen,' said Chief Superintendent Colin Jepson. The divisional commander had joined the enquiry team for half an hour to watch the broadcast. He sat stiffly on a chair among the detectives, trying for an air of informality.

'Well, quite, sir,' said Hitchens.

But Cooper wasn't sure about that. He looked around the room for the reaction of the rest of the team. For him, Andrea Lowe had performed well at the press conference. She'd been articulate and compelling, her manner suggesting strong emotion barely restrained. But her brother, Simon? There had been little from him throughout. This time, he'd left Andrea to do all the talking as he sat, tense and uncomfortable, uttering only monosyllables of agreement.

Cooper found himself wondering about the nature of Simon's relationship with his father. He'd been fifteen years old at the time of Carol Proctor's murder, and the trauma must have gone pretty deep. Cooper knew how difficult it could be to deal with conflicting emotions about a parent. In Simon Lowe, he was looking at someone who was almost a mirror image of himself.

'You know we're going to get every busybody in Derbyshire phoning in, don't you?' said the Chief Superintendent, as Hitchens killed the TV picture with the remote. 'Everybody will want to think they've seen Mansell Quinn. Within twenty-four hours, you'll be nobody around here unless you've had Quinn lurking in your back garden. You won't be able to hold your head up with the neighbours if you haven't stood next to him in the queue at the chippy at least once.'

'We are rather relying on the public, sir,' said Hitchens. 'We don't have any other options at the moment.'

'All we can rely on the public to do is to tie up all my resources.'

'It *will* use a lot of resources manning the phones and checking out the sightings,' said Hitchens. 'But we need the help of the public. We've got to catch this man before he strikes again.'

'Strikes again?' said Jepson. 'Are you writing headlines for the newspapers these days, Hitchens? Have you taken a sub-editor's course at the *Derbyshire Times*? Are you going to start talking in words of one syllable?'

'Sorry, chief. I meant, we're gathering community-based intelligence in our efforts to establish the location of the principal suspect prior to a recurrence of his offending behaviour.'

The Chief Superintendent went rather red in the face. Watching him, Cooper shifted uneasily in his chair. He hadn't yet learned to overcome the awe for his divisional commander that he'd felt ever since he was a trainee PC. Hearing somebody provoking him so blatantly was rather shocking.

'You know who's going to get the blame for all this?' said Jepson.

'Sir?' said Hitchens.

'Me.' The Chief Superintendent sighed. 'But quite frankly, it goes with the job description. As divisional commander, you have to be ready to take all the flak that people want to fire at you. And believe me, it comes in from every direction.'

'Yes, sir.'

'But it doesn't worry me,' said Jepson. 'In fact, I take it as a compliment. If people are permanently having a go at you, at least it means they think you're big enough to be a target.'

'You ain't nobody unless you've been booed some time,' said Hitchens.

Jepson stared at him. 'Sorry?'

'It was something Bob Dylan said.'

'DI Hitchens, I haven't the faintest idea what you're talking about.'

'Sorry, sir. I thought Bob Dylan might have been your era.'

Jepson went a little red around the ears. 'For your information, Hitchens, as a young man I was already an enthusiast for Italian opera. I suspect you're being facetious, Inspector.'

'Not at all, sir. Just trying to help with the cultural references. It's so easy to get out of touch, isn't it?'

'Perhaps it's time you were back at work on the Quinn case. There's must be a great deal to do.'

'Yes, sir.'

It was obvious why everyone was on edge. Progress had ground to a halt. Painstaking legwork and hours of phone calls had established Quinn's route from Sudbury Prison. He'd used buses as far as Hathersage, then a train the short distance to Hope. After that, he seemed to have been on foot, because the information from the public transport system had dried up.

Most worrying of all, it was now Friday, and there had been no reported sightings of Quinn since Wednesday night, when he'd called on Raymond Proctor at the caravan park.

Cooper watched the DI stand in front of the maps and run his eyes over the geography of the Hope Valley for the hundredth time, perhaps considering the futility of sending the helicopter support unit up to cover the ground. They'd be looking for one man in a landscape scattered with hikers and in villages thronged with tourists.

Hitchens turned and looked at Cooper. 'What do you think, Ben?'

'He's still in the area somewhere,' said Cooper.

'Why?'

'He hasn't finished what he came back for yet.'

Will Thorpe had walked out of Wingate Lees caravan park as soon as he thought no one was looking. He would have preferred to be in a hostel. At least he'd have had no problem with the accommodation, or the people who ran the place. They were usually civil enough.

But the idea that everyone knew where he was had started to make him feel nervous. He felt trapped, pinned down, expected to wait helplessly for the arrival of anyone who chose to find him. Within minutes of arriving at Wingate Lees, he'd known he would have to get away. He had noticed Connie Proctor watching him. Next day, she'd have got Ray to tell him to leave anyway.

Thorpe remembered the abandoned field barn. He was pretty sure he'd used it before. He didn't mind the smells. In fact, he hardly noticed them any more. They were simply a sign of the presence of humanity nearby, a warning that he should go carefully and be on the alert.

The stone building stood between Dirtlow Rake and the quarry of the cement works. Thorpe could hear the growl and squeal of machinery in the quarry and the rumble of the excavators. From the doorway, he could see a dumper truck driving along the ridge, throwing up a trail of dust.

Inside, the field barn was divided it into two bare rooms, connected by a doorway so low that he had to stoop to get under the lintel. The dirt floor was uneven and scattered with lumps of limestone that had fallen out of the walls, as well as crisp packets and screwed-up tissues left by the last people in here. There were round beams above head height and openings high in the wall – one of them looked as though it had been a fireplace, with ventilation through the wall into a chimney.

Thorpe looked around doubtfully. The building had no doors, and the empty windows narrowed from a foot to a couple of inches on the outside, like arrow slits. There would be no escape for anything through these holes, either animal or human.

The roof was mostly sound, though, and Thorpe could see from the dirt floor that the rain came through in only one spot. Unless there was a storm, when the wind would drive rain through every nook and cranny. It was exposed up here, and even now the wind gusted raggedly around the building with a noise like someone battering on the walls.

Thorpe found a piece of corrugated tin lying in deep nettles in front of the building. It must have been there for some time, because the nettles were growing through the bolt holes. The tin crackled loudly when he walked across it, and he decided to drag it across the open doorway, just as a precaution.

He was very tired, and all he really wanted to do was sleep. Sometimes he wished he were like a bird – they didn't sleep the way people did, but were able to shut down just one half of their brain at a time, while the other half remained on the alert.

He wouldn't be staying long here anyway. Tomorrow, he'd move on, get away from the area altogether. It wasn't safe for him here any more. But it had been an exhausting day, and he needed sleep.

Outside, the dumper truck rumbled back across the ridge. The dust it threw up turned yellow as dark clouds gathered in the east, swallowing the evening light. But Will Thorpe was no longer aware of it.

Diane Fry could stand it no longer. That evening, she looked up Ben Cooper's phone number and called him at home.

'Oh, Diane, it's you,' he said. 'What's happened?'

'Nothing.'

'Nothing? I thought perhaps Quinn had been found. Or someone else . . .'

'No. Nothing.'

'Right.'

There was an awkward pause. It was one of those pauses she'd promised herself she wouldn't allow to develop, in case she felt obliged to fill it with the usual: 'Well, I'll let you get on, then.'

But Cooper filled the pause himself with some inconsequential chatter about his landlady and people they knew at the station. There was even something about snails that she didn't understand. Fry was trying to judge whether he wanted to talk or was just trying to get her off the phone by boring her to death.

She'd almost decided to put the phone down and stop bothering him, when Cooper took her by surprise.

'Diane,' he said, 'would it be possible for me to come round and see you?'

'What?' she said, struck by the sudden change in his voice.

'If you don't want me to, it's OK.'

'Well . . .'

'Or you could come to see me, if you like. Or we could meet somewhere else. Whichever you prefer. Only, it's a bit difficult on the phone.'

'What is, Ben?'

'Talking. I mean, talking properly.'

Fry could feel herself smiling. She was smiling so hard that her cheeks were hurting. 'You want to talk about something, Ben?'

'Yes. Look, I know it's an imposition. You won't want to bother. But if you could spare a bit of time. Just half an hour. Do you think you could? Spare a bit of time for me?'

'Yes, Ben,' she said. 'Of course I could.'

She heard him sigh with relief.

'Thank you,' he said. 'There's something I really do need to talk to you about.'

Will Thorpe was woken by the rain. Even in his half-asleep state, he knew that something was wrong, but it took a few seconds before he could figure out what. Then he began to wonder why the rain was falling on his face. He vaguely recalled that he was in the field barn, and that he'd chosen his spot carefully to be in the dry. But water was definitely dripping on him.

Thorpe groaned and cursed. The wind must have changed direction during the night and now the rain was blowing in on him. If he didn't move, he'd be soaking wet by morning and his joints would be so stiff that he'd hardly be able to walk. And he had to be away early. He had to get away from the area, because it wasn't safe.

Nevertheless, he lay thinking about it for a second or two longer. Perhaps the rain would stop and save him from having to move. But he could hear it falling steadily on the roof of the barn. Instead, Thorpe listened for the wind – it might be

324

just a passing squall that was blowing the rain in. Against his will, he felt his brain become a little more alert, his senses stirring sluggishly in response to some anxiety. He screwed his eyes tight shut and listened again. There was no wind.

Thorpe's eyelids creaked open. At first, he could see nothing. His vision was unfocused by sleep, and his surroundings unfamiliar. He recognized the smells he'd fallen asleep among – stale cigarette butts and urine, damp concrete and soil. But he detected something new, too, something that hadn't been there before. The smell of another human being.

Another drop of water fell on Thorpe's cheek. And with a lurch of terror, he became aware of the figure looming over him, a dark shape bending downwards, water leaking from its black angles, and invisible eyes staring at him in silence.

Thorpe began to scream. The noise came from deep in his belly, almost bypassing his exhausted lungs, shocking him with its volume. At the same time, he thrashed around in his blanket, trying to sit up, free his hands, or roll away from whoever was standing over him. The noise of his screaming filled the field barn, cracking an echo off the stone walls and the ancient beams in a derisive imitation of his fear.

The figure had been still until now. But the yelling jolted it into action. Two black arms slipped towards his face and hands covered his mouth, crushing his lips against his teeth and forcing his head back against the dirt floor. And Thorpe's screaming stopped.

30

'Who's that at the door, Sis?' said Angie Fry.

'It's Ben Cooper.'

'Hey, how's he doing? I'll say hello to him.'

Diane Fry stared at her sister, who made no effort to move from the settee. 'For God's sake, put some knickers on, at least,' she said.

'Oh, sorry.'

Angie fished around in the pile of clothes on the floor, and found a white scrap of material that she pulled up her legs. Fry turned her eyes away. She was worried that she might see on her body some telltale mark of addiction that she couldn't ignore.

Cooper came through the door of the flat hesitantly. He'd been here only a couple of times before, and the second time he couldn't even remember what had happened. But Fry watched him carefully for signs that he disapproved of the mess.

'Hi, Ben.'

'Angie,' said Cooper cautiously.

'Good to see you.' Angie smiled, and patted him on the chest. 'I'd love to stop and chat, but I know I'm in the way. You two have police stuff to talk about, I bet.'

Angie walked back towards the sitting room, and Fry looked on stonily as Cooper turned to watch her. She supposed he couldn't help it. The T-shirt Angie was wearing failed to cover her buttocks, and the knickers she'd put on did little more.

At least Cooper had the grace to look embarrassed when he met Fry's eye and found her watching him.

'If you've finished staring at my sister's bum,' she said, 'we've got somewhere to go.'

But before she reached the door, Fry was sure she caught a glimpse of her sister peering around the corner from the sitting room, pulling a face at Cooper. That moment of secret communication between the two of them, no doubt some ridicule at her expense, made Fry flush angrily. She ran down the steps into Cavendish Road, pulling her unbuttoned coat across her chest, and left Ben Cooper to catch up with her in the rain.

They went to the Light House, a famous pub that sat on top of a hill on the Buxton road out of Edendale. It wasn't a long drive from Fry's flat, and the evenings were light enough at this time of year for them to enjoy the spectacular views for an hour or two. They managed to get a table on a terrace that had been converted into a conservatory, sheltered from the first drops of rain that were already falling. Cooper bought the drinks, trying to hide his surprise when Fry asked for a vodka.

'You've seen the files from the Carol Proctor case, Diane,' said Cooper. 'What do you think? I can't understand why there were never any serious questions about Mansell Quinn's conviction.'

'Well, nobody wants a successful prosecution thrown into doubt, do they?' said Fry.

'Nobody?'

'Almost nobody. And especially when the convicted person

has already spent a number of years in prison. It makes things a bit unpleasant all round.'

'I've been trying to imagine what the effect of this might have been on Quinn. I don't think we understand what's going on in his mind.'

Fry snorted. 'But I bet you think you've got closer to his mental processes than anybody, don't you, Ben?'

'At least I try,' said Cooper.

'And what conclusion have you come to?'

'I think he's a righteous killer.'

'A *what*?'

'A righteous killer.'

'Where on earth did you get that expression from?'

'I can't remember,' said Cooper. 'I heard it somewhere, and it seems to fit.'

'So what does it mean exactly?'

'It means someone who thinks he's doing right, not wrong. Someone who thinks his actions are morally justified. Maybe he even thinks he's achieving justice.'

'We're the ones whose job is to achieve justice, Ben.'

'Yes.'

But Cooper knew that wasn't right. The job of the police wasn't to achieve justice but to gather enough evidence to obtain a conviction. There was a big difference.

'Ben, your empathy is legendary,' said Fry. 'But you're going too far this time. Surely you can't have fooled yourself into empathizing with Quinn? You can't think there's any justification for what he's doing?'

'That wasn't what I was trying to say.'

The next pause in the conversation was so quiet that he could hear the ticking of his watch above the sound of the raindrops on the glass roof. To demonstrate his calmness, Cooper picked up one of the drip-mats and used it to brush the crumbs off the table. He concentrated on doing it, clearing the space around him with the air of having found a task that was as important as anything they might have been talking about. He took his time. But he could feel her watching him impatiently.

'So what is it that's really bothering you?' said Fry.

'What you might not have noticed about the Carol Proctor case was that the arresting officer was my father.'

He watched Fry open her mouth to make a smart comment, but then hesitate as she remembered that Sergeant Joe Cooper was dead – and how he had died. He didn't know why, but he'd noticed that his father's memory was one of the few things that had the power to soften her sharpness. He'd seen the way she handled the photograph over the mantelpiece that one time she'd visited his flat.

Now, her mouth stayed open slightly, but no comment came out. A tiny drop of vodka slid from her upper lip, like a tear.

'So that's why,' she said. 'DI Hitchens knows, of course.'

'Yes.'

'Tell me about it, Ben.'

So he told her. He left out none of the details. Fry listened well when she wanted to, and she said nothing while Cooper talked. When he'd finished, she fetched more drinks and took a sip of her vodka. Her first question took him by surprise.

'The other officer who attended the scene with your father, the PC . . .'

'Netherton,' said Cooper.

'Where is he now?'

'I don't know.' Cooper put down his glass and sat up straighter. 'Damn.'

'He's the only other person who was there at the time,' said Fry. 'Apart from Mansell Quinn, obviously.'

'Diane, that's exactly what I need. Another brain, a second pair of eyes. You've put your finger on something I couldn't even see, because I haven't been thinking clearly.'

'It's because you're personally involved, Ben. I've told you and told you: don't get so personally involved. You need to take a step back –'

'I know, I know. But it's difficult in this case. I think I'm getting a bit obsessed.'

'Oh, I know all about your obsessions.'

Cooper decided to let that one pass. 'I really can't see what Dad did wrong – if anything. But even the slightest grey area seems to take on the worst possible interpretation. I'm sure it's all in my mind, Diane. Why can't I be objective, as I would if it was anyone else?'

'What did Mr Hitchens say?'

'He told me to keep my ideas to myself.'

Fry nodded. 'It's good advice, more often than not. Don't forget that Quinn pleaded guilty at trial. Even if your father did interfere with evidence, it might be considered noble cause.'

'Noble cause,' repeated Cooper. It was a long time since he'd heard the expression, once used to justify the actions of police officers who 'improved' evidence to ensure the conviction of someone they were sure was guilty.

'You're not above noble causes yourself, are you, Ben?' said Fry.

Cooper watched her take another drink. He didn't expect any sensitive insights from her, but he hadn't been able to think of anyone else he could explain his feelings to, outside the family. At least he'd been able to say what he wanted to. It didn't really matter if she didn't understand, or care.

'You need to prove that your father wasn't perfect, don't you?' she said.

'What?'

'That's what everybody tells you. You must hear it endlessly. I certainly have, since I came here.'

'Yes, of course.'

'It's always the reaction when someone dies. Sergeant Joe Cooper has become the great hero, the ideal copper. And you can't accept that, can you?'

'Wait a minute. You don't think that I hated my father –'

'No, that's not what I'm saying. But, in a way, your memory of him has been taken over by this heroic image that you keep having shoved down your throat. Ben, you won't be able to reclaim your own memory of him as your father until you've proved he wasn't the paragon of perfection that everybody says he was, until you've shown that he was flawed. That he was human.'

'Maybe.'

'People must have flaws before you can love them properly,' said Fry.

Cooper stood up a bit too quickly, knocking the drip mat on the floor.

'I think I'd better fetch some more drinks,' he said.

Lying on his back in the abandoned field barn, Will Thorpe rolled his neck from side to side, wincing at the pain. He had been used to pain for a long time, but this was different. This was a pain mixed with fear and shock. He knew his lip was bleeding, and the back of his head felt sore where it had hit a stone. He'd wet himself, too – he could feel a warm, damp patch in his trousers. But at least he was sitting up now, his back against the wall, the blanket pushed down to his knees to free his arms.

'I'm sorry,' said a voice. 'But you mustn't make so much noise.'

'I did what you wanted me to do,' said Thorpe.

'Oh, yeah. But who else did you tell?'

'Nobody.'

'I don't believe you.'

'It's true.'

'Who did you tell, Will?'

'I'm choking,' said Thorpe, tugging at Quinn's hands. 'You're choking me.'

'And why shouldn't I?'

331

'Mansell, I'm a sick man. You know that.'

Thorpe knew Quinn would be able to hear the rasp of his breathing, growing louder as he became more stressed. He opened his mouth wide to let the sound escape more clearly, making full use for once of the damage to his lungs. He couldn't see Quinn's expression, but he felt the fingers loosen slightly on his throat.

'I ought to kill you,' said Quinn. 'I ought to put you out of your misery, like an animal.'

But Thorpe was feeling more confident. He knew Mansell Quinn. And Quinn had never been a clever man, as far as he was concerned.

'I'm your mate, Mansell,' he said. 'Remember?'

'Crap. You shafted me, like everyone else.'

'No.'

'Mate? Some mate.'

For a moment, the fingers had tightened again. But Quinn's grip had no conviction any more. Thorpe gasped air in and tried to force himself to relax. His hands dropped away from Quinn's wrists as if he had lost the strength to support his arms. Quinn immediately let him go, and Thorpe fell back, gasping loudly and fingering his throat.

'Don't make such a fuss,' said Quinn. 'You're not dead yet.'

'It's my chest. It's a real mess, the doctors said. I don't suppose I'll live much longer.'

Quinn leaned closer. 'If you're lying to me, Will, you won't live for another day. I'll make sure of that.'

'Yeah, OK, Mansell. OK.'

With a sudden thrust, Quinn grabbed a handful of Thorpe's jacket and banged his head against the wall.

'You'd better believe me,' he said. 'Because I mean it.'

'OK, I said I believe you.'

Quinn sat back on his heels, and there was silence. Thorpe could hear the water dripping from Quinn's waterproof and the faint rustling as he moved. He turned his head to the side, hoping to see the other man's face. But all he could make out was a black shape against the faint rectangle of the doorway.

'You told Rebecca, didn't you, Will?'

'That wasn't my fault,' said Thorpe. 'Look, the police told me she was killed. Did you – ?'

He heard Quinn take a sharp breath, and he stopped. Perhaps he didn't want to ask that question, after all.

'You talk too much, Will. That's a pity,' said Quinn.

'What do you mean?'

'It comes of spending too long on your own, I suppose. You never learned to control your mouth. Remember when you came to visit me at Sudbury, and you talked to me about what it was like back home? You even told me the places you doss. That made you much too easy to find, Will.'

Thorpe tried to laugh, but the noise came out as a wheeze, and his mouth filled with bile. He wanted to spit it out, but was afraid that Quinn would take it as a deliberate insult.

'I should have known better, shouldn't I, Mansell? Giving away my position. What an idiot, eh?'

'You told Rebecca, didn't you?'

'Yes.'

'Who else did you talk to?'

Thorpe didn't reply. Quinn shifted his position, so that the darkness of his eyes became visible for a moment inside his hood.

'I've got all night, Will. And it could be a long and painful night.'

Drawing a laboured breath, Thorpe raised a hand in an appeasing gesture. 'There's no need to be like that, Mansell,' he said. 'I'll tell you what you want to know.'

Ben Cooper swirled his beer, watching the foam rise over the lip of the glass. He was aware of the pub getting busier, more and more voices raised in conversation around him as the Eden Valley landscape withdrew into the darkness.

'So will you help me, Diane?' he said. 'I need your emotional detachment.'

'My *what*?'

Cooper realized he might not have put that in quite the right way. 'You know what I mean,' he said.

Fry sat back and gazed out of the window at the rain falling over the Eden Valley.

'This would be entirely unofficial, I suppose?'

'Yes. Officially, I've had advice about the potential threat from Quinn, just like the others on the list. But that's as far as it goes. Officially.'

'I see. A personal favour, then?'

Cooper nodded. He was starting to feel like a small child in the head teacher's office, asking for time off school.

'What do you say, Diane?'

She continued to stare at the view across the valley. She'd learned to control her responses so well that Cooper sometimes wondered whether she'd heard him at all. She had a trick of waiting just the right amount of time, so he had to start working out for himself what she was thinking. Invariably, of course, he was mistaken. And so she wrong-footed him every time, just as she did now.

'There might be a deal we can come to,' she said.

'A deal?'

'I don't suppose it occurred to you to wonder why I phoned you in the first place tonight, did it?'

'Er . . .'

'Some of us might have personal concerns of our own, you know. Despite our emotional detachment.'

'Yes, of course, Diane. But –'

'It's about Angie,' she said.

'Oh.' And because Cooper thought that might sound pathetic and inadequate, he added, 'You mean your sister?'

Fry reached a hand to take hold of her glass. It was a carefully controlled movement, but Cooper sensed that she needed something to occupy her attention. Still she kept her head turned away, with the shadow of the rain-streaked roof across her face, her eyes too dark to read their expression when she spoke.

'You know damn well I mean my sister.'

Cooper winced at the hint of venom in the sibilants. He'd heard that tone of voice before, and the subsequent conversation had never been comfortable.

'I'm sorry, Diane.'

'Oh, yeah? Sorry for what?'

Cooper threw up his hands. 'For interfering. It was none of my business. I had no right to interfere in your life. You told me that yourself, and you were right. But I just went blundering on. All I can say is that I thought I was doing the right thing. The right thing for you, I mean.'

'And I'm supposed to say "thank you"?'

'Of course not. You're angry with me. And you have every right to be.'

Fry raised her shoulders and took a deep breath. Cooper braced himself for the anger that he thought was about to come. He'd given her the cue, after all. And it would be better once it was all out, once the storm was over. The air would be left clear, and they might be able to carry on with whatever relationship they had before, instead of the constant nervous uncertainty, the treading on eggshells in case he said the wrong thing.

But the outburst didn't come. Fry let out the breath. Her shoulders slumped. She took a drink of her vodka and watched four people get out of a Volvo in the car park and walk towards the terrace.

If they'd been able to sit outside, at least there would have been a bit of breeze – a breath of air to ease the humidity. Cooper could use it now. His neck and forehead prickled uncomfortably. Diane Fry's intense concentration on him had always made him sweat and feel claustrophobic. He was worried she'd judge his responses disappointing, his manner lacking in signs of enthusiasm or understanding, or whatever else it might be that she was expecting of him.

But Fry seemed to have made a decision and she wasn't going to allow anything to distract her from her purpose, however distasteful the task she had in mind.

'What do you know about her?' she said.

'About Angie?'

'Yes. You remember – my *sister*.'

'Not very much.'

'But you know *something* about her. She talked to you. She came to your flat.'

'Yes, she did.'

'She stayed the night.'

'Yes. But Diane – I did it for you.'

'And what do you mean by that, Ben?' she said.

'Just . . .' Cooper raised his shoulders, flapped his arms helplessly. He couldn't say to her that she ought to understand the importance of relationships and family and friendship – she, who had been so cruelly deprived of it. Shouldn't her past experiences have made her more understanding, more aware of what she had missed?

Somehow Cooper's hopeless gestures seemed to communicate more clearly what he meant than any amount of embarrassing sentences. She could have tuned out his words, refused to listen, cut him short with a few painful expletives and left him floundering. But she couldn't defend herself against the sudden jolt of comprehension that leaped between them, like a charge of electricity from a badly earthed connection. Her eyes widened, a faint flush crept along her injured cheek. Cooper saw that she knew what he meant, after all. She'd read it in his mind, translated it from his eyes without the need for words.

But he didn't expect Diane Fry to respond. He expected her to do exactly what she did next: to turn away, unable to meet his eyes. There was nothing else she needed to say.

'Diane, I've said I'm sorry. I don't know what else I can do.'

Fry leaned across the table towards him. Her face was pale, as if she had been living out the summer in the darkness of the caves below Castleton instead of in the open air.

'Ben, how much does it cost to get a private detox?'

Cooper looked startled. 'I don't know.'

'About two grand, would you say?'

'Thereabouts. What is it you want from me?'

'I want you to find out more about her,' she said. 'I want to know what she's been doing these last fifteen years. I need to know who she was mixed up with in Sheffield. I need to know what she's doing *now*.'

Cooper sat back in his chair. The movement was partly to give himself a little more distance from Fry's fixed stare, which he found unnerving. But it was also to provide a moment to think. He already knew more about Angie Fry than he'd told Diane. He supposed he'd tried to push the information to the back of his mind, in the hope that he would never have to tell her.

'I don't understand, Diane. She's your sister. You haven't seen her for fifteen years. You must have talked to each other since you met up again –'

'We've hardly done anything else but talk. I've told Angie everything about myself, everything that's happened to me since Warley. And she's told me a lot about herself, too.'

Cooper shook his head, puzzled. 'So what's the problem?'

'I don't believe her.'

'What?'

Fry seemed to have trouble getting the words out a second time, as if her lips had gone numb.

'I don't believe her. I think she's lying to me.'

She took another drink, then held her glass up to the light. It was empty. A bluebottle buzzed closer, attracted by the smell, and Fry swatted at it with a vicious side-swipe of her hand.

'Why would she do that?' said Cooper, trying to put conviction into his voice.

'I don't know. That's what I'd like to find out.'

'Have you told her you don't think she's telling you the truth?'

'Of course not.'

'Why not?'

Fry sighed. 'You don't understand. I've just found her after all these years. Or *you* found her for me . . .' She paused and looked at Cooper, who tried to meet her gaze, but failed and dropped his eyes. 'I might be wrong, and I can't risk ruining it now. She's my sister, and I love her very much. I don't want to lose her again. But I need to know. I need to know the truth. Do you understand that, Ben?'

'I think so.'

'I could be wrong,' said Fry. 'But I don't think I am.'

Cooper was aware of a fly in the ointment here. His best bet was to say 'no' to what Fry wanted him to do and hope that he could keep out of the situation entirely.

'If you're worried, you could make enquiries yourself,' he said.

Fry shook her head. 'There's a big risk of her finding out that I'm checking up on her. I'm frightened she'd just walk away again. I get the feeling she's on a knife edge, that she hasn't quite decided whether to stay or leave. She might just disappear from my life again. I couldn't stand that.'

'No.'

'But you – I don't think she'd be surprised if she found out that you'd been checking up on her. It would only confirm her opinion of you.'

'I see. Basically, you want me to be the fall guy if anything goes wrong?'

'Basically, yes.'

Cooper began to shake his head. But Fry fixed him with her direct stare again.

'I think you owe me this, Ben,' she said. 'You owe me this, at least.'

He dropped his eyes. He'd always found it difficult to meet her stare.

'Believe me,' she said, 'if there was anyone else I could trust . . .'

Cooper hesitated a moment longer. Perhaps it was a moment too long.

'I'm sorry, Diane. I don't think I can do that. I've already interfered enough, as you said yourself just now. My getting more involved wouldn't do either of us any good.'

For the last few minutes Fry had been sliding her glass backwards and forwards across the polished surface of the table, as if intrigued by the sound it made against the wood, or the patterns formed by the streaks of condensation. But now, her hand became still.

'I knew this would happen,' she said. 'It's been like this all my life. No matter what you think you want, it turns out to be a disappointment when you finally get it.'

She looked at her glass as she spoke, addressing the remaining mouthfuls of vodka as if it were the spirit that had disappointed her, as if its taste was just one more thing that hadn't come up to her expectations.

Will Thorpe heard the sound of a car engine on the road outside, climbing slowly up the hill above the cement works from Pindale. Quinn heard it, too. He let go of Thorpe's jacket and straightened up. Thorpe watched him stoop under the connecting doorway and slip into the shadows near the entrance to wait for the car to pass. He suspected Quinn

339

wouldn't have a car of his own, and wouldn't want to risk walking along the road, where he'd be seen too easily. He would be intending to navigate his way across the fields back to Edendale or Castleton, or wherever he was heading next.

Thorpe smiled in the darkness. Quinn hadn't taken the trouble to check what he had in the pack under his blanket. He hadn't considered his old friend a threat.

As quietly as he could, Thorpe slipped the carrying case out of the pack. The zip made a noise that sounded loud to him. But a few feet away, Quinn didn't react. His concentration was entirely on the vehicle approaching up the hill.

Thorpe knew he couldn't risk Quinn wandering around loose any longer. While Quinn was around, he would always be in danger. He'd never be able to sleep safely again for the rest of his life.

With a surge of excitement and fear that gripped his chest and made him gasp, Thorpe slid the crossbow slowly out of his pack. He had already snapped out the arms and unfolded the stock, and he was thankful that he'd left the weapon cocked before he went to sleep, with the automatic safety on. But when the string was pulled back and locked into the trigger, it made an audible click that even the sound of the car engine wouldn't have covered. Quinn could have heard that.

Now Thorpe's hand shook as he fumbled for one of the eighteen-inch bolts he'd taken from Ray Proctor's house. It was a long time since he'd handled a crossbow, and he prayed his aim would be good. Relying almost entirely on his sense of touch in the darkness, he placed the bolt under the front sight bracket and on to the track unit, then felt for its fletches and turned one down into the track groove. Lastly, he slid the bolt back under the retainer and into the trigger mechanism.

The car passed by. Its headlights swung briefly across the front of the building, and Thorpe could see Quinn for a moment as a blacker shape in the darkness of the barn, a momentary glitter of rainwater on his smock picking him out as a target.

Quinn raised his head only when he heard the safety button released on the side of the trigger. The noise was distinctive, and Thorpe could picture the puzzled frown on his face, perhaps even the first hint of fear.

Thorpe sighted into the darkness towards the low door-way, holding his breath and feeling for the trigger a little more quickly than he should have.

'Mansell,' he called. 'I believe you.'

And Thorpe waited one second for Quinn to start turning, before he shot him.

31

Saturday, 17 July

When Ben Cooper arrived at Siggate, a uniformed inspector from Traffic section was practically spinning on the spot. The reflective hoops and patches on his yellow jacket flashed and flickered in the lights as he paced along the tape. He was listening to the crackling voices from his radio, shouting instructions to somebody at the other end, then glaring at the field barn as if it had delivered a personal insult.

'We can't sustain this situation for long,' he said. 'We've had to close the road all the way back to Castleton and all the way up to Bradwell so we can operate diversions for the traffic. Highways have got the carriageway up in Castleton for repair work. I'm warning you, it's going to be complete chaos for twenty miles in every direction in a couple of hours' time. We'll bring the whole of North Derbyshire to a halt.'

The inspector swore when he was ignored and went back to his radio.

The exact time a motorist had called in on his mobile phone to report the body had been logged by Control, but it wasn't necessarily a reliable indicator of when the incident had occurred. The road was quiet at this time of the morning.

And even if other drivers had passed by earlier, they had either seen nothing or not bothered to stop.

The body was out of sight of the road, inside the abandoned field barn. The motorist might be wishing he hadn't called it in, now that he was being asked to explain what he'd stopped for.

Cooper found himself quite by accident standing near DCI Kessen, who'd just arrived and was being briefed by the Crime Scene Manager.

'There's a good bit of blood inside,' said the CSM. 'And splashes of it in the nettles, and between the building and the gate over there.'

'What about the road?' said Kessen. 'Traffic was still going through for a while – enough to contaminate the scene?'

'I'm not too concerned about the road. It looks as though your man came and went on foot.'

'Really?'

The CSM pointed towards the gateway. 'We'll be able to see things a lot better when it's daylight, but Liz has found some traces leading off into the field there. The poor bugger inside obviously never made it as far as the gateway, so it seems a fair bet that it's going to be your suspect's exit route. The field is nice and empty, thank God. There's nothing worse than a herd of inquisitive cows trampling a crime scene. They're even worse than a bunch of heavy-footed coppers, and that's saying something.'

'Any ID?'

'There doesn't seem to be anything on him. You might have a better chance of identifying him when you get him to the mortuary.'

'Sir, could I get a closer look?' said Cooper. 'I might recognize him.'

Kessen nodded. The CSM kitted Cooper out in a scene suit and guided him to a point where he could see the face of the dead man.

The body lay in the inner room of the field barn, sprawled on its back on the dirt floor. Cooper had to bend almost double to duck through the doorway on the stepping plates laid by the SOCOs. Lights had been set up in two of the corners, illuminating the victim like an exhibit in an art gallery. The floor around him seemed to glitter where flecks of quartz in the limestone reflected the lights.

The smell was pretty bad in here. Cooper wasn't sure how much of it was the effect of extreme violence and death on the body's natural processes, and how much resulted from whatever had gone on in the field barn previously. Some SOCO would have the pleasure of analysing the screwed-up tissues and crisp packets.

There were bloodstains, too, and a lot of disturbance of the ground. But Cooper's attention was drawn to the face. It was dark red, almost purple in the artificial light. What he could see of the neck was marked by deep, black bruises, the result of far more violence being used on the victim than was necessary.

'Any luck, Cooper?'

'Yes, I know who it is,' he said. 'It's William Thorpe.'

DCI Kessen sighed and turned to the officers waiting by their vehicles.

'All right,' he said. 'Why have we still got the road closed? Isn't there anyone here from Traffic?'

He was always like that. Whenever we had a row, I'd think it was all over and forgotten about. But he . . . Mansell would go away and brood about things. It seemed as though he turned everything over in his mind, everything that I'd said in the heat of the moment. He picked my words apart, analysing them, making himself more and more angry. There were a lot of things that I didn't mean, of course. But he never seemed to understand that. He took everything to heart and stored it up. His memory was unnervingly accurate, too – I could tell he'd rehearsed my words over and over, letting them eat away at him from the inside. Then he would come back to the subject after a while – the next morning, or two or three days later, or longer than that even. And by then he'd built up the whole thing in his mind, turned it into something else, something far worse. When he came back to it, he was angrier than he'd been while we were arguing. I called it his 'slow burn'. It was like he had a really long fuse that took time to burn down before the explosion came. It was really quite frightening. Because I never knew when it might happen.

Mansell was never physically violent towards me. It was only words. When the explosion did come, it was just that – an explosion of anger. What I would still call the heat of the moment. An outpouring of emotion, something he had to get out of his system. I wouldn't describe him a cold, calculating man. Not at all . . .

Statement of Rebecca Quinn, October 1990

Ben Cooper was tired, and ready to go back home. It was three o'clock in the morning, and it was still raining. It was also his birthday.

He stared blearily out of the window of the CID room, wondering how much rain had to fall before Peak Cavern flooded. He was picturing the parties of tourists running to get out of the cavern, foaming water rushing behind them through the passages, roaring like all the devils in Hell were after them. He knew it wouldn't happen in real life – there would be plenty of warning before anyone was caught by a flood.

Cooper had read Rebecca Quinn's statement before, but this morning her analysis of her husband's character seemed particularly ironic. Perhaps he was just tired, but she seemed to be talking about a different man altogether.

He guessed Rebecca wouldn't have been allowed back into her own home for a while after that day in October 1990 – not until the SOCOs were satisfied that they'd done all they could to collect the available evidence. Her sitting room had probably still been prohibited to her then, even if she'd wanted to enter it.

Cooper tried to imagine what it would be like to go back into your house knowing someone had recently died a violent death in your sitting room, and that your husband was probably the killer. Would it still feel like your own home? Or would everything have changed? He suspected it would feel as if some alien presence had invaded your space.

There would have been a horrible temptation to open the door of the room where it happened, to look for some sort of explanation among the familiar surroundings, to hope that the whole thing had been a bad dream. But all Rebecca Quinn would have seen were the markers left by the SOCOs, the holes cut out of the carpet to retrieve the bloodstains, a dusting of powder on the window frames and door handles. She might have smelled latex gloves, and the sweat of people working indoors in crime scene suits. She might have noticed that the bottle was gone from the table, the cushions from the settee, and the poker from the hearth. All very prosaic, in a way. But all signs that the room had been the setting for a violent crime.

Cooper looked through the statement list for an interview with neighbours called Page. Alistair Page had been only sixteen at the time, but if his parents were still around they might be worth talking to. If they'd lived quite close, they ought to have known the Quinns pretty well in a place like Castleton. And independent witnesses were distinctly in short supply.

But there were no Pages on the list. Cooper made a note to ask Alistair about his parents. Then he turned back to Rebecca's statement. She recalled leaving the house at eight thirty that morning to go to her job as a secretary in a solicitor's office in Hathersage. Normally, she wouldn't have returned home before five thirty, but she'd been phoned by the police earlier in the afternoon. She said she'd been too shocked and confused at first to understand what she was being told.

Rebecca had stayed at her sister Dawn's house that night. Neighbours had looked after the Quinn children when they arrived home from school, until they, too, had gone to their aunt's house. Cooper looked for the name of the helpful neighbours. Townsend. Maybe they were still around, at least.

There was a statement from another neighbour on the opposite side of the road, a woman called Needham. But neither she nor Mrs Townsend remembered seeing anyone enter the Quinns' house until Mansell Quinn himself arrived home, driving his Vauxhall estate. It wasn't clear from their statements how good a view either of them had of the house.

Cooper began to gather up the statements to put them back into the Carol Proctor case file. Then he noticed a photograph of an evidence bag. According to the label, it came from Room 1 Sector B, and it carried the identification code PM24 – a scene of crime officer's initials, plus the number of items of evidence he'd collected from the scene. He didn't know who 'PM' was – not one of the present SOCOs at E Division anyway. After fourteen years, it was probably someone who had left the force or retired.

The bag contained a Coke bottle. It looked like the bottle that had been sitting on the Quinns' table in the crime scene photographs. Cooper could see the fingerprint dust on the surface.

Faithful old fingerprints – they were sometimes sniffed at these days by forensic experts who described them as an art, not a science. But the team attending 82 Pindale Road in 1990 had dusted the bottle for prints. And they'd found them, though they were too smeared to get a match. That was odd

347

in itself – glass was perfect material to lift fingerprints from. Unless it had been deliberately wiped.

With a weary sigh, Cooper put the file down and looked at his watch. He wondered if he'd ever get chance to take a look at the Quinns' old house in Pindale Road.

Finally, he saw Diane Fry coming into the room. She looked as tired as he felt.

'William Edward Thorpe,' she said. 'He started off as one of your actions, didn't he, Ben?'

'Yes.'

'In fact, he was a TIE – to be traced, interviewed and eliminated.'

'We traced him and interviewed him.'

'But somebody else managed to eliminate him.'

'Mansell Quinn?' said Cooper.

'It seems a good bet. Looks as if DI Hitchens was right – Quinn *has* got a list.'

'Thorpe was the odd one out, though,' said Cooper.

'How do you mean?'

'We know where all the others on the list are.'

'Always assuming,' said Fry, 'that Quinn's list is the same as ours.'

'But this one doesn't feel right,' said Cooper.

'Why?'

Cooper was looking at the map showing Quinn's appearances in the Hope Valley. 'It's in the wrong place somehow. But then, the pattern is probably just accidental.'

'Of course it is. Quinn isn't planning all that carefully, is he?'

'No,' said Cooper doubtfully.

He remembered descending Siggate into Pindale from the field barn. He'd been able to see all the way to the top end of the Hope Valley, where the yellow street lights glowed along the A625. He'd made out the dark belt of trees that marked the route of the railway line from the cement works.

348

It passed Hope Valley College and swung towards the main line near Killhill Bridge.

A little to the east, he'd seen the lights of the Proctors' caravan park, Wingate Lees. But the lights had looked dimmer there. They were half hidden by the railway embankment and the slope behind the site, as if trapped between the shadows.

'What are you reading that's making you look like that?' said Fry.

Her voice sounded nasal and muffled. She had a tissue pressed to her nose, and her eyes were red.

Cooper showed her Rebecca Quinn's statement.

'There you are,' she said. 'Quinn's wife said he was the kind of man who stored things up.'

'For days, she said. Not fourteen years.'

'It might have been a shorter time if he'd had the opportunity to get the anger out of his system. But he didn't have the chance on the inside. He has now, though. Now that he's out.'

Cooper shook his head. 'It still doesn't feel right, Diane. Tracking people down one by one isn't an explosion of rage. It's far too calculating. Too cold. Exactly the things Rebecca said Quinn wasn't.'

'Ben, nobody doubts Quinn's guilt.'

'Don't they?'

'The evidence was pretty convincing – at least, the jury must have thought it was.'

'It's all circumstantial,' said Cooper.

'One piece of evidence wouldn't have been enough to get a conviction on its own, I grant you. But, taken as a whole, there was enough to make a substantial case. The jury decided it went beyond the possibility of coincidence. Quinn was there, Ben. Right on the spot. He had Carol Proctor's blood on his hands.'

'But what exactly is the evidence that Quinn killed his ex-wife on Monday night?'

'There were no signs of a break-in. Somebody came into the house who knew her, or who had a key. Unless she left the back door unlocked.'

'There's no way Quinn would've had a key to Parson's Croft.'

'Maybe not.'

'Are there any traces that identify him?'

'You know we don't have his DNA on record, Ben. There are some fibres at the scene that might be from his clothing, but until we locate him, we can't attempt a match.'

'It's all conjecture, isn't it?'

'He's a convicted killer, Ben. He was released from prison that morning, and promptly disappeared. We know he turned up shortly afterwards in the Hope Valley area – we have plenty of hard evidence for that. There are witnesses, we've got him on film. And then his wife is killed within a few hours. He came back to the area for a reason, Ben.'

'Like I said, it's conjecture.'

Fry sighed. 'Rebecca Lowe knew she was at risk from him. She had a phone conversation with her daughter about it that afternoon.'

'Actually, Andrea said that her mother insisted she wasn't worried.'

'And she went on to say that her mother was just putting on a brave face for her benefit.'

'It means nothing either way. Not as evidence.'

'Ben, your trainspotter got a photograph of Quinn within half a mile of Parson's Croft that evening. Does that mean nothing?'

'Perhaps.'

'All this will become academic when we find Quinn himself.'

'You hope,' said Cooper.

'What else we can we do in the meantime?' She laughed when she looked at his expression. 'Unless you have another suspect in mind?'

Cooper flushed a little. 'I think it's odd that we have no witnesses who saw Quinn in Aston. He would have been conspicuous.'

'And you think the fact that no one saw him proves he wasn't there? You can't prove a negative, Ben. It was dark when he left – no one would have seen him crossing the fields. Everyone who was outside would have gone indoors. No croquet players, no dog walkers. He planned it carefully. But he had a bit of luck, too. That's the story, Ben, right?'

'OK.'

Fry glared at him. 'I'd ask you what your problem is, but I know already, don't I?'

Cooper reached for his jacket. 'If it's all right with you, I'm going home for a few hours. I think I've had enough for now.'

'Haven't we all?'

He headed for the door, conscious that Fry was watching him all the way. He was almost out of the office when she called his name, and he stopped.

'Yes, Diane?'

'By the way,' she said, 'happy birthday.'

32

Mansell Quinn cut off the forelegs at the first joint and scored the skin of the belly, careful not to pierce through to the gut or bladder. Then he loosened the skin around the back legs. Keeping one end of the hare's body taut against the other, he pulled the skin down towards the stumps of the forelegs. It was stiff in places where it clung to the body, but slowly it peeled away, uncovering the layers of muscle and sinew. Finally, the skin came cleanly over the head of the animal in one piece.

Quinn gutted the animal carefully, wiping the blood and fluids from his fingers so that the knife didn't slip in his hands. He wanted to save the liver, which was valuable protein. When he'd finished, he buried the stomach and intestines under a tree and washed his hands in the stream. He watched the thin swirls of blood curling downstream on the surface of the pure, cold water. The smell of the gutted hare would linger in the vicinity for a while, but it couldn't be helped.

He'd built a small fire to cook the hare. He could survive for a while without food, as long as he could get water. But he mustn't go hungry for too long, or he'd start to lose his strength and his mental alertness would be blunted. Already, he was feeling a little light-headed. It left him a bit detached from reality, and that was dangerous. It would be too easy to make a mistake if he wasn't fully alert.

He was pleased with the results of his practice with the crossbow. He'd used one before, many years ago, before he'd gone inside. The strange thing was that he remembered Ray Proctor as the one who'd been interested in them. Ray's father had let him have an air rifle from an early age, and Ray had bought himself a crossbow as soon as he could afford it on his wages from the building site. He was forever persuading his friends to go with him on to the moors and into the old quarries to shoot rabbits and pigeons. Once, Ray had shot a swan on the river and broken its wing, which had sickened Quinn. But Will Thorpe had been keen on that, all right.

Quinn lifted his shirt to look at the wound in his side. The blood had almost dried now, but he'd have to wash the stains out of the shirt if he was going to avoid being too notice-able when he went down into Castleton again. The cut was clean. The crossbow bolt had penetrated the layer of fat above his left hip – almost the only fat on his body these days. He was lucky that Will Thorpe's hand had been none too steady when he fired.

In fact, Will had been in a pretty bad way. Quinn told himself that he'd done him a favour, really. There came a point when it wasn't worth living any more.

To eat his meal, Quinn moved to a vantage point on an outcrop of limestone. It was a narrow valley with thickly wooded slopes and a river running in the bottom. In places, its sides rose into vertical cliffs riddled with small caves and old mine workings. It would take him days to do a proper recce, but he hadn't prepared for it. It had been the sight of the police swarming in the Castleton car park that had forced him to find a refuge out of the town. Someone must have recognized him leaving the toilets.

After he'd cooked the hare and eaten the thin strips of

meat, Quinn washed himself in the stream. He still felt hungry. He had that same gnawing in his belly that hadn't gone away for days. In fact, it had been there for months. For years.

Later that morning, Quinn noticed the sheep. It was a young ewe that had somehow scrambled through the fence at the top of the slope, no doubt thinking it had spotted some tidbit the others couldn't reach. Now it was teetering on the rocky edge, finding the ground too unstable to get back up, and too frightened to go any further down. There was always a suicidal sheep or two in any flock. This one would become weaker and weaker until a fox found it or the crows pecked out its eyes. He'd be doing it a favour.

Quinn positioned himself against a horizontal branch and slipped a bolt into the crossbow. With luck, there would be mutton on the menu tonight.

A moment later, he scrambled down the slope to where the sheep had fallen. His bolt had gone through its neck, and its legs were still kicking when he reached it. The twitching hooves were gouging holes in the leaf litter. He grasped a handful of wool and pulled the sheep's head back, then drew the blade of his knife quickly across its throat, feeling the skin part and the blood vessels sever. As blood gushed on to the leaves, he withdrew the crossbow bolt from its neck and wiped both bolt and knife carefully on a fistful of damp leaves.

Then he stopped and raised his head to listen. He could hear voices somewhere to the west, two females at least, coming his way. He reckoned they must be on the path that ran alongside the river further down the slope. The sheep wasn't within view of the path, and he if lay still the women probably wouldn't see him. It was a risk, though.

As they came closer, one of the women seemed to raise her voice and call to someone. A child, perhaps? But then Quinn heard an answering bark. It didn't sound like a large dog –

something like a terrier, perhaps. But that was bad enough.

Reluctantly, he packed everything away and backed up the slope towards the denser woods, kicking the leaf litter over his footprints until he was on dry ground. When he reached the first limestone outcrop, he used the rocks for cover and increased his pace to put distance between himself and the dead sheep.

Within a few minutes, Quinn was out of the dale and over a stone wall into a field. It was a pity to leave, but he could come back later when it was safe. Perhaps after nightfall, when there was no risk of being interrupted.

33

Despite the cattle grid that narrowed it to a single track, Winnats Pass was the main route from Castleton through to Chapel-en-le-Frith and the whole of the western side of the Peak District. It hadn't always been the case, though. Just down the hill, Ben Cooper could see the remains of the old A625. A landslip from Mam Tor had swept it away after years of battling by the highways department to protect the tarmac from its unstable shale slopes.

Diane Fry looked tired. He wondered if she'd managed to sleep at all before the early morning call to the abandoned field barn above Pindale.

'These hills are an odd shape,' she said, as they drove up the steepest part of the pass.

'It's a coral reef,' said Cooper. 'Well, a limestone reef.'

'Sorry?'

'There was a tropical lagoon here. It stretched right down to Dovedale and Matlock, with a few volcanoes in the middle, and these reefs were the outer edge of it. The reefs were formed by algae and shells, the fossils of molluscs and corals. Fish teeth and scales, stuff like that.'

Fry said nothing. She sniffed and scratched her nose irritably.

'Of course, that was when Britain lay south of the Equator,' said Cooper.

Silently, Fry got a tissue out of her pocket and blew her nose.

'You're not impressed?' said Cooper.

'I'm waiting for you to start making sense again.'

'But it's true.'

'Yeah, right.'

And it *was* true. The lagoon had existed here three hundred million years ago, and masses of shells had collected on the fore reef, where it shelved down towards the valley. It was one of the things Cooper had learned during his school project.

He could still remember his own incredulity when he read the description in the work pack. But the sight of the limestone reefs in Winnats Pass had convinced him – even before he found his first fossils, the perfectly preserved imprint of a spiral shell in a piece of limestone, and the outline of a tiny fish in the face of the cliff.

'Your birthday *is* today, isn't it?' said Fry.

'Yes, why?'

'I was wondering if you're old enough to be grown up yet.'

Carefully overtaking a cyclist who was going purple in the face on the climb, Cooper drove over the top of the pass. It had just occurred to him that Fry had taken the trouble to remember the date of his birthday – but he had absolutely no idea when hers was.

'So it was too late, then?' said Jim Thorpe. 'He'll never come home now.'

'No, sir. I'm sorry.'

Mr Thorpe looked beyond morose today. Ben Cooper couldn't even think of a comparison. The old man had been crying, and he looked as though he might begin again at any moment.

'It wasn't your fault, Mr Thorpe,' said Cooper, shifting uneasily. Maybe he was undergoing an unnecessary guilt trip, but he had a sneaking suspicion that it *had* been partly his own fault.

'I had to identify him,' said Mr Thorpe. 'I hardly recognized him at first. But it was William all right.'

'He was staying at a caravan park near Hope, but he decided to leave. That was a mistake.'

'A caravan park?'

'Belonging to Raymond Proctor.'

'Oh, yes. But why there?'

Cooper already felt guilty enough. 'We agreed he'd be safer there, among other people. And I suppose he *would* have been safer, if he'd stayed.'

'Why did he leave?'

'I don't know.'

The cat was sitting in the middle of the room, glaring at the visitors. Cooper sensed that it didn't feel it was getting enough attention. It clawed at the carpet a bit, then clawed harder when nobody told it to stop. It came closer, and began to shred the table leg.

'You never know what's going to happen, do you?' said Mr Thorpe. 'It's a bit like the weather in these parts. The sun might be shining one minute, but the next second you can be drowned by rain. Nobody can tell what's going to come next.'

'I'm sorry, sir,' said Cooper.

Thorpe looked at him sadly. 'You said you met my son, didn't you?'

'Yes, sir.'

'But you never answered my question.'

'What was that?'

'I asked you what you'd call him. A loner, an outcast, a tramp?'

'No, sir. He was just a man who was lost without an institution to look after him.'

358

Cooper said it without having thought the idea through. But it sounded right. Leaving the army, Will Thorpe had been like a prisoner released after a long sentence, with his carrier bag full of clothes and no idea how much a bus fare home was. Thorpe and Quinn hadn't been all that different.

As they left Rakelow House, Cooper noticed one more thing. The house stood on the western side of the hill. It meant that old Mr Thorpe would always be able to see the weather coming off the moor, if he took the trouble to look.

Gavin Murfin had been teamed up with a PC in plain clothes, and they had toured shops in Castleton with their photos of Mansell Quinn. Old-fashioned legwork, Murfin called it. He looked more exhausted than Ben Cooper had ever seen him, and he was stuffing a beef and mustard sandwich into his mouth with an air of desperation. Yet Murfin also seemed remarkably pleased with himself as he patted the PC on the arm like a friendly uncle and sent him to fetch the coffees.

The reason soon became obvious. Murfin had brought back another CCTV tape, and officers were gathering round the screen as he slotted it in.

'This is from one of the craft shops in Castleton. It's on the main street, near the car park.'

'Near the bottom of the riverside walk to Peak Cavern?'

'You got it. The staff recognized Quinn from the print we got off the camera at Hathersage. They remembered him coming in the shop on Thursday afternoon.'

Somebody leaned forward to press the button and run the tape, but Murfin wanted to do it himself.

'Here we go.'

The view showed the interior of a small shop, crowded with shelves and display cases. The dark shapes glimpsed through the glass were objects made of Blue John, the spectacular mineral that was found only in one hill above Castleton. In the foreground, small items of jewellery glittered under a glass-topped counter. There were other kinds of stock, too: mugs and aprons, tea towels and postcards, the inevitable tourist stuff.

A group of girls were in the shop. They were jostling around the cabinets in a scrum of bare arms and white hips, with small rucksacks hanging from their backs. But after a moment or two, the crowd cleared, and a solitary figure was revealed behind them.

Murfin froze the picture. He approached the screen and pointed a finger at the figure.

'Here – see?'

When he took his finger away from the screen, it left a greasy smudge of butter obscuring the very area he'd been trying to draw their attention to.

But Cooper had no doubt at all that he was looking at Mansell Quinn. The man was standing right at the back of the shop, completely still, so that the throng of girls seemed to break like a wave against a rock, passing on either side of him. Quinn was dressed only in shirt and jeans, his shirt open across his chest. Cooper thought he could see a scatter of thunder flies in the sweat on his throat and along his collar bones. Two straps could be seen under the folds of shirt, as if he were carrying the rucksack, too. Quinn wasn't looking at the Blue John or other items displayed around him; he was staring straight ahead, as if his attention was fixed on something underneath the camera lens.

'They're only those tiny cameras,' said Murfin. 'You know the ones – like a little eyeball on a bracket? So the quality isn't too good.'

There were a few mutters, but the conversation died down as Quinn's gaze moved. He looked up slightly, and was staring directly at the screen. There was no doubt this time.

'He's a cocky bugger, isn't he?' said someone.

'You can say that again,' said Murfin. 'Very sure of himself.'

Cooper saw a member of the shop staff move across in

front of Quinn and pause for a moment. She must have spoken to him, because Quinn turned to look at her. She was probably asking him if she could help. Was there anything he was looking for in particular? He looked at her as if he didn't understand, and shook his head. She spoke again. Perhaps she spoke more slowly and clearly this time, taking him for a foreign tourist. Quinn turned away from the assistant towards the door, and the rucksack became visible on his back.

Despite the grey, grainy nature of the image, Cooper felt he could read Quinn's expression. Not cocky or sure of himself. Not that at all. Quinn looked like a man who was looking for something. But it was something he knew perfectly well he'd never find.

The moment DI Hitchens returned to his office, Cooper knocked on the door and asked to speak to him.

'What is it, Cooper?'

'The Carol Proctor case, sir.'

'Look, I thought we agreed –'

'It's only one thing. I just wondered – were there no other suspects considered?'

Hitchens sighed. 'Well, the husband was looked at, obviously. Especially when some of the victim's friends said there had been arguments between the couple.'

'Arguments? What about?'

'We don't know. But all married couples have arguments at some time, don't they?

'I suppose so.'

'Anyway, it wasn't considered significant enough to follow up. If there had been any evidence against the husband, it might have been different.'

'It might have been,' said Cooper.

Hitchens looked at him closely. 'I know, I know. It sounds as though we had our sights set on a likely suspect from the

361

beginning. We were sure we'd get a conviction against him, and we didn't find it necessary to look elsewhere. But the forensic evidence eliminated the husband. That's why he dropped out of the frame.'

'Sir, it seems to me there was precious little forensic evidence.'

Hitchens sighed. 'I know. But that was then, and this is now.'

'There's one other thing, sir.'

'Yes?'

'The Quinns' children, Simon and Andrea – where were they at the time?'

'At school, of course. They were aged fifteen and twelve.'

'They must have been due to arrive home about then.'

The DI had started to tap his fingers with impatience, but frowned at the question. 'It's a long time ago, but I've a feeling the girl went to her aunt's house. The boy turned up later on, though. I remember that. Somebody intercepted him and took him to a neighbour's.'

'Much later? How soon after the murder happened?'

'Well, it must have been pretty soon. He only had to come from the college at Hope.'

'But, sir –'

'The case against Quinn was sound, Ben. He pleaded guilty in court.'

'Yes, I know he did.'

'Well, then. The fact that he confessed should put your mind at ease.'

'Funnily enough,' said Cooper, 'that's the one fact that worries me most of all.'

'Two murders in a week,' said Gavin Murfin. 'It's too much excitement for me, at my age.'

Diane Fry sat on the edge of her desk facing them. She'd just come back from a strategy meeting upstairs and was looking pleased with herself.

'Just think yourself lucky, Gavin,' she said. 'You could have ended up working in Northern Ireland, where they have eighteen hundred unsolved murders on the books.'

'If I was so stupid,' said Murfin, 'I'd have joined the army instead. At least I could have got shot at in a nice climate.'

Fry swung her legs impatiently. 'Anyway, listen to this, guys. The pathologist confirms that William Thorpe died of strangulation. The blood came from someone else – a trail of it between the body and the doorway of the field barn, as well as the splatters we saw outside, in the nettles. So it definitely looks as though Quinn is injured.'

'Maybe that'll slow the bastard down, at least,' said Murfin.

'Alerts are going out, in case he seeks medical treatment of any kind.'

'Did you hear that, Ben?' called Murfin across the office. 'Quinn was injured.'

Ben Cooper was opening a few birthday cards that had been left on his desk. One was from his colleagues in CID, another from Liz Petty in scenes of crime, signed 'Hugs, Liz'. Somebody had tied a couple of silver helium balloons to his in-tray. They bumped gently against each other in the draught from Fry's desk fan.

'If that's who it was that killed Thorpe,' he said.

'We have a sample of Quinn's DNA now, Ben,' said Fry.

'No, we have *someone's* DNA. We can't say it's Quinn's until we find him and do a comparison.'

'Yes, all right.'

Cooper looked up from his cards. 'So how far did the trail of blood go?'

'They couldn't follow it beyond the gate. But if it *is* Quinn's blood, it looks as though he's made another mistake.'

'Another?'

'Being caught by two security cameras. Not to mention the trainspotter at Hope station.'

'Yes, if Quinn went up there intending to kill Thorpe, he

363

planned it very badly,' said Cooper. 'Getting angry and losing control of the situation, now that's a different matter. I can believe that.'

'This victim obviously fought back, anyway,' said Fry. 'That could be our breakthrough.'

'Yes, Thorpe was the wrong person for Quinn to choose.'

Fry looked at him. 'Still a bit doubtful, Ben?'

'Thorpe wouldn't have been any problem for Quinn, if he'd planned and executed his attack properly. The fact that Thorpe was able to fight back suggests bad planning. I'm surprised that Quinn even gave him the opportunity to resist.'

'You make it sound like a spur-of-the-moment thing. But that isn't possible. It's not as if he came across Thorpe in the street. Quinn went to find him, just as he did Rebecca Lowe.'

'Not quite the same. Unless Quinn had somehow got hold of a key, Rebecca must have let him in. There were no signs of a break-in, remember?'

Fry sighed. 'Perhaps you're right. But so what? What if Rebecca Lowe *did* let him in? Quinn might have tricked her into opening the door. Or she might have been taken by surprise to see him standing there on her doorstep. We can't reconstruct the scenario clearly enough to know what happened immediately prior to the attack.'

Cooper pictured the abandoned field barn. He wondered if there was a spot where Quinn might have stood and watched it before approaching. But the site had been too open for that. He would have had to strike in complete darkness, which made things as difficult for him as for his victim.

'Well, we'll be making sure of one thing from now on,' said Fry. 'No other potential victims will be taken by surprise to find Mansell Quinn on their doorstep.'

She had that look on her face – the one that told Cooper she had something else to tell him, some parting shot. But before she got it in, he needed to mention another subject that was on his mind.

'Diane, did you read the Neil Moss story?' he said.

'I had a look at it,' said Fry. 'But it doesn't seem to have any relevance.'

'You don't think so?'

'No. It was a terrible tragedy, but it happened forty-five years ago, Ben. And there's no connection between Moss and Quinn, is there?'

'Well . . .'

'They're not related, and Quinn can't possibly have known him. It was too long ago.'

'That doesn't mean there isn't any connection between the two,' said Cooper. 'But it does mean the connection is a bit more . . . psychological.'

'Oh, my God.'

Fry looked at him with that exasperated expression he'd grown used to. 'Would you care to explain that, Ben?'

'Look, you have a man serving a life sentence in prison for a crime he says he didn't commit. As far as he's concerned, he's there because his friends betrayed him. And then his family stops visiting him. He's completely isolated, right? Locked up in a cell for the rest of his life. Walled up.'

'OK, I think I see where you're heading.'

'And he reads the story of Neil Moss, who really is walled up. Moss died in complete isolation because no one could reach him.' Cooper spread his hands, inviting Fry to share his thinking process. 'In prison, people develop obsessions. They start finding things that seem to have immense significance, things they think relate specifically to their own lives. God knows, it happens to enough people outside prison. It's so easy to let that grip on perspective slip.'

'Well . . .' said Fry doubtfully.

'Look, when you were a teenager, wasn't there some song in the pop charts whose words seemed to sum up your emotional state at that moment? So much so that you were convinced the song was actually *about* you.'

365

'Heaven is a Place on Earth,' said Fry.

Cooper paused. 'Really? Belinda Carlisle?'

'Yes.'

Fry began to looked irritated again, and Cooper decided not to pursue it.

'Well, I think it's possible that Quinn saw the Neil Moss story as some sort of metaphor for his own life,' he said. 'A symbol, if you like. And all the more meaningful because Moss is still imprisoned there in that shaft in Peak Cavern. He never got the chance to return to the outside world. He died in isolation and darkness.'

He saw Fry shudder. But he wasn't sure whether she was reacting to the thought of Neil Moss dying in his limestone tomb, or to the childhood memories he'd inadvertently stirred up. 'Heaven is a Place on Earth'?

'So,' said Fry, poking half-heartedly among the papers on her desk, 'Mansell Quinn loses touch with his family and friends. He's starved of normal communication. Then he finds this book in the prison library and he responds to a dead man's voice speaking to him across the space of forty-five years – is that it?'

'Something like that.'

'Well, to be honest, it's a bit more cosmic than anything I'd have come up with.'

'I know, Diane.'

'But there's one thing that might not have occurred to you.'

'What's that?'

'As I understand the story of Neil Moss, he ended up trapped in that shaft as a result of his own voluntary actions. He was there because of something he did, a miscalculation or a combination of unlucky circumstances. But he walked into it with his eyes open. It was a risk that he was prepared to take for his own reasons.'

'Yes, I think that would be right,' said Cooper thoughtfully.

'Anyway, enough of the philosophy. You can hand in your thesis later. I thought you might like to know what else the SOCOs found in the field barn where Will Thorpe was killed, apart from the blood . . .'

'Oh, what?'

'The floor was packed dirt. Dry dirt – or it would have been. Ironically, it seems Quinn brought the rain in with him and created a couple of wet patches.'

Cooper felt his heart sink. It was an illogical reaction, but he knew Fry was about to prove him wrong again.

'Footprints,' he said.

Fry nodded. 'They're a bit trampled, but the SOCOs lifted a couple of good impressions from the sole of a right boot.'

'And?'

'They match the impressions from Rebecca Lowe's garden.'

She handed him the report. A photograph of the dirt floor slid out, grainy and scattered with small stones, like the surface of the moon. He could make out the footprint clearly. The SOCOs must have been delighted. Even at a glance, Cooper could see they would have no trouble making a comparison.

'What do you say now, Ben?' said Fry.

Cooper blew out a long breath at the helium balloons. They bounced against each other, as if applauding quietly. 'OK, what's the next move?'

'We're hoping that he's weakened by his injuries and the loss of blood. Quinn can't have got far, so we're going to hit all the places where he might be lying up.'

'Such as?'

'Peak Cavern, for one.'

When he came back to the place, the dead sheep had gone. Mansell Quinn quartered backwards and forwards across the area, but he was sure he had the right spot. His sense of direction was excellent. Above him he could see the limestone outcrop and the ledge where the sheep had been trapped. From below, he could hear the river, and he knew the path the women had walked on was near it, though he couldn't see it. And here was the patch of leaf litter beneath the tree where the animal had fallen.

Clutching the wound on his side, Quinn crouched close to the ground. At least two pairs of boots had trampled the area since he'd left it, and there were signs of something heavy having been dragged down the slope.

He made his way downhill, stepping carefully to avoid tripping over rocks and tree roots. Suddenly he emerged into the open and found himself standing on a smooth surface made of compacted earth. The path here was wide enough for a small vehicle, perhaps an ATV of the kind that farmers used for getting around the furthest corners of their land.

Quinn grimaced. Because of the interruption, the sheep he'd killed had been found too soon. Anyone who took a close look at the carcass would be able to see that it hadn't died by accident. Soon, the search parties would arrive in his dale.

Well, so be it. Quinn patted the crossbow in its bag across his shoulder. This meant the time was past for taking risks, for spreading fear among those who ought to be afraid. The time had arrived to finish the job.

34

'You're convinced he's back in Castleton?'

'Who?'

Alistair Page laughed. 'Mansell Quinn. That's who you're looking for, isn't it? It's hardly a secret by now. It's been all over the papers and TV.'

Ben Cooper nodded. 'Yes, OK, you're right.'

'As a matter of fact, I didn't really need to ask. I know somebody who works at the craft shop down the road there. They said he was in the shop, and he got caught on the security cameras.'

Cooper sighed. 'There's no point in trying to keep anything secret in a place like this, is there?'

'Absolutely no point.'

Page's mannerism of speech seemed more pronounced today. Perhaps it was a sign of excitement. He had certainly seemed agitated at the sight of the police officers entering the cavern, and the fact that it had been temporarily closed to the public.

'And at the height of the season,' he said, shaking his head. 'They won't like it.'

'It's routine,' said Cooper. 'We have to check all the possibilities.'

'Do you really think he might come to Peak Cavern?'

'As a matter of fact, yes.'

Some of the task force officers were returning from a trip down the Devil's Staircase to the River Styx and into Five Arches. The knees and elbows of their overalls were covered in the brown silt that coated the floor and the walls down there. One of the last officers up was covered from head to foot, and the front of his overalls glistened with mud. Even his hands and face were liberally splashed with it.

'It can be really difficult to keep your footing down there,' said Page. 'I wonder if anybody told them it would be easier to walk in the stream bed.'

'Probably not,' said Cooper.

The task force officers smelled, too. As they passed, Cooper got a whiff of the ancient sludge that had been sucked out of the nooks and crannies of the cavern system over many thousands of years and left in the passages to add to the fun for cavers.

'They ought to have come with proper equipment,' said Page. 'I hope they're not planning on trying to go any further than Five Arches.'

'Would he be likely to get that far in?'

'There are food dumps in Treasury Chamber and Picnic Dig for cavers who get trapped by flooding,' said Page. 'But there's no way he could reach those unless he has diving equipment. There are sumps in the way.'

'No matter. He could survive for days without food, provided he can get access to water.'

'There's plenty of that. In fact, there might be too much.'

'What do you mean?' asked Cooper.

'These thunderstorms we keep getting. They're depositing a lot of water into the system. If we get another one like Thursday night, the cavern could flood.'

'In July? I thought the floods happened in winter.'

'Mostly. But it wouldn't be the first time the system has

flooded in summer. People don't realize that July is one of the wettest months of the year in this area.'

'Flooding. That's all we need.'

A cave system like Peak–Speedwell must be the nearest anyone would ever see to Hell. Cooper felt full of admiration for the cavers and cave divers who had been mapping the system – let alone those who had first set out to explore it, with their primitive lamps and equipment. Some of them had free-dived through sumps and flooded chambers, not knowing how far they'd have to swim before they found the next pocket of air, blinded by zero visibility in the cold, silty water. There had been no diving suits and oxygen tanks in those days; the divers had found their way underwater on a single lungful of air. If they failed to reach the surface in time, they died.

'He hasn't killed anybody else, has he?' said Page. 'Do you think he's planning to kill again?'

'Sorry, Alistair, I can't tell you things like that.'

'Oh, right.'

Cooper supposed he shouldn't be surprised at Page's interest. Probably everybody in Castleton was agog by now. Some people would be looking suspiciously at every tourist who passed. Others would remember Mansell Quinn and the Carol Proctor killing. Memories were long in these parts.

'I'm sure nobody's in danger from Quinn unless they had some connection with him in the past,' said Cooper.

'Oh,' said Page. He didn't look entirely reassured.

'Of course, we're advising people not to approach him. They should just call us.'

'Approach him? As if I would.'

'Good.'

'But do you mean he's got a hit list of some kind? It wasn't just his ex-wife he came looking for?'

'A hit list? It's one theory anyway. As a precaution, we've been warning anyone who might be on such a list.'

371

'Like Ray Proctor and Will Thorpe?'

Cooper looked at him, openly surprised now. 'You really are familiar with the details of the case, Alistair. Did you know Proctor and Thorpe, too?'

'Oh, I looked the names up. I was interested.'

Cooper watched him polish the glass of his lamp on a corner of his jacket. He was going to ask Page why he was so interested in the case, other than morbid curiosity, when his mobile phone rang – a summons back to the office.

'Yes, just about finished here,' he said.

Page was watching him keenly. 'What's up?'

'I've got to go,' said Cooper. 'But I'll speak to you later.'

'Do you think it's safe here?' said Page anxiously.

Cooper was already moving away. He stopped to look back at Alistair Page, and saw how anxious he was. It was strange that a man could venture willingly into those claustrophobic caves in pitch darkness, and yet still be the sort of person who worried unnecessarily about dangers that would never come his way.

'As you long as you take care,' said Cooper. 'And remember – if you do see Mansell Quinn, stay clear of him.'

'So,' said Gavin Murfin when Ben Cooper got back to the office in Edendale. 'I hear we've even got a Beast of Bradwell now. What's the place coming to?'

'A what?'

'Beast of Bradwell. One of those mysterious giant cats that roam the countryside during the silly season. Apparently, it's been savaging sheep. It's in the bulletins.'

'I haven't seen them yet.'

Cooper read the reports. Predictably, a team of firearms officers had been called out to search the area where a sheep had been found with its throat 'ripped out', according to the report. The site was close to a path used by walkers and their dogs, so someone considered there might be a threat to the public. But as far as Cooper was concerned, sending coppers with guns into the woods was more of a risk to the public than any type of wildlife they were likely to encounter, real or imaginary.

'It wasn't in Bradwell,' he said. 'It was in Rakedale.'

'That's no good,' said Murfin.

'Why not?'

'It doesn't begin with a "B". The Beast of Rakedale doesn't have the same ring. No good for a newspaper headline.'

'Accuracy was never your strongpoint, was it, Gavin?'

'I've always thought I might make a good journalist. Anyway, it's near enough, isn't it?'

Cooper read through the report again. Rakedale was a narrow, meandering limestone valley on the other side of Bradwell Moor from the Castleton area. It joined the Eden Valley further south, passing within a mile of Bridge End Farm. Cooper was very familiar with its wooded sides and limestone cliffs, and the pure stream running through it. He also knew it had many small caves, and some old mine workings.

'It doesn't sound as though anyone has taken a proper look at the victim yet,' he said.

'Eh? You're expecting a postmortem? Mrs Van Doon would have kittens if we sent her a sheep.'

'I was thinking of a vet. They ought to get a vet to look at it. Someone will have thought of that, won't they?'

'Maybe.'

'I'll mention it to the officer in charge,' said Cooper.

'But what else could rip a sheep's throat out? A dog, maybe?'

'A dog wouldn't do so much damage. They'll chase sheep, but they lose interest once they stop running.'

'Has to be a big cat, then,' said Murfin confidently.

'Not at all.'

'What then?'

'There's one other species that would inflict that kind of damage on an animal, and do it just for sport. The human species.'

Cooper watched one of the incident room staff place a new marker on the map. Mansell Quinn's trail through the Hope Valley had reached Castleton, almost at the head of the valley. Cooper felt sure there would be a second location to add soon. But he had no doubt at all about Quinn's final destination. *Death Underground* had some meaning for him and, somehow, he was intending to enter the cavern system. But he wouldn't do that until he'd finished what he'd come to do. And they still didn't know what names had been on Quinn's list.

Raymond Proctor seemed to have aged ten years. Ben Cooper and Diane Fry found him at his desk, staring into space. Though no bottle was visible, a smell of whisky hung in the air. The office looked more untidy than ever. Only the rows of keys remained neat and orderly, as if Proctor thought their orderliness could resist the spread of chaos.

'I'm really sorry about Will,' he said. 'But there wasn't anything I could have done, was there?'

Fry didn't seem inclined to ease his conscience.

'Certainly. If you'd called us when Quinn came here on Wednesday night, we could have had him out of circulation and your friend would still be alive now.'

'Yeah.' Proctor looked towards the old filing cabinet. Maybe that was where he kept the whisky.

'Also, if your crossbow had been properly secured, Quinn wouldn't now be in possession of a lethal weapon. Would he, sir?'

'No.'

'Mr Proctor, do you have any idea who else might be in danger from Quinn? Did he say anything that might give us a clue?'

'No, he didn't.'

'Because I'm sure you wouldn't want another death on your conscience, would you?'

'No.'

'Please think carefully then, sir. What did he talk about?'

Proctor stared into space. 'He talked about coming out of prison and things being different.'

'Yes?'

'He mentioned somebody else living in his old house.'

'His old house? The one on Pindale Road?'

'I suppose that's where he meant.'

'What else did he say, Mr Proctor?'

Proctor frowned. 'He must have been thinking about Rebecca. That house in Pindale Road was their home – his and Rebecca's. But she couldn't wait to get away from it after what happened. Can't say I blame her.'

'Did you know her well, Mr Proctor?'

'I did back then. She left the valley for a while when she married the second time, you know. She wanted to move back, but she had to have a brand-new house, which isn't easy to get planning permission for. Anyway, they managed it, and Parson's Croft was the result. Only trouble was, the new husband had a heart attack before the house was finished.'

'That must have been tough.'

'Not for Rebecca. She was quids in. Very comfortable.'

'Comfortably dead.'

'Well, yeah. She is now.'

'She'd have been better off spending some of her money getting away from the area. Moving down south, or out of the country altogether.'

'Probably. But you can't help wanting to come back to where you belong, can you?'

Fry watched him. He did seem to be trying to help this time. 'Anything else, sir?'

Proctor shook his head. 'Nothing I can remember.'

'We'd better have a word with your wife, then.'

'She won't remember any more than me,' said Proctor. 'She hardly saw him.'

'He was saying something about children when I came in here,' said Connie when she was called into the office. 'That's all I remember. It was such a shock seeing him. But I knew straight away who he was.'

'Whose children?' said Fry.

'Not Jason and Kelly, anyway – he's never met them, thank God. In fact, he'd never met me until that night.'

'It must have been his own children he was referring to, then? Simon and Andrea.'

'Yes, I suppose so. But they don't even live in the Castleton area any more, do they?'

'No, that's true.' Fry looked disappointed. 'Oh, well. We're leaving a patrol car at the entrance for the time being.'

'My guests won't like that.'

'Don't bother telling me. I don't care any more.'

'Well, you were right about the Beast of Bradwell, Ben,' said Gavin Murfin, when Ben Cooper got back to the office. West Street was a bit quiet, and Cooper thought the senior officers must be in a meeting somewhere.

'Oh? No beast?'

'The vet's report says the sheep's throat wasn't ripped by teeth. It was cut with a sharp knife.'

'There you go, then. Another sicko wandering the area. A few years ago it was horses, remember? Doesn't sound like a professional poacher – they're much more organized, and they take entire flocks rather than slaughtering an individual animal in the woods like that.'

'This was in the daytime, too. Two witnesses came forward who thought they heard something run off when their dog barked. Or someone.'

Cooper noticed that Murfin was looking too smug.

'Anything else happened, Gavin?'

'Good vet they got,' said Murfin. 'Almost as good as a pathologist.'

'What do you mean?'

'He said the sheep had been shot. With a crossbow.'

'My God. Have they –'

'Everybody's out there now,' said Murfin. 'Didn't you notice how quiet it is?'

The search party was working its way along the sides of Rakedale, but the going was slow. The trees on the slopes were too dense, the caves too deep, the holes and crevices in the limestone too numerous to count. Armed officers went ahead of the main group, and their caution slowed the search down even more. But without them, the task force officers would have been too vulnerable, because their attention had to be focused on the ground and on their immediate surroundings. They were looking for traces of recent occupation in the caves, or in the ruins of the old mine buildings that were scattered along the northern side of the dale, almost overgrown with ivy and brambles.

'It's much too slow,' said DI Hitchens. 'If he's in here, he'll see us coming half a mile away.'

'There's no way we can speed the search up,' said DCI Kessen. 'The troops are too exposed already. If Quinn should be waiting up on one of those limestone cliffs, he could do a lot of damage.'

'That's if he's still armed. We don't know that for certain.'

'I'm not taking the chance.'

'The dogs seem to be all over the place,' said Hitchens.

'They don't know what they're looking for. We have nothing of Quinn's to give them.'

'The helicopter should be here soon, though. Its thermal camera will identify any bodies hiding among these trees.'

'In the trees, perhaps. But not in the caves.'

'And what about the public?' said Hitchens.

'They're a nightmare . . .'

At the bottom end of the dale, several families were enjoying the sun by the water. Half a dozen Mallard ducks sat in a row on a log submerged in a green pool, watching the children rushing about on the grass.

'. . . but there's no way we can get rid of them altogether.'

The search didn't reach the end of the dale until early evening. The co-ordinator called a halt where the trees petered out and the limestone sides gave way to a patchwork of fields criss-crossed by stone walls.

'He's not here. Not any more, anyway.'

Kessen and Hitchens gathered around him for a hasty conference. Two officers carried over a pile of bin liners filled with evidence bags.

'I don't want to see all that,' said Kessen. 'What have we got that's of any significance?'

'Someone camped out in one of the caves recently. About halfway along the valley on the south side. You can't see it until you get right up to it. It isn't big, but it's dry, and there's a sort of ledge at the back where you can lie up and be out of the weather, as well as out of sight.'

'What traces are there?'

'A couple of the SOCOs are going over it now. I'd say they'll get no more than some wax and ashes, and a few scuff marks in the dirt on the cave floor.'

'Nothing we can get a DNA sample from?'

'I doubt it.'

'He must have defecated and urinated somewhere.'

The search co-ordinator shrugged. 'This man is very careful. There's no sign of anything in the vicinity of the cave. My guess is he'll have gone deep into the woods some-where, a different location each time, and concealed the traces in a scrape in the ground. We'd never find anything like that.'

'Here's the helicopter at last,' said Hitchens.

'Much good it'll do.'

In the briefing room, Ben Cooper could see that DCI Kessen and DI Hitchens were frustrated at Mansell Quinn's ability to move freely around the Hope Valley. The tone of the newspaper and radio reports was reflecting the public's incredulity. An incredulity echoed by senior officers in Ripley.

'He's too unpredictable,' said Hitchens. 'One minute he's living rough in some remote bit of woodland, and the next he's mingling brazenly with the crowds in the middle of Castleton. It makes us look like complete prats.'

'I'm not happy about these CCTV pictures,' said Kessen. 'It looks as though he's taunting us. He's constantly one step ahead, and he knows it.'

Cooper studied the photo of Mansell Quinn taken from the camera at the gift shop. To him, Quinn didn't seem to be laughing at all.

'And the weather is too good,' said Hitchens. 'What we need is rain. The heavier the better.'

The DI was right there. If the weather stayed the same, there would be chaos on Sunday. Traffic would be gridlocked in Castleton, just as it would in Dovedale and at Matlock Bath. On summer weekends and bank holidays, visitors would queue in their cars for hours to get to the honeypots and mingle with crowds of other tourists, until they were so thick on the ground no one could move for ice-cream cones and frisbees.

Castleton would be busy every day now for the rest of the summer. It boasted five of the Peak District's ten most popular attractions, and the show caves alone brought in thousands of people every weekend. But the tea rooms and gift shops would soon empty if the tourists became aware of a multiple killer at large in the area. What if a tourist got killed? Or a child? It would be a disaster for the tourism trade – worse even than the foot and mouth outbreak.

Watching his senior officers fretting, Cooper shook his head. Surely the chiefs were worrying more than necessary? It was obvious that Quinn had specific targets in mind, and he wasn't about to start attacking strangers. And this man was no predatory paedophile or child killer. He could have no possible reason to harm a child.

35

Mansell Quinn's hands trembled slightly as he ran the sights of the crossbow back across the same stretch of undergrowth, looking for the movement. He focused on the base of a tree and gripped the shaft in his other hand. Despite its lightness, he knew it had the power to bring down an animal the size of a deer, if necessary. It was silent and deadly, too. He could even retrieve the bolt from the body with his knife, and no one need ever know how his quarry had died.

Despite the trembling, his motions were slow and steady. He made another sweep across the ground. There was the movement again. Now it had come into the open, and he could see what it was. A little girl was running down the slope. She was no more than eight years old, wearing a bright blue dress, with brown hair tied into bunches and her feet shoved into over-sized trainers. Her face was screwed up in concentration as she ran. Quinn noted every detail – her thin white legs, a scab on her left knee, an imitation gold bracelet around one wrist.

Of course, her mother wouldn't be far away – she'd be among the other adults and children enjoying the sunshine. But this child was independent. She'd decided to go exploring on her own, tempted away from the safety of the adults by

381

a glint of water through the trees, or just an urge to run down the slope in the sun. Quinn liked independence. He thought it was one of his own best characteristics.

Quinn tried to imagine what people would be saying about him now. They'd be judging him, and he couldn't stand the thought of that. Everyone had always judged him when he was inside. Prisoners were each other's jailers, in a way. If you weren't guilty when you went in, you soon convinced yourself you were. It was too easy to turn that anger on to yourself.

He was glad to have got the chance to wash in the stream. Sometimes, he thought he'd never get the smell of prison off his skin – that stale stink of a place filled with too many bodies, where fresh air never blew. Now and then, he'd taken the chance to inch a bit closer to a prison visitor, to see if he could detect the smell of someone who'd stroked their pet dog, or walked in their garden that morning, or touched a child. The tiniest whiff of a remembered smell could bring the outside world back. It kept the connection from breaking entirely.

The girl stopped at the bottom of the slope, poised on the edge of the water. She looked up at the hillside, staring directly at where Quinn was positioned. He held his breath and didn't move; there was no way she could see him. Her child's eyes weren't good enough to pick him out, and she couldn't yet have learned to recognize danger so easily.

Then, inexplicably, the girl smiled. Quinn's heart gave a lurch. She must have been smiling at a particularly pleasing pattern of trees, or a bird glimpsed in the branches above him. After a moment, she lost interest in whatever it was and began to poke around among the small stones at the edge of the stream. He could see her white trainers beginning to turn darker at the edges as the water soaked into them. When her mother found her, the girl would be in trouble for getting her feet wet.

382

Quinn lowered the crossbow for a moment. Where *was* her mother? The girl shouldn't have been allowed to wander off alone like that. It was dangerous.

The girl suddenly broke into a run. Quinn watched her trot along the slope, her arms waving to keep her balance, and her blue skirt blowing in the breeze. The girl's bare legs were white and streaked with dirt, and she stumbled as she dodged the bigger stones. She was moving fast now and changing direction, heading diagonally across in front of him. In another thirty seconds she would reach the flat area of grass and be into the trees, and then he'd no longer be able to see her clearly.

Quinn squinted against the low sun, focusing on the blue skirt, assessing the trajectory of the bright scrap of colour as it travelled across his range of vision. Slowly, he lifted the crossbow back to his shoulder, and slid a bolt into place.

36

Isabel Cooper was waiting in the lounge of the Old School nursing home, wearing her best coat and her best shoes, and looking expectant. Somebody had joked with her that she must be going to a wedding, and now she wasn't quite sure whether she ought to be wearing a hat.

The staff of the nursing home knew Ben. He visited regularly, and more than one care assistant had been ticked off for spending too much time talking to him. And today Cooper's mother recognized him, too. She got up to greet him, and he bent to give her a hug and a kiss.

'I need to find a hat before we go,' she said.

'No, Mum, you'll be fine as you are.'

'Are you sure?'

'We're only going to Bridge End.'

She didn't answer, and he knew she'd noticed the careful way he referred to the farm. It was awkward trying not to say 'home'. He would always think of it as her home, and he was sure that she must, too. But the family had an unspoken agreement that it was a word they should avoid saying out loud.

She brightened up when they got into the car and drove out of Edendale. After they passed through a shower, the evening sun broke through again and lit up the fields and wet trees, revealing fresh colours in the landscape. In town, Cooper quite liked the odour of hot pavements dampened by rain. But on some days, after it had rained, parts of the valley would steam like a tropical swamp as water vapour rose through the trees.

'I've got you a present, Ben,' said his mother. 'It's your birthday.'

'Yes, I know. Thank you, Mum.'

He was aware of her opening her handbag and rummaging among the tissues and spare glasses, Polo mints, family photographs, and whatever else she kept in there.

'I think we'll have to go back,' she said. 'I've forgotten to bring it.'

'No, you haven't, Mum. It's at the farm. Matt and Kate have got it. You can give it to me when we arrive.'

'Oh, yes. I remember.'

Kate was very good at organizing these things. She planned ahead so that they could anticipate what Mum might do and make things easier. Most things were accepted without question, or any need for lengthy explanations. His mother knew that she forgot things a lot.

'Your Dad and I can give it you together,' she said.

Cooper's heart sank. 'What, Mum?'

'It'll be nice to see Joe. He hasn't managed to visit me this week. I suppose he's too busy.'

He didn't answer. A moment later, she began to hum quietly to herself. She was happy as they passed familiar landscapes – the houses of friends she remembered, the old cottage hospital where she'd worked for a while, the stone bridge over the river where Joe had once scraped the side of the car against the parapet and she hadn't been able to open the door to get out.

And then something brought out another memory. Cooper had no idea what it was – a glimpse of a particular hill, or the look of someone's face in a car going the other way, or maybe just something floating to the surface of his mother's mind, like a rotting leaf disturbed from the mud on the bottom of a stagnant pond.

'I heard that Mansell Quinn is out,' she said.

Cooper almost lost control of the car and steered into a field full of Friesians. They'd have got as big as a shock as he'd just had.

'What?'

'Mansell Quinn. Do you remember, Ben?'

'Yes. Yes, I do, Mum.'

Isabel frowned. 'You must have been quite young at the time. We tried to keep it from you.'

'You didn't keep as much from me as you thought.'

'Oh.'

Cooper hesitated, but couldn't resist asking the question. 'How did you know he was out?'

'Somebody at the Old School mentioned it.'

'Do you remember the case? I mean, the murder?'

'Murder?'

'Mansell Quinn killed a woman. Do you remember, at the time, did Dad . . . ?'

Cooper turned to look at his mother as he spoke, and saw a look of terrible anguish on her face. He could have been looking at a child facing some unseen terror in the darkness.

'Ben,' she said, 'your dad's dead.'

Ashamed, he faced towards the road again and took the next bend a little too fast, forgetting to brake, or not bothering.

'Yes, Mum,' he said. 'I know.'

Two minutes later, Cooper swung the car up the hill towards Bridge End Farm. On the upper slopes, the leaves of the limes and sycamores shone almost yellow against the background of dark clouds still shouldering their way across the moors. He thought it would probably rain again later.

When they arrived in the farmhouse, Cooper was immediately surrounded by a scrum of family. There seemed to be more of them than he remembered. His sister Claire was there with a new boyfriend who said he was a doctor but looked more like a car salesman. Uncle John and Aunt Margaret were there with a whole gaggle of cousins. And of course there were Matt and Kate, and Kate's parents. But it was his nieces, Josie and Amy, who insisted on crowding in first to deliver their presents.

When Cooper had made all the right noises and a birthday cake had been cut, the fuss finally died down and he found himself sitting among a pile of wrapping paper and cards with a glass of beer in his hand. One of those momentary quiet spells had descended, allowing him a second or two to think. But Cooper looked up and found Josie standing at his elbow, waiting patiently for him to notice her.

'Uncle Ben, I've got the poem,' she said.

'What poem, Josie?'

'The one the man was talking about at Peak Cavern. It's by Ben Jonson.'

Cooper smiled when he heard Josie call the place 'Peak Cavern', hoping that he would notice she'd used the polite name. Her sister Amy took pleasure in saying 'the Devil's Arse', for the opposite reason. Or perhaps it was for the same reason – to get his attention.

'What was the poem called again?'

'Well, the man said it was *The Gypsies Metamorphosed*, but that's the name of a book, not the poem. Anyway, the poem's called "Cock Lorrel". Do you want to read it?'

'Er . . .' Cooper looked at the book Josie was holding, and then at her face. 'OK. Thank you.'

He took it and read the first verse of the poem aloud:

> '*Cock Lorrel would needs have the Devil his guest,*
> *And bade him once into the Peak to dinner,*
> *Where never the fiend had such a feast*
> *Provided him yet at the charge of a sinner.*'

He began to read the second verse, then paused. 'Did you read this, Josie?'

'Yes. It's a bit gruesome, I think.'

'Yes, it is a bit.'

Silently, Cooper scanned the rest of the poem. It seemed to be a catalogue of the dishes enjoyed by Cock Lorrel and the Devil during one of the notorious cannibalistic feasts in the cavern – the Beggars' Banquets. There was: 'A rich, fat usurer stewed in his marrow,/ And by him a lawyer's head and green sauce' and 'Six pickled tailors sliced and cut,/Sempsters and tirewomen, fit for his palate.'

'What are tirewomen?' said Josie, effortlessly following his progress through the poem.

'I don't know. You'll have to look it up.'

Then Cooper wondered whether that was the right thing to have said. For all he knew, tirewomen could be some kind of prostitute. Matt would be thrilled if he thought his brother was encouraging his daughters to do that sort of research.

But the passage that made Cooper stop was roughly halfway through the poem. Ben Jonson had really managed to hit a nerve with this one:

> *Then carbonadoed and cooked with pains,*
> *Was brought up a cloven sergeant's face:*
> *The sauce was made of his yeoman's brains,*
> *That had been beaten out with his mace.*

With an effort to appear calm, Cooper handed the book back

to his niece. He smiled, knowing as he did it that she'd be able to read every emotion on his face.

'You did a great job finding the poem, Josie,' he said. 'A *really* great job.'

At West Street that night, Diane Fry was working late. A shift had gone off duty, and another had come on without her noticing. The noise and chaos of changeover would normally have irritated her, but tonight it passed her by. She was sitting at a desk in the CID room with a pile of papers on either side of her, turning over pages with one hand and making notes with the other. Occasionally, Fry looked up, slightly disorientated. Nobody who came into the room even tried to speak to her, though they looked at her curiously. The expression on her face was enough to deter them from asking her why she was sitting not at her own desk, but at Ben Cooper's.

If anyone had dared to ask, Fry would probably have said that she was reading the documents from the Carol Proctor case because she had nothing better to do. Earlier, Angie had surprised her by phoning her at the office.

'Hi, are you busy?' she'd said.

'I'm always busy.'

'Right. You never stop trying to climb that slippery ladder, do you, Sis?'

'What do you want?' said Fry. 'Is something wrong?'

'No. It's just that I didn't see you this morning before you went out. How did you get on with nice Constable Cooper last night?'

'Angie, I haven't time for this –'

'OK, OK.' Angie's tone had changed. 'I want to let you know I'll be out tonight. Just in case you start getting worried about me.'

'Where are you going?' said Fry, conscious that she was sounding like a fussy parent again.

'I've got people to see, that's all. I do have a life of my

own, Diane. It went on without you for fifteen years, and it doesn't just stop.'

Fry hadn't pressed her any further, though she knew she'd spend the night worrying. She wanted to ask Angie what time she'd be home, but she managed to hold back the words.

So tonight, Fry needed something else to think about, to take her mind off her sister. The hay fever was making her feel rough enough without the extra stress. The trouble was, the material that she was reading on the Carol Proctor case wasn't making her any happier.

Mansell Quinn smiled. He released the pressure on the trigger and swung the sights of the crossbow past the running girl and back to the windows of the house. The more he handled the weapon, the more confident he felt with it. The perfect balance and the feel of its stock in his hands helped to counter the pain in his side.

Quinn slid his hand inside his shirt to check the bleeding. Will Thorpe had taken a three-inch gouge out of his skin with the bolt he'd fired in the field barn. It hadn't been too bad a shot – not in the dark, at a moving target, with no time to aim properly. Quinn knew he was lucky to be alive.

He looked for movement in the downstairs windows one by one, then raised the sights of the crossbow to the first floor, watching the play of light and shadow carefully as the evening light faded. He shifted slightly on the grass, conscious of several small stones lying against his ribs. The movement sent a stab of pain through his side that made him wince and catch his breath.

The wound would slow him down, of course, and that might have been a problem when he was going to be faced with someone much younger than himself. But now he had the crossbow it wouldn't matter so much. If he'd wanted to, he could have killed the girl. If he'd missed the first time, he could have fired two or three bolts into her, and no one would have known where they came from.

He froze for a moment, focusing all his attention on one of the windows. But the movement he could see was only the lengthening shadows of the trees on the opposite hill, outlined by the low sun.

Quinn let out his breath. Of all the things he'd worried about until now, he had never doubted that he would recognize the moment when it came, and recognize the man. Despite the difference in age, he would know him. Like father, like son. Wasn't that what they said?

Shortly after one o'clock in the morning, Ben Cooper decided he needed some fresh air. The party was still going strong, though only members of his family were left, his friends and Matt's in-laws having sensibly set off for the drive home.

The serious drinkers had moved into the kitchen among the rows of empty bottles and stacks of washing up that would be left for the morning. The conversation had drifted into unlikely areas. Matt was trying to get everyone to recite their favourite funny lines from TV comedy shows, while Uncle John had startled a few people with his imaginative solutions to the country's asylum problem.

Meanwhile, those who were up past their bedtime and were beginning to flag had propped themselves up in the sitting room with a jug of coffee and the remains of the birthday cake, and were watching an old *Star Wars* video. The girls had been watching it the day before, and they'd left it in the video player. It hadn't occurred to anyone to change it for something quieter, and now the older members of the family were having difficulty nodding off because the sound effects were so loud. His mother had long since been helped to bed and was sleeping in her old room.

Nobody noticed when Cooper slipped away to stand in the back garden, where he could look up at the trees on the hillside and see the stars. It was a bit cooler out here. He'd started off the evening drinking beer – mostly Budweiser and Grolsch, and some obscure Continental brands that Matt had bought in. Later, he'd found himself switching to white wine, simply because it was there. That had probably been a mistake. He didn't feel drunk, just sort of fuzzy and detached from reality.

Of course, someone had asked about Mansell Quinn. None of the family had lived in Castleton, but everyone seemed to have friends who did. It was Uncle John who couldn't believe that Quinn had been let out of prison.

'Life?' he said. 'Thirteen years isn't life. I've had dogs that lived twice as long as that.'

And that had started Matt off. He had a regular grumble about prisons, which he said were subsidized competition for dairy farmers. Prison farms produced twenty million pints of milk each year, not to mention goal nets for most of the English league football clubs.

'And taxpayers like me shell out twenty-five thousand pounds a year to keep a prisoner inside doing that work,' he said. 'I'm paying to put myself out of business. Make sense of that, if you can.'

When the rain began to fall again, Cooper was surprised how good it felt. For a while, the splashes dried on the ground as soon as they'd fallen. And then the rhythm increased, and soon the drops were hissing through the trees and into the grass. Cooper held out his hands and let the rain gather in his palms, the way he'd done as a child.

Somehow, he seemed to have taken a long time to get to the age of thirty. The years since he was eighteen had lasted forever. The death of his father had begun to feel as though it had happened in an entirely different existence, from which he was only now emerging, like a man staggering from the water after a cross-Channel swim. The trouble was, he wasn't quite sure whether this was a good or bad thing, whether he wanted to leave the old life behind or needed to hang on to it for safety.

Cooper walked along the side wall of the yard, where he knew he'd be out of range of the movement sensors that set off the security lights. Matt had installed the lights a few years ago after a spate of thefts from equipment sheds in the area. He'd lost a generator one night, and that had been the last straw. But the sensors couldn't cover every corner, so they were directed on the main approaches and weren't designed to catch people slipping away between the jumble of buildings, as Cooper was now.

He passed the end of the tractor shed and found himself among the old byres and pig sties. They stood unused now, rotting away quietly until Matt decided he needed the space for a new milking parlour or silage clamp. Cooper liked the smells down here – the scent of moss-grown stone and ancient wooden beams, and the ingrained odours of the animals that had lived and breathed in these buildings for generations. They were the smells of his childhood; he'd spent much of his spare time here, trying to help out, or simply hanging about and getting in the way, observing everything.

Cooper wished that Mansell Quinn hadn't been mentioned, not tonight. And not here at the farm. On the face of it, his fear made no more sense than Alistair Page's nervousness earlier that day. But he thought that unlike Page he might have good reason to be afraid – the history that existed between Quinn and Sergeant Joe Cooper might have been enough to set Quinn on his trail.

But Joe Cooper had two sons. Of course, Matt ought to be told about the situation, but Cooper didn't know how he could broach the subject. There was no way he could tell Matt there might be a risk without explaining the reason. His own memory of his father might be tarnished, but spreading the contagion to the rest of the family was a different matter. He owed his father something, at least. And all Joe Cooper had left now was his reputation.

Cooper's head turned sharply. A security light on the garage door had come on. It bathed the gate and the top end of the driveway in light. Cooper watched for a moment, expecting to see a cat that had set off the movement sensor. But nothing moved in the area picked out by the light. Beyond the light, the lower part of the drive now looked like a black hole into which anything could vanish, or from where anything could appear. The rain continued to hiss all around him. A tapping had started somewhere – a drip of water from a blocked gutter, or the overflow from a water butt falling on a metal drain cover. The steady tap-tap-tap sounded like someone drumming their fingers with increasing impatience.

He waited a few minutes, and the light went off. He blinked to readjust his eyes to the darkness. Behind the stone buildings was the stream. Cooper could hear it rushing over the stones, more noisily than usual because of the amount of rain that had fallen. And beyond the stream, the trees climbed up the hillside in dense, black clumps.

A public footpath ran through the fields here, and the sheep were used to people. They didn't move or bleat as walkers passed, especially in the dark. Most of them didn't even stop cudding.

When he looked across the stream, Cooper felt disorientated by the utter darkness, and he swayed a little, reminded of how much he'd had to drink. He had felt fine when he first got out into the fresh air, but he certainly couldn't describe himself as sober, and suddenly the effects of the beer and wine seemed to be catching up with him.

'Oh dear, that doesn't feel too good,' he said, feeling his stomach lurch as if someone had punched him in the gut.

And then, across the stream, he thought he saw a movement. He realized straight away that he was imagining things. He shook his head, but that only made him feel worse. Peering into the trees, he found his eyes drifting out of focus and had to concentrate to get them back into position. Ahead, where a rock formed an elbow in the bank of the stream and the water foamed as it flowed round it – was something there? In the blackness he thought he saw a darker glistening, the uncertain outline of a shape formed by water swirling in different directions. Droplets of rain gathered and trickled sideways, while others lay glittering in random patterns on horizontal surfaces before running downwards again. In the centre of the outline was a void, where no rain touched.

Cooper took a step forward towards the stream, but stopped when he heard brambles crackle under his feet. He squinted into the trees, now no longer sure if he'd seen anything, or whether he was simply imagining the way a scatter of raindrops passed in and out of the light, etching a silhouette in the darkness.

He pictured a black hood and a pair of shoulders streaming with rain, and the vague features of a human face, with eyes set too deep in shadow to be visible. It was a figure that had been moving through his mind all week, as if a ghost had been following him.

And then even the suggestion of a shape was gone. Cooper narrowed his eyes to peer into the darkness again, but could no longer make out a thing. He hadn't seen any movement, or even heard a noise. There had been no footsteps, no crackling underfoot, no rustling of clothes. It had been nothing more than an illusion created by the rain and his imagination.

Cooper realized his head was spinning. The buildings and trees swayed around him, and he had to sit down suddenly to avoid falling over. He put his hands to his head and groaned. Then he rolled over on to his stomach and was sick into the stream.

Now Cooper was oblivious to everything around him. He wouldn't have noticed anyone, not even if they'd been moving towards him from the trees and across the footbridge, moving slowly and deliberately, dripping water from a black hood in which he couldn't see a face.

37

Within a few minutes, Mansell Quinn was too far in to feel the movement of air. He noticed the stillness by the lack of sensation in his hands, an absence of touch on the skin of his face. For the first time, he was beyond the breathing.

He shone his torch on to the sides of the passage. He had no spare battery, and the light wouldn't last long. It was better to use it just to orientate himself, to be sure that he didn't fall into some unseen shaft as he felt his way along the walls. There was no need to go too far. There would be nobody along this way to find him. Not tonight, anyway. Nor would there be anybody to bring him out safely if he fell and broke his ankle. Not tonight, or any other night.

Moving through complete blackness was like walking through the dreams that came whenever he managed to sleep. That was the only darkness Quinn had ever found terrifying, the darkness behind his eyes when he lay down at night. And that was because too much light filtered through his eyelids, creating pictures, shapes dancing and gesturing, dim figures silently playing out scenes of a life he didn't recognize. The shapes were like those of people on the TV screen in one of his prisons, when the reception had been so bad that the picture was a fog. Behind his eyes, those figures might be no more than a faint glow of colour, the suggestion of a human shape. What were those people doing, there behind his eyes?

Quinn moved on a little further, going gradually deeper. In *Death Underground* there had been a map of the Peak–Speedwell cavern system. All those miles of branching and winding tubes resembled a huge set of lungs. That set him thinking about Will Thorpe and his emphysema. It had been a mercy to kill him, really. He pictured the postmortem, imagined Will's lungs being taken out and examined. They would be a shrivelled black mass, the disease-ravaged lung tissue replaced by fleshy pustules.

He felt a jolt of pain in his side, and touched the reassuring weight of the crossbow over his shoulder. It hadn't been right tonight, but he could wait a little longer. For now, he was enjoying the feeling of calmness within himself. It felt good, as if the deep, dark mouth of the cavern had sucked the anger from his blood.

Down in a cave, cut off from the real world. Quinn repeated it to himself. Yes, he was cut off from the real world. Whatever the real world was.

He was splashing, head-bowed, through an underground river bed, the noise of his boots echoing on the walls as he rattled over the stones. He moved to the sound of constantly running water. It cascaded out of holes in the roof, ran down the walls and trickled into rock pools.

If you stood still in here, it could get chilly. Some of the chambers had a bad atmosphere, too. From time to time, he had the conviction that he must be following someone, because he could hear noises ahead, like another person's boots dislodging stones or splashing in a pool. But Quinn ignored the noises and the illusions, taking his time, feeling his way along the walls as he walked through the stream, the water sometimes over and inside his boots.

What would it be like if the cavern flooded? He thought of white foam and the roar as the water rushed over the rocks, the rumbling as it grew in volume and reached the roof.

Quinn reached another pool and turned on his torch. He saw flickering movements in the water and realized that life existed down here after all. Minute creatures were wriggling along on their sides, like tiny fragments of fingernail. Troglodytic shrimps, living in an environment free of predators. He wondered why they didn't they get washed out when the caves flooded.

Here, the floor was covered in flowstone with water running over it. Quinn crouched close to the ground. He could hear voices all the time now, though he knew it was just the echoes of the cave. These caverns should be as remote and unaffected by man as the furthest reaches of the planet. Time meant something here, because the cave had gone through millions of years like this, experiencing the slow dissolving of rock in water. It made him feel tiny and transitory.

Yet the curtains of flowstone had been splattered and smeared with mud by hundreds of pairs of cavers' boots over the years. He'd read about members of one of the caving clubs going into Moss Chamber with scrubbing brushes to restore the flowstone to its original gleaming whiteness. Apparently they'd not been here, for he could see imprints left by the recent passage of many boots. If he wanted to, he could leave his own mark. The mud would stick to him, too. It would cling to him like a dirty memory.

Now he was here, he knew the cavern was the right place. He could have waited above the house in Castleton and made the shot whenever he wanted to, but it wouldn't have felt right. He'd waited so long that another day was nothing, if it meant doing it properly.

Quinn knelt to take a drink from the pool in his cupped

hands. Unlike the water from the well in Edendale, this was freezing cold, and it made him gasp. It left an aftertaste on the back of his mouth – a strange, acid bitterness. It was the bitterness of stone.

38

Sunday, 18 July

Diane Fry sat back in her chair at West Street, staring at the notes she'd made. It was a pity that they didn't have Mansell Quinn's DNA profile. There ought to be something – some identifiable trace of him that would remove the doubts Ben Cooper had raised. They were the sort of baseless doubts that Fry would normally have dismissed as a wild-goose chase. It was Cooper's kind of obsession, not hers.

Somebody had opened the windows again in the CID room, though Fry had asked them not to. Already this morning she could sense nature sneaking in. Every seeding patch of grass in the Peak District was sending its pollen in her direction right now. Though she'd taken the antihistamine tablets, she could feel the membranes in her nose beginning to swell.

At least authorization had come through for her to get information from Human Resources on PC 4623 Netherton, Arthur. According to his file, he'd received the Chief Constable's Commendation and a Royal Humane Society Testimonial for rescuing a woman who'd been threatening to jump from a bridge over the River Derwent some years ago. Another hero, then.

But Arthur Netherton had retired from Derbyshire

Constabulary in 2000 after thirty years' service, and had moved to Spain. Death benefits under his pension provision had been paid to his widow three years later. Netherton had died of a heart attack in his mid-fifties. Too much of the good life in too short a time, perhaps? Fry suppressed a surge of jealousy. Too much of the good life? Chance would be a fine thing.

With both of the uniformed heroes gone to the great dress parade in the sky, her options for a first-hand account of events at 82 Pindale Road in October 1990 were limited. Mansell Quinn was unavailable, while Carol Proctor was the most silent witness of all.

And now Rebecca Quinn was dead, too. What might Rebecca have been able to tell her? Anything useful? Well, perhaps Quinn himself had thought so – or somebody had. Whoever stabbed her with the carving knife had made sure she wouldn't talk.

Fry sighed. She was starting to sound like Ben Cooper. Quinn was guilty, and no one should have any doubts.

So who was left? The Quinns' neighbours? She pulled out the Hope Valley telephone directory, but found no listing for any Townsends at 84 Pindale Road. She tried calling a couple of possibilities in Bamford and Bradwell, but they were the wrong Townsends and no relation – or not admitting to it. Then she dug out the electoral roll for the Castleton ward. The current residents of 84 Pindale Road were a family by the name of Ho.

Great. So it looked as though the Townsends had left the area, too. The world was full of people trying to put the past behind them. And some of them were doing it more successfully than others.

The gala was over in Hathersage. As Diane Fry drove through the village, workmen were taking down the bunting, and the bus shelter had reverted to its normal boring state.

On the Moorland estate, children were playing on the grass and adults were washing their cars. This time, Fry found herself taking notice of small things here and there – a clown puppet hanging by its strings in an upstairs window, a rabbit with long golden fur in a hutch on a front lawn. There was a '*Not in my name*' poster in a bedroom window, left over from an Iraqi War protest, while across the street someone had painted a smiley face on their wheelie bin. A lady sat outside at a plastic table reading a newspaper, with a collie dog asleep at her feet.

Enid Quinn had a distracted air today. She had been standing in a corner of her garden, wearing her yellow rubber gloves to dead-head the roses.

'I know it's hard having to go over it again and again,' said Fry. 'But you must understand how necessary it is.'

Mrs Quinn wouldn't look at Fry, but watched the children on the grass across the road.

'Of course it's necessary,' she said. 'I know that. It's all absolutely bloody necessary.'

Fry watched her carefully from the corner of her eye. The woman's voice had taken on an unfamiliar edginess that might be the first sign of a crack in her composure. The people who seemed most in control were often the ones who disintegrated in a big way when the stress finally became too much. She didn't want that to happen to Mrs Quinn.

'We could go and talk somewhere else, if you like?' she said. 'Perhaps we could go in the house and have a cup of tea?'

'No, this is fine.'

The scent of the roses was too strong for Fry. The smell hung around her like cheap perfume. But it was grass pollen that triggered her hay fever, so she might be OK.

'The thing is,' said Fry, 'we need to go over the past, because it may be the only way of figuring out what's going through your son's mind.'

'If it's Simon and Andrea you're interested in, you should be talking to them, not me. I don't remember anything. I wasn't there.'

'I've made an appointment to see them later today. But I think there are things you may be able to tell me, even though you weren't there. Simon and Andrea are your grandchildren, after all.'

Mrs Quinn looked back towards the house with a half-shrug of her shoulders, as if it wasn't important. Fry frowned at her, trying to divine her thoughts, and failing. She wasn't a psychologist, she was a police officer. Her own experiences didn't give her access to the mind of someone like Mrs Quinn.

'Andrea is all right,' said Mrs Quinn. 'A bit too serious, and she doesn't know how to enjoy herself properly. But she's a sensible enough girl. The most sensible one of the family, probably.'

'And your grandson?'

The old woman sighed. 'Simon had a tough time of it. He was already going through a difficult phase when he was fifteen. And when it all happened, he got very mixed up. I think he still is. It was bad enough for a lad of his age when his father was convicted of murder. Simon still admired his father. He had loyalty. But it completely knocked him for six when someone told him –'

She fastened her gaze on a climbing rose and snipped at one of its flowers angrily, though to Fry it hardly seemed to have begun to wilt.

'Told him what, Mrs Quinn?'

'Someone told Simon that Mansell wasn't really his father.'

Fry raised her eyebrows. 'Who would do that?'

'Someone trying to stir up trouble, obviously.'

'But who? Do you know?'

'I'm . . . well, I'm not sure. You know what people are like. They love to be malicious.'

'And was it true?'

403

'It was possible,' said Mrs Quinn. 'That was the worst thing, I suppose. It was possible.'

It was late afternoon by the time Ben Cooper started the Toyota in the yard at Bridge End Farm. The dogs, recognizing the sound of the engine, ran towards him. But Cooper sat in the car for a few minutes, looking at the farmhouse, the place that was so familiar and yet no longer his home.

In some ways his father still lived here. He still walked in the shadow of the barn, or sat in a quiet corner of the kitchen. Every time Cooper entered the house, he knew he'd be able to smell his father's presence. No amount of fresh paint and wallpaper could cover up the memories. Joe Cooper's spirit had seeped into the walls, and it would stay there until the day the farmhouse was demolished.

The dogs barked in a puzzled way for a while, but settled down in a gateway and waited for the car to move. In the cold light of morning, Cooper was sure that his experience in the early hours had been the result of too much alcohol combined with the worries that had been preying on his mind. At the first opportunity, he'd gone to look for footprints in the wet ground by the stream, but had found only his own tracks, crazily wandering and confused. He hoped he was right, because he didn't know how he could ever tell Matt and Kate that they might be at risk. Nothing that he said would help them to understand.

On the other hand, he would never forgive himself for not warning them, if he turned out to be wrong.

> *Then carbonadoed and cooked with pains,*
> *Was brought up a cloven sergeant's face:*
> *The sauce was made of his yeoman's brains,*
> *That had been beaten out with his mace.*

Whatever logic told him, Cooper couldn't resist the feeling that the poem Josie had found was somehow about his father. Sergeant Joe Cooper had died when his head had been kicked in by drunken thugs in Clappergate while trying to make an arrest without back-up. A cloven sergeant's face.

At first, Cooper had been puzzled by Mansell Quinn's conversation with Raymond Proctor at the caravan park on Wednesday night. Quinn had been talking about children, particularly about sons. And Proctor hadn't been sure whose son he meant.

What if Quinn had been thinking of Sergeant Joe Cooper's son? What was that line from the Bible? The sins of the fathers. It must be somewhere in the Old Testament, which had a lot about vengeance and blood. An eye for an eye, a tooth for a tooth.

'You're telling me Rebecca Quinn had an affair?' said Diane Fry. 'But it must have been some time ago?'

'Yes. It was before she and Mansell got married – while they were engaged, in fact.'

Enid Quinn put down her secateurs and stripped off the yellow gloves, revealing her thin hands and pale skin like lined parchment. The smell of hand cream mingled with the scent of the roses.

'It wasn't a long engagement,' she said. 'Mansell was madly in love with her, and he was impatient to get wed. So it was all a bit of a rush, not at all what I would have wanted for him, if I'd had my way. I like things to be done with all due consideration for what's right and proper. I don't think either of them had really thought things through. I said so at the time, of course, but he didn't take any notice. That was Mansell in those days: impetuous.'

'He seems to have learned better now.'

'What?'

'Nothing,' said Fry. 'Nothing important. And then a child

405

came along – but that must have been after they were married, surely?'

'Yes, but not too long after – six months. Mansell had no suspicions. I'd heard the rumours, though, so I wondered about it. For me, there was something about the boy that wasn't right, and there always has been. Simon never looked like Mansell, you see. Not in any way. But that wasn't the sort of thing Mansell would notice. And I wasn't going to be the one to ruin my son's happiness.'

'So how did Mansell find out? Did he start to suspect? Did he ask Rebecca?'

'No. Well, that would have been difficult. If he really *was* the father, it would have caused problems in the marriage if she knew that he doubted her. And if he wasn't . . . would she have told him the truth?'

'I see what you mean.'

'He didn't want to lose Rebecca, you see. That was the last thing Mansell wanted. But still, he needed to know the truth.'

'So what did he do?'

Mrs Quinn sighed wearily. 'It doesn't matter now. It can't matter, can it? I'm tired of it all. I think you should leave me alone.'

Fry felt a momentary twinge of sympathy for the old woman. Then she heard a lawnmower start up in the neighbour's garden. Within minutes, the air would be full of spores from freshly cut grass – one of the triggers she'd been warned to avoid. Soon, she'd be feeling like death again. The thought made her unreasonably annoyed.

'Mrs Quinn,' she said, 'you visited your son in prison. In fact, you were the last member of his family to see him, weren't you? What did you talk about?'

'I told you, it doesn't matter any more. Go out with your dogs and helicopters and hunt my son down, if you must. But why do you have to persecute me?'

'Did Mansell ask you to do something particular for him, Mrs Quinn?'

The old woman waved a hand in front of her face, as if swatting away a wasp.

'Look, I thought it was wrong,' she said. 'He shouldn't have been digging up the past like that, trying to get dirt on someone who was dead.'

'Especially someone he'd killed himself, perhaps?'

Mrs Quinn pursed her lips at the comment, and decided to ignore it. 'I helped him because . . . well, I thought it would be the last thing I'd do for him. "This one thing and no more," I said. That's what I told him. "If I do this for you, Mansell, that's it. I'm never coming to visit you in here again."'

'And he accepted that?'

'He had no choice, did he?'

'It must have been something very important to him. He was condemning himself to years in solitary confinement, almost.'

'Yes, it was very important to him. It had become an obsession. If you'd read the letters he wrote to me, you'd realize that.'

'Where are those letters, Mrs Quinn?'

'I burned them.'

Fry sighed. 'OK. And what exactly was it your son asked you to do for him?'

'He wanted to have a paternity test done to prove if Simon really was his son. You can get sampling kits, and send them away for testing. Rebecca never knew about it. This was all ten years ago.'

'Ten years,' repeated Fry thoughtfully. 'Just about the time he started to claim that he wasn't guilty of the murder.'

'About then.'

Fry knew the type of kit Mrs Quinn was talking about. They contained two sets of buccal swabs for scraping cells

407

from the inside of the cheek – one for the parent and one for the child. It was very simple to do, and perfectly safe. The reports were pretty comprehensive, and conclusive, one way or the other. They gave either a 100 per cent certainty that there wasn't a paternal relationship, or a 99.5 per cent probability that there was. It was enough to stand up in court, if necessary.

She imagined Quinn in his prison cell, looking at tables of allele numbers, identification markers and chromosome locations. He'd probably had a long wait for the test results. Back then, there had been no UK laboratories doing paternity tests, so the samples would have gone to a lab in the USA or Australia. It would have cost him a few hundred pounds, too.

But then she frowned again. How had he obtained a sample from Simon without Rebecca knowing? True, there were companies who would extract DNA from hair roots, toothbrushes, disposable razors, or dried blood and saliva. But Quinn had no physical access to his son in prison, except at visiting times.

'Was that why his family stopped visiting him?' said Fry.

Mrs Quinn just looked at her. Her hair had become disarranged in the breeze on the hillside. Fry remembered something Dawn Cottrill had said about Quinn upsetting his family during visits, trying to grab his son, tugging at his hair until he cried. Hair didn't contain cells, but its roots did. Had Quinn been trying to get a hair with the root still attached for DNA analysis? But that was too soon, surely?

'You need to have a DNA sample from both father and son to do a comparison,' said Fry.

'Yes, I know that. The kit Mansell had ordered came with things to scrape inside your cheek. They were a bit like Q-Tips, only longer.'

'Buccal swabs.'

'If you say so.'

'But what about Simon?'

'That was my part in the business.'

'How?'

'I stole a comb of Simon's. His hair was a long, tangled mess in those days, so it wasn't difficult to get some. It had to have roots on it, Mansell said.'

'That's right.'

'I wasn't very proud of what I did,' said Mrs Quinn.

Fry remembered there had been talk of a new law to prevent estranged fathers from secretly taking material from their children for paternity tests. It was claimed that some of them did it to escape responsibility for child-support payments.

But it wasn't possible to be in intimate contact with a child without taking away a bit of their DNA. It would surely be unfeasible to create a new law that made it an offence to remove a child's hair from a hairbrush, to take a sticking plaster off a cut finger, or pick up a bit of chewed gum, a used handkerchief, or an old toothbrush. Any one of them could contain DNA.

'And all to establish whether Simon was his son?' she said.

The old woman turned away towards the house. Fry tried to manoeuvre to keep eye contact, but the path was too narrow and her sleeve caught on the thorns of the roses, holding her back. Mrs Quinn managed to get a few paces away.

'Well, that was the idea, Sergeant,' she said. 'Mansell wanted to have peace of mind. He said it was the one thing he had a chance of being certain about. But there isn't really anything you can be certain about in this life, is there? Not in my experience.'

Fry listened carefully to her tone of voice, because she was unable to see Mrs Quinn's face. She pulled the thorns from her sleeve, feeling a sudden prick on her thumb and seeing a bright spot of blood appear.

'You asked me a minute ago how Mansell got the idea that Simon might not be his son,' said Mrs Quinn. 'It was Simon himself who told him, when he visited him in prison. I think it was the last time he saw him, in that prison in Lancashire. After that, it preyed on Mansell's mind. It still does, I think.'

Fry shivered. She remembered Simon Lowe the first time she'd seen him. His words came back to her: 'He's not my father. He was once, but not any more.' She couldn't believe that it had taken her all this time to understand. Damn. Why couldn't people say what they really meant?

'Mrs Quinn, when we first came here to speak to you, you told us that you believed your son was guilty of Carol Proctor's murder.'

'That's right, I did.'

'But that wasn't true, was it?'

'You mean, you don't believe I think he was guilty?'

'No.'

'You think I was lying?'

'Were you?'

'It would be a strange thing for a mother to do. If I were going to lie, wouldn't it be to stand up for my son, to protect him? Isn't that what mothers do in your experience, Sergeant?'

'Of course. There's only one reason you'd lie about him being guilty.'

'And what's that?'

'If there was somebody else you thought needed protecting even more.'

'Like who?'

'In my experience,' said Fry, 'grandmothers can get ridiculously protective of their grandchildren. Especially if they get the idea that the parents aren't doing the job properly.'

'Grandchildren?'

'Yes. Grandchildren.'

'Sergeant, I don't know what you mean.'

Fry took a deep breath, and immediately regretted it. She could taste the sharp tang of the vaporized sap spraying from the neighbour's lawnmower. She could feel the grass pollen settling on the back of her throat.

410

'I'm suggesting that when he had the DNA tests done, Mansell found out he wasn't Simon's father,' she said. 'Which meant he'd taken the blame for someone else's son. Isn't that right, Mrs Quinn?'

Enid Quinn stared at her for a moment, then began to laugh. Tears welled from her eyes. But Fry was sure she couldn't have been all that funny.

'Well, you've got that wrong,' said Mrs Quinn. 'Wrong on both counts.'

39

Ben Cooper had intended to head straight home, but somehow he never quite made it into Edendale. It was almost as though the Toyota steered itself away from Hucklow towards the Hope Valley.

When he reached Castleton, he carefully negotiated the market place and passed the Saxon-style cross to reach Pindale Road. The streets were narrow, and there seemed to be cars parked everywhere – not to mention the groups of visitors ambling in the roadway, as if they didn't expect to encounter traffic. Uniformed police officers stood in pairs on the corners, watching the crowds.

The former Quinn home stood near the top of the road, above Hope View House. When he'd lived here, Mansell Quinn had probably parked his Vauxhall estate at the roadside, as everyone else did. Castleton was one of the places where residents got seriously wound up when they couldn't park near their own homes because of the number of visitors' cars. The little town had been laid out many centuries before motor vehicles had been invented.

Pindale Road became narrower the further up the hill he went. It would be possible to get a good view of number 82 from the houses across the road, if you happened to be looking out of the right window.

Cooper had to go a long way past the house and almost to Siggate before he found a wide enough verge to turn round. He drove back down the hill and parked in the gateway of an empty house, then knocked at the door of number 84, where the Townsends had lived in 1990.

But the helpful neighbours of the Quinns were long gone from Pindale Road, and had left no forwarding address.

Cooper drove back down the A625 through Hope and turned up Win Hill to Aston. In rural areas like this, his street atlas was vague about what was a road or a farm track and what was merely a footpath or bridleway. He wanted to see if the track that ran parallel to Rebecca Lowe's garden ended at the nearby farmhouse, as it seemed to on the map, or whether it diverged at any point towards Parson's Croft.

Sure enough, he found it was possible to get a car off the farm road. The track was wide enough to drive along the back of Rebecca Lowe's hedge. It would be too muddy in the winter perhaps, but at the moment the surface was fine. A car could be parked unseen, and there were gaps in the hedge where anyone could approach the back door of Parson's Croft.

But who would have done that? It was all very well having a feeling that Mansell Quinn didn't fit the crime, but who else was there? Diane Fry herself had asked him if he had another suspect in mind. And, of course, he didn't.

Raymond Proctor drove a bright red Renault van with the caravan park's logo emblazoned on the side. It wasn't the sort of vehicle to go unnoticed in the lanes of Aston. William Thorpe might have made it up to the house on foot. But if the Newbolds' sighting was genuine, he'd already been to see Rebecca two weeks previously. Why would he come again? And why wasn't he seen a second time – a passing vagrant would be sure to attract attention in this sort of neighbourhood.

That left only one person who was close enough to Rebecca Lowe. In fact, the only person who would logically have a key to let himself into the house. Granted, there wasn't a glimmer of a motive that Cooper could see. But motive often came later, and could be surprising.

He still remembered a case from several years ago, where a seventeen-year-old boy had murdered his mother. Friends of the family had said the two of them always had a good relationship. But on that particular night, the victim had refused to let her son borrow her car to go out with his friends. So he'd killed her. Sometimes, it was impossible to understand what was going on in other people's minds.

Simon Lowe lived in Edendale. Could he have been in the Hope Valley area when his mother was killed? There had been sightings of cars reported by residents, but what sort of car did Simon drive? Perhaps the information was recorded in the incident room. He could get someone to do a check.

Thinking about Simon brought Cooper back to the events of 9 October 1990. The transcript of the police interview with Mansell Quinn had been very frustrating. All those silences from Quinn when he was asked to back up his claim that someone else had been there. On paper, his silence had implied an inability to substantiate a false version of events. But Cooper would give anything for a video tape of the interview, so that he could watch Quinn's face during those silences. He wondered if he would have been looking at a suspect caught out in a lie – or a man suddenly realizing the implications of what he'd seen and heard that day.

Obviously, he needed to know more about Simon Quinn. But who else could he ask, apart from the family?

As if on cue, his mobile rang. It was Diane Fry.

'Ben,' she said. 'This Alistair Page – what address did he live at in 1990?'

'I don't know.'

'But he was somewhere in the Pindale Road area, wasn't he? Do you have a house name?'

'Sorry.'

'He's not on the list of statements from that time, you see.'

'He'd have been too young at the time,' said Cooper. 'Fifteen, he said.'

'I see. So how did you meet him?'

'Well, he came to find me one day when I was on duty at West Street.'

'When was this?'

'Only a couple of weeks ago. I think one of my friends must have mentioned my name to him. I suppose they thought I might be interested in liaising with the cave rescue organization.'

'I suppose so. It's not as if you're Mr Anonymous around here, is it?'

'Well, no.'

'What's he like? Reliable? Do you think he's worth talking to about the Quinns?'

'The impression I get is that he was a bit traumatized by the whole business. He's desperately keen to know what's going on, but he shied away when I asked him directly about Simon.'

'They might have known each other quite well, then?'

'It's possible.'

'I might talk to him, in that case. An independent view would be useful.'

'Diane, is this –'

Fry was silent for a moment. 'It's relevant to the official enquiry,' she said.

'I see.' But Cooper wasn't sure what she meant. 'You've been looking at Simon Lowe, then?'

Fry hesitated. 'He seems a bit of an enigma, that's all.'

'I agree.'

'He was supposed to be at school that afternoon, but as

415

far as I can see he turned up at Pindale Road much later than he should have done if he'd come straight home. Nobody seems to have asked him where he'd been.'

'And why would they, in the circumstances?'

'Exactly.'

Cooper gazed out of his car window at the back door of Parson's Croft, trying to picture another house at another time.

'How about this?' he said. 'I know it's speculation, but . . .'

'Go on.'

'Well, if Mansell Quinn had been having an affair with Carol Proctor, it would have been devastating for the family to find out, right?'

'Of course.'

'What if they did find out?' said Cooper. 'Or rather, one of them did.'

'Rebecca? You think she knew?'

'No, not Rebecca. I mean Simon.'

'Simon?'

'What if he bunked off school that day and went home, not expecting anybody to be in. But he found Carol Proctor there.'

'You mean if he'd walked in and found her lying dead on the floor? But why didn't he phone?'

'No,' said Cooper. 'That wasn't what I meant.'

Fry was silent for a moment. 'Do you have Alistair Page's number?'

'Diane, let me talk to him myself.'

'All right. But let me know how it goes. As soon as you can, Ben.'

Fry rang off. Cooper wasted no time. He had the number he needed in his mobile phone already.

'Alistair,' he said, 'I'm sorry to bother you about this, but I don't know who else to ask.'

'What is it, Ben?' said Page. 'Still worrying about radon? Or scared of getting trapped in a flooded cave?'

'Neither. I want to talk to you about Simon Lowe. The boy you knew as Simon Quinn.'

Page seemed to go away from the phone for a moment, or to put his hand over the mouthpiece. But it could just have been a fade in the signal on Cooper's mobile.

'Simon?' Page said when he came back on the line. 'You want to know about Simon? Well, what can I tell you? We hung around together a bit as teenagers.'

'He seems rather quiet and intense. And secretive.'

'Secretive?'

'He's been trying to keep quiet about the fact that Mansell Quinn is his father,' said Cooper.

'I think we'd all do that, in the circumstances. It's not something I'd want everyone to know about – that my father was a murderer.'

'It would give you a lot of street cred in some circles, Alistair. If you lived on the Devonshire Estate in Edendale, it would get you elected king.'

'Not Simon. That's not the sort of street cred he'd be interested in,' said Page. 'Actually, as a teenager he was unpredictable, and he had a bit of a temper. You could never be sure what he would do if you aggravated him. I suppose he got that from his father.'

'Possibly.'

'Alcohol was a problem for him too, I remember. A few drinks, and he could flare up in a moment. And we drank quite a bit as teenagers. We had no problem getting booze when we were fifteen or sixteen.'

'Bunking off school at lunchtime?'

'Yes, now and then.'

Cooper tried to picture Alistair Page in his little cottage. He didn't know whether Page was in a relationship, or even if he had children somewhere. He'd never mentioned anything about himself, except that he'd lived near the Quinns when he was a youngster.

417

'Have you seen much of Simon recently, Alistair?'

'No. I didn't keep in touch with him very much after we left school, because I never really felt comfortable in his company. To be honest, I started to find him a bit scary.'

'Why?'

Page was silent for a moment. Cooper could hear music playing in the background. It was a CD from Alistair's collection: 'I Still Haven't Found What I'm Looking For'. Very appropriate.

'Ben,' said Page, 'if you want to know more about Simon Quinn, I think you'd better come to the house. Can you make it tonight?'

'Yes, I think so. But not too early.'

'That's OK. At the moment, I'm doing a final security check at the cavern about nine o'clock each night, just before it goes dark. Come to my house after that.'

Dawn Cottrill hovered over Simon and Andrea Lowe like a mother. She had them both sitting alongside each other on the sofa in her lounge, looking out of a big picture window into the conservatory. Diane Fry and Gavin Murfin were ushered into armchairs opposite them, conscious of the light behind them and the sun on their backs of their necks.

Fry was struck again by the similarity between the brother and sister. They were both dark-haired, as Rebecca had been, though Simon was slightly lighter in colouring and a few inches taller. He hardly looked the dangerous type. Yet even before Fry spoke to him, she could see him undergoing those ominous dark flushes, as if waves of anger were surging through his veins.

'How are you feeling now, sir?' she said.

'I'm fine. I had a headache for a couple of days, a few bruises, that's all.'

Andrea patted his arm gently. 'I don't suppose you're any nearer catching him?' she said to Fry.

418

'The person who attacked your brother? No. We think he used an edging stone from one of the graves in the church-yard, but we have no other leads, I'm afraid.'

'Oh well, you'll just have to write it off as an attempted mugging, I suppose,' said Simon, flushing a deep red. 'Some character spotted me in the pub and thought I looked worth robbing. It's the obvious conclusion for our wonderful police force.'

'Simon, don't get stressed,' said Andrea. 'It won't do any good.'

Fry waited calmly, observing how Simon reacted to his sister. Andrea was obviously the person he listened to. The closeness between them was palpable.

'I've been talking to your grandmother, Mrs Quinn,' said Fry, now addressing Simon without a pretence of including Andrea.

Neither of them reacted, but Dawn fussed along the back of the sofa behind them, then stopped and stared at Fry, as if she had just noticed something wrong with her.

'I gather your father became concerned about whether you were his real son.'

'Sorry?' said Simon.

'He seems to have had doubts about whether you were his son. Genetically speaking.'

'Never mind "genetically speaking" – I know what you mean,' said Simon, his face darkening again.

'And do you have any idea why your father should have had doubts about your paternity?'

Simon sighed. 'I suppose it was something I said in the heat of the moment. I didn't mean it literally.'

'You didn't?'

'No. This is a very strange line of conversation, Detective Sergeant. When you asked to see us, we were hoping you might have some news for us. Good news – the news we've been waiting for ever since our mother was murdered on

Monday night. But apparently that isn't what you've brought us.'

'No. I'm sorry, sir.'

He nodded, with a tremor of agitation. 'Well, I don't know what it is you're talking about, and I don't see what possible relevance it can have to my mother's death.'

'You do believe Mansell Quinn is your father, then?'

'Unfortunately, yes.'

'So there wasn't any need for you and your sister to change your surname?'

'No.'

'I understand why your mother would have wanted to change to your step-father's name, but you didn't have to. You were old enough to say no, and keep your own name.'

Simon leaned forward a little, as if to focus attention entirely on himself. As far as Fry was concerned, he didn't need to do that. But she noticed Andrea exchange an anxious look with their aunt over her shoulder.

Fry didn't know what she was expecting. Enid Quinn had told her that the DNA tests proved Simon really *was* Mansell's son, so she had to come up with some other reason why Quinn should start to claim that he was innocent of Carol Proctor's murder. The theory she had begun to form was in pieces.

If Mansell Quinn hadn't committed murder in 1990, he must have had some idea in his mind who did. He surely hadn't suspected Rebecca, who had been at work at the time with a dozen colleagues as witnesses. Yet she had become Quinn's second victim on his release from prison.

And Simon? Had he, too, been an intended victim? Had Quinn been the one who attacked him outside the pub in Castleton on Tuesday night?

There was undoubtedly some missing factor that Fry couldn't put her finger on. It was almost as if someone was absent from the equation – someone who provided the vital link.

420

'Detective Sergeant,' said Simon, growing impatient at her hesitation, 'the fact is that we just didn't want people to associate us with an unpleasant incident from the past. The name Quinn has connotations around here, a lot of history that goes with it. People still recognize it.'

'I understand. But, from your father's point of view, it must have looked like a betrayal.'

'What do you mean?'

'I mean, the fact that his only son had disowned him.'

Simon raised his eyebrows. Then he surprised Fry by smiling, as if she'd said something funny again. In that moment, he reminded her of his grandmother, Enid Quinn. But she suspected she'd get even less out of Simon.

'I wonder if I could ask you about the day Carol Proctor was murdered?' she said.

'What?'

'I know it's many years ago now, but I'm sure it must still be clear in your mind.'

Simon had gone very quiet, but the two women began to make protesting noises. Fry tried to over-ride them.

'You were at school that day, weren't you, sir? Could you tell me what time you left school to go home?'

'Detective Sergeant, please – ' said Dawn Cottrill.

'You were at Hope Valley College, as was your sister. Why did it take you longer than her to arrive home that day?'

Simon opened his mouth, but only one word came out.

'I . . .'

'I'm sure you must remember,' said Fry. 'We usually find trivial details like that are imprinted on people's minds after a traumatic event.'

But Simon Lowe's face had closed like a trap. His jaw clenched, and the veins throbbed in his temples as colour rushed to his neck and cheeks. In that second, he convinced Fry that he was a man possessed of a barely restrained temper, a man capable of violence.

'I'm not answering any questions about that,' he said. 'It's all in the past. Finished with. I won't answer any more questions, and nor will my sister.'

Fry looked at Andrea, who nodded sharply.

'Very well, sir. It's your prerogative.'

Simon began to get up. 'Now, if you don't mind, Detective Sergeant, I have somewhere to go, and I don't want to be late. If you do happen to have any news you think I'd want to hear, my sister will know where to find me.'

'Not the sort of lad I'd want as *my* son,' said Gavin Murfin on the way back to Edendale. 'Not that we fathers get any choice in the matter.'

'I grant you Simon Lowe isn't very appealing,' said Fry. 'But, to be fair, he may not always have been that way.'

'We need someone who can tell us, don't we?'

'We've already got someone,' said Fry. 'Oh, damn.' She poked at the buttons on her mobile.

'What's up?'

'Ben Cooper never phoned. He was supposed to talk to an old schoolfriend of Simon's, some bloke called Alistair Page. But there are no messages from him.' She dialled Cooper's number, and cursed. 'And now he's switched his mobile off. There's no signal.'

Murfin laughed. 'You know our Ben,' he said. 'He's probably in a cave again.'

40

There was no bell tolling in Castleton tonight. As darkness came, Ben Cooper had expected to hear it. The memory of its sound came back to him as he crossed the road and followed the riverside walk.

Cooper had visited Castleton twice as a child. Not on a school trip the second time, but with his family. It had been during the evening, and in winter, too – perhaps they'd come to see the Christmas lights, he wasn't sure. He'd been with his mother and father, and he knew it was winter, because he remembered the bell: a single note repeated over and over. He'd heard it rolling out from behind the buildings as they walked along Cross Street, getting louder as they turned the corner to the church. The bell had a sharp after-note – a bitter, unhappy sound that echoed off the walls of the George and the Castle Hotel, where tables and chairs had stood on deserted patios.

A man in one of the shops had told them it was called the Curfew Bell. It was rung in Castleton every evening during the winter, marking the hour when the villagers should put out their fires and lights for the night. The tradition dated back to a time when people had lived in wooden huts with thatched roofs. Now it served only to recall the past.

But this was July, and the night was quiet as Cooper walked alone by the river under the subdued light of the streetlamps. Yet his father's presence had been evoked for a moment by his memory of the bell.

He could see into the brightly lit rooms of cottages that lay close to the path, squeezed into the lower end of the gorge. At one point, a black chasm appeared between them. Judging from the noise, much of the water that poured out of the cave system must emerge here. Its roaring rose into the high spaces between the walls, its sound the only thing to fill the dark void except his imagination.

Cooper felt like an intruder as he walked in silence towards Lunnen's Back. The past still clung to the stones here. It had a powerful grip, which many decades had failed to shift. Some of the houses gave the impression that they hadn't quite made it into the twentieth century, let alone the twenty-first. They might have central heating and satellite TV, but these seemed transitory things that hardly touched on their real existence. These houses had been carved out of the sides of the limestone gorge. And as darkness fell, they seemed to be retreating into the hillside, slowly shuffling back into the rock, edging away from the modern world, as if they came out only in the daylight. With each step Cooper took towards the cavern, he felt he was walking into the past.

A few minutes later, Cooper was knocking on Alistair Page's door but getting no reply. He banged harder. Rock Cottage was such a small house that he ought to be able to hear somebody calling or even moving around inside, but there was nothing.

He peered through the window, feeling like one of those intrusive tourists. There was a light on in the kitchen extension at the back, but he could see no sign of Page. Cooper tried banging on the window, but got no better result.

He pulled out his phone. He didn't have a mobile number

for Alistair Page, but Page had rung him the other day, so his number should still be logged in his last ten calls list. But no – Cooper remembered that Page had rung him at the office, not on his mobile.

Then he noticed an old lady watching him. She had come out of one of the other cottages – perhaps the white one with the black door, or the empty-looking place with crumbling stonework. She was grey-haired and neat, and she reminded him of Enid Quinn in the cemetery at Hope, tending her husband's grave with her rubber gloves and hearth brush.

'It's no use trying to phone young Alistair, if that's what you're doing,' she said.

'Why not?'

'You won't get through where he is.'

'Has he gone up to the cavern? Oh, of course, he does a security check, doesn't he? But he said that was at nine o'clock. He should have been home long since.'

The old lady shook her head. 'He went off and hasn't come back, anyway.'

Cooper looked up at the sides of the gorge. He had a sudden image of Mansell Quinn watching him from the edges of the cliff, or from the trees near Peveril Castle, or from the mouth of Peak Cavern itself.

'Of course. Could I use your phone, please?'

The old lady retreated a few feet. 'I don't let anybody into my house. I don't know who you are.'

'Very sensible. But I'm a police officer.'

'Have you got any identification?'

'Yes, of course.' Cooper patted his pockets, but it was a warm night and he'd left his jacket in the car, all the way back in the main car park, knowing there was nowhere to leave it in these narrow alleys. 'Damn. I'm sorry, I haven't.'

'We've been told to watch out for strange men hanging about here at night,' said the old lady. 'There's a prisoner on the loose, you know. A man who did a murder.'

'Yes, I know. Look, if I could just use your phone.'

'Not without showing me your identification. That's what the policeman said who came to talk to us at the Darby and Joan Club. "Don't let anybody in without identification," he said.'

'It's very good advice normally.'

'He gave us some little plastic cards, too. I've got one stuck to the inside of my door, so I know what to do, if I forget.'

'Yes, but –'

Then Cooper heard a phone ringing in Rock Cottage. He turned towards the sound, listened to it ring four times, then stop, as if an answering machine had cut in.

'Do you happen to know –' he said.

But the old lady had gone. She'd faded silently back into the jumble of stone cottages and left him on his own.

As she walked back into the office at West Street, Diane Fry considered the irony of what Mansell Quinn's mother had told her. A DNA profile of Quinn had existed after all. Ten years ago, he'd used a buccal swab on himself and had his own sample analysed. But the result of a private DNA test couldn't be obtained by the police, even if it still existed, which was unlikely.

There were no messages from Ben Cooper at the office. Fry tried his phone again, but still got no signal. If he'd been in one of the Dark Peak's notorious black spots, he ought to have come out of it by now. Cave, indeed. Cooper was trying to avoid her.

Did that mean he'd got something useful from Alistair Page? If Cooper had gone off on some crusade of his own without telling her, she'd have his guts for garters this time. Enough was enough.

Fry picked up the Carol Proctor file and looked through the list of statements again. There was definitely nothing from anyone called Page. Maybe his parents had had a different name; perhaps, like Rebecca Lowe, his mother had remarried.

Of course, if the Carol Proctor enquiry were taking place now, there'd be a searchable index of houses and their occupants, the kind of index the HOLMES system provided as routine. Every name that cropped up would have been entered, and links established automatically by the computer. There would be indexes, too, for vehicles, street names, telephone numbers. A major enquiry could produce thousands and thousands of entries. On some enquiries, there were so many entries you'd think the SIO was going for the *Guinness Book of Records*.

But no such luck in this case. It was like delving back into the Stone Age.

Fry hesitated. Perhaps she should get the name checked out by the current HOLMES team anyway, and see if something came up.

She went through the files one last time, flicking through the questionnaires and statements again, looking now not for the name Page, but just for a boy of the right age. There was Simon Quinn, of course – himself now with a new identity. In his case, there had been no real need to change his name except for a desire to put the events at Pindale Road in the past.

Finally, she came to a halt. Apart from Simon, there appeared to have been only one other fifteen-year-old youth in the immediate area. A youth called Alan. He was Raymond and Carol Proctor's son.

'My God, why has nobody mentioned *him*?'

Fry hardly knew where to start. The phone book showed no Alan Proctor anywhere in the Hope Valley; the electoral roll had no one by that name either, and certainly not living at Wingate Lees caravan park with Ray and Connie.

She reached for the phone. She really didn't want to have to speak to Raymond Proctor right now, but there was no choice. Alan Proctor was what she'd been looking for – a missing piece in the equation.

427

Then Fry stopped and withdrew her hand. No, he wasn't missing at all, just there in a different form, a man who had adapted his identity. She was quite certain that Alan Proctor and Alistair Page were one and the same person.

But before she could figure out exactly what that meant, Gavin Murfin stuck his head round the door.

'Diane, are you coming?'

Fry stared at him. 'Where?'

'There's been an alarm at one of the show caves in Castleton.'

'Peak Cavern?'

'No, Speedwell. The troops are all revved up to go. They think it could be Mansell Quinn.'

The lights ended at the last cottage, and the rest of the path was in darkness. As Ben Cooper reached the head of the gorge, with the streaked cliffs towering above him, he couldn't help tilting his head to look up. A cluster of spindly trees on the edge of the cliff framed one of the brightest stars in the sky.

By the time he stood at the gates of the cavern, he could hear water dripping raggedly on to the roof of the ticket booth inside. The concrete floor was damp where the water gathered and ran away to join the stream further down the gorge.

Cooper felt very small standing at the entrance to the cavern. The outer gates were black wrought iron, topped with spikes. A steel mesh fence on either side was backed with thick rushes and strung with barbed wire, and it ran down into the stream bed to meet the wall of the cliff. Not an easy prospect for climbing over.

The constant chattering of the jackdaws overhead had begun to resemble the cry of seagulls at the seaside. The sound had that same harsh, high-pitched quality.

Cooper jumped as a stone dropped from the cliff and

thudded on a wooden table between the ticket booth and the ropemakers' house. Maybe the stone had been dislodged from a ledge by one of the jackdaws. Perhaps the cliff face was even more dangerous than it looked.

Looking at the black mouth of the cavern, Cooper knew it must have been a perfect place for outlaws. Who would venture into those depths to face them? Who'd want to leave the daylight far behind and pass along the stream bed, feeling that change in the air on the descent into the Devil's Dining Room? By flickering candlelight, they'd have seen the stalactites like black hooks in the roof of the chamber, and watched shadowy shapes moving in the walls as the River Styx rushed far below.

He shook his head. No one who was superstitious or claustrophobic would dream of entering. But Cock Lorrel and his outlaws had been beyond the normal bounds of society, associated in the imagination with the Devil, and with every evil practice that people could think of – including cannibalism.

That reputation must have been relished by the gypsies and tinkers who'd come to the cavern each year for the Beggars' Banquet. In fact, they had probably cultivated the myth, knowing it would ensure they'd be left alone.

A deep rumbling he'd been hearing came closer, and Cooper saw lightning over Castleton. He touched the handle of the iron gates. There should have been a chain and padlock, but the gates swung open easily at his touch. He could see several footprints at the top of the first terrace, where water running from the cliff face and splashing off the ticket booth had softened the surface.

'No way,' he said. 'There's no way I'm going in there again. Not on my own, in the dark.'

He fingered his phone, remembering that he'd have to walk all the back into the village to get a signal, or talk his way into someone's house.

Cooper was about to turn away from the gates, but stopped. The last shreds of light from the lamps on the path reached a few feet past the ticket booth before being swallowed up in the blackness of the cavern. As his eyes adjusted to the darkness, he could make out the shapes of the abandoned ropemakers' equipment on the terraces – the sledges and winders, and the jack with its rotating hooks.

And a few yards along the top terrace, he could see a human figure, motionless, slumped over one of the pulley-poles.

He pulled out his torch and shone it on the figure, illuminating a hunched back in a dark jacket, and legs that dragged on the floor at an unnatural angle. It hung on the edge of the darkness that led to the Devil's Dining Room, and he knew he was looking at no one alive.

Carefully, Cooper moved over the terrace towards it. He touched the shoulder, already feeling a prickle of apprehension from the knowledge that something wasn't right. His hand rested on the dusty fabric, and sank in. His fingers pushed into the shoulder as if it had been reduced to shreds of straw. The figure sagged and slipped sideways. Dust fell out of its sleeves, and a pale, shapeless face rolled towards him, painted eyes staring past him towards the soot-blackened roof.

Somewhere in the darkness of the cavern, Cooper heard a metallic scrape, the drawing back of a powerful spring.

'Put down the torch and turn round,' said a voice. 'Or you're as dead as that dummy.'

41

Outside Speedwell Cavern, Diane Fry could see the road that ran up into Winnats Pass. The sides of the pass certainly looked a peculiar shape, but no doubt there was some sound geological reason for that. Coral reefs and tropical lagoons, indeed.

Ben Cooper had also told her a story about the old A625 being closed by landslips from Mam Tor. She'd found it hard to believe, having spent most of her life among roads that stayed pretty much where they were put. But, from Speedwell, she could see the collapsed slopes of the hill, where the shale had been loosened by the vast amounts of water that fell in these parts. It was obvious even to her that thousands of tons of rock had slithered down into the valley, carrying the road with it, ripping up yards of tarmacked surface as if it had been so much black crepe paper.

A member of staff was waiting for them in a room at the top of a steep flight of steps. He made them put on white safety helmets from a heap on a table.

'Was it you who called in?' she said.

'Yes.'

'And what's your name, sir?'

'Page.'

'Mr Alistair Page?'

'That's right.'

Fry studied him for a moment.

'I'd like to talk to you later, Mr Page,' she said.

A guide took them down the steps, which ran back under the road, descending steeply into the hillside. The arched roof was low, as if constructed with small men in mind. Fry found it impossible to get into her stride as she went down. She had to take the steps one at a time for fear of losing her balance and pitching headlong to the bottom, where even her hard hat might not save her. Behind her, Gavin Murfin clutched cautiously at the handrail, which meant he had to stoop rather than walk in the middle of the steps where the roof was high enough to stand upright.

'And how far does this canal thing run?' Fry asked the guide.

'Over half a mile. The old lead miners cut southwards from here to intersect the veins that run east to west through this hill. Some of the veins are still visible in the tunnel we'll go through.'

'We're not here for the tour, by the way.'

'Fair enough.'

When they reached the landing stage at the bottom, two members of the task force dressed in boots and overalls were already sitting in a long punt-type boat. In front of them was the mouth of a tunnel cut through the rock. Once they entered it, they would find their heads only an inch or two below the roof.

'There isn't much weight in this boat, so it's going to ride a bit high in the water, I'm afraid,' said their guide. 'You'll have to duck as we go through the tunnel. Also, it might go a bit too fast for me to control properly. But don't worry – it's perfectly safe.'

He switched on an electric motor and the boat began to move. The low hum of the motor was no louder than the

432

splash of water and the bump of the hull against the walls. They ducked their heads to avoid the roof, but couldn't avoid the occasional scrape of a helmet on rock. Around them was the smell of cold, wet stone. And the tunnel was dead straight. All Fry could see ahead were two rows of lights fixed to the walls, reflecting in the slowly moving water like elongated candles. They made the tunnel seem endless, and the entrance to the cavern unreachably far away.

Ben Cooper watched Mansell Quinn closely for a clue to his intentions. He knew he was trying to look for humanity in a face hardened by despair. The creases at the corners of Quinn's eyes hadn't been there in the old photographs, and his hairline had receded a little from his forehead. But his hair was still much the same colour – still that sandy blond, like desert camouflage.

Quinn was very lean, but the muscles in his shoulders were well defined. Apart from his hands and face, he had remarkably fine, translucent skin. He'd taken off his shirt, and his ribs and collarbones were visible, their fragile shapes like scaffolding under plastic sheeting. Blue veins snaked across his shoulders and along the insides of his arms, and gathered in clusters in the crooks of his elbows. Above his left hip was an angry wound, about three inches across, that wept trickles of blood.

'I'm Detective Constable Cooper, Edendale Police. Please put the weapon down, sir.'

Quinn didn't respond. His torso was wet, as if he'd been washing, perhaps trying to clean the wound. He was standing a few yards away on one of the terraces where the ropemakers' sledges and winders stood abandoned. Cooper guessed he'd been down to the stream in the bottom of the cavern.

The crossbow was pointing steadily at Cooper's chest. Quinn nodded towards the interior of the cavern.

'Walk straight ahead on to the path.'

'This isn't a good idea, Mr Quinn. Put the weapon down.'

'Don't tell me what is and isn't a good idea.'

Cooper hesitated. The usual advice was to keep the subject talking in a situation like this. But he saw Quinn's reaction and remembered his reputation for violence and a quick temper. It might be best to co-operate, or seem to.

'It *is* Mr Quinn, isn't it?' he said.

'Walk straight ahead. Don't step off the path. And don't stop until I tell you.'

'I'll need the torch,' said Cooper, gesturing at his feet. 'The lights are off in there.'

'No. There'll be all the light we need. Just move.'

Cooper looked at the crossbow in Quinn's hands. The bolt was about eighteen inches long, with a wickedly sharp point. A draw of a hundred and fifty pounds, and a hunting range of forty yards. The statistics had seemed academic at the time. But not now.

Cooper turned towards the path, and walked into the darkness.

'There's Poor Vein, then Pocket Holes,' said the guide. 'They found blocks of lead ore in there weighing several pounds, buried in yellow clay. We're four hundred and fifty feet below the surface now.'

'I did say –'

'I know you did. But I thought it might help if I keep talking.'

Diane Fry silently cursed the man for noticing that she was having a problem. Once they'd entered the tunnel, she'd begun to feel the rock closing around her. She knew without the guide telling her that they were getting deeper, the weight pressing down harder and harder as they slid through the water.

The darkness ahead was unnerving, too. Despite the lights,

she couldn't see an end to the tunnel. The walls converged slowly, but vanished in the distance before they met. There was still a long way to go before she could get out of the boat. Fry looked down into the water.

'How deep is it?'

'Only three feet.'

Enough for her to drown in, if she had a panic attack and went over the side of the boat. She didn't have much hope of Gavin Murfin saving her, if that happened. Fry looked at Murfin on the next seat. His shoulders were hunched and his head was down. He was very quiet.

'Enjoying it, Gavin?' she said.

He shook his head, squinting at the sides of the tunnel. The bow swung to the right and hit the wall with a bang, shuddering the planks in the bottom. The guide pushed against the rock face to get it back into the centre. But with no more than a few inches' clearance, the boat bounced off the opposite wall almost immediately.

The guide looked back into the boat at his passengers.

'There's no way anybody could get in here. You can see that.'

'We have to check,' said Fry.

He shrugged. 'Just here is Halfway House – it's a branch canal, made so that two boats can pass in the tunnel. It's only a few yards long.'

Fry dipped her hand in the water. They'd been told the temperature down here was a constant nine Celsius, but the water itself was a few degrees colder.

'How does it stay full of water?' said Murfin.

'There's a dam up ahead in Far Canal.'

'Another canal?'

'It's more of a continuation of this one, further into the hillside. But we don't go as far as that. We stop at the Bottomless Pit.'

'Thank God for that,' said Murfin. 'I think.'

*   *   *

The cavern system was full of flowstone curtains, delicate calcite dams, and little gour pools holding crystal-clear water. Irregular fragile growths hung on the passage walls, while stalactites and stalagmites grew from the roof and floor, forming drip by drip from the evaporation of dissolved calcium.

But Ben Cooper saw none of it. Mansell Quinn had the only torch, and he kept it pointed at the floor so they could see where they were putting their feet on the uneven flights of steps and slippery patches of wet limestone. The light didn't seem very strong to Cooper. He wondered how long Quinn had been using the battery. A torch wasn't on the list of items he'd bought at Out and About, so where had he got it? Was it something his mother had kept in a kitchen drawer in case of emergencies? Cooper prayed that Quinn at least had a spare set of batteries. Peak Cavern wasn't a place to be without a source of light.

And it was clear that they were heading deeper into the cavern. They had bent double as they passed through Lumbago Walk and into the Great Cave. The dome-like avens in the roof far above had gone by unseen as Cooper tried to listen for the echoes that identified the acoustics of the Orchestra Gallery. But the familiar cascade of water still caught him by surprise, and he was unable to turn his head away in time to avoid it. Roger Rain's House.

In a flicker of Quinn's torch, Cooper saw the moss around a fibre-optic light on the wall, growing from spores that had been carried into the cavern on visitors' clothes, or that had drifted in on the air.

'OK, stop,' said Quinn a few minutes later.

Another second of light, and Cooper saw the yellowish-white calcite sheets glistening on the walls, and tiny black hooks hanging from the roof. Then the torch turned away, and there was only darkness around him again. The surface was four hundred feet away now, through solid rock.

Cooper realized that his skin was tingling in the cool air.

All his attempts to engage Quinn in conversation had failed so far. Maybe he could think of something that would force him to answer.

'Sit down,' said Quinn. He pointed with the torch. 'On the floor.'

Quinn had the torch in his left hand, on his injured side. But the crossbow was gripped firmly in his right, his index finger curled close to the trigger. Cooper sat cross-legged on the floor, immediately feeling the chill of the damp rock through his trousers. He hadn't come dressed for this. In fact, he hadn't come equipped for it, either. Like the most fool-hardy of amateur cave explorers, he had no equipment, no proper clothing, no food or water, and now no light of his own. And he hadn't told anybody where he was going. What an idiot. Alistair Page was the only person who might think of looking for him in the cavern.

Quinn sat on a boulder across the chamber, at a safe distance and above Cooper's level. He was taking no chances. But Cooper saw that Quinn hadn't put his shirt back on. It would be difficult for him to do that now without losing control of the crossbow or the torch, or both. His body had dried, but he must be feeling the cold.

'Why did you confess to killing Carol Proctor?' said Cooper.

His voice jarred the silence. He'd never heard himself sound so small and tinny. As the cavern swallowed the sound of his words, he was overwhelmed with a sense of his own insignificance in the vastness of the cave system.

But at least it had worked.

'Because I was guilty,' said Quinn.

'That's not what you said at first.'

'I changed my mind.'

'Why?'

The torchlight flickered. Quinn put the torch down on the boulder next to him, flexed his left arm and gripped the shaft of the crossbow to steady it. Cooper saw that he was shivering.

437

'Why did you change your mind? Was it because your friends let you down, didn't give you an alibi for the right time? Without that, your defence wouldn't stand up, would it?'

Quinn didn't answer. So Cooper tried again – he had to keep him talking.

'Or was it because of what you remembered during the police interviews, Mr Quinn?'

'What do you mean?'

Cooper leaned forward and talked a little more quickly and insistently, focusing Quinn's attention on him.

'I think it must have been very traumatic going into your own house and finding your lover dying on the floor. The shock would've driven everything else out of your mind. You couldn't think properly, could you? I can see that's how it must have been. But some things came back later, didn't they? Details, impressions. They came back when the detectives asked you questions.'

Quinn stared at him. 'I don't understand how you can know that. You weren't there.'

'I've read the transcripts, Mr Quinn. I think I could tell where it happened – where the memories came back to you.'

'You can't know something like that. You're making it up.'

Quinn shifted the butt of the crossbow a little. It must be very uncomfortable, pressed against his naked shoulder like that.

Cooper leaned an inch or two closer. The torchlight was definitely failing now, but Quinn didn't seem to notice. The gradual fading of light could be indiscernible, until it was too late. Until you realized it was already too dark to see.

'What was it you saw that day?' said Cooper. 'You noticed something in the room, something that surprised you. It shouldn't have been there. What did you remember seeing?'

Quinn's eyes were drifting away, and he was losing concentration. The nose of the crossbow dipped a little. Cooper

438

realized that Quinn must be exhausted. He'd been sleeping rough for the past few nights, and constantly on the move during the day, always looking over his shoulder for a police car or a CCTV camera. It was almost over for him now; he was drawing on his last reserves of energy.

'The Coke bottle,' said Quinn, as if talking in his sleep. 'I smelled it first. There was a Coca Cola bottle on the table. It wasn't quite empty.'

'What was wrong with the Coke bottle being there?'

'Carol didn't drink Coke. She hated it. The bottle shouldn't have been there.'

'And what else?'

But Cooper couldn't get out the next question before Quinn cut across him.

'And there was a light – a light from upstairs. Carol wouldn't have gone upstairs. She wouldn't go near the bedroom, not even to pass it on the way to the loo.'

Cooper wanted to hold his breath, so as not to disturb Quinn's recall. But he needed to ask one more thing.

'There was something you heard?'

'Music. There was music in the house.'

Cooper hadn't expected that. A voice, a footstep, the sound of a door closing, perhaps.

'Music? What music?'

'I knew it,' said Quinn. 'Not at the time. But later, I recognized it. It was U2.'

'U2?' Cooper closed his eyes. It had been there in the transcript of the interview, after all. But he hadn't understood it. Nor had the interviewers. As far as they were concerned, Mansell Quinn had said, '*You, too.*'

'Somebody else had been in the house before you arrived,' said Cooper. 'Why didn't you say so?'

'Only the kids drank Coke. And the light was from Simon's room. He used to draw the curtains and put the lamps on, even in broad daylight. He played U2 all the time up there, and it drove me mad. When he had it on too loud, I got angry with him. Too angry.'

He turned his attention back to Cooper, who sank reluctantly back on his heels as the crossbow straightened up again.

'I've been angry all my life,' said Quinn.

42

When the torchlight finally became too low, Mansell Quinn reached into his rucksack with one hand and withdrew a round foil packet about eight inches long, which he opened with his teeth.

Ben Cooper couldn't make it out properly. 'What's that?' he said.

At least Quinn had become calmer now. For a moment, Cooper had feared he'd pushed the man too far. But instead he'd withdrawn into silence again, wrapped up in his own thoughts.

'Light sticks – high intensity,' said Quinn, taking the end of one of the sticks in his teeth and removing it from the packet. 'They last thirty minutes.'

'Thirty minutes?'

'It's enough,' said Quinn.

Out of its foil, the light stick itself was a translucent yellow tube full of fluid, capped at one end and with a small hook at the other. Quinn bent the tube in the middle until the inner section burst with a snap. The fluid made contact with the crystals in the cap and began to glow. It threw a greenish-yellow light around the chamber that would have been bright enough for Cooper to read by if he'd held it close to his face.

Its glow was almost fluorescent, and it threw complicated shadows on the walls and roof, and on the faces of the two men.

Quinn found a level part of the floor and stood the tube upright on its cap. Lit from below, his features seemed skeletal and demonic. But Cooper thought he probably looked the same way himself.

He gazed at the yellow glow. 'You bought a packet of two light sticks at the outdoor shop in Hathersage.'

'Yes,' said Quinn. He didn't seem at all surprised that Cooper should know.

'Two light sticks,' repeated Cooper.

'That's right.' And Quinn paused. 'The other one is for me.'

Cooper sneaked a glance at his watch, tilting it to catch a gleam of light, wishing that it had a luminous face. It seemed important to know the exact position of the hands. In thirty minutes' time, there would be no more light. One way or another.

'What are you waiting for?' said Cooper.

Suddenly, Quinn focused on him properly, as if he'd just been woken from a dream.

'What did you say?'

'I asked what you're waiting for. You *are* waiting for something, aren't you? Or someone?'

Quinn nodded.

'A killer.'

The pool of bright green water was a long way below. Diane Fry experienced a moment of vertigo as she looked down from the edge of the platform. She saw a scatter of white safety helmets lying on a sort of stony beach at the edge of the water, and instinctively raised a hand to hold on to her own helmet as she leaned over the iron rail.

The colour of the pool looked garish and unnatural in the

442

electric lights, but the guide had already explained that the green was caused by the high lead content of the water. Superstitious lead miners had named it the Bottomless Pit because the forty thousand tons of rubble they'd hurled into it from the walls of the cavern had failed to raise the level by an inch. According to the guide, the miners had concluded that it connected directly to the underworld, where the Devil was presumably unfazed by the amount of rock falling on his head.

There was also some legend about a giant serpent that would emerge from the water and squirm its way through the caves and passages looking for anything warm and alive to eat. Fry shook her head. Those old miners must have lived in constant terror of what they would find around the next boulder.

Most of the task force had reached the cavern ahead of them in another boat, and were now spread out on the rocky slopes above the platform, shining their lamps into the nooks and crevices. A diver's head broke the surface; green water ran from his wetsuit and mud slid across his mask. He raised a gloved hand to wipe away the muck and clear his vision. He gave a thumbs down to a colleague on the shore.

'How far is it down to the water from here?' said Fry.

'Seventy feet.'

'Does anybody ever decide to take a dive off the platform?'

'That would be suicide. The water is full of rocks.'

'Well, yes.'

The guide shrugged. 'There are some weirdos who say they get an irresistible urge to throw themselves off whenever they're in a high place with a sudden drop, like this. They say it's something inside them they can't help, a bit like vertigo.'

Fry drew her feet back from the edge of the platform. She'd been imagining launching herself into the air and plunging into the green pool, enjoying the feel of the cool air as she fell, and savouring the sensation of the water as it burst over her head. The rail was no barrier, if she'd wanted to do it. There was nothing to stop her at all, if the urge grew too strong.

'Those people are really weird, though,' said her guide.

When the lead miners had blasted the last few feet of rock and emerged from the wall of the cavern, would they even have been able to see what was down there, seventy feet below? Wouldn't it just have been a black hole disappearing into the earth? Giant serpents might easily have sprung to mind. Fry looked up. They wouldn't have been able to see the roof of the cavern, either.

'What happens when it rains heavily?' she said.

'The lake down there floods right up to where we're standing.'

'I see.' She took another step back from the edge.

'There isn't enough rain today,' said the guide. 'But we get thirty-six inches a year – a million gallons of it on every acre of the hill up there.'

'What's further on?'

'More canal. There used to be the remains of some old boats, though I don't know if they're still there. But I told you – there's no way anyone could get in here, except down the steps.'

Fry watched the task force officers clambering fruitlessly over the rocks and peering down into the green water. She thought of Ben Cooper, who'd gone to talk to Alistair Page and hadn't reported back. Now Page was here at Speedwell, so where was Cooper?

She remembered Simon Lowe leaving his aunt's house in Castleton. Where had Simon been going? She should have asked him, but she had no power to make him tell her. Then she thought of Mansell Quinn finding somewhere to lie up like an injured animal. A dangerous animal.

Finally, Fry recalled the moment back in the office earlier

444

this evening, when she'd discovered that there was no Alistair Page listed among the Quinns' neighbours back in 1990. The only fifteen-year-old, aside from Simon Quinn, was the Proctor's son, Alan. Then she remembered Gavin Murfin joking about Cooper being in a cave.

'Gavin,' she said, 'I think we've made a big mistake. We're in the wrong place. We've got to get out of here.'

Even before half an hour had passed, the glow from the light stick was beginning to fade. The blackness of the cavern was creeping back towards them, inching across the rock floor and running down the walls, like a dark tide filling the chamber.

Soon, the roof had disappeared and the walls had receded beyond Ben Cooper's vision. For a while, he could see only Mansell Quinn and a few feet of floor between their feet. Quinn's face had seemed to sag, the skin slipping away from the bones as the shadows thickened and lengthened. His eyes sank into his skull, the whites turned yellow and dull. There was almost too little light to show whether he was still alive.

Cooper was sure he must look that way to Quinn, too – like a man sitting upright, but dying slowly. And that was the way he felt. He knew that Quinn couldn't let him live beyond the last glimmer of yellow light.

Although he was still watching from across the chamber, Quinn had been quiet for a long time. He seemed to be chewing something that he'd taken from his pocket. Cooper could hear the occasional crack of his teeth.

'Did you say your name was Cooper?' said Quinn at last.

'Yes. I'm Detective Constable Cooper.'

Cooper felt he was being assessed, analysed down to the soles of his boots. If this was some sort of test, he didn't know what the right answers were, or what he should do to appease Quinn.

But eventually Quinn simply nodded. 'You look a lot like him.'

'Who?' said Cooper automatically. But he'd heard things like that said to him so often that he really didn't need to ask.

'Sergeant Joe Cooper. I suppose he was your dad?'

'Yes, he was.'

'Like father, like son. Isn't that what they say?'

Quinn shifted the butt of the crossbow, leaving a red imprint in the damp skin over his collar bone. Cooper couldn't help dropping his gaze to Quinn's right index finger, where it lay against the trigger guard. The end joint of his finger flexed a little. Had it moved a fraction closer to the trigger on the mention of Joe Cooper's name?

'I know about what happened to him,' said Quinn. 'He died.'

'Yes.'

'I was very sorry to hear about that.'

Cooper felt as though the breath had been sucked out of him. It was the last thing he'd expected to hear.

'Sorry? You were *sorry*?'

'I didn't know about it until I read that plaque in Edendale. I was sorry about it. Really sorry. It's no way to die.'

Cooper knew it must be sarcasm. Quinn was taunting him. Yet the man's voice was flat, and Cooper could detect no emotion behind his taunt. In fact, Quinn's words seemed to falter and die in the air of the chamber, as if they lacked enough conviction to reach the walls. They sank quietly, like carbon dioxide settling to the lowest point of the cave, and their meaning was swallowed up by the layer of silt on the floor.

Of course, Quinn was a man who had stifled any real feelings long ago. Any feelings except that deep, consuming anger.

Quinn tensed, watching him intently in the yellow light.

'I just wanted to tell you that,' he said.

Against his will, Cooper closed his eyes. He knew it was

going to happen now, and he didn't want to see the look in Quinn's eyes as he squeezed the trigger of the crossbow.

In that moment, Cooper felt his senses heighten. He could feel his clothes sticking to his body with sweat, and the bite of the underground chill on his hands and face. He could taste the dampness of the air in his mouth. Around him were the smells of mud and rock, and water draining through layers of earth, like the odours of the grave.

Cooper listened for the sound of breathing, but couldn't even hear his own. He heard only the faint hissing of the light stick and the trickle water from the roof, as he waited for the thud of the bolt leaving the shaft.

43

By the time Diane Fry found Alistair Page's house in Lunnen's Back, she was feeling sick. Her spell in the cavern had built up the pressure in her head until she thought it would explode. She couldn't blame the hay fever alone, although it had left her feeling rough for days. Now it was compounded by anxiety. Not anxiety – fear.

When the boat had finally brought them back to the landing stage, they'd climbed the steps only to discover that Alistair Page had disappeared. And she still had no idea where Ben Cooper was.

'Mr Hitchens isn't happy,' said Gavin Murfin as he finished a call to the West Street station. 'He wants to know what your justification is for diverting the task force from Speedwell. He says you don't have the authority, Diane.'

'I'll give him justification,' said Fry. 'Let him wait.'

'Is that Page?' said Murfin.

'Where?'

'On the corner there, just below the house. There's somebody lurking underneath the street lamp.'

'No,' said Fry, 'but it's somebody I want to talk to. It's Raymond Proctor.'

* * *

After a few moments, Ben Cooper opened his eyes, expecting to find Mansell Quinn still there, his face yellow in the glow from the light stick. But Quinn was gone, and so was the light. Around him was darkness. Real darkness.

Cooper stood up. It was the only thing he felt confident enough to do. Even so, he almost lost his balance. His head swam dizzily, and he had to flap his arms as he struggled to orientate himself. Without light, there was no way of knowing which way was up or down. But after a moment of panic, he calmed down. He practised standing still for a while to ease the pins and needles in his legs. The damp rock he'd been sitting on had chilled him through to the bone.

He had no idea which direction Quinn had taken. In fact, it was impossible to tell which way the passage ran. All he could do was find the wall and feel his way along it. It would be slow going, but it was the best he could do for now. He might at least be able to work out whether he was going up or down – out of the cavern, or deeper into it. All Cooper knew was that he was in the Devil's Dining Room. In the light from Quinn's torch, he'd recognized the black stalactites in the roof: the Devil's Hooks.

He began to move in the darkness, then stopped after a few paces, feeling anxious about bumping into something hard. He waved his hands in front of his face, like a blind man. Maybe the more sensible course would have been to stay where he was and wait to be rescued. But he was wet from the cascade of water, and when he stood still he began to feel very cold. He knew hypothermia was a real danger if he was down here too long. There was no Little Dragon handy to provide warm air for him to breathe.

He started to move again. It felt as if the darkness had diminished his powers of logic and perspective, as well as disrupting his physical senses. He tried to remember how far he was from the place where Neil Moss had died, trapped in the limestone and running out of air. It had seemed a long way into the cave system on the map, yet Moss's presence felt suddenly very close.

And who knew *what* could be around him in complete darkness? The chamber could be full of dead bodies, stacked to the roof sixteen deep, heaps of buried carnage that no one would ever see. The damp smell in his nostrils could be the stench of their bones, picked clean by pale, fat insects that had fallen off and died in the pools of ice-cold water, bloated with human flesh. If Cooper reached out a hand, his fingers might not touch stone at all, but the smoothness of a skull, the crevice of an eye socket, the dusty fragments of a young man's hair.

Cooper felt like a man walking through his own dreams, stumbling across a darkened, illusory landscape, where anything could be true, or everything could be false.

He stopped when the toe of his boot hit a solid obstruction. He felt around with his foot, and stretched a hand out, moving it carefully downwards through the air to judge the height of the obstacle. It was a low boulder, no more than two feet high. If he hadn't been moving so slowly, he would probably have tripped over it. He could feel nothing but empty air on the other side.

It dawned on Cooper that he'd expected the cavern to be silent. Darkness and silence seemed to go to together. But he'd been wrong. The river that ran deep in the limestone was a long way below him, but he could hear its roar through the rock. And water was running through the streamways, trickling over sheets of flowstone, seeping down the walls, dripping from the roof. Water was moving constantly everywhere.

But there was something else, too – something that he heard only if he concentrated hard. It was a more subtle sound, a gentle rhythm that might have been caused by the movement of air, or could have been inside his own head. It was the swishing and pulse of a distant tide, invisible in the endless darkness. As he stood in the depths of the cavern, deprived of sight, Cooper found the sensation oddly reassuring. The sounds he heard around him were like the liquid stirrings of a womb, and the distant beat of a mother's heart.

Of course, there was no such thing as silence. Not on Earth, anyway. Even the movement of the atmosphere made the planet hum, made it ring like a bell at a frequency beyond the reach of human hearing. If you were able to listen closely enough, you might be able to pick up the vibration. But of course, it was never quiet enough to do that. You'd always be able to hear the wind and the movement of the trees, the beating of your heart, and the sound of your own breathing. There was no such thing as silence.

And that meant it would be very easy to hear voices in here. There were strange echoes among the murmurings and tricklings of the water. He wondered if cavers were superstitious and populated the caves with their own ghosts and demons. He wondered if they ever thought they heard Neil Moss, calling them. Heard Neil Moss, breathing.

Cooper could hear a voice now. It sounded a long way off, but it bounced softly off the walls, drawn towards him on the cool air.

'*You should never have come back. You should never have come back into my life.*'

He didn't recognize the voice. Its resonance was distorted and flattened by the rock, and the words were overlain by echoes. Cooper turned his head from side to side, trying to locate it, to identify the direction it had come from.

'*But you knew that I would, one day.*'

A second voice. This one was Mansell Quinn, he was sure. In Quinn's case, the flatness of tone wasn't entirely due to the acoustics. It was an intonation Cooper had been listening to during the last hour – the voice of a man on the edge.

'Yes. And I knew what you'd do once you were out of prison.'

'Of course you knew. You're just like me.'

'Like you? The hell I am.'

Cooper began to edge cautiously towards the voices. He mustn't be too hasty, or it could be disastrous. If he was heading towards the entrance of the cavern, then somewhere ahead of him would be the slippery limestone floor and ice-cold pools of Roger Rain's House. He didn't want to die face down in water with tiny, blind shrimps in his hair.

'Yes, you're just like me. Except that you really are a killer.'

'What? You're kidding.'

'They shouldn't have let you out. They kept me inside for years, but they let you out.'

'A few months in that place was enough for me. There's no way I'm going to end up like you, Quinn. I'm not going to spend half of my life inside, the way you did.'

'Not much chance of that, Alan. You aren't going to live that long.'

The voices were louder now. Cooper couldn't tell if it was because he was closer to them, or because the two men were getting angry, or both. Groping his way round an angle of rock, he felt the first spatter of water in his face. Damn the sheep urine. This time it felt good – it meant he knew where he was at last.

Then Cooper's foot slipped on the wet surface, and he hit the ground hard. He felt his ankle twist, and his knee cracked against the sharp point of a rock. He lay still, winded for a moment. In total darkness, the fact that he was lying on his back made almost no difference to how he felt. Except for the pain in his leg.

'Are you threatening me, Quinn? You're an old man now. Prison has destroyed you. I can see that in your eyes. You're frightened – terrified of your own shadow. Why else would you be hiding down here? Hiding away from the light.'

And suddenly Cooper recognized the second voice. It was the last word that did it – that final 't' spat out like an audible

452

exclamation mark. As if there were always an apple pip stuck between his teeth.

Diane Fry had pinned Raymond Proctor against the wall of one of the cottages. A couple of vehicles went past her towards the cavern, lights flashing and engines groaning in low gear up the slope.

'Alistair Page –' said Fry '– is your son, Alan. He changed his name, didn't he?'

'Yes,' said Proctor.

'I suppose he didn't want people reminding him of his mother's murder all the time? Understandable, considering he was responsible for it.'

Proctor said nothing. He wasn't paying full attention to her. She could see his eyes wandering towards the cavern entrance and the activity around it.

'Ten years ago,' said Fry. 'It was ten years ago that Mansell Quinn started telling the prison authorities and his fellow prisoners that he wasn't guilty after all. That was a stupid thing to do – it could have been a factor in his parole hearing. Suddenly, a third of the way through his life sentence, Quinn was in denial. You see, it's usually the other way around – when prisoners change their story, it's to admit their guilt. Showing remorse helps them get parole.'

'I know all that,' said Proctor.

'Of course you do. But it didn't make sense to me. At first, I thought it was because Quinn had found out that Simon wasn't really his son, and he wasn't going to take the blame for another man's child. But Enid Quinn put me right on that. Simon *is* Mansell's son, and the DNA test proved it.'

Proctor shook his head. 'What's that to me?'

'It wasn't Simon who killed Carol, was it, Mr Proctor?' said Fry. 'That was what Mansell found out somehow, ten years ago. And he was pretty much the last to know, wasn't he? No wonder he's so angry. He's spent more than thirteen years in prison. I'd be pretty bloody angry with people who did that to me.'

Proctor heard her out with a puzzled expression. But he didn't ask what she was talking about. He had his own concerns.

'Where's Alan?' he said.

Fry drew in a long breath. 'I don't know, Mr Proctor. But we're going to find him. Let's hope nobody else has suffered to protect your son.'

'He isn't my son,' said Proctor.

'*What?*'

'Alan is Mansell's son. I've known that for a long time. All the gossip about Rebecca and the stuff about paternity tests, it made me laugh. Mansell was worried that he had no son, but he has two. I'm the one that has no son.'

Fry stared at him. She could see that Proctor was sweating heavily from fear or anxiety, or both.

'So why did you protect him?'

'I'd lost Carol. In fact, I'd already lost her before she died. I may not have any real family now – but Alan is the closest thing I've got.'

Proctor tried to move away then, but Fry took his arm.

'Does Alan know who his real father is?'

'Yes,' said Proctor. 'I thought he ought to know, so I told him when he was eighteen. It didn't do any good. We were really close until then, but it seemed to destroy our relationship. I never understood why, exactly. I mean, you can be close to somebody without being related by blood, can't you? Blood doesn't always have to be thicker than water.'

'And Quinn? Is he aware that Alan is his son?'

Proctor shook his head. 'Not unless Alan has told him.'

44

Mansell Quinn's hand shot out and grabbed Alan Proctor around the neck, forcing his head back. If Alan had expected him to move more slowly, he'd been wrong. Prison hadn't destroyed Quinn physically, at least. He threw his weight forward, and Alan crashed backwards, his head hitting the water of the pool.

'You stupid bastard. Get off me!'

Quinn plunged Alan's head back into the pool. He kept it under for a few seconds longer this time, watching the other man's face disappear in a swirl of silt from the bottom. When Alan came up again, he was coughing and spitting out streams of brown water. Quinn waited until he opened his eyes. He read the fear in them, the knowledge that the next breath Alan took could be his last.

He tightened his grip on a handful of collar.

'You're mad,' said Alan. 'Let me get up.'

Quinn heaved him up on to his knees then and stood back, bringing the crossbow smoothly over his shoulder.

'You deserve everything that's coming to you. Don't you think so, Alan? Do you think you should get away with it completely? You killed Carol. For God's sake, you killed your own mother.'

'I don't know what you're talking about. You're mad.'

Quinn sneered. He pulled a bolt out of his rucksack, cocked the bow and loaded it. 'I suppose you think you've suffered,' he said. 'Did you spend years expecting the police to come for you? Even after I went to prison, were you convinced someone would realize there'd been a mistake? Did you think there'd be a knock on the door one night, or somebody would be waiting for you when you were called out of class? If a car you didn't recognize was parked on the road, did you believe it belonged to somebody who was watching you? I hope so, Alan.'

'I didn't kill her,' said Alan. 'When I heard you coming home that night, I ran out of the house. I was in a panic, not thinking about anything except getting away. It was only afterwards I remembered I'd left the Coke bottle on the table and a tape in the cassette player. Simon had bought *The Joshua Tree* that week. It was still playing when I left the house. I can still hear it now, when I think about it. It was either "I Still Haven't Found What I'm Looking For" or "With or Without You". It was playing, right there in the house. You must have noticed. There are some things you can't help but notice.'

'But there was no reason for you to worry yourself,' said Quinn. He slid the bolt back into the trigger mechanism and released the safety. 'Not once they'd got me sent down.'

'Listen,' said Alan, trembling now with cold and fear, 'I don't know what you're talking about. You've got this all wrong. What I told you in Gartree – that was true. There weren't any other men with Mum at the same time as you. I really am your son. I'm a bastard, but I'm your bastard. You can't do this to me.'

But Quinn just shook his head.

'You should start running now,' he said.

Ben Cooper knew the two men weren't far ahead of him. But his leg wouldn't support him any more, and he could only drag himself a few inches at a time through the darkness.

He'd be glad now even to see a glimmer of Mansell Quinn's light stick, though he was sure Alan Proctor must have come into the cavern with a lamp. He craved any kind of light.

The words the men spoke were hardly penetrating Cooper's brain. But phrases stuck in his mind, and he knew they had meaning. The Coke bottle he remembered. Somebody had wiped the fingerprints from it – wasn't that it? So had they been Alan Proctor's fingerprints, not Simon's? Quinn had remembered Simon playing U2 in the house. But Alan was a fan of the band, too. He had their CDs in his rack.

Cooper gasped with the pain, but almost laughed at the same time. 'I Still Haven't Found What I'm Looking For'. It had been playing in the background when he phoned Alan. What day had that been? Back when he still thought of Alan Proctor as Alistair Page, anyway. And that was something else funny – Will Thorpe had almost told them the truth before he was killed. It was Alan who'd made a new life for himself. He'd even changed his name.

The voices had stopped. Cooper tried to listen, but could hear only his own breathing. And then there was a loud *snap* and something whistled over his head. Then he heard a crack and clatter as it began to ricochet violently between the walls of the passage behind him.

The echo hadn't died away before there was a second *snap,* followed by a dull thump and a slap, like a butcher's cleaver slicing a piece of steak.

Cooper kept his head down. If he'd been standing upright, the first bolt might have gone straight through him. He waited for more noises, but there were none. The natural sounds of the cave began to creep back, the trickling of water and the distant rumble of the river. They were impressions that he would carry with him for ever, if he got out alive.

While he waited, Cooper tried to make sense of what he'd heard – the Coke bottle and the music, signs that a teenager had been there at the scene of Carol Proctor's murder. He thought of the ten minutes that Sergeant Joe Cooper had been alone at the Quinns' house, securing the scene. He was an observant man, so he'd have picked up the clues of another person's presence in the house. There were some things you couldn't help but notice.

Finally, Cooper decided it was safe to keep moving. He seemed to be crawling for a long time, but he had covered only a few yards. He sensed an obstruction in front of him and stopped again, feeling tentatively around the object. Illogically, his hopes rose. He thought at first that he'd somehow found his way back to the dummy of the ropemaker lying near the cavern entrance. But that would have meant he'd passed through the Orchestra Gallery and Lumbago Passage without noticing them.

Then logic took over and told him that if he was in the cavern entrance he would be able to see the light of the streetlamps in Riverside Walk.

But there was no light, only darkness. The body on the floor was too solid to be a dummy. And it wasn't dust that leaked from its clothes, but blood.

Diane Fry hadn't stopped being angry. The search team had reported the discovery of the dummy, the series of footprints going into the cavern, and the police-issue torch abandoned on the terrace. Armed officers had arrived, and they were heading further in, using caution, though now they at least had lights. Cave rescue were on their way, in case casualties needed to be recovered from the cavern. DI Hitchens had arrived, and DCI Kessen would be on the scene soon. It was no longer her responsibility.

A cheer went up from the team in the cavern entrance. The task force officers had succeeded in entering the ticket booth and locating the main control panel for the lighting. High on the cave walls the fibre-optics began to glow.

* * *

A short while later, Ben Cooper experienced a series of familiar sounds and movements – a swaying and tipping, the heavy breathing of effort and discomfort. The constriction was familiar, too. And the darkness, the occasional flash of light across the rock surface. And there was the constant trickle of water. Splashes of it landing on his face.

And at last, he felt a change in the temperature of the air, and heard a babble of voices and clatter of machinery filling a much larger space around him. The DCRO rescue party had brought him to the cavern entrance.

'I bet you're glad to be out in the daylight at last,' someone said.

Cooper nodded, but couldn't speak. He'd been so far into the darkness that the light hurt.

From the waiting room at Edendale General Hospital an hour later, Cooper made a call on his mobile to Bridge End Farm. He told Matt part of what had happened, and reassured him he was OK.

When he ended the call, he looked around the waiting room. There was no sign of him getting near the front of the queue yet. Gavin Murfin had set off to fetch him a cup of tea, but had been gone a long time. Cooper imagined he'd found a cafeteria and was putting away a quick pie and chips before he returned.

His next call was to Diane Fry.

'How is Alistair Page? I mean, Alan Proctor?'

'Dead,' said Fry.

'Damn.'

'Yeah.'

'And Mansell Quinn?'

Fry's voice lowered to little more than a whisper as she failed to hide her disappointment and tiredness.

'We lost him.'

Cooper tried to sit up straight, but a jolt of pain shot through his ankle and up his leg.

'Lost him? You're kidding.'

'I wish.'

'Do you think he got out of the caves?'

'I don't see how, Ben. But if he did, he'll turn up somewhere.'

'There's one other possibility. Maybe Neil Moss is about to have company.'

Formations, stals or pretties – those were the names the cavers gave to the calcite deposits in the caverns. Somewhere there might be cave pearls, the tiny calcite spheres lying in their own nests. Mansell Quinn remembered the petrified bird's nest that his father had shown him, its eggs apparently turned to stone. But down here was real stone, millions of tons of it. No question of the slow smothering of new life. Here, life could be crushed in a moment.

He raised the light stick above his head and looked at the translucent yellow sheets covering the rock. Flowstone, they called it. Well, it might have flowed at some time, many thousands of years ago. But now it was solid and hard, flowing nowhere. If he chipped a lump out of the wall, would the remaining calcite flow over to fill the hole? Not in a million years. The hole would stay right where it was, and the broken lump would crumble in his hand. It hung in great, dead sheets in the darkness, untouched by the outside world. It was beyond the breathing.

Quinn stepped to the edge of the black void. He took hold of the crossbow by the butt and threw it into the darkness. It vanished from sight instantly, but took a long time to fall. He listened patiently to the silence until the weapon hit the water with a distant splash. Then the rucksack followed, and the waterproof, and the bloodstained shirt. He didn't need them any more.

He thought about the early cave explorers, back in the 1950s, using primitive diving equipment, walking on the bottom of flooded passages in weighted boots. In a sump, you couldn't come up for air. There was only one way out – the way you came in. Quinn knew that in those circumstances the only thing to worry about was fear. You could die with nothing wrong, simply because you'd panicked.

He had expected to be cold, but he didn't feel chilled any more. The temperature was warm enough down here to attract new life into the cave system – the bats and spiders and insects. But some were accidentals, like himself. They fell in through the cracks in the rock, or were washed in by the underground rivers or the water soaking through the hill. Others just followed the movement of air, the irresistible pull of cave breathing. They drifted with the current, taking the easiest route – until they found themselves out of their environment, isolated from their own world. They'd been drawn in by the breathing. And there was no way to return.

Quinn lifted his arms above his head like a high diver. He felt the wound on his side break open and begin to ooze blood, but he ignored it. The yellow glow was fading at last. The light was almost gone.

Then Mansell Quinn took one last breath. And the darkness rose up to meet him.

45

Monday, 19 July

Simon Lowe had been lucky to get this house, all right. In fact, Diane Fry could see that he'd be the envy of many a first-time home buyer in North Derbyshire.

The house stood in the middle of a traditional stone terrace on a side street off Meadow Road, one of the few parts of Edendale where property hadn't moved up into an unreachable price range. The street ended at the fence that enclosed a school playing field. In common with all the older areas of town, there was almost nowhere to park.

A lot of the tension and anger seemed to have gone out of Simon since Fry had spoken to him at his aunt's the day before. As she watched him move a roll of carpet aside so they could squeeze down the narrow passage into the house, she remembered how alike he and his sister had seemed on the day they identified the body of their mother at the mortuary. How alike, and how close.

But after days of studying photographs of Mansell Quinn, she could see Simon's father in him now, too. He had the same colouring and the same slightly wary look in the eyes.

'Watch where you walk,' said Simon. 'Sorry about the mess. There isn't a habitable room in the house at the moment.'

462

'It's no problem.'

Fry turned to see where Ben Cooper had got to. He was still coming up the path, though it was only a few feet from the pavement to the door. He limped awkwardly over the step, smiling at her as though his leg wasn't troubling him in the least.

'Are you sure you wouldn't prefer to stay in the car, Ben?' she said.

'No, no. Don't worry about me, I'm fine.'

She tried to rein in her irritation. Cooper had practically begged to come in on this interview, and she knew she'd made a mistake in agreeing. She didn't really need him now, not once she'd picked the relevant information out of his statement. She'd let him come because she felt sorry for him. But if he was going to be a martyr, it was just too much.

All the rooms of Simon Lowe's house seemed to smell of old floorboards and stale plaster. When he led them through into a back room, Fry could see why. There were no carpets down, and most of the wallpaper had been stripped. Wires protruded from holes at skirting-board level.

'Have you been in this house long?' she asked.

Simon laughed. 'A couple of months. I suppose you think it isn't possible to live here when it's in this condition, but you get used to it.'

Well, at least there was furniture. A three-seater settee stood opposite a TV set, and Simon whipped off a couple of dust sheets to reveal matching armchairs.

'There's a lot of work to do on it, of course,' he said. 'It'll have to be completely re-plastered and re-wired, and it needs a new floor in the kitchen. And you ought to see the bathroom – you couldn't go in there without a decontamination suit when I first saw it. It'll all have to be ripped out. But I can do most of it myself, given time.'

Cooper was having difficulty lowering himself into one of

463

the armchairs, because his leg didn't seem to bend properly. Fry hoped she wouldn't have to help him up when it came time to go. She might prefer just to leave him there.

'Do you live here alone, then?' asked Cooper.

'For the moment. But I'm engaged, and my fiancée and I are planning to get married next April. We'd already been saving up for a while, so when we saw this house on the market we snapped it up. It has three bedrooms, so we can start a family as soon as we want. We were very lucky.'

'Yes, you were. But you're taking a lot on, aren't you?'

'I'm nearly twenty-nine,' said Simon. 'It's time I settled down.'

Fry heard a noise in the kitchen. 'Is your fiancée here?'

'No, that's Andrea. I presume it's all right my sister being here?'

'Yes, of course.'

Simon glanced towards the kitchen. 'You know, we've always been very close. Well, not always, perhaps. I didn't appreciate having a little sister when I was in my early teens. But after what happened with our father, we became close. And now, after all this, well . . .'

'There are times when you need to turn to members of your family for support,' said Cooper.

'Exactly.'

Fry looked at Cooper, but he wasn't paying her any attention. He was gazing around the room, as if memorizing the entire contents. If he could have moved more easily, she thought he would have got up to count the videos and CDs, and inspect the magazines in the rack by the telly.

'Mr Lowe,' she said, 'I have to ask you some serious questions.'

Simon's face fell. 'Go ahead, then.'

Andrea came into the room then, as if on cue, and sat next to her brother on the settee. She nodded at Fry and Cooper, but said nothing.

'For a start,' said Fry, 'did it ever occur to you that it might not have been your father who killed Carol Proctor?'

Simon looked shocked by her directness. She saw the first hint of that rush of colour to his face, but it died away again.

'No, it didn't.'

'It's a pity. But the scapegoat was too obvious, wasn't he? Too obvious, and too easy.'

'That's uncalled for.'

'It doesn't matter,' said Fry. 'We were all the same. It helped everybody to believe that your father was guilty.'

Simon leaned forward. 'Look, I honestly believed he was guilty. I mean, he *did* kill Carol Proctor, didn't he?'

'We can't be entirely sure of that, in the light of recent events.'

'Oh?' Simon and Andrea looked at each other. 'And what's your evidence for that?' said Simon.

Instead of answering, Fry changed tack, trying to keep him off balance.

'You bunked off school a lot when you were about fifteen, didn't you, sir?'

'So what? Everyone does it. It means nothing.'

'I know. Believe it or not, I did it myself.'

'Where is this leading, Sergeant?'

'The day Carol Proctor was killed, you both bunked off school together, didn't you? I mean, you and your good friend Alan.'

Now Simon looked really surprised, and Fry knew she was right. Until that moment, she hadn't been entirely sure.

'Well, not *together* exactly,' he said. 'We were supposed to sneak out separately and meet up at my house. We were just going to drink Coke and listen to some music, it was as innocent as that. But Alan managed to get away from school and I didn't. One of the teachers spotted me and sent me back. I was supposed to be preparing for my GCSEs, you see. I didn't want a bad report going back to my parents. They wanted me to do well – you know what it's like.'

Fry nodded as if she understood. But proud and ambitious parents were one pressure that she'd never had to suffer.

'So Alan went to your house and waited for you to turn up. But he got into the house, didn't he? How could he have done that?'

Simon sighed. 'There was a spare back-door key under one of Mum's garden ornaments – a concrete rabbit with a hollow base. She didn't trust me or Andrea not to lose keys of our own, so she always left one under the rabbit for us in case we came home when no one was in. Alan knew about the key. He'd seen me get it from there before. That day, he waited outside for a while, but it started raining, so he got the key and went into the house. He knew I wouldn't mind – we were good mates.'

'I see.'

'You know, Mum carried on doing that, even after we left home. She used to say wherever we all were in the world, her house was still our home.'

Fry watched him for a moment, fearing a show of emotion that she'd have to pretend to sympathize with.

Then she realized that Cooper had tensed and was sitting forward in his armchair. She gave him a glance, but he was concentrating on Lowe. At least he wasn't going to interrupt at the wrong moment.

'So let's go over that again,' she said. 'Alan Proctor had gone into your parents' house to get out of the rain. He was waiting for you, but you didn't turn up. So what did he do with himself?'

'He got a bottle of Coke from the fridge, then went up to my room, drew the curtains and put some music on the stereo. That's what we would have done anyway, if I'd been there. There was nothing wrong with that.'

'OK. And then?'

'He waited a bit, until eventually he realized there must be something wrong. After a while, he knew there was a chance

466

of my father coming home, and it would look odd him being in the house without me. So when he heard somebody coming up the path, he scarpered.'

'Out of the back door?'

'I suppose so.'

'So whoever he heard must have been approaching the house from the front?'

Simon shrugged. 'I imagine he heard my father parking his car and coming in through the gate. Maybe Alan actually saw him – my room looked out on to the street. Dad had a bit of a temper, and he didn't like Alan very much. He thought he was a bad influence on me – you know the sort of ideas parents get.'

'Did Alan tell you all this himself?'

'I'm sure he told me some of it – about going into the house anyway, then leaving sharpish.'

'When did you see him to talk about it?'

'Oh, it was days later.' Simon frowned. 'In fact, it must have been weeks. Andrea and I stayed at our Aunt Dawn's for a while, and we didn't go back to school until nearly the end of term. My memories of that time are all a bit vague. I was thinking mostly about my father, and worrying about my mother. The shock, you know . . . To be honest, I don't think it even occurred to me at the time that Alan would have been at the house. Everything else seemed so unimportant.'

'And when you did see Alan again, did you ask him about it? Or did he volunteer this story?'

'He volunteered it. Like I say, I hadn't even remembered that he was going to the house. When he told me, I just thought he was so lucky that he'd got out of the way in time. If my father was drunk and lost his temper, he might have attacked Alan too.'

Fry studied him. Concern for a friend was all very well, up to a point. Had Simon Lowe's sense and judgement been influenced by his feelings for the people involved? Well, why not? Everyone else's had.

'But I don't understand why you call it a story,' said Simon. 'Don't you believe it?'

'Surely you can see there's something wrong with your friend's version of events?' said Fry.

'What do you mean?'

'According to all the evidence, your father didn't arrive at the house while Alan was there – or, at least, he wasn't the first to arrive. The person your friend would have seen coming up the drive was Carol Proctor – his own mother. When she came into the house, he must have realized she was having an affair with your father.'

'You don't think he would . . . ?'

'I don't know,' said Fry. 'What do *you* think?'

But Simon Lowe said nothing.

'OK. So let's try this – who told your father about Alan Proctor being there?'

'I don't know.'

'Don't know? Mr Lowe, there's only one person it *could* have been. Apart from Alan Proctor himself, you were the only one who knew.'

She could see Simon was sweating now. If she'd made him uncomfortable, she'd achieved at least part of her aim in coming here.

'My father wrote to me from prison once,' he said. 'His letter sounded almost reasonable.'

'When was this?'

'About nine years ago, or a bit less.'

'So you told him about Alan?'

'He asked me what I remembered of that day. He said his memories were very vague and fragmented. Well, I understood that. I was like that myself for a long time after it happened. Shock can do that.'

'Yes, Mr Lowe. So you told him?'

468

'I told my father what I could remember. None of it seemed important, especially after all that time. And I never heard from him again, so I put it out of my mind.'

'Why do you think he didn't write again?' said Fry.

'I don't know. I supposed he hadn't really wanted to make contact with me, but just needed the information.'

'Well, there is another possibility.'

'What's that?'

'Perhaps your father concluded that you knew who'd really killed Carol Proctor, but you'd let him go to prison for it, as everyone else had.'

'Oh, but –'

'And maybe,' said Fry, 'he thought *your* betrayal was the greatest of all.'

Simon glowered. 'I hardly think betrayal is a word you can use in the circumstances.'

'No? Didn't you try to tell your father at one point that you weren't his son?'

'That was just something I said in the heat of the moment. I was only a teenager, and I was upset.'

Fry paused for a moment, conscious that it made Lowe nervous about what was coming next.

'Did you know that Alan Proctor was your half-brother?' she said. 'Your father's son?'

Simon looked as though all his fears had been realized. 'What? My father – and Carol Proctor? I don't believe it. That can't be true, can it?'

'You know it can,' said Fry. 'Ask Raymond Proctor. He believes it. And Alan found out later, too.'

'That would have devastated him. He thought the world of Ray.'

'Yes, I think the feeling was mutual. It was a dangerous kind of love, though, as it turns out.'

'I really don't understand what you mean, Detective Sergeant. This is all too much to take in.'

Fry knew it was time to leave, and she studied the Lowes for the last time. The brother and sister always looked so close that it made her wonder what it would take to split them apart and set them against each other. There'd be something, no doubt. There always was.

'What I mean, sir,' she said, 'is that DNA isn't everything. As Raymond Proctor said to me himself only yesterday, blood doesn't always have to be thicker than water.'

When he saw Ben Cooper back in the office, Gavin Murfin was the first to slap him on the back, as if he were some sort of hero. But Cooper knew perfectly well that he wasn't anything of the kind.

'Well, we don't need to do a DNA test on you, Ben,' said Murfin. 'There's no mistaking who your father was. You're so like him it's unbelievable.'

Cooper smiled. It was the reaction expected of him, and he'd practised it.

'So they tell me, Gavin.'

'I don't mean just the way you look. It's the way you go about the job. Joe Cooper was the same – he wanted to know everything about everybody. Who was doing what to who, how often and what with. It seems a bit of an old-fashioned idea to us modern coppers, but I suppose it has its advantages. He knew Mansell Quinn. And I'll bet he knew Alan Proctor, too.'

'What makes you say that?'

'I gather he was a bit of a teenage tearaway, always getting into fights. I wonder if your Dad ever pulled him in for anything?'

'I don't know, Gavin.'

'Away, when he was nineteen the magistrates finally lost patience and he got sent down for twelve months. He was past the age for youth detention centres by then, so he got a spell in Gartree. And guess who he ran into there, among Her Majesty's guests?'

'Mansell Quinn.'

'Right in one. And it was Quinn who knocked Alan Proctor's front teeth out. He had to wear dentures after that. It must have been a right bugger for a lad in his twenties. According to the records at Gartree, Quinn would never give a reason for the assault. But they obviously had something between them. Who says they don't let men form close relationships in prison?'

Cooper could see Diane Fry busy at her desk. She seemed to have shaken off the hay fever, or at least the drugs were working. She looked less tired this morning than he'd seen her for days. At Simon Lowe's house, Fry had been very much back on her old form – combative, direct and getting results. But missing all the subtleties.

'Thanks for letting me come with you this morning, Diane,' he said. 'I appreciate it.'

'That's OK, Ben. As long as you don't take it into your head to have any more outings. You need to rest that leg. Stay in the office. Do some paperwork.'

'Yes, all right.'

'Simon Lowe is coming in later on to make a formal statement and have a chat with the DI. You can bet Lowe wasn't very happy about it, but that's too bad. I thought we got a lot out of him, didn't you? It seems to tie up a loose end or two, anyway.'

'Oh, yes,' said Cooper. 'That's what it does.'

Fry looked thoughtful. 'It's a pity we can't interview Will Thorpe again, though. He was very important in all this, wasn't he? Thorpe felt under an obligation to Quinn.'

'Of course he did, Diane. He made a choice fourteen years ago – Quinn hoped Thorpe would lie for him, but he didn't. Even when you've made a right decision, you can still feel guilty about it. That was why he agreed to do favours for Quinn when he was due out of prison.'

'Right. For a start, he got addresses for him. But when

Thorpe actually saw Quinn, he started to worry about what he'd do when he got out. So Will Thorpe must have told Rebecca Lowe the truth, mustn't he?'

'All of the truth?' said Cooper, frowning. 'Everything that he knew from Quinn – including about Alan Proctor having killed Carol?'

'Yes, why not? He was trying to clear his conscience, I suppose. He knew he hadn't got much longer to live.'

'Let's hope it worked, then.' He frowned again. 'But wait – did Will Thorpe die knowing that Rebecca had been murdered, or not?'

'Oh yes, Ben,' said Fry. 'Don't you remember? We told him ourselves.'

Cooper closed his eyes for a moment. 'Yes, we did.'

He'd been standing at the window of the CID room, but now he limped back to his desk. His leg wasn't too painful, but he was resigned to being stuck on desk jobs for a week or two. He wondered about asking Fry if he could move his desk next to the window, so he could get a bit more light.

Cooper was well aware of his own role in the death of Alan Proctor, and it didn't make him a hero. The only reason that Alan had entered the cavern that night was because his elderly neighbour told him Cooper had gone there to look for him. Maybe the old girl really had thought he was a suspicious character, and had laid it on a bit thick. Otherwise, Mansell Quinn might well have waited in vain for Alan to appear on his security check, thanks to the false alarm at Speedwell.

It was nothing if not ironic. At one stage, Cooper had imagined that Quinn was trying to draw him into the cavern. But he had never been Quinn's intended victim. Alan Proctor had. And, in the end, Cooper had made it possible for Quinn to achieve his aim.

And now where was Quinn himself? It seemed as though the caverns had simply swallowed him and digested him.

Cooper looked at Gavin Murfin. What was it Murfin had said a few minutes ago? 'Like father, like son.' Quinn had used the same words that day in Peak Cavern. At the time it had seemed he was talking about Cooper and his father, and he'd meant it as a compliment.

He thought about fathers and sons while he tried to clear up some of the stuff that had gathered in his trays. You didn't have to retire from the job for your desk to become everybody's dumping ground around here. The layers of accumulated paper were as deep as the pile of the carpet at Rebecca's Lowe's house. Nothing had protected her at Parson's Croft. But then, she hadn't known what direction the danger would come from.

'Diane,' said Cooper.

He heard her sigh. 'Yes, Ben?'

'What about Rebecca Lowe? Why would Alan Proctor have killed *her*? Why is there no forensic evidence? And what was his motive?'

'We'll never know, thanks to Quinn,' she said. 'With all three of them gone, the relationship between them is impossible to figure out.'

'Yes, I suppose so.'

Cooper moved a stack of paper aside and found a packet of photographs. What were these? He slid one out. 'The City of Aberdeen', hurtling towards distant hills and an evening sky ominous with thunderclouds. He'd forgotten to send the trainspotter's pictures back.

The photo of Mansell Quinn on the westbound platform at Hope was missing, of course. But the photographer had been right – the light had been interesting that night. Over to the right he could see the slopes of Win Hill and Lose Hill, and in the centre the distinctive shape of Mam Tor stood out against the sky. Mam Tor meant Mother Hill. But it was a father who'd been most important in this case. *Like father, like son*. And there was something else that Diane Fry had

473

said today. Something about a dangerous love. *DNA isn't everything.*

Cooper dropped the photos suddenly and stared out of the window at the sunlight on the roofs of Edendale. It was a nice day again out there. But they'd had an awful lot of rain recently.

He spun round to see if Fry was still there.

'Diane,' he said.

'What now?'

'I know you said I shouldn't think about outings . . .'

'Yes, Ben?'

'But do you have time for a drive?'

She turned to stare at him as if he'd made an indecent suggestion.

'Where to?'

'Well, first of all, I'd like to call at the Cheshire Cheese in Castleton.'

'A pub? It's a bit early, Ben, isn't it?'

Cooper shook his head. 'No, it's late enough. I just hope it isn't too late.'

46

Beyond the railway line it wasn't much of a road, more of a dirt track. But it had been well constructed, and it didn't have too many potholes to gather mud when it rained. It passed a farm entrance and skirted the edge of Win Hill before petering out in a gateway. From there, the route marked on Ben Cooper's street atlas was actually a public footpath that crossed a stile and ran along the edge of a field, where it was barely visible but for a line of flattened grass.

'OK, the times fit all right,' said Diane Fry. 'Ten o'clock at the Cheshire Cheese, and the journey between the two locations is what – fifteen minutes?'

'Yes,' said Cooper. 'And it's only a short walk from here.'

'It's been too long to get any impressions from the track, Ben.'

'And too wet. Shall we walk to the house?'

'What about your leg? Are you sure you can manage?'

'Well, that's part of what we're trying to find out.'

They followed the faint outline of the footpath, keeping a few yards to the side of it. And within ten minutes they'd reached the hedge of elm saplings.

'Do we have to push our way through it?' said Fry doubtfully, looking down at her clothes.

'No need. There's a little gate, look. I never knew that was here.'

'It doesn't appear to have been used much.'

Cooper eased open the gate in the hedge, wincing as it creaked on its hinges. 'It needs oiling,' he said.

'OK, so we're in the garden. What now, Ben?'

'This way.'

Fry followed him as he walked round the side of the house. Cooper crossed one of the lawns, then stopped.

'What are you looking at?'

'The concrete heron,' he said.

'We came all this way to look at a concrete heron? Why? You don't even have a garden of your own, Ben.'

'No. I wonder if it was made out of cement from the Hope works, though.'

'Does it matter?'

'Not in the least.'

Cooper put on a pair of latex gloves and grasped the heron's head. It took the indignity with a stony glare.

'Ben, what are you doing?'

'If I take the weight a bit –' he said. 'Diane, I can't bend too well at the moment. Could you . . . ?'

Fry crouched to look.

'The base is hollow,' she said. 'Wait a minute . . .' She reached out a hand.

'I shouldn't touch it. Fingerprints, you know. But I take it there's a key under there?'

'Yes. It's the back-door key, I suppose. But this means some-body could have used it to get into the house.'

'Yes.'

Fry shook her head. 'No, Ben.'

'What do you mean, no?'

'If somebody used the key to get in and kill Rebecca Lowe, why would they put it back?'

Cooper gently lowered the heron back into position and removed his gloves.

'Habits die hard,' he said. 'If you're used to handling keys all the time, it's important to get into the habit of putting them back exactly where you got them from.'

Fry nodded. 'All right. I'll get someone up here to check for prints.'

'I think the concrete is probably useless for prints, especially after all the rain.'

'But the key is perfectly dry.'

Slowly, Fry walked back to the hedge and looked through it at the path they'd used to cross the field.

'And you're right,' she called. 'If he came under the railway bridge and parked where we have, it's just a short walk.'

'I had no trouble, despite my injured leg.'

'No, you didn't.'

'So it would be easily manageable,' said Cooper. 'Even for a man with a touch of arthritis in his knee.'

Fry nodded again, and Cooper went to stand alongside her at the hedge. Below the embankment of the distant railway bridge, he could see a row of static caravans, and the rustic log walls of the nearest holiday lodge.

Then Cooper saw what he hoped for. He saw Diane Fry smile for the first time in days.

'I think I'm going to enjoy this bit,' she said.

And then, after all that, she sent him back to the office to put his feet up and rest his leg. He wasn't even allowed to be present at the arrest or take part in the search. Ben Cooper had never taken inactivity well. Now he felt like an invalid who had to be kept out of the way. A liability.

Somebody had brought him a coffee, but he let it go cold on his desk while he sulked. He didn't want to appear to be enjoying himself when they came back from the caravan park.

Then, when he finally saw Diane Fry coming through the door, Cooper threw his legs off the desk and couldn't suppress a small gasp of pain.

'Well, we found the knife,' said Fry. 'Do you want to guess where?'

'In one of the old caravans,' said Cooper, rubbing his leg. 'Did he try to blame it on Iraqi refugees, by any chance?'

'Not this time. But you're right. Connie seems to have watched him like a hawk, so his options for disposing of it would have been limited and I suppose the old 'van seemed as good a place as any to hide it. Nobody else went there except him.'

'And Will Thorpe, when he was staying at the site. And us, when we asked to see inside them.'

'Poor Mr Proctor – he must have been sweating bricks for days. Well, it was obvious all along that he was frightened. But it wasn't Mansell Quinn he was frightened of. He told us that himself, several times.'

'I don't know if you noticed,' said Cooper, 'but when we were in the office that day he made a bit of a fuss about finding the keys for the old 'vans.'

'So he did.'

'I thought it was odd, because the rest of the keys were all neatly organized and labelled on their hooks. But there was one key that he had to get out of a drawer. That's why he made a performance of it.'

'I thought he was just being awkward.'

'Also, Proctor tried to pretend he didn't know Quinn was coming out of prison last Monday. But he must have known – he'd spoken to Rebecca Lowe earlier in the day. I checked the phone records – it was the office number at Wingate Lees that Rebecca rang, not the Proctors' home number. It would have been Ray she spoke to.'

'It seems likely. Connie told us he kept her out of the office.'

'And it wasn't a short call. So I wondered what else they might have talked about.'

Fry took off her jacket. She looked warm, but not dissatisfied with the day's work. 'Sounds as if you've been doing a bit of thinking while we were out, Ben.'

'There wasn't much else to do.'

'And?'

'I think that when Rebecca Lowe phoned, she told Ray Proctor she knew about Alan, and that she was going to tell Quinn the truth, if he came back.'

'Tell him that it was Alan who killed Carol? But Quinn had already figured that out for himself years ago, thanks to Simon.'

Cooper nodded. 'Yes. But neither Rebecca nor Proctor knew that.'

'Are you sure?'

'How can I be? We'll never know what was going through Will Thorpe's mind, or how much he told Rebecca. This is total conjecture, Diane, but it's the only way it makes sense.'

'You mean Ray Proctor had no reason to shut Rebecca up? It achieved nothing?'

'Nothing,' said Cooper. 'If only Will Thorpe had told her the whole truth, it could have saved both their lives.'

Fry sat down suddenly and stared at him. 'But, instead, Rebecca's threat must have upset Proctor badly.'

'So badly that he needed a drink. We know Ray Proctor drank at the Cheshire Cheese. He always has done, and he's never altered his habits. Some people never do. He was out drinking that Monday night – Connie mentioned it. She said he came back late.'

'Yes, she did.'

'The landlord confirms Proctor was in the Cheshire Cheese that night. Which means he'd have seen Quinn – remember, Quinn was in the bar from about ten o'clock.'

'Well, perhaps he did see him,' said Fry.

'Yes, I think he did. Quinn checked in and went up to his room, then came back down to the bar later. I think Proctor saw Quinn come into the pub, and so he made a quick exit.'

'And he went to Parson's Croft?'

'To see Rebecca Lowe,' said Cooper. 'He thought that's where Quinn would go, so he wanted to get there first.'

'You've got it all worked out.' Fry looked at him. 'It's almost like the Carol Proctor case all over again, isn't it?'

'He'd been drinking heavily for a while by then. And he was desperate to stop Rebecca telling Quinn the truth.'

'But the boot impressions, Ben – they matched the prints at the field barn where Will Thorpe was killed. Quinn was definitely at Parson's Croft that night. You can't escape that fact.'

'Yes, he was there all right. It's ironic, but by the time Proctor saw him in the pub he'd already been to Parson's Croft. And Rebecca was still very much alive when he left. I'm sure he just stood at the bottom of the garden and never even approached the house, let alone went in.'

'But why?'

Cooper remembered the images of Quinn captured on the security cameras at Hathersage and Castleton. His expression had been difficult to read at the time, but it came back to Cooper now.

'I think he was frightened,' he said. 'His courage failed him. I think he couldn't face Rebecca after all that time.'

'He couldn't face her sober, you mean?'

'Maybe.'

'So Rebecca was alive, you think?'

'Yes,' said Cooper. 'If his courage hadn't failed him at that moment, Mansell Quinn might have saved her life.'

Fry was silent for a moment. 'It remains to be seen how co-operative Raymond Proctor will be. Without his prints on the back-door key for Parson's Croft, we'd have had no evidence to justify the search. We knew Rebecca Lowe made

480

a phone call to Proctor that day, but so what? They'd known each other for years. OK, so Proctor was drinking at the Cheshire Cheese that night, where he might or might not have seen Mansell Quinn, and he might or might not have left the pub when he did. Again, so what? Why shouldn't he get out of the way rather than risk a confrontation? We have no witnesses to say Proctor went to Parson's Croft, no one who saw his vehicle on the farm track, and no tyre impressions. There was no DNA at the scene, nothing. If Proctor had used a bit of logic and kept the key, or just wiped it, or worn gloves, he'd still have been waiting for the right moment to dispose of the knife.'

'Logic doesn't necessarily work at a time like that, does it?'

More members of the team were arriving back in the office now. Their voices could be heard in the corridor, loud and excited. Downstairs, Ray Proctor had been processed, booked in and allocated his cell. Cooper wondered whether he'd be sent to Gartree to start his sentence. And whether, in fourteen years' time, he'd find himself walking out of the gates of HMP Sudbury, abandoned by his family and about to slip through the cracks in the system.

'I'll tell you what,' said Fry. 'Proctor must have been really worried about Will Thorpe. Full marks to your persuasive powers for getting him to take Thorpe back again, Ben.'

'Proctor made sure he didn't stay, though.'

'And Quinn finally sorted the problem out for him.'

'I suppose we still haven't located Quinn?' said Cooper.

'No. But he'll turn up somewhere. Not even Mansell Quinn can slip through the cracks completely.'

Gavin Murfin came in, smiling and sweating. 'Hey, Ben,' he said, 'We don't need to do a DNA test on you. Did I ever say that?'

'Yes, you did say that, Gavin.'

'I know, but it's amazing. Did you check to see whether your Dad ever pulled Alan Proctor?'

'No. But Dad would have given any fifteen-year-old boy a second chance,' said Cooper. 'He always did with youngsters.'

'Yes, I've heard that, too,' said Fry.

She'd perched on her desk as the room filled up, looking relaxed and enjoying the atmosphere. Or at least, that's what Cooper thought she was doing.

'I heard he preferred to take the initiative into his own hands and just give them a ticking off, or a bit of friendly advice,' she said. 'Like Gavin says, a real old-style copper. You wouldn't get away with it these days. Not for a minute.'

Cooper turned to face Fry. He managed to hold her gaze for once, despite the fact that he knew she could see straight through him.

'Everyone deserves a second chance,' he said.

'Not quite everyone, Ben.'

He wasn't sure who she was referring to. Who didn't get a second chance? Mansell Quinn or Alan Proctor? Or was she referring to *him*? Or even to herself?

It reminded Cooper that he'd come nowhere near to understanding Diane Fry the way she seemed to understand him. At times, he felt as though he was getting closer to an insight into her mind, but she always drifted away again, like something too fragile to be grasped in the hand.

He couldn't remember which of the Castleton show caves contained a well-known calcite formation – a stalactite and stalagmite that had grown towards each other until they were only four centimetres apart. Just four centimetres away from touching, and merging together. But geologists had calculated that it would take at least another thousand years before they finally met, if ever.

Cooper cast around for something to say that would take her mind off the subject, something that might restore the personal understanding they came so close to now and then.

482

'How is Angie, by the way?' he said.

Fry slid off her desk. She came towards him slowly and leaned her face towards his, touching her hand lightly on the sleeve of his shirt, where it lay like a branding iron against his skin.

'Ben, did you happen to get any additional information out of Mansell Quinn, anything that would help us to clear his name and prove that it was Alan Proctor who killed Carol?'

'No,' said Cooper. 'I didn't.'

She stared at him, and Cooper still couldn't tell what she was thinking.

'OK.'

Of course, the one mind that Cooper had no trouble understanding was his father's. He and Joe Cooper were very much alike, as everyone pointed out. They both believed in a second chance. For Mansell Quinn and Alan Proctor, it was too late. But had Sergeant Joe Cooper attempted to conceal the presence of a fifteen-year-old boy at a murder scene? It seemed possible that someone had stopped the music, turned off the upstairs light and wiped the Coke bottle. Had those efforts been in vain? Cooper hoped not. And he didn't know if he'd undo what his father had done fourteen years earlier, even if he could.

He felt a sudden chill run up his spine and along the back of his neck, as if someone had opened a fridge door behind him, and he turned to the window. It was open, but the air coming in was no icy draught. What he'd felt was a gust of air from a world where it was much colder than a humid summer in Edendale.

The window looked down on to the car park, and Cooper saw Simon Lowe walking to his car. He must have completed his formal statement, and had probably been kept waiting around for a while. Andrea was waiting in the car, and she got out of the passenger seat to meet him as soon as he

483

appeared. There was another woman sitting in the back of the car, somebody Cooper didn't recognize. The fiancée, Jackie, perhaps? They had a wedding planned for next April, and an awful lot of work to do on their new house if they were going to start a family.

'Diane,' said Cooper, 'did you ever track down the teacher who caught Simon Lowe bunking off school and made him go back in?'

'No,' said Fry vaguely. 'He gave me the man's name, but it turned out he retired years ago, and has since died of a heart attack. Funny – it reminded me of your father's partner, PC Netherton. Why?'

'Oh, nothing. It was just the last loose end, really.'

'It's good to clear up loose ends. But you were wrong about one thing, weren't you, Ben?'

'What's that?'

'None of it had anything to do with your father. So that's one problem out of the way.'

'Yes, Diane.'

But Cooper didn't think that was right. For a moment, his father had walked back into his life, to remind him that he was dealing with people, and not with a sequence of numbers and chromosome locations on a DNA profile. He was in no doubt that it was Sergeant Joe Cooper himself who'd crept up behind him a second ago and breathed that icy breath on the back of his neck. His father had sent him a message with a single cold touch, an unspoken word in his ear.

Cooper watched Simon and Andrea Lowe standing together for a moment by the car. They weren't touching or speaking, just looking into each other's faces, communicating the way you could with a sibling. Then they threw their arms around each other and hugged so tightly it must have been painful.

At last they got into the car, reversed carefully among the police vehicles, and turned out on to the road towards

Edendale. Simon drove a little too fast, as if afraid he might not get a second chance, after all, if he didn't get away soon.

Cooper had heard of a Chinese religion called Taoism. Its members believed you were born containing all the breath you'd ever possess in your life. For them, every exhalation was a step nearer death. When you used up your last breath, there was no more.

But Cooper had thought about it in the last few days, and he knew they were wrong about that. There was always one last breath.

Speedwell Cavern, 10 September 2004
It was towards the end of the summer when a party of retired college teachers from Virginia climbed slowly down the steps at Speedwell Cavern to take the underground boat ride.

When they disembarked on to the platform above the Bottomless Pit, they straightened their safety helmets and looked up into the roof of the cavern hundreds of feet above their heads, where the remains of primitive wooden ladders still protruded from the rock.

Then they gazed down into the green water far below as the guide told them about the lead miners who'd hurled tons of rock into it. They listened politely to his stories about the Devil, who the miners believed had lived at the bottom of the lake, and about the giant white serpent that was supposed to emerge from the water and roam the passages, seeking human prey.

'And, of course, it's the high lead content of the rock that gives the water its green colour,' he said.

The guide was about to turn off the lights and lead his party back to the boat. But one visitor had been leaning over the parapet and staring closely at the water. He was an old physics professor, and he had a question.

'Excuse me, sir,' he said. 'I understand it's the lead that makes the water green. But what causes the bubbles?'

Puzzled, the guide looked over the parapet. 'What do you mean?'

'The bubbles, see? Oh, and another thing – the smell?'

The guide wasn't a man to be frightened by his own stories of giant white serpents. But even he could see there was something in the lake seventy feet below. It was pale and bloated, and it almost shimmered in the lime-green water as bubbles of gas burst around it.

And one thing he was sure of. The thing was rising slowly to the surface, gradually re-emerging from the depths of the Bottomless Pit.